YOUR
DARK
SECRETS

Also by ELLE MARR

The Missing Sister
Lies We Bury
The Family Bones
The Alone Time

CHAPTER ONE

ADDISON

PARIS, FRANCE | AUGUST 17

The truth? I have never met a situation I can't spin. After as many years as I've logged as a top public relations pro in SoCal, I've seen them all. High-profile CEOs caught swiping from the till? Rebranded by yours truly as modern-day Robin Hoods intending to direct funds to charities. Respected members of Congress who sent partial nudes? Budding photographers whose only crime was forgetting an artistic filter across the shot.

And here in Paris, the City of Light, where my client, an actress whose stellar career made her spokesperson for an iconic perfume from La Fumée, has vomited onto the custom Chanel dress she's wearing, I'm ready to flex that impressive skill set.

"Madame?" the line producer of the shoot squeaks through my phone. "What should I . . . uh . . . How can we . . . um?"

"Yves, I'm going to need a full sentence. Try again," I demand.

When I first answered his call, the line producer updated me on my client's sour stomach. Then he shared that a production assistant was snapping pictures on his phone of my client bent over. I ordered the producer to confiscate all cell phones on-site. I tabled the instructions I was giving the costume designer in the courtyard, then began marching up a centuries-old staircase beneath a vaulted cupola dripping in Renaissance influence.

"Bien sûr. Of course," the line producer adds. "Well, it's just that . . ."

"Quickly now."

"Well—Madame, your client is drunk. I can smell the cognac wafting from her pores from here."

At the entrance to a grand marble foyer, I pass between stately columns twined around by sculpted palm fronds reaching toward the heavens. "The organic shampoo infused with copper and oak samples from Indonesia?" I laugh into the speaker. "She orders that shit by the barrel."

Truly, as the commanding echo of my heels announces my imminent arrival—a punishing soundtrack by which to set expectations as I reach the east wing, where the shoot is in progress—today feels like just another Thursday.

I plant my feet in the doorway of a ballroom full of production veterans collectively rolling their eyes at my client, now retching on all fours. Only a young man and an older woman flirting in the corner seem oblivious to the scene. I tuck back a strand of black hair that's escaped my high pony. Survey the crushed-velvet settee surrounded by oversize cotton balls meant to evoke the clouds of heaven and invite consumers to purchase a new variation of the flagship scent from this brand. I smooth down the blue satin dress I bought at top dollar. Then I turn to the nearest key grip.

"What is going on?" I say, not shout. Addison Stern doesn't need to shout.

The line producer I spoke with over the phone, Yves, approaches with all the trepidation of Quasimodo. "Bonsoir, Ms. Stern. You asked that no one leave until you got here."

Obviously. "I meant, why has no one helped my client up? Someone get her sparkling water. Now. The carbon dioxide will help settle her stomach."

His eyes bug out, as if debating whether to argue with me. Yves turns toward the staff lined up on chairs and seated on the floor along the mirrored walls, then bellows an order. A wise decision.

"Where is that PA who took photos of my client? I want that person fired," I add. "Strip him of all responsibilities. I have a lot of friends in this industry, and he should know that he'll never work with this level of talent again."

In truth, professional contacts I have in spades; "friends," less so. Unless you count the executive board at Ovid Blackwell, the PR megafirm I've been with for the last three years. Then, if anyone asks, I have two best friends—the president and vice president of the company—who each insist I use their personal jet when I travel domestically. A small perk in exchange for my skills.

Yves's eyes dart between me and the exit to the main hallway. "You can . . . repeat, please?"

Seventh-grade French, don't fail me now. "Where is the

production assistant who took photos? Qui a pris les photos? Il s'appelle comment?"

He nods to two young men and a woman, standing wide-eyed against the mirrors. "Henri, then Antoine and Isabelle took pictures. And perhaps others."

"Others?" I glower. My client moans, then voms onto the polished eighteenth-century tile where François the XVIII choked to death on an olive pit.

"It all happened so fast. Everyone saw her—sees her. Anything near a phone is fair game these days, yes?" Yves offers up three smartphones like he's making a sacrifice to the publicity gods. "Do you want to delete the photos yourself?"

I smile, and the line producer shrinks backward. "You think I'm going to give the phones back?"

Lifting my head to address the room, I glide forward on my red-soled heels. "Each of you will hand over your phone now. You'll file for unemployment tomorrow because you're all fired."

Outrage ripples across the room. Without blinking, Yves approaches each person to collect devices in a basket.

"You can't fire us. The paperwork takes forever in France, and not something you can do with a snap of your entitled fingers." The set designer, a woman with brown curls, sneers.

"The marketing firm running this campaign is a special collaborator of mine." And well acquainted with the wrath of Addison Stern. "They won't want to be associated with such amateurs and will do what it takes to relieve you of your duties."

"The actress is the one hungover and unprofessional!"

I mime a swollen belly. "Enceinte. Did you really think I'd let you exploit this poor woman by taking pictures of her while she's pregnant?"

All eyes flit to my client's flat stomach as she lies on her back on the floor. Faint snoring rumbles from her throat.

The set designer smirks. "You think you can take our phones—fire us—but you can't keep us quiet."

Yves returns to me with a full basket of shiny touchscreens.

"Actually, that is my job. None of you will breathe a word of today's excitement, because I now hold your entire lives in my hands. For those of you dumb enough to forgo a lock code, I have all the blackmail I need. For the rest of you, I have a team already digging into the background checks you submitted prior to being selected for this shoot. While I know some photos may be up in a cloud, if any images from today make it back down, I will personally blast your browser search histories to your entire contact list."

The woman gapes at me, matching each flabbergasted slack-jawed face in the room. Ah, my favorite kind of reaction: stupor.

"What else am I missing? Oh! The icing on my mille-feuille." I smile, baring my teeth. "The roster of this production can kiss any photo shoots relating to my client Emilia Winthrop, and any of her Hollywood colleagues, goodbye. After all, word travels fast."

The director of the shoot, Annick, rushes forward. An angry little pixie. "Look, I knew that you would be upset about everyone taking photos, but this is unacceptable."

"Is it? What's unacceptable is your hand-selected crew and their embarrassing behavior around a celebrated movie star. Or maybe you've never worked with anyone this big before?"

"I've worked with the biggest names in French and American cinema and have never—"

"No problem." I give her a hard pat on the cheek. "You won't have to worry about that kind of pressure ever again."

Annick seethes. "You have no authority to come in here and bully us. You don't even belong to the French film union."

The young man I saw earlier cuddling up to Annick in the corner delivers a coffee to a producer I met on my last visit to Paris.

"How clever," I deadpan. "I may not be in the union, but I can report you to the creative authorities and my contacts in the French media for sexually harassing subordinates on the job. You should know that I have the authority to do whatever it takes to protect the image of my clients. Up to and including destroying every last voyeur here."

Facing the rest of the crew, I throw them a grin. "In case anyone asks, you'll say the shoot was rescheduled to take place with more experienced personnel. I'll answer questions now. Anyone? No? Pas de questions?"

When no one raises a hand, I step to Emilia's side—she really was exquisite in this summer's erotic thriller—to wipe spittle from her cosmetically enhanced lips. "Let's order pâté from your dressing room."

"Addison," she whispers, struggling. "I'm not pregnant."

"Sweetie, I know. And if anyone suggests otherwise, they'll be laughed out of the media landscape. Have you seen your abs?"

She throws me a weak smile as I help her to her feet. "Thank you. You are a queen, Addison Stern."

As we take halting, echoing steps to the powder room of this stately French manor, a twinge of regret pinches my ribs. Although I dislike using pregnancy as an excuse, it was the best I could think of in the moment. After all, there are worse things than being hungover—or hungover and pregnant. There's poverty. Destitution and desperation. And I will do what it takes to keep my crown at Ovid Blackwell. Addison Stern will never know those plights again.

CHAPTER TWO

ADDISON

LOS ANGELES | AUGUST 18

The flight home the next day is a long eleven hours, but I relish the time to work uninterrupted. While everyone else in first class is watching Meryl Streep nail another emotional arc, I'm drinking champagne and reviewing the sordid affairs of the Paris production crew that my assistant uncovered. They should know better than to cross me at this point, but I like having my insurance at the ready.

Without a doubt, there's nothing tastier than leverage.

Switching gears, I tap the open browser tab on my tablet detailing tonight's event. The Pharma for Female Gala has been in the works since last year's election, when Californians voted in the first female governor—a onetime client of mine, pre–state legislature, when she was merely heiress to a skin-care empire. My current client, Phinneas Redwood, will be introducing Madam Governor, the guest of honor. Every detail of his appearance needs to be perfect.

"Miss Stern, we're about to land at LAX. Hot towel?" A flight attendant dressed in a mauve skirt suit balances a tray of terry-cloth egg rolls.

"Thank you." I pluck one from the top of the pyramid.

Across from me, a one-year-old girl who has been babbling for most of the flight sneaks a peek at me from beneath a fringe of her mother's auburn curls. I couldn't help watching as she toddled up and down the aisle—no one could, given her shock of red hair and sharp brown eyes that kiss at the edges. A mixed baby—Asian and white, probably—just like me. She gurgles to me, but I continue scrolling on my tablet.

No time to pause for pretty faces, sweetheart. In my line of work they are a dime a dozen.

Phinneas has endured the roller coaster of fame as the now-disgraced CEO of Thrive, Inc., a company that kicked off the diet fads of the eighties, and as one of the most recognizable little people in the world. A young buck then, he didn't anticipate the lawsuits that would follow the company for the next three decades or the toll it would take on his personal relationships and emotional health. Still, to Phinneas's credit, Thrive, Inc. staved off self-destruction and is one of Ovid Blackwell's oldest accounts. When Peter Huxton, my VP, personally assigned me the account for their relaunch—with a wink and "I know you're up for the challenge"—I understood the opportunity at hand: Turn this scullery maid into a princess and I may finally land the partner title that I'm owed.

The plane lands, jolting me forward. I bite back an f-bomb.

"Are you all right?" the mother across the aisle asks. Her toddler squeals, as if delighting in the terror plastered on my face like bad Botox.

"Yup. Fine, fine." I give a tight nod, then stare out the window at the twinkling lights of the runway.

Customs is inundated with travelers, per usual. I glide forward to the empty line reserved for frequent, important fliers and pass through even before my flight crew.

Post-security, I slip on red trousers and a white sleeveless top in the restroom before searching out my chartered Escalade. The driver whisks me toward the 405 freeway. Traffic is packed tighter than a model before a weight-loss enema, and I direct the driver to cut through Culver City and up to Beverwil Drive to Wilshire; I send Phinneas a message letting him know I'm running behind.

Sports cars and SUVs crowd the final stretch before we reach the Beverly Hilton. I scroll on my phone to check Phinneas's progress. He should be on the red carpet by now, following our plan to hit all the major outlets before the ceremony begins.

Livestreams on social media confirm the entrance is stacked with big names of the pharmaceutical industry, all dressed to kill. Behind each nerdy-yet-polished individual follows someone dressed in a neutral ensemble speaking into an earpiece or checking their phone—the PR brigade. My people.

I swipe up through the hashtags. Hopefully the reporter from CherieTV—a women-first conservative news network—goes easy on Phinneas tonight. They've criticized him relentlessly as a "toxic male leader" for months but seem to have cooled their take on him recently.

I pause to watch a video of a gray-haired woman in Alexander McQueen parading her tattooed boyfriend before a crowd, then swipe again to an entertainment reporter beaming into the camera: "We've seen the company leaders behind the eye cream that's taking down filler injections, but where is Thrive, Inc.? Controversial CEO Phinneas Redwood was supposed to arrive an hour ago, but this reporter has yet to get the five-minute interview she was promised."

"Shit," I breathe. I had to bribe the reporter's rabbi with the Valley's best challah bread to get that early time slot. I text Phinneas again. Then I notice he didn't reply to my last message.

"Everything okay?" my driver asks above the Latin pop music on the radio.

"Keep going. Past the Hilton. We need to head into Benedict Canyon. And pick up the pace while you're at it."

I give him a new address to punch into the GPS. The incline sharpens as we enter one of the many luxury neighborhoods nestled between Hollywood and the San Fernando Valley. Another client of mine, a tech buff, lives a quarter mile away on the Bel-Air border.

If Phinneas has lost track of time because he's had another burst of inspiration or he's still passed out from last night's bender—both equally plausible for him—I'm going to be livid. We spent three days last week going over his speech for the gala, his outfit, and his key points to push during interviews on the red carpet.

When Operation Scullery Maid began back in the first quarter, I targeted write-ups and print features to rehab Phinneas's image and get public confidence—and stock-market perception—back on track; written interviews offer me the most control. Now, at the middle of Q3, the *My Fair Lady*–makeover I forced on him is complete, and tonight was meant to be his debutante ball—his reentry into society in person, with plenty of time to establish his presence in the industry again before his new product launch in November. But not everyone is as confident as I am that he's ready. Three media appearances scheduled for next week are dependent on how well—how sober—Phinneas appears on camera tonight.

One smart-ass at CNN said he didn't think Ovid Blackwell took on charity cases. I had to personally vouch for Phinneas in front of my VP. As the Escalade pulls to a stop outside a dimly lit one-story house, I'm beginning to wonder if I shot back too soon.

"Wait here," I tell the driver.

Fairy lights illuminate the pebble path leading to Phinneas's front door. Curated desert plants flank the north side and rise like sentries against a wooden fence. The Spanish archway is dark, leaving Phinneas's brass doorknocker in shadows. As if no one is home.

My heels crunch up to the porch; then I rap my fist against the thick oak door. Listen for movement inside. Nothing. I touch the handle, and the door swings inward.

"Phinneas? You here?"

A backward glance confirms the driver isn't paying me any mind. The ghostly glow of a phone screen reflects on his pale cheeks.

"Dammit, Phinneas, you're late." I teeter forward, knowing how much is riding on tonight. Maybe he's driving in the canyon where reception is spotty and we passed each other on the road.

A quick look around the corner of the house, past the pair of palm trees that Phinneas calls "the twins," confirms his black Mercedes remains beneath the carport.

Something feels off. Why isn't he answering? Why didn't he return my text messages?

I smooth down my red trousers, my go-to power pants. "Ready or not, here I come."

White oak hardwood floors appear like bone as I step inside. A night-light activates behind an aquarium, casting the foyer in an eerie green glow. Tiny fish swim along the glass.

"Phinneas? It's Addison Stern. Are you here?"

Behind me, the triangle of light from a streetlamp narrows. The door moans as it closes shut.

To the left is the spacious kitchen and marble breakfast nook at which Phinneas and I outlined tonight's speech last week. The stool he stood on as he redlined my notes at the breakfast table—the audacity—and the reacher he used to grasp a bag of coffee grounds from a top shelf each remain where I last saw him use them. On the granite counter, a closed laptop is positioned next to some kind of meal—pasta—which sits untouched. Beside it, a bottle of wine is uncorked.

Did he run out in a hurry? Forget to lock his door and take his cell?

Is he actually drunk, after swearing to me he would keep a clear head tonight?

I turn in the opposite direction and withdraw my phone from my clutch. Still no texts.

Floor-to-ceiling glass walls of the great room offer a view of manicured topiaries in the expansive backyard. A birdhouse dangles from a tall fir tree, jostled by the canyon wind.

"Phinneas?" I call again. With each hollow click of my heels against the hardwood, a knot in my stomach coils tighter.

Something is wrong. The hair beneath my braid stands on end and I snap my gaze back to the topiaries outside. But the shadows are too dense to tell if anyone is lurking.

I step forward. Another night-light at my ankle activates. A yellow glow. Framed accomplishments line the hallway at my chest level, with only a single matted photo of Phinneas, standing beside his mentor from UCLA.

The sound of trickling water grows. I nudge open a door left ajar to my right to reveal the deep bathroom I've seen before. A toilet, bidet, stand-up shower, and jet bathtub spread along the heated tile.

Continuing farther into the house, I confirm the next door hides a bedroom with crisp bedcovers, and a stepstool at the bed's edge. No Phinneas.

The final door is closed.

Phinneas is probably passed out, exactly as the media outlets suspect. Irritation wrestles with the fear palpitating in my chest.

I turn the handle, then wield my cell phone as both a weapon and flashlight. The office is tidy but for the three bankers boxes stacked on a desk in the center of the room. Emboldened by the night-light in the hall, I step inside.

Burbling water cascades in the corner of the room, a tall waterfall behind shaded glass. A stout bookshelf harbors a series of trinkets—an empty pint glass, a helmet, a model car, and a framed photo of Phinneas and a woman—and no books. Paper with embossed letterhead covers the desk, between the bankers boxes. The black ergonomic chair behind them is empty. He's not here.

Striding forward to the desk, I read the heading of the paper on top: *Coastal Children's Hospital*. A checkbook is wedged between one stack of forms and another, like a bookmark. Beside the pile, handwriting covers the back of a business card: *A.S. 131023*.

My initials are A and S. Is that a note for me?

"Well, Phinneas. If you skipped out to Vegas, I hope you brought your credit card." Turning on my heel, I notice something behind the chair. A sock.

The sharp tang of iron stings my nostrils. I lift my cell phone's glow for a better view, and the sock disappears beneath wide gray pants and a UCLA hoodie covered in blood—the yellow letters of the university logo turned orange.

A body. Phinneas's body. His distinct Roman nose is covered— caked in a layer of blood, forming a mask on the face I planned to splash across social media tonight.

Horror licks down my back. He's not stuck in the canyon somewhere. Not in Vegas. He was attacked, judging from all the blood, and it looks like I'm the first person to taint the crime scene. My mind reels, recalling the doorknobs I touched throughout his home, my fingerprints mingling with the killer's.

I whirl to the door, to the faint light that glares from the hallway. Is the killer still here?

Did I hear movement when I passed the great room and its floor-to-ceiling glass windows?

Were the night-lights already illuminated when I first stepped onto the white hardwood of the foyer? Or not until after, when I triggered the sensors?

Cold air encircles my neck. Am I truly alone with Phinneas's body?

I snatch the cardstock that bears my initials, some burst of paranoia—intuition, perhaps—driving me to pocket the writing.

Walking as quickly as I can to reach the Spanish archway doors, I then march to the Escalade, not daring to look behind me until I am safely tucked into the back seat.

By the time the police arrive, I've made all the calls. Called the VP of Ovid Blackwell, who called the Ovid Blackwell lawyers, who called me. When I recounted my evening to them and what I found within Phinneas's office, my driver hit the automatic locks. In the rearview mirror, fear skittered across his face, the total opposite of my own.

Tonight was bad. A tragedy—for all of the pharma industry. Or something like that.

The truth is that as soon as I hung up with my boss, my mind was flitting ahead, strategizing next steps. This is not my first dead body, not even close—though it is the bloodiest. So how to announce the untimely, tragic death of Ovid Blackwell's friend and client Phinneas Redwood? How to salvage this headline in the media?

I rub my temples. The sweatshirt logo, turned orange, that Phinneas died wearing returns to mind. A shiver pinches my neck, the threat of career disaster looming nigh. How to spin this news in order to benefit Ovid Blackwell—and me?

Red and blue lights flash from the main road.

A man in a dark uniform knocks on my window. "Ma'am? Please step onto the sidewalk."

I slide out from the back seat's leather. "Addison Stern, with Ovid Blackwell Public Relations. I came here to check on my client, Phinneas Redwood. He's inside. Dead."

The officer nods, unfazed. "Sergeant Ames. Start with the time you arrived. Walk me through your path inside the house."

After I recount the circumstances of my night, then repeat

the story for a lieutenant, Sergeant Ames tells me to take a seat on the curb. I laugh, then remain standing. Not in these pants.

Sergeant Ames squints at me, exaggerating a vein in the middle of his forehead. But he doesn't comment on my reaction. Instead, he disappears into the house, following personnel who wear black coveralls.

The first reporter arrives a few minutes later. Their kind is always so punctual when it comes to these types of events. "Addison Stern?" she asks, wearing a pinstripe suit from last season. "You're the deceased's publicist?"

Casting an eye at a detective who's speaking with a neighbor, I shake my head. "I can't confirm anything."

"Of course," she says. "But if you could. What was the last thing Phinneas Redwood said to you? What would you say is his legacy? Anything to give people a sense of what you're feeling right now?"

Recalling the checkbook amid the pile of paperwork I saw on his desk, I offer a weak smile. Search for the right words to hit this curveball out of Dodger Stadium.

"Redwood . . . along with his company, Thrive, Inc. . . . . is a philanthropist to his core," I begin. "He wrote a check to a children's hospital just recently."

The reporter makes a noise of quiet awe. "Wow. What a guy. He really turned things around, didn't he?"

I dip my head. Allow myself a moment of thoughtful reflection. "Yes, he did."

She types notes on her phone. "Do you think you'll have to stay here much longer? Seems way beyond your job duties—on a few levels."

I offer another forlorn smile, aware that I am always

representing Ovid Blackwell, always interviewing with future CEOs, real estate moguls, and heirs to questionably amassed fortunes. No matter how batshit crazy the situation might be.

"It's simple, really," I reply, as a helicopter surges overhead. "I'd do anything for my clients."

CHAPTER THREE

CONNOR

LAS VEGAS | AUGUST 19

I haven't been this screwed since Post Malone's New Year's party in Bangkok, when I did priceless thousand-year-old shrooms by accident. Waving my worthless ticket in my hand, I stare at the mega big-screen of the Bellagio's sports wing, at the triumphant jockey clutching the trophy that should belong to another guy—mine, on whom I placed a bet comprising the last of my life savings. Big Dipper, the odds-on favorite for this year's Belmont Stakes, lost to So We Win Again by barely a flick of a horsetail.

No, not just screwed. Royally manhandled. Squeezed like an orange and told to turn my head and cough by an intern with sweaty palms.

"How'd you do?" a waitress asks. She clears empty drinks from beside a slot machine. Pauses to give me a once-over, probably admiring the tailored button-up and chinos I bought three years ago, back when I was rolling in cash. Working as a private investigator, poking into the lives of anyone my wealthy patrons were curious about or nursed a grudge against, yielded more money than I thought I would ever need.

"Yeah, not so great. I lost—" everything, but this waitress doesn't need to know that. "Seems like I can't get a break lately."

"Buck up, guy. Maybe the next bet will be a winner." She winks, all heavy eyeliner and fake lashes.

"I doubt it," I mumble. "Hey, uh—any chance you can leave those drinks? They look half-full."

I wince, hearing how pathetic I sound.

The waitress wrinkles her button nose. "They've been sitting out for the last hour while I was serving a bachelor party in the high rollers' room. That's not liquor, it's melted ice."

Casting me another stink eye, she turns away. I crumple the square of paper in my hand, then toss it in the trash. The remainder of my life savings was pretty pitiful to begin with: $371. I suspect the sum would have been more impressive had I not moved to Las Vegas. Being here, after I was forced into early retirement at the age of thirty-four, made everything feel surreal. Limitless. Without consequences beneath the blazing desert sun.

I take a seat and pretend to put money into a slot machine that features the Kardashians walking a runway. Maybe a different waitress will arrive so I can order a fresh drink for free.

A pop-up window appears in the corner of my screen. A news segment. The host of the show, a leggy blond in a barely there halter dress, stands beside aerial camera footage of a house.

"Thanks for joining your digital news source, LVIN. Just last night, CEO and controversial onetime playboy Phinneas Redwood was found dead in his Benedict Canyon home. Although police have not yet released further details, celebrities and business tycoons alike are weighing in on the tragedy."

The footage cuts to some bodybuilder from the eighties expressing his regret, but the split screen continues with a camera zooming in on a house. A woman in bright red pants and a white top stands on the sidewalk beneath a helicopter spotlight while police officers mill around her.

I suck in a breath. "Holy shit."

"Can I get you anything?" a new waitress, older and with blue eye shadow, asks at my elbow.

"Uh, yeah. Martini. Extra olives."

She leaves me to gape at Addison Stern, dripping style outside a crime scene. Beautiful black hair wrangled into a French braid accents high cheekbones, dark red lipstick, and her perfect neck that, years ago, used to be her favorite place for me to kiss her. It was mine, at least.

Well, it was alternately my favorite place to kiss her and where I wanted to strangle her, but I digress.

"Of course you'd be working with that scumbag, Addison." I scoff at the screen as the memories come rushing back. The scent of her lavender shampoo. Her love of James Dean. Her deep belly laugh that sounded like a machine gun if the moment hit her just right. The late nights and late mornings lying in bed together.

Her bloodlust for finding the best angle of a story to benefit her client. Her inability to see black and white—she was myopic, only seeing the gray area as it suited her needs. The way she betrayed me, stole information from me when I let my guard down, to fuck over my own client to help another Ovid Blackwell campaign.

When I had to cop to the blame to my client, the damage to my reputation as a private investigator ended my career, three years ago—which didn't seem like the worst thing, until I discovered online poker. A few successful hits gave me the bright idea to move to Vegas. For a while, it was the good life. The cheaper cost of living held an obvious advantage over Los Angeles—but only if you stayed out of the casinos. Bottom line, it's Addison's fault that I'm stuck here in Vegas with a lousy betting streak. While she's scrubbing clean the images of the worst companies and schmucks in the country. And looking gorgeous on TV.

"Martini, extra olives." The waitress returns with a glass brimming with gin. I take it, then throw her my last fiver on the tray.

"Oh, wait. Uh, could I have that back?"

The waitress lifts both eyebrows. "Excuse me?"

"Sorry, I mean—you don't have change, do you?"

She purses thin lips, then reaches into her apron pocket and produces five one-dollar bills. I take them all, then hand her a single, pathetic George Washington. Burning shame climbs my throat.

The waitress leaves, and I gulp down half the drink. The TV host moves on to another segment—the latest movie to be filmed along the Hoover Dam—and I stand to walk the diamond-patterned carpet. Cigarette smoke is thick on a Saturday afternoon in summer. Tourists and bachelor parties rolled in yesterday like a selfie-tsunami, as they do every Friday night.

I amble past a pair of dancers in a cage. Pause to admire the tassels and sequins.

Another sip of my drink goes down easy. A retired couple hits the blackjack table beside me, and a group of preteen girls wearing heavy makeup livestream their afternoon on social media. Vegas: Where anything goes, and one second you're up—and the next you're considering stealing garnishes from the bar for dinner.

The group of preteens disperses. A man in a black hoodie leans over a bistro table behind them. Staring at me.

"Hey, Connor, right?" His voice is gruff. I don't recognize it.

"Uh, yeah?"

He moves toward me. Hulking shoulders, thick eyebrows that connect in the middle, and a glare that I last saw in the dead of night on the Fremont Strip come thundering closer.

Spinning on my heel, I walk. Quickly, at a speed just below a sprint, I begin weaving my way through the crowd.

Gianni's muscle. Gianni was a guy I knew better than to place bets with, but who was the only bookie who'd accept such little collateral as I had to give before last week's boxing match.

I down my drink, then toss it on a cocktail tray. High-pitched bells peal from a gambling arcade game, screams and moans burst from a craps table that I pass, and drunken conversations all blur together to make listening for my pursuer's approach impossible. I sneak a glance behind me, and he's closer than I remember. Faster than I gave him credit for. He's already passing the craps table.

HIGH ROLLERS ROOM. The illuminated sign overhead is a beacon of safety, and I cut right. Slipping between a pair of burly women with sun hats, I withdraw from my wallet the VIP card I earned when I was at my financial peak, then disappear past the glass doors.

I whirl to watch Gianni's goon turn in a circle. He doubles back toward the craps table.

My shoulders drop. I lean my head against the glass. He's going to come back—they always do. When they return with their open hands, I'll still have nothing to offer them. How did I end up here? How the hell am I ever going to dig myself out of the quarter-million-dollar hole I'm in?

"Connor. Connor Windell?"

A woman's gravelly voice calls from behind. The back of my neck prickles in a wave of déjà vu. I know that sound.

Seated at an empty blackjack table, wearing a flowy, mid-length black dress and blunt heels, Mrs. Genevieve Aspen balances a slender cigarette holder between two delicate fingers—delicate in size, but wielding more power than most grown men could hope for. She's a widow-turned-venture-capitalist and used to keep me very gainfully employed. Anytime she thought her employees, new boyfriends, lovers, or children were up to something, she gave me a call, then had an envelope of cash dropped in my mailbox. I could usually count on her paranoia to fund a trip in December, my own year-end bonus.

"I thought that was your shapely behind," she says, matter-of-fact. With a flick of her wrist, she invites me to join her. "It's been ages."

I slide onto the plush velvet chair opposite her. The dealer raises his eyebrow, waiting for me to ante up; I shake my head.

"How are you, Gen?"

She sweeps a glance down my face, taking in the sweat dotting my brow and my chest still rising and falling too fast.

"I suspect better than you, my dear."

"You always were perceptive. What are you doing in the desert?" I sneak a glimpse at the glass doors. Still no linebacker shoulders. Not yet.

23

She puffs on her cigarette. Red lipstick leaves rings around the paper. "I needed a getaway. Business is good, of course. It's my family."

"Oh?"

She pauses mid-inhale to eye me. Zero in on my cornea from close range. "Tell me, Connor. Was that just babble I heard, that you sold out your client? Simply your excuse to leave Los Angeles and the game? Or did you really betray your professional ethics?"

"You know, it's a funny . . . Well, the thing is—"

She slaps the air with her taloned hand, interrupting me. "No, don't say. I make my own decisions, and you always delivered with me. More importantly, I have a proposition for you that I can't entrust to anyone else. I confess—I came to Las Vegas to find you. I deleted your number after that scandal, but I heard you were a regular at the Bellagio these days. I figured sooner or later you'd turn up among the high rollers, so here I am."

My mouth opens. Hope flutters in my chest like a baby bird. "Gen, what do you need?"

She taps her smartphone where it sits on the green felt tabletop. A photo of Genevieve and a spritely young woman fills the screen.

"My daughter, Hyacinth, is engaged to a man who I believe has been unfaithful to her. I need you to find out whether my suspicion is correct."

"What makes you think that?" I ask.

The white security-tint envelopes from the past flash to mind, and I can almost smell the crisp hundred-dollar bills within. I've dreamed about a moment like this, a chance to start over and leave the money pit of Vegas, ever since my luck started to change a year ago—and yet . . .

"And why do you think I can help? I'm an outcast back in LA. My bridges are all burned there, I'm sure you know. I'm . . . I'm done with all that. I hurt a lot of people."

Being on the receiving end of Addison's double cross brought a lot into perspective—although I didn't come to grips with the way my actions destroyed lives until a long time after. It was the jagged little pill I swallowed eventually.

Gen fixes me with a stare. "Security footage caught my daughter's fiancé sneaking another woman into my guesthouse. There's the pudding for you."

I whistle. "That is compelling."

"And you are the right man for the job because I say you are. No one else was ever as efficient, discreet, or creative as you. You don't have to hurt anyone. You'd be making everyone's life better by uncovering the truth. Most of all, my Hyacinth's."

"I'm not sure about that."

"Then if he is cheating on Hyacinth," Gen continues, tapping her cigarette in a gold-flecked ashtray, "you have the choice to secure additional payment."

I lean away in the short-backed chair. "Do you want me to investigate the mistress?"

She levels me with a sneer. "I want you to bring the affair to an end, using whatever means you deem necessary. And I don't want to know a scrap of detail about how you do it."

My shoulders slump. Genevieve Aspen wants me to do something I've never done before: meddle. Sure, I've poked around in other people's lives, their bank accounts, and real estate records, and that has led to trouble. But I've never altered anyone's path or deliberately harmed someone—until Addison did on my behalf. Other PIs I knew, friends of mine, who got too involved in their client's personal affairs wound up missing, or outright dead. Messing with someone's relationship—even a poorly functioning one, if he is cheating—could be more hassle than it's worth.

I sigh. "Look, Gen, I appreciate you coming all the way out here, but I can't do that. My answer is no."

Gen lifts a finger. Signals to a cocktail waitress dressed in a white beaded floor-length gown. "How much money do you have in your checking account, Connor?"

"Excuse me?"

"It can't be much." She pauses as the young woman delivers a martini to the table. Extra olives. "It's been, what, three years since you left and forced me to work with your subpar competitor PIs? I can offer you a signing bonus, if you will, and bring you out of the red—whatever it is. Judging from the sheen across your temples when you burst through the doors, it must be a significant figure."

She slides an olive off a toothpick, then bites into it with a dull pop. My stomach rumbles.

"What's the guy's name? The fiancé," I ask.

"Devon Lim."

"The tech buff?" Years ago, he was Addison's client; he still could be. We drove past his megamansion once, somewhere over in Bel-Air.

Genevieve scowls. "The tech buff embarrassing my daughter and my family."

Although I know it shouldn't, learning I could do some damage to Addison's carefully curated world adds a twinkle to the job offer. A sparkle. An extra sequin on a drag queen's bustier. Plus, Gen's offer of a signing bonus might get Gianni off my back. And ensure he doesn't break it.

"So, deep thinker. What's your decision?" Genevieve polishes off the last of her three olives, then plunks the toothpick in her full martini glass.

I wave a hand to the waitress, ready for my own gin-soaked fruit. "All right, I'll do it. But I'm going to need something from you first."

CHAPTER FOUR

ADDISON

LOS ANGELES | AUGUST 24

Palm trees dot the cityscape visible from the fifth floor of this Sunset Boulevard high-rise—permanent pom-poms cheering me on to do what I do best: dominate.

Someone knocks on my office door, jarring me from reflections on my success and the amazing view that came with it. Peter O. Huxton, VP of Ovid Blackwell, peeks his head in. The *O* stands for Olivier, but *overwrought* might be more appropriate this week.

"I scared you, Addison? Sorry about that."

I exhale through my nostrils, seated in my ergonomic, black smart chair. The massage setting should kick on automatically when in range of such anxiety. Peter has been in nonstop calls with the Ovid Blackwell team of lawyers, our media allies, and the Los Angeles Sheriff's Department since Phinneas's death.

"Not at all. Just strategizing my next steps."

He frowns. Hazel eyes dart to the floor. "Of course. Do you have a minute?"

Although each of mine is invaluable, I nod. "What can I do for you, Peter?"

He steps inside, peering out the window at the view I was awarded after six months of working here, when I convinced MSNBC to cover my client's daughter's quinceañera, then I secured high-priority info on a different client's competitor. Getting the dirt on the rival came at a hefty personal cost, but I gained this incredible office. No regrets.

"Total tragedy to lose Phinneas Redwood like that," he says, not for the first time. "Awful that you were the one to discover him that way."

"It was."

"I remember when he was just a young thing—back when I was," Peter muses. "He went by 'Red' back then, but everyone used different names in the eighties." Peter strikes me as a placid lake: still on the surface, but rippling underneath. What would his different name have been? Reader Peter? Peter Peter Pumpkin Eater?

"Were the police asking you about Phinneas—about when he first became our client?" Peter adds. "Maybe I could add more color there. I don't want the burden of representing the firm to fall solely on you, Addison."

I dip my head. Peter is usually hands-off, as busy as a partner and VP at Ovid can be, but this last week he's been in overdrive. Checking in with everyone to make sure that our barge weathers this unexpected storm.

"Thank you, I appreciate that. I've told the police everything I can."

Peter lifts an eyebrow.

"Well." I smile. "Everything that our lawyers advised me was pertinent."

He tips his weight onto his heels. "Good, good. It's been stressful, to say the least, to have the police interviewing so many of our employees this week. I should have known you'd be managing just fine."

"Clearly."

Peter chuckles. "Well, come join us in the hub when you have a moment. The team has something to say to you."

With a sideways glance to me, he turns and exits my glass-walled office.

"Nice work in Paris, Addison. You really saved the day with that pregnancy bit," I grumble to myself. Although I've been grateful for the support from Peter and the board of directors—with no mention from them of the suspicious comments flying across news outlets and social media, questioning my involvement in Phinneas's death—a proper pat on the back for my work last week would be nice. A promotion to partner, for instance.

The rumor mill has been brutal since the weekend, both inside and outside Ovid Blackwell. The police expanded their orbit, asking my colleagues if Phinneas had any illicit activities or known enemies, and word leaked online that blue uniforms have been at our office each day this week. Lately, things at Ovid Blackwell are looking worse than the day after a bender in Malibu.

I rise from my chair. Smooth the pleats in my chartreuse skirt. Prepare myself for more searching glances and darting looks.

Although HR advised me to take off a whole week, to regroup after the trauma I experienced in discovering Phinneas postmortem, I came back after three days. I was going stir-crazy in my West Hollywood condo, anxious to ensure my other clients didn't get neglected in my absence or snatched up by an enterprising coworker. I was too tense as I scrolled my news app for updates on Phinneas's investigation. On his killer.

The lobby of this floor—aka the hub—connects the two wings of Ovid Blackwell: public relations on the north side, support functions on the south. Today, everyone seems crowded into the modern space, wedging between the coppertop reception desk and the bamboo garden that lines the opposite glass partition.

"What's going on?" I ask Malina, our social media manager and my assistant. I join her beside a table stacked with cookies, handheld strawberry tarts with the crumbly crust—my favorite—buttery croissants, and enough alcoholic drinks at ten in the morning to make a bartender blush.

"Are we celebrating something?"

She turns to me, powdered sugar on her lips. "Oh—she's here!"

"Congratulations, Addison!" The room erupts with my colleagues' voices and thunderous applause. Peter strides to the front of the pack, facing me. A performative smile tightens his jaw.

"What is this about?" I ask. Ovid Blackwell doesn't carelessly spend money on its employees. Something is up.

Am I being forced out? Did someone scapegoat me for this mess with the police? The memory of someone else I knew who was forced into early retirement flickers, but I push it down.

"Oh, you know." Peter chuckles, then steps to my side. Malina slides out of frame as someone else—another social media teammate—comes forward and snaps a photo of Peter and me.

I force a smile. "Should we be throwing a party when the police are still hovering?"

"We've been lying low for almost a week, Addison, and we issued our public statement of mourning on Monday. Our competitors and our clients need to know that we're rolling forward, business as usual, despite ongoing difficulties. And we're celebrating you and your success!" He turns to me, his voice now elevated so even the mailroom clerks can hear.

"Peter, I'd prefer—"

"For your hard work in Paris," he continues. "Thanks to your quick action on set, you narrowly avoided bad press and handled the threat of a confidentiality breach at La Fumée. Emilia Winthrop's perfume campaign and the week she spent in Versailles have been all that anyone is talking about. Internet chatter is raving about her every move, restaurant choice, and outfit—with no mention of her club-hopping or a possible pregnancy. Best of all, according to our friends at her production company, buzz is high for Emilia's indie release next month, coming off a successful festival run. Ovid Blackwell continues to lead in global public relations with you raising the game. Cheers to Addison!"

The room lifts champagne flutes as a full glass is placed in my hand. Though unclear on Peter's strategy, I take a sip anyway. Cool liquid douses my fight-or-flight instincts.

This is a party. For me, apparently. Not a goodbye party or an indictment suggesting I could be homicidal. Scanning the crowd of Ovid acolytes and their laughter, I find the Photoshop fail: Through the glass wall of the adjacent conference room and halfway down the building, I see people carrying bins of paper down into the fire stairwell—probably to the shredder that we keep on hand for disposing of old marketing materials. This isn't a party for me. It's a distraction—to rid the firm of incriminating documents while the police continue to snoop around.

Peter leans in close. "You do deserve a party, Addison. This one just happens to be dedicated to cleaning house."

I huff. There's the Ovid I know so well. "It's a smart move. Besides, when I'm promoted to partner, we'll need a much larger venue to celebrate. Maybe that rooftop bar in Downtown."

"About that, Addison. The board announced that Hiram Benson will step down at the end of Q4, but they haven't decided whom to name as a new partner. Simply maintaining Emilia's image won't earn you that title."

I swig more bubbles. "It's true, Phinneas was the meatier job. But he had secrets and enemies, obviously. Not my fault. Who's the next client in need of image rehab?"

Peter raises an eyebrow. "I'm rooting for you, Addison. Ever since you got the Archdiocese of San Diego to endorse that ex-convict Bitcoin genius, I've been touting your abilities to the firm."

"Everyone was." Fake humility is beneath me. That was a damn good coup.

"But I heard you personally vouch for Redwood's progress, that he would be ready for this week's round of interviews," Peter continues. "Not only did he not appear for them, he was killed before his first in-person event. As his publicist, you should have known the ins and outs of his life better than he did. You should have known who was gunning for him before even his killer decided he was dead. It raised a lot of eyebrows in the executive office that he wasn't kept out of trouble."

Goddammit, Phinneas. "I'm sure it did. But Mr. Griffin and

the other board members know I'm the best they have on their roster. They'll get over it."

"I'm not so sure, Addison." Peter ducks his head. "Griffin texted me from the Bahamas, pretty concerned—"

"Look, Peter. I'm a publicist, not a clairvoyant. If I were, I'd be able to warn the admins which one of them should expect Mr. Griffin's unwanted sexual advances when he returns."

Peter chokes on his drink. "Keep your voice down, Addison."

"We all make mistakes, Peter. It just so happens his are muffled by NDAs."

A moment passes between us in which neither of us breaks eye contact. When he finally blinks, I know the ax is about to drop.

"Addison, you're not making this easy—"

"Because it wouldn't serve me."

"Then I'll be more direct: The board wants you to take a step back from all high-profile clients and events."

"Excuse me?"

Peter sighs, as if I forced the confession from him. "It would be good for you, Addison."

"Because you care so much?" I smile, showing my teeth. Regardless of what bombshell Peter detonates on me, I won't be unsettled. My colleagues continue to sip champagne and nosh on my favorite pastries, none the wiser to the rage brewing in my chest.

How could Ovid Blackwell sideline me? They should put their star publicist front and center to dispel the rumors, not fuel them by setting me aside. The board of directors is composed of industry professionals, each of whom has an equity stake in the firm's success. It must be amateur hour for them to be spooked by a few circling badges.

Peter shrinks backward, but he doesn't retreat. "Of course

I care. I've watched the impact you've had in only a few years, and I worry what this overexposure might do to your career."

"Tell that to Miley Cyrus. Tell that to Paris Hilton."

"Look, I've fought just like you're doing, Addison. I had to struggle up from the bottom to get where I am, and I know you can do the same."

Peter mentors young publicists just starting out. He's made a name for himself, not only as a PR leader, but as a compassionate guide who donates his time and energy to the next generation. A fact I've always considered quaint. Like honesty, when speaking with a CPA.

Peter sighs. Lifts his glass to his temple as if he's nursing a headache. "Well, there is Reed Song. He's got an event in Hong Kong next week for the unveiling of his new architectural project in Wan Chai. It needs an Ovid Blackwell member on the ground."

"Hong Kong?"

"His mistress has gotten pretty aggressive at public events, his drinking is interfering with appearances, and the media is decrying how he's single-handedly forcing low-income families onto the street. Go there and get him some good press saying that he's been misrepresented. Convince the local outlets, if you can. They're adamant he's the problem."

Hong Kong. A metropolitan city where expats of all backgrounds gather to make career moves.

I lift my chin to the room of people celebrating me. "Okay. Fine. I want what the board wants."

Peter raises an eyebrow. "That's very amenable of you. Am I missing something? You're agreeing to be sent overseas to manage a locally important unveiling that won't move the needle here on your quest for partner."

I fix him with a penetrating stare. "Reed Song deserves the very best. And that happens to be me."

"Addison." Peter hesitates, scanning the room. "Los Angeles Fashion Week will be here in six weeks. We need all eyes on our clients—the live ones—at that point. I know you'll do everything in your power to restore the balance long before then. So do us all a favor and lie low when you get back home."

The elevator dings. Two men in generic short-sleeve button-ups step forward. They take in the party, scanning the crowd, starting at the reception desk to where I stand beside the food and drink buffet. Both men are probably early fifties. Though far from twins, their shared demeanor is remote, steely.

"Shit," Peter mutters. "Not these guys again. Aarin!"

Conversations hush. Aarin Williams, resident counsel at Ovid Blackwell, pokes her head up from a conversation over by the bamboo. Natural dark curls form a halo around her determined gaze. The lobby's usual jazz soundtrack slinks across the gray marble tile.

"Gentlemen, back so soon. What can we do for you?" Her tone could freeze the La Brea Tar Pits.

"We want to speak with Addison Stern." The taller one, who wears a slender tie bearing eight balls, fixes me with a blank stare. "We went by her apartment, and her neighbors shared that she'd already returned to work. Pretty quick after discovering such a gruesome scene, Ms. Stern."

Aarin takes a step forward. "As counsel for this firm, neither it nor its employees have anything further to say on the matter. Unless you'd like to produce a formal subpoena."

Convince the local outlets, if you can. Peter's challenge continues to ring in my ear—its misplaced doubt of my abilities.

"No, it's fine, Aarin. I'm happy to chat with the police."

Peter throws me a warning glance that I return coolly. I gesture toward my office. "Gentlemen."

"You really don't have to do that, Addison," Aarin says. "They're federal agents."

I stifle my surprise. What would the feds want with me? Why care about Phinneas?

The music abruptly ends, no doubt at Peter's quick command, and we leave the party. Silence in the hub is so much more conducive to eavesdropping.

"What can I do for you? I've already spoken to the police extensively." I slide into the chair behind my desk, deliberately facing the agents with my back to my hard-earned view of palm trees. The picture of success. Power.

The taller one, with patchy gray stubble, clears his throat. "I'm Special Agent Jonas and this is Special Agent Tremor. We were hoping for more detail about your *relationship* with the deceased, Phinneas Redwood."

"We weren't romantic."

A wry smile tweaks his stubble. "I didn't say you were. But it's interesting you jump to a defensive line."

Tremor lifts both eyebrows. "Who would want to harm Redwood? Let's start there." The good cop.

"Frankly? Just about every woman who took a diet pill in the eighties."

"Could you elaborate?" Tremor withdraws his phone. He taps notes into an app.

"Lawsuits were rife in his company, Thrive, Inc., when it first exploded onto the diet scene. Mostly due to weight gain, enhanced acne, and the occasional infertility. Women were not pleased."

"And what was your role in Redwood's life, exactly?" Jonas asks.

"To try to downplay the negative history of his reputation. To assist him along his path to greatness."

"For a cost," Jonas adds. "A hefty one, if my sources can be believed about Ovid Blackwell's price tag."

"Nothing in this life is free, Agent."

"If your job is to know Redwood and his issues, who in his life would have motive and opportunity to kill him?" Tremor lifts his gaze to mine.

Ah, this question again. The blame that the board of directors lobbed at me returns to hover above my designer blouse. "Honestly, Agents, I don't know. I spent several months with him as my client, and the list of disgruntled customers, business associates, and family members was too long to itemize. I had more important tasks at hand."

"Such as?"

"Getting Phinneas sober. Getting him presentable. Having him wake before noon most days."

More note-taking. "Did you see anyone outside of Redwood's home when you arrived last Friday night?"

"No."

"If you had, do you think you could recognize any of those disgruntled individuals?"

Phinneas's darkened stoop seemed ominous when I pulled up in the Escalade. I recall goose bumps pricking the skin of my neck, but I pushed forward, pushed through, per usual. No one was lurking out front. Or beside the carport.

The tang of iron stings my nose in a fit of sensory memory. Phinneas had been recently killed when I found him; the window of time between my arrival and the killer's departure must be narrow. Was that person lurking nearby, watching me, still dripping with Phinneas's blood? Did I see the outline of a man's—or woman's—shape?

"Doubtful. I still can't understand why you care," I add. "A likely homicide took place within LAPD's jurisdiction. What did Phinneas do that would catch the interest of the federal government?"

Agent Jonas tips his chin. "Maybe we're not investigating Phinneas. Maybe we're investigating his death as a hate crime under federal law. As a high-profile little person, he could have caught the interest of certain prejudiced aggressors."

I scoff. "Right. You're harassing me now because you want social justice."

"Ms. Stern," Agent Tremor begins. "Mr. Redwood was shot twice, once in the chest and once in the head. We need you to tell us anything that might be relevant to solving his murder. Did you see anything unusual at Mr. Redwood's home, or did you disturb anything? Maybe an open door that you shut. A payment that Redwood left for you that you, understandably, took. Something you're not telling us?"

The white cardstock with its messy handwriting flits to mind. "No. I saw nothing at all."

Agent Jonas leans forward. "Your fingerprints are all over the crime scene, Ms. Stern. Were you really there to pick him up for some event, or did you have something else planned?"

A long pause follows. Agent Jonas looks giddy, as if he's caught me somehow, and my patience begins to wear thin.

"You and the LAPD don't have any leads, do you?" I counter. "The FBI really must be clueless to be wasting time in here with me, a publicist, when it's been almost a week since Phinneas was killed—murdered in cold blood."

"It's highly usual to question the person who discovered the body," Agent Jonas says.

"Sure. But I've answered your questions, and those of local police officers. I'm getting sick of repeating myself. Now get out there and find Phinneas's killer. And stop wasting my expensive time."

Even Agent Tremor regards me coldly. "So this is the tack you're taking, Ms. Stern?"

I push back from behind my desk. "Well, as Ovid Blackwell's attorney might reply: I am not at liberty to say. Thanks for the visit."

They exchange a glance. Then the federal agents rise to leave.

\\\\////

Between emails, phone calls, and planning strategy for Reed Song, the afternoon passes quickly. Questions from my conversation with the feds linger in my mind, but I do my best to ignore them. This chapter is finished; Phinneas is dead. There's no reason to dwell on any of the details of his life or death, as far as I'm concerned. As his publicist, I've done all I can.

At four o'clock, I pack up. Home is where I need to be, where I can begin researching Reed Song's mistress with a glass of red in hand. Maybe toss back an Ambien in a few hours.

When I reach my doorstep, thirty minutes and three miles later, it's with visions of the French cheese I smuggled home in my suitcase. I insert my house key, and it turns with ease.

Too much ease, in fact. The dead bolt wasn't locked.

Chills spiral down my back. I'm a thirty-two-year-old woman, whose quick thinking has elevated her professionally but who lives alone in WeHo with only a baseball bat under her bed; I always lock my door. A quick swipe on my phone to the security app for my Ring doorbell reveals the battery is dead. And I last charged it a year ago. Shit.

Withdrawing the pepper spray I carry on me, I enter the house. Slanting sunlight reflects across my blue hardwood floor. I take a step forward. Inhale. The kitchen and front sitting room still smell like the coffee-and-protein shake I downed for breakfast. Nothing appears out of place.

A floorboard creaks from somewhere deeper within. From the bedroom.

Hair on my neck stands on end, and I'm reaching behind me for the exit when a body appears in the bedroom doorway. The silhouette of a man.

"Who are you?" I demand. "How did you get in here?"

The man—government agent? Hit man from Phinneas's past? Killer who watched me enter a crime scene?—takes a deliberate step toward me. He passes the framed photos on the wall of me with clients, of the first check I ever received as a publicist.

Sun angles through my kitchen window to strike a pair of scuffed loafers. It travels along tailored chinos, then highlights broad shoulders in a plain white tee. When the man fully emerges from the shadows, I suck in a sharp breath. Rage tightens my chest.

"*You.* What are you doing here?"

Connor Windell grins like a smug tick. He holds up a single house key. "I guess you never changed your locks."

CHAPTER FIVE

CONNOR

WEST HOLLYWOOD | AUGUST 24

Addison Stern glares at me from the doorway. Sleek black hair reaches her elbows, and she wears a satin shirt and pencil skirt that probably cost as much as the first-class flight I asked Genevieve to book for me out of Vegas. With the dusk behind her adding a fiery glow, Addison looks every bit the goddess of wrath.

"You made a key to my home?" She seethes.

I can't help gloating. "You're not the only one double-crossing people at night."

"And what does that mean?"

"Exactly what you think. You stole my password and hacked into my phone while I was dead asleep. I made a copy of your house key in case I ever needed it."

"Why? Why are you here, Connor?"

I lean an elbow against her granite counter. "An old friend can't pop in for a visit?"

"Old friends could do that, if I had any."

A fringe of hair falls into my eyeline. I make no move to brush it back. "C'mon, Addison," I purr. "Is that any way to greet me?"

A smile plays on her mouth. "You have five seconds to explain yourself or I'm uncapping the pepper spray."

"Fine. Fact is, I'm feeling generous. I have a business proposition for . . ."

Before I can finish the sentence, she's smirking. "You? What could *you* offer *me*?"

I arch an eyebrow. "We both know I used to offer you a lot of things, Add. In a few different places."

This kitchen, for one. Her back porch. The carport. Griffith Park. A bathroom stall at the Viper Room.

"Is that what this is about?" she asks. "You're broke and have taken up selling your wares door-to-door?"

"I'm proposing a partnership. You've got a dead client—oh, don't make that face, everyone knows by now—and could use someone on your side. While the police are still searching for the killer, or a name to pin this on, you might want someone away from Ovid Blackwell to watch out for you."

Addison rolls her eyes. She nudges the door closed with a stilettoed toe, then throws her purse on the counter. She places the small canister of pepper spray to the side. A warning.

"Please. The firm doesn't want me to go to jail. I make too much money for them."

I tap my chin. "Wait, remind me. Wasn't I the one living in a desert mirage the last three years?"

Addison doesn't say anything, which means she knows I'm right. She strides to the wraparound kitchen counter, past bare walls, then uncorks a half-empty bottle of Merlot.

I lean toward her. Soften my stance. "Despite everything that happened between us, we always worked well together."

She snorts. Red wine sloshes inside a deep glass that's all set and ready on the counter like this is her routine. "Okay, you've outlined half your partnership. What's in it for you?"

"Not much." I shrug. "Just some information."

"On?"

"Devon Lim. He was your client a few years back. I'm betting he still is."

She tosses a sheet of black hair over her shoulder. That's a yes. "You know I would never betray my clients, past or present. My answer is no."

"Really? Even after the way we parted?"

Addison lifts both eyebrows, as if I just asked where to find the local Food4Less. "I'm not sure what you mean."

"Oh no? Quick recap: You seduced me to get what you want—like always, to benefit your career—then royally screwed me out of my own."

She shakes her head. "I was involved there, but you left LA by yourself."

"Addison, everyone believed I was the source of the information leak against my client when you stole the information from my phone. Just to give yourself another leg up—clout with Ovid Blackwell."

She bats her eyes. "It wasn't all in the name of ambition, Connor."

"Cut the shit, Addison," I snap. "It's been three years. If you think I don't see you now for exactly who you are, you're a worse publicist than I thought."

She dips her chin. "So, now that you have my answer, should I call the cops to report a B and E, or will you leave on your own?"

Zero remorse. Of course. Addison doesn't give a rat's anything about the damage she causes or the lives she ruins. Least of all mine.

"It's not breaking and entering when you have a key, Addison."

"Let's see what the police think about that."

Anger grinds my jaw, my calm splintering. "Devon Lim hasn't been to his Bel-Air home for the last week, and no one knows where he is."

Addison swirls her drink. She leans against wood-trimmed cabinets along the kitchen's back wall. "You mean none of your former contacts knows where he is. Or maybe they know but they won't share with you because you can't be trusted."

"Addison. *You* are the reason no one trusts me."

"If I recall correctly, you car-dialed the president of the American Federation of Labor—"

"That's not what happened."

"—while we were getting *intimate* in your back seat because you wanted to humiliate me to an Ovid Blackwell client. No one trusts you, because you're a pompous show horse, constantly trying to mount the next goal."

"I told you, I don't know how the AFL president was called. I swear. My foot must have hit the touchscreen, then scrolled to my contacts list. And besides, that wouldn't justify you hacking into my phone and stealing—"

Addison huffs. "This song and dance again? Look, Connor. Devon is a very important leader in the tech industry. He's always up to some new project at some undisclosed location. I don't have that information on hand."

"You know more than a simplistic rundown I could get from Google. And I can't do my job unless I have consistent tabs on him."

She takes a long, slow glug of wine. "Do you really think I'd help you sabotage one of mine?"

"Who said I was—"

"You were a private investigator, Connor. And a pretty good one. The only reason a client of yours would be interested in Devon Lim is to smear his good name and all the hard work I've put into maintaining it. If you really came here presuming I'd help you, you are rusty."

Hope drains from me like a poolside cocktail in the hands of a preteen. "Addison. This is my shot to get my life back."

"I see that." She stands upright, as if gaining strength from my show of weakness, exuding grace and hunger. "But why would I hurt my career to jump-start yours? No, I think I'll watch and see how this plays out on its own."

I sneer at this woman's indifference. A person I thought I loved, albeit a long time ago. "Fine. Have it your way. But when we meet again, you're going to wish you had helped me without hesitating."

Pale pink lipstick parts in a smile. "I doubt that very much, babe. In our world, Connor—the world of ulterior motives—it's survival of the fittest; you know that. And from where I'm poised, it looks like the hyenas are circling your carcass. Again. Now, if you'll excuse me, I have bodies to bury for a certain Chinese architect."

She stares pointedly at the door, unwilling to spend another second with me.

"Fine. I'll go. Before I do, remind me. When did you take that life-changing trip to Fiji? Was it 2006 or 2007?"

Addison pauses. Her hand twitches toward the counter where she abandoned the pepper spray in favor of the Merlot. "Why do you ask?"

"Oh, that's right. It was 2010," I muse. "You kept talking about it the night we got all-you-can-eat sushi with bottomless sake bombs. You remember that? You were raving about the food, the culture, the scenic views of the islands."

Tension cuts deep across Addison's face. Her eyes dart to the bedroom, to where she keeps her personal laptop hooked to the charger on the nightstand.

I take my time. "No, you know what? It was 2012. A good year for travel. And an embarrassingly simple combination for a password—Fiji2012—considering you have folders on all past and present clients on your desktop, accessible to anyone who's been paying attention. Who am I to judge, though? My password is my childhood dog's name. But then, you knew that."

Addison Stern is speechless.

"Oh, don't worry, babe." I cross to the front door, relishing the moment. "As soon as I catch up to Devon Lim in his vacation home in Santa Barbara, I'll be sure to let him know you told me where to find him."

I toss the house key I used to get in here to the floor like discarded trash. It clatters on the hardwood as the door slams shut behind me. It was a good litmus test; I had the Santa Barbara address when she walked through the door, but there's a stupid, naïve part of me that needed to see her in all her ruthless, unyielding glory—to have her reject any semblance of aiding me, a person she once said she had feelings for. As I march to where my rental Rover is parked on the street, I know I got both the information and the closure I needed.

Addison Stern was the driving force behind my last three years of pain. It's time the debt was repaid.

CHAPTER SIX

PHINNEAS

BENEDICT CANYON | JUNE 12

PHINNEAS REDWOOD: *It sucks to be dead. You don't get any free drinks, no recognition for all the people you helped—or screwed—during your lifetime, you can't enjoy watching a bartender sweat and cry for six minutes while they make the fresh mojito you ordered, and after you're gone, people warp your life into whatever format and content fits a ninety-minute made-for-TV movie. All these reasons, and more, are why I decided it's finally time to do it. Write my memoirs.*

I hope this is recording.

Okay. To my future editor, to whom I will pay an exorbitant fee, no doubt—welcome. I've been toying with the idea of recording voice notes for a while now, and I'm glad this morning's Bloody Mary finally gave me the liquid courage to start. [Glass clinks]

Okay, let's try again, for serious this time—Addison Stern is going to be here any minute, and I really want to get a few ideas down while I'm focused. That woman is visually and audibly distracting. And she scares the hell out of me.

My name is Phinneas Eugene Redwood, and I was born knowing that I would be the best at whatever it was that I wanted to do. Really. Trouble is, I decided I wanted to be a world-class drunk for most of my early life. But once I got through grad school and earned my chemistry doctorate, I realized I wanted to do something else—besides disappointing my mother that I wasn't a chess prodigy. I wanted to make money. Not just enough to fill up my tank or buy a nice suit. I'm talking French Riviera yacht money; college-admissions-scandal money; rig-an-election money. And I didn't give a shit who I had to hurt in order to get it. Because the world had already hurt me plenty.

[Doorbell rings]

Ah, crap. [Muffled] *Just a minute!* [Footsteps] *I'm coming, I'm coming.*

ADDISON STERN: [Muffled] *Phinneas, how are you?*

PR: *Good, good, Addison. Come on in.*

[Door shuts]

AS: *Well, where should we get to work? We have a lot to cover now that all our print interviews are published and being reviewed positively. People are excited to see you in the public eye again, and the pharma gala will be the perfect occasion to demonstrate how you're ready to resume the spotlight. Have you started up an account on Boom Boom yet—that video platform everyone is talking about?*

PR: *Boom Boom? Sounds like an adults-only playground. Which might be more lucrative than this whole pharma thing, if you wear the right ensemble, you know?* [Laughs]

AS: *I'm guessing that's . . . a no.*

PR: *Um. No. I have not started the account. But I will.*

AS: *I see.* [Pause] *A place to work?*

PR: [Coughs] *Yup. Yup, right over there. The breakfast table. There's electrical outlets right behind that— Yup, you found them. And just close my laptop there. That eyesore of a spreadsheet was me planning out my tax breaks for next year. I'm pretty terrible at keeping finances straight.*

AS: *You know, Phinneas,* [rustling] *I'm not big on social media. Personally, I don't see the point in blasting my personal information wherever possible, just for fun. But from a professional perspective, it is a necessity. Especially if you're selling something to the masses, as Thrive, Inc. and you are. And aren't you excited to promote your new, groundbreaking pill before it launches this fall?*

PR: *Definitely. For sure, for sure. But I'm pretty certain* *if I post a video about a "new pill that excites me," the Boom Boom algorithm will lump me back in with the adult-playground people, you know?* [Laughs] *C'mon, it's funny.*

AS: *Hardly.* [Sniffing] *Is that— Phinneas, have you been drinking? Ah. So that's what this is. I thought you said you were going to cut back.*

PR: *I—*

AS: *Phinneas, it's eight in the morning.* [Deep sigh] *Okay, where is your coffee machine? I'm making us lattes.*

PR: *Fine. Probably for the best.* [Rustling] *Hey, have you ever had a caffè corretto—*

AS: *I'll be direct, because my time is expensive.*

PR: *Uh. Mine is, too. I am the CEO of a multibillion-dollar company.*

AS: *Exactly. You are the leader of quite possibly the most well-known pharmaceutical company of the new millennium. Not only did you captivate the country in the eighties and nineties with your first diet pill—*

PR: *Which I designed myself, by the way.*

AS: *I am aware. Not only did you do all that with your first attempt, but you also ensnared the public interest with your . . .*

PR: *Douchebag antics?*

AS: *I was going to say colorful relationships, public appearances, and that one interview that you gave to GQ magazine* *where you insisted that "thinning is winning." But since we agree our time is costly, yes. Douchebag antics.* [Coffee machine sputters] *Your diet pill and this next pill are each desirable commodities in their respective markets. But don't forget, Phinneas: You are a commodity as well.*

[Pause]

PR: *So . . . I should be on pay-for-play websites after all?*

AS: *So you should want more for yourself. You have all this potential to really use your platform and your incredible intellect for good.*

PR: *Whoa, hey, Addison.* [Chuckles] *I didn't think I hired an idealist in you.*

AS: *At the risk of being trite, I do think you deserve more than . . . getting drunk before noon on a Monday. But you need to believe that.*

PR: *Huh. I mean, what you're saying does hold water. I guess I just didn't realize you were so sentimental, Stern.*

AS: [Laughs] *Well. There's power in owning one's potential. My core beliefs lie there.*

PR: *Okay. Well, I guess I could do more to . . . own . . . my potential. These days, some days, it feels like the only direction left to me is up.*

AS: *And what could you do—something simple—to start on that trajectory? As we are mapping out your summer schedule and publicity strategy.*

PR: *I guess get on Boom Boom.*

AS: *That would be a start.*

PR: *And . . . I guess . . . quit drinking before noon?*

AS: *Quit drinking, period. Full stop.*

PR: *Ooooh. Yeah, that's going to be a hard sell, Stern. Anything else?*

AS: *Quit drinking in public, then.*

[Pause]

PR: *I can do that. For the launch of this next pill—which is a really good one, by the way. It's in line with your talk about owning my potential—I will stop drinking in . . .*

AS: *Public. Say it out loud. You can do it.*

PR: *I will stop drinking in public. Hoo boy! I said it. Yikes. Not sure how long that is going to stick.*

AS: *Well.* [Pause] *I will make sure that face-to-face interviews are the equivalent of a unicorn sighting this summer.*

PR: *Pretty sure that is a sexually charged hashtag on Boom Boom. C'mon now! Up top!*

AS: *Oh, for fuck's sake— Hey. Are you recording us? Is your phone—?*

PR: *Oh, sorry. Yeah, wow, will you look at that? Sorry about that. I'll go ahead and delete that right n—*

CHAPTER SEVEN

ADDISON

HONG KONG | SEPTEMBER 1

Warm car exhaust sweeps across the jade-green jump-suit I chose for tonight's unveiling of Reed Song's newest architectural feat when I step outside my luxury hotel. Mandarin, Cantonese, and some English are audible through the open windows of passing cars, and the mixture brings back memories of holidays with my extended relatives—before my parents divorced, that is. By the time my dad left I was barely allowed to go to the store by myself, in case my mother—who put the "ow" in Munchausen's—needed me, let alone attend gatherings on my father's side of the family.

Traffic hums across three lanes in the dense urban cityscape of Hong Kong, but a sleek black car dares to stop along the curb before me. I breathe deep the fumes of the island's evening rhythm and allow the noxious air to clear away the memories.

The back door opens. Reed Song shoots me a mischievous grin from against red leather seats. "Addison. Usually when I pick up women from the sidewalk, it's dark and I have to be more furtive."

I wrinkle my nose as I slide into the car beside him. Sharp cologne—no, the scent of vodka—stings my nostrils, envelops me. "Reed. I hope you're not planning to use that joke with reporters tonight."

Skyscrapers quickly fill the scenery of the drive as we speed off toward the center of Wan Chai, the financial district of Hong Kong. Chrome windows that resemble eyes all seem to follow our path. Rightly so.

"And betray all of your helpful tutelage, Addison? Never," Reed replies, his crisp *T*s emphasizing a Cambridge education. He retrieves notecards that we prepared together earlier today from his jacket pocket. The last week has been intensive, both for the effort I've taken to get his answers just right—about his personal life and the tenacity of his work ethic—and the meetings I've led with Hong Kong's chief media outlets, both in English and in my subpar Cantonese. Although each person here has assumed I'm a local, I have disappointed them all with my clumsy American accent. Their judgment mingles with confusion when they comment how I appear "so Chinese, though."

No matter. I have other priorities. Bonding with strangers over any shared culture is at the bottom of my list.

Ovid Blackwell's board of directors removed me from all high-profile clients and events, a fact that stung—but only for two shakes of an ingenue's tail. When Peter dangled Reed Song's architecture unveiling over my head like some consolation prize to be won, I recalled a better reason to head to Hong Kong, beyond Ovid Blackwell's ulterior motive to keep me out of sight of the feds. Sure, there is the real possibility of impressing Mr. Griffin with my work here in Hong Kong, but there is another, more stylish purpose.

Camera flashes ignite as we turn the corner to arrive at the architectural equivalent of a pincushion, Reed Song's latest creation. People clamor at the edge of the sidewalk underneath the large domed structure, whose trio of elevated glass orbs at the top provide 360-degree views of the island. A red carpet leads up broad steps to a double-door entrance adorned with gold ribbon. News-media personnel, a few social media influencers I found on Weibo while researching public opinion of new construction, and several government officials who seem half-dead of boredom hang farther back along the carpet.

As I switch seats with Reed to allow him to exit first, I catch a petite blond figure in a blue sparkling minidress straining from the back of the throng. Reed's mistress, Mei Zhen.

"Well, here goes," Reed says, slipping his hand inside the inner pocket of his black tapered suit. A shiny travel-size bottle emerges. Vodka.

"Ahem. What did we agree upon, Mr. Song?" I smile, not yet baring my teeth.

Reed has the grace not to roll his eyes. "No drinking tonight."

"More specifically?"

"No drinking, and you'll ensure Mei Zhen doesn't disrupt the event. Or piss off my wife."

When I landed five days ago, Reed was already waiting at my hotel, eager for help in cleaning up his mess. Yet instead of accepting my expertise, he gave me his mistress's phone number to "reel in her crazy" and make sure she behaved. I nearly walked myself out, seething from the dismissal, then remembered Peter's subtle challenge: *Go there and get him some good press saying that he's been misrepresented. Convince the local outlets, if you can.*

Reed tucks the bottle back into his jacket pocket—bringing it with him instead of leaving the tiny publicity bomb inside the car, as I would have preferred. I sigh, not bothering to hide it. I am a glorified babysitter tonight, but if that leads me to my due reward of greater recognition at Ovid Blackwell—and allows me to elude those federal agents' attention—then so be it. Addison Stern knows that every chance to impress the board is an opportunity to squeeze like a lemon.

Shouting rises from the sidewalk as Reed steps from the Escalade. His entrance goes smoothly, with Reed pausing for photographs, waving to a few reporters, and ignoring the small crowd of protesters decrying the latest metallic installation to sully their island.

"Reed! My love!" Mei Zhen shouts in Cantonese. I catch the eye of the tallest of the three security guards I hired to bar the woman from the reception inside. The trio of men moves to block her from view. A few members of the media turn toward the sound.

"Reed!" I take up, moving to my client. "We're on a tight schedule, everyone. Time to move along."

I usher the man of the hour to the building's threshold and keep my expression neutral when he pauses to wave to Mei. So long as he doesn't ask for a photo op with both his wife and his mistress, I'll allow the brief acknowledgment.

Reed disappears into the foyer of the building he designed as the band that his firm hired begins playing a bass-filled number. "My better half," he says loud enough so the reporters outside can hear, no doubt greeting the supermodel-turned-housewife he married seven years ago.

As the individuals with approved lanyard passes hurry to join the party, whimpering reaches my ears. The mistress.

"You didn't have to do that, you know," Mei Zhen says in English. Fierce brown eyes, still safely barricaded behind security, meet mine.

"And what is that?"

"We're women. We should be sticking together. Not doing the bidding of men."

A smirk twists my mouth as I take in her frustration, now directed at me. "Darling, I do my own bidding."

"I love him," she shouts, pushing against a sturdy chest. "You know what it is to love someone, don't you? To be stupidly, blindly in love and willing to make a fool out of yourself, if only you can be near that person?"

I look at her anguished face—the eyebrows pinched tight and the cupid's bow quivering. Have I ever loved someone to the extent that this woman describes? Would I even want to? Why on earth would anyone subject themselves to the gut-punching vulnerability of loving someone that much?

A tiny seed of doubt sprouts in my mind at seeing the ardent passion on her face. Connor's angry expression as he left my apartment last week flashes across my vision. Once he was gone, I stared at my front door for a full minute. I was outraged that he managed to sneak into my home and leave with—probably—a full thumb drive of my client files. I was irritated with myself for the small part of me that enjoyed seeing him.

I brush those feelings aside. The band switches to a slower jazz medley. Reed's speech is about to begin.

Casting a glance at the woman over my shoulder, I reply, "No, sweetie. I don't."

\\\\\////

Inside a spacious lobby the size of an airport terminal, guests at the reception mingle near their assigned tables and at satellite bars throughout. The building is meant to be a community workspace for creative thinkers, leaders of tomorrow working to build their brands and fine-tune their endeavors—hence the avant-garde pincushion-design exterior. Or, as I said when talking to the local media conglomerate, this building is "a place where new and unconventional ideas can be refined, without the stagnant limitations of yesterday."

Reed takes the stage, his elegant wife beaming her approval from the round tabletop closest to him. As he opens with an anecdote about his humble upbringing and the appreciation it gave him for designing opulent structures such as this, I scan the room for public opinion. Several men in suits are nodding—his financial backers and an architecture firm that has been courting him for months—and most everyone appears intrigued by what Reed has to say, a few even raising their champagne glasses.

I purposefully ensured only media outlets that have covered him favorably were invited, along with a reporter from the democracy-driven platform *The People's Word* who stares listlessly at the opaque glass wall that lines the street—Kwong Lin. He might need to be convinced, considering the paper he works for has complained that Reed is forcing low-income families onto the street with his "eyesores." Peter Huxton would have my collection of jade jewelry if he knew, but my strategy has always been more direct than his: Engage with the loudest naysayer head-on, then bend them to my goals. Or break them.

Reed finishes his speech to roaring applause. Only two guests in the room fail to clap as Reed exits the stage: a woman who sits at the bar and Kwong Lin, who begins to play some game on his phone.

Servers scatter among the white tablecloths, carrying silver trays of the first course of ten, as another speaker, the owner of the building, takes over the podium. Lin barely raises an eyebrow.

Fuming, I turn toward the main bar, which was installed behind the building's reception desk. A woman with jet-black hair fading into subtle highlights, the other non-acolyte present, sips her gimlet facing the dinner.

"Not your kind of party?" I ask with a smile.

She raises two thick eyebrows. "How did you know I speak English?"

"I knew you were American when you thanked the bartender for your drink—a knee-jerk response for many of us. It's not expected here culturally."

"Well, well, well." She smiles. "Another expat."

"Addison Stern. I'm Reed Song's publicist." I nod to where Reed is seated and whispering in his wife's ear. "You're not enjoying yourself."

"I'm not?"

"No, you're here out of professional curiosity. To see whether Ovid Blackwell can handle a large-scale PR campaign from a distance. You're Velvet Eastman."

"Am I?" Velvet purrs.

I take a sip from my own champagne coupe—everyone in this room is toasting to Reed's accomplishments—then raise the glass to this woman. "You're Chicago's foremost female entrepreneur of the decade, maybe even of the century."

Velvet throws me a wry glance. "No need for flattery. I prefer 'madam.'"

I dip my head. "A defender of women. Protector of those working in the oldest industry known to man. Madam to some of our country's most innovative leaders. A purveyor of beauty, but more importantly, a survivor of the times."

Velvet seems to recognize me now. "You had a reason to talk to me when you sidled up to the bar, didn't you?"

"I did." If she thinks I didn't have a name and pre-researched face attached to each body that sauntered into this train wreck of a building, she is really in need of better help. That's where Ovid comes in. And, more importantly, me.

"I have been a fan of yours for some time," I continue. The band resumes playing music after the final speaker vacates the stage, while waitstaff in white coats deliver steaming plates of roasted duck browned to perfection. Savory soy sauce, sweet glaze, and green onions perfume the lobby, making my mouth water, but I don't turn from Velvet's tense stare.

"Honey, are you here to deliver a message from Ovid Blackwell? Because I just hired them via video conference. I'm meeting with someone named Peter next week who said he was going to manage the PR for my new fashion line."

Reed Song laughs louder and longer than anyone else behind me, clearly drunk. A quick glance around the room confirms that no one seems to care, however. When Peter first suggested

I manage the unveiling of Reed's latest design in person, I was miffed that the offer came with a demotion from the more prominent events at home. Then I remembered Peter mentioning a proposal a month ago for Ovid to court Velvet Eastman as a client—including a summary of her background: a native Chicagoan, purveyor of fantasies, relocated to Hong Kong. I had Malina check the administrative calendar and realized that Velvet planned to fly to our offices while I was away. Peter would be meeting with one of the most well-known tabloid headliners—without me.

Quickly, I arranged custom mooncakes featuring the Chinese characters for *good luck* and *auspicious partnerships* as an invitation to Reed's event and sent them to Velvet. She accepted, then contacted Ovid Blackwell to push out the meeting in the USA to the following week. Peter should know by now: I never let an opportunity to wow a client go by. Although Eastman isn't one I sourced myself, there's no reason I shouldn't be considered as her publicist. Not even a murder investigation.

"Your fashion line deserves nothing short of PR excellence, Ms. Eastman. And I'm part of the Ovid Blackwell team that's going to give you that. Just look around you."

Gold-embroidered red drapes hang from the second floor, surrounding the two dozen dinner tables in the center of the lobby. Red envelopes sit at each plate, thanking the guest for being there and announcing a donation made in their name to equitable-housing groups on the island. Normally grumpy Kwong Lin now grins into his cup, seated next to representatives from the Fair Housing Ministry, fans of Reed's work who reject Kwong Lin's criticism that Reed's designs are bad for the neighborhood. Members of the media discuss the speakers of the evening, each of whom was selected based on their convincing support of design innovation, particularly Reed's. This room is eating out of my hand as if it were a bowl of my grandmother's congee.

Velvet takes in the scene. Her dark lipstick—ombreux, the latest shade from La Fumée—curls in a smile. "It is all very convincing."

Connor's voice returns to my mind, like an unwanted ringing in my ears. *Cut the shit, Addison.* I lean forward, undeterred. "Ms. Eastman, success is convincing."

"But what about—" Velvet drops her voice. Smattered English mixes with Cantonese as loud laughter erupts from the table closest to us. "Your firm—you, my dear—have had some trouble lately. Redwood was his name, right? He was known among the Hong Kong elite. The man was a heavy drinker."

I maintain a tight gaze on Velvet's intrigued expression, but inside my thoughts are churning. How far-flung is Phinneas's negative reputation? How many enemies did the CEO have?

"Mr. Redwood's death was unfortunate. Full stop. And if he had been honest with me about his enemies, I might have been able to support him better." I allow my gaze, lowered in regret, to rest on the bar top. "When he was discovered, I had actually just flown home from Paris, where I was doing PR for a new perfume campaign with La Fumée."

"Really?" Velvet leans closer. "La Fumée is one of my favorite brands. I love their products, their marketing, their print ads."

Velvet lifts a manicured nail to the bartender. "Another drink, please. This time with more chipped ice. I need something to toast my new publicist."

I allow my lips to part. "I thought Peter would be managing your campaign."

"I'll consult him, since I liked what he had to say in our meeting. But I rely on the senses to make decisions. And this"— she surveys the room that I tailored to her specific likes, not Reed's—"this I can taste, smell, see, hear, and feel. I want you."

I raise my coupe. Adrenaline brings a flush to my cheeks, the way it always does when I bag my prize. Peter and the board won't be able to deny a powerful client like Velvet her preference—exactly as I planned. "I won't let you down."

"God knows it will be good to have a team of professionals behind me as I start this chapter." Velvet smooths back a curtain of long, loose black hair. "That Phinneas didn't know when or where to draw the line on his own shenanigans. He pissed off more people in the nineties than even I can name, globally, and I don't plan to make the same mistake."

I give a pert nod in return. Victory should be coiling through me, hugging me like a new, ethically sourced fur coat: Reed's event is a success, and I managed to impress Ovid's shiny new toy away from prying eyes. Instead, at hearing a new take on the polarizing antics of my deceased client—someone I thought I knew—a frisson of anxiety ripples along my frame.

CHAPTER EIGHT

CONNOR

SANTA BARBARA | SEPTEMBER 2

Ocean waves roll across the shoreline of the beach, like Las Vegas cage dancers undulating to show off their curves. The scene is idyllic. Serene. Relaxing. It's exactly what most tourists dream of, but I've been chugging coffee, playing Six Degrees of Kevin Bacon, and chomping down Pringles for the last two hours, trying to keep from drifting off to sleep.

I fumble with my phone, the sudden light piercing my vampire eyes in the darkness of my car, then scroll to my old list of surveillance music. High-pitched electric guitar erupts from my earbuds, and I'm wide-awake. Wider than I used to be when I was on Adderall and first starting out in the PI game. Drugs never had the desired effect for me, though. I learned other strategies.

"Denzel Washington." Nodding to a drum solo, I scan the back balcony of Devon Lim's vacation home. No lights have flickered on since eight p.m., but my old contact at the post office said that Devon has been receiving mail here. And Addison turned spotlight-white when I told her I already had the address.

No, someone is in there. I'm sure of it.

"Let's see. Denzel was in . . . the movie *Philadelphia* with Tom Hanks. Tom Hanks was in . . . *Apollo 13*—with Kevin Bacon. Boom. Denzel with a Bacon number of two degrees of separation."

From where I am parked, Devon Lim's picturesque cliffside condo resembles a frame from a movie. Palm trees overlook the water from two hundred feet up, teetering precariously as moonlight shimmers on the waves beneath. Broad glass walls provide unobstructed views, and on the opposite side, the narrow one-lane road leading to the front door is flanked by cameras on all sides. When I saw those—from one surveillance lover to another—I had to give a little golf clap.

Two more hours go by, and then the sun emerges from behind a hillside of bushes, still lush before the start of Southern California's brief autumn.

Another hour. Traffic begins to pass along the road behind the empty beach parking lot where I'm waiting. A school bus. A pickup truck toting a metal ladder and stacks of buckets. Then a white van rumbles up Devon Lim's dead-end street, the words MARY'S CLEANING SERVICE painted across the side.

A few minutes crawl along. The drapes beside the glass door of the balcony stir. A man and a woman in matching white uniforms step out to clean the railing, while another man in a button-up shirt who I know to be Devon Lim's personal assistant gestures to a dirty spot on the glass. He must have stayed overnight. Has

Devon been at this property at all in the last few days?

"Timothée Chalamet." I take a break from the car to stretch outside. "Old Timmy was in . . . *Lady Bird* with Laurie Metcalf. Laurie Metcalf was in . . . *JFK* with Kevin Bacon."

Food wrappers clutter the footwell of the driver's seat. I search for the rest of the sandwich I packed before I left my two-star motel, but I forgot—the empty cellophane streaked with mayo doesn't even hold a crumb. I ate it all.

My stomach grumbles. "Where are you, Devon? I've been watching this place for three nights, and nothing yet."

Another reason to hate Addison Stern. She knows more than what I discovered on her laptop, yet she's forced me up here to learn for myself that Devon is somewhere else.

"Arnold Schwarzenegger was in that jungle alien movie with Carl Weathers. Carl Weathers was in *Toy Story 4* with Annie Potts. Annie Potts was in . . . ?"

White wings of a seagull glide along the beach toward a pile of driftwood. Approaching something—a crab, backed up against the log. The bird stills, as if sizing up its options. Then it attacks, diving at the wood. Sand explodes in a cloud as the two struggle in a fight to the death.

There must be another way to compel Addison to cooperate. The woman doesn't have an ounce of remorse for the way she did me, so a good conscience isn't going to help.

I text an old friend, Rex, a defense lawyer and Southern California's premier source for interested parties like me who offer—used to offer, in my case—information in return; despite my banishment to the desert, he's one of a few who didn't completely cut me out. When I ask whether he has any dirt on publicist pain-in-the-ass Addison Stern, he replies within minutes:

More than you'd guess. Can't write it out,
though. Need to talk on the phone. Give
me a ring later today.

"Bingo." I slide back into the driver's seat, then I hit the ignition button. Cast another eye at the balcony. Drapes that frame the glass door twitch as if someone moves behind them.

"Annie Potts was in . . . *She's Having a Baby* with Kevin Bacon. Bacon number of three. Boom." I slap the steering wheel.

But what was that jungle aliens movie called—the one with Arnold?

Another ten minutes go by. Thirty. No one emerges.

\\\\\////

"I'm really sorry. I'm not allowed to give out the personal information of our customers." The young woman standing at a glass counter purses her lips. Beneath a chalkboard advertising the season's discounts, bouquets of brightly colored flowers line a shelf behind her. Vanilla scents the air, like she just spritzed before I entered.

"No, I wouldn't expect you to," I answer. "But Devon Lim is my boss, and he got into a fight with his lady because the purple roses he ordered never arrived. I just need to know the address of the last order he placed. Make sure he knows I sent it to the right place, and that the delivery guy must have messed up. Could you help me out—please?"

Rifling through Lim's alley-side garbage can here in Santa Barbara earned me a weird look from the neighbor's shih tzu and a florist receipt soaked in wine. The date was from last week, which could be consistent with an "I'm sorry" delivery sent to Hyacinth Aspen, Gen's daughter—especially if he wanted to get away, after Gen accused him of cheating—or to the woman with whom Devon is cheating on Hyacinth.

I adopt a lopsided grin and aim for charming. Once, a million lifetimes ago, I could flash a smile and talk my way into any VIP room across the Sunbelt states. Either I knew someone inside, or I knew the security dude barring the entry. I was in everyone's good graces back then, or, if not, they owed me a favor.

"I don't know. Honestly, I'm up for a promotion and I don't want to do anything . . . I don't know . . . weird?" She begins picking at a blue polished nail.

"No, no. Definitely not." A flicker of remorse hits me as I recall all the times I lied to people—hurt them. In Vegas, I swore I was done with living that way. My granddad said that acting with integrity is the only way to greet each day—that our reputations are all that survive us. I did his memory dirty for years, ignoring the sage advice, and look where it's gotten me. But this is a random cashier, and a little white lie. Right?

Act with integrity. Whatever the hell that means.

A pop song fills the awkward silence as I pretend to scan the glass case. The young woman's phone lights up on the counter above a bouquet of baby's breath. A picture of a teacup animal—a dog, or cat? I can't tell from here—is her lock screen. Some kind of banner with writing frames the photo: SANTA BARBARA FRIENDS OF PETS.

I try again. "Hey, can you tell me what plants a cat would be allergic to? I don't have one anymore—mine died a while back—but Roxanne would always throw up after nibbling on my houseplants, and I was never sure which one."

The young woman peers at me a moment. Which I get. I'm not sure I'd trust me, either. Thick white eyeliner creases in the corners of her eyes.

"Household flowers?"

"Yeah. I was always picking them up in my last job." Working private events scoping out a client's entourage, roaming red carpets listening for information that served a client, or doing surveillance at parties, I would end up taking the perfectly fine bouquets of flowers home before they were dumped in the trash after last call. And Roxanne, sweet chubby cat that she was, enjoyed most of them.

"Were they kind of slender?"

"Her favorites were."

The cashier nods. "Probably tulips. They're the ones that usually end up indoors. Owners don't realize the adverse effect on curious kitties."

"Yeah, I was in the dark about that. If I were to get a cat in the future, what kind of flowers should I allow in my house?"

"Hm." She drums long fingernails on the glass counter. "Air plants are always a good bet."

"Air plants?"

"Yeah, let me—I think we have some in the back." She disappears past a door painted solid white, leaving me alone in the shop.

I hesitate. Then I spin around the counter, beneath the chalkboard, and take in the still-unlocked computer screen. The store's address book is front and center on the monitor.

A cardboard box falls down somewhere behind the white door. "Shit," the store clerk swears.

I tap *Devon Lim* into the search bar, and his most recent order history, with an address, pops right up: 3326 Trail Ridge Court.

Genevieve's address. Rats. Devon must have sent flowers to Hyacinth. This information does nothing to point me toward a possible mistress.

A car door slams somewhere close by. Footsteps approach quickly from the stockroom.

I jump back in front of the counter, just as the clerk opens the door to the shop. "Any luck?" I ask.

She presents a beige geometric planter filled with thick, vibrant green blades of grass. "Tillandsia. Nontoxic to cats and pretty hardy in case a cat does get ahold of it."

I smile. Resume the role of dedicated assistant and animal lover. "I'll take it. Thanks for the help."

I pay for my new plant, actually looking forward to bringing it back to my Airbnb in LA. As I push open the glass door facing the highway, the clerk's voice cuts through the accompanying chime: "No more tulips, if you get another cat!"

Waving goodbye, I turn toward the tiny roadside parking lot, then stop dead. A dozen cars speed past, and in my peripheral vision people in matching leggings jog on the opposite side of the street. Seagulls cry somewhere overhead, but my gaze is drawn to the In-N-Out diagonally across.

A tall, lean guy wearing a beige jacket and a black hoodie faces away from me. Standing beside a boxy car, he examines the small rectangle of paper—a red splotch in the center, the same wine-soaked receipt I discarded minutes ago—that had been left exposed on the top of Devon Lim's trash pile. The man shifts his frame to the left, then right, searching for something. His full profile is distinct: a thick nose, long chin, and beady eyes that scan the block. When he reaches inside his jacket for something, the edge flaps up, revealing a black handgun wedged between his belt and his jeans.

Spinning on my heel, I race to my rental car to duck out of view in front of the hood. My heart beating like a slot machine's bell—*ding ding ding ding ding*—I peer around a tire and watch as the man approaches the florist shop. He steps inside.

Unbidden, the memory of a gruff voice in the casino pricks my ears: *Hey, Connor, right?* That guy, Gianni's goon, had thirty pounds of muscle on this one. I've never seen this man before in my life, but Gianni is known for his deep bench of players.

By some gut instinct, I'm certain he is now chatting with the florist, asking her if she's seen my face recently, not knowing I'm currently cowering behind a blue Land Rover. I jump to the driver's side. Slide behind the wheel and jam the ignition's start button. With another glance at the now-empty florist entrance, I pull the car onto the 101, then drive forward like I haven't a care in the world.

Boutique businesses along the water pass. Shops catering to college kids of the area blur by, but their images don't register with me. Not with the way that I continue to check my rear-view mirror, staring, waiting for a brown beater car from two decades past to surge through traffic and follow me back to my rented room.

The buildings become sparse. The view of the ocean and the tapering beaches could resemble a postcard from fifty years earlier—all nature, no neon signs advertising cheap stays and student discounts. As I reach the edge of Santa Barbara and approach Goleta, I pull off to a viewpoint and park facing the way I came. Just in case.

I thought I escaped Gianni that night when Genevieve approached me. And even though I sent him 10 percent of what he's owed, thanks to Genevieve's down payment, I know he's waiting for me back in the desert. He'd happily track me down out here if he had any indication that Santa Barbara is where I'm hiding—but how would he know that? I'm a Las Vegas resident, to his knowledge.

Snooping out Devon Lim and his infidelities won't be as straightforward now.

I pull away from the viewpoint, then circle back the way I came. A sign for the Santa Barbara city limits comes into view as the answer to my most recent Kevin Bacon game pops into my head—the title of the jungle alien movie: *Predator*.

The block of shops where I saw that guy's lanky build appears, and I switch to the fast lane. The brown beater sedan I saw him standing beside is gone; I search my rearview for it. Instead, a modern lime-green VW bug rides my bumper, some teenage girl with oversize pink sunglasses at the wheel.

CHAPTER NINE

PHINNEAS

THIRTY THOUSAND FEET | JUNE 24

PHINNEAS REDWOOD: *And we're back! Only instead of my house, make it international. That's right, I am currently flying overseas to Hong Kong during the longest flight known to man—or known to me, anyway—and on my way to meet with Thrive's Asia-affairs team. And see the lovely Annalise Meier.*

FLIGHT ATTENDANT: [Muffled] *Hot towel? We have almost arrived to Hong Kong International Airport. Will you be needing a customs form?*

PR: *No, thank you. Oh, excuse me. Could you send a glass of champagne back to seat 16A? The cute redhead.*

Thank you. Oh, definitely tell her it's from me. Yup. Thanks.

So anyway, I thought I would use the flight time to dive into the beginning. I guess, fittingly enough for my destination right now, it all did kind of begin with Annalise. Annalise Meier, the beautiful wrecking ball of my heart, girlfriend in college, and also, you know, billionaire heiress to the plastic corporation of East Asia, who agreed to show me around a bit when I told her I'd be in Hong Kong for work this week. I haven't been before, but Annalise is a German Hong Konger, and she agreed to give me the highlights tour in between my business meetings.

Excuse me? Can I have another one of these? [Gulps] *Ready. Thanks.*

Yes, memoirs, although I did tell Addison Stern I wouldn't drink in public, I think we can both agree she meant in public *on the ground. Am I right?*

So Annalise and I met at Stanford and instantly fell in love. Well, on my part it was instant; she was beautiful and pedigreed, but her compassion and creativity were what made me fall for her. She took a bit more time to fall in love with me, but a few exquisitely written love letters moved things along. Annalise is the catalyst of so much in my life.

Growing up, I was fairly confident in myself. I knew I was the smartest in my class, and funny, but I never felt . . . I don't know . . . great. No, that's not right; I mean, I never felt . . . good enough. My parents were overjoyed by my birth—they tried for a long time to have me—even though my size was a surprise to them. It was the other disappointments they endured—that my mom did—that cropped up in my childhood and led to the rift between us: the realization that I didn't have an ounce of desire to be an actor, a comedian, an athlete, or even a chess prodigy—which really pissed my mom off, because I was actually pretty good. Won a few tournaments for kids under age ten. But my dad—a cameraman—and my mom—a set designer—were crestfallen I didn't give a care about the movie industry or anything else that could make me famous. I loved books. Science. Creating stuff in a petri dish. That was my jam. And they just could never get on board. By the time I actually was becoming famous, for chemical engineering, the wounds had never healed, and I hadn't spoken to my parents in years. I wasn't about to turn around and accept their superficial form of love at that point.

No, I wanted something greater. And I found that in Annalise. All the feelings of inadequacy, and the judgment that I felt from a tender age and was heaped on me by the world— their presumptions as soon as they laid eyes on me—she undid all of that the very first time she said, "I love you, Phinneas." [Sniffs]

[Gulps] *We were all set to get married—I had the ring picked out and everything—when she met someone else. Devastated doesn't fully describe my feelings about our breakup, but I never could stay mad at her. Even when she was featured in tabloids in China, kissing this new guy. I actually hired someone to take him out—like, out out—but then decided against it at the last minute. Asshole never knew how lucky he got.* [Chuckles] *Addison Stern would kill me if she knew I just put that in a recording. Did I mention that I've been drinking?*

Holy shit! Did you feel that? [Muffled] *That was wild! Is the pilot drinking, too? What was that?*

Turbulence? Biggest fucking round of turbulence I've ever been in.

Have you ever seen a UFO up here? No? But, like. Maybe a little one. No? Hm.

FLIGHT ATTENDANT: [Muffled] *Sir, please, sit down.*

PR: *Sorry. So, back to Annalise and me. We were insepa-rable in college, then she met this guy. I never understood what she saw in him that would make her leave me—leave what we had and move on to the next. Especially when my pharma business took off.*

It was good timing, though. Instead of wallowing in bed, steeped in depression, I was meeting with investors. Researchers. Money managers. Initially, investors were hesi-tant. They didn't understand the magic that I had created, and I sympathized with that, I did. Compounds that I engineered could block a specific enzyme to shrink fat cells *in the body, and that's not something anyone else had accomplished then. Not all fat cells, mind you. But around 10 percent of them, uniformly distributed throughout. Are you following? Instead of a pill that shrinks only your butt, or your boobs, or your fatty ankles, you've got consistent overall fat reduction. It was a miracle! Or so my advertisers later said. What I loved about my pill was that it could make someone change into another version of themselves, practically overnight. The idea of such a drastic, speedy transformation was intoxicating to me. And, I guess, to others as well.*

Everything was cool. I was content to pitch my product to boardrooms until the right group of investors came along—people who could grasp these concepts for the solid-gold value they held. Benefactors along the way kept me afloat and allowed me to stay at their global vacation properties while I kept refining my recipes. And meeting with pompous venture capitalists gave me something to do while I nursed a broken heart and wielded a few handles of liquor against my liver. [Gulps] *Until Farron Greystone. When he introduced me to some interesting characters, shit hit an industrial fan.*

Hey, excuse me, do you Boom Boom? [Laughter; muffled] *The video platform. All the kids are uploading videos doing dances or lip-synching to audio tracks. Yeah, my publicist is on me to start an account. I don't know. She says it will help me gain greater exposure.*

FLIGHT ATTENDANT: [Muffled] *How fascinating. Another fill?*

PR: *Yeah, that's great.* [Gulps] *Make it two, though. God gave me two hands for a reason, right?* [Laughter] *Thanks. You have no idea how much I needed this.*

CHAPTER TEN

ADDISON

DOWNTOWN LA | SEPTEMBER 5

"Addison, you vision. Which do you prefer?" Velvet Eastman lifts two leather swatches in greeting, one mauve and the other a burnt red. The plastic cup of boba beside her is nearly drained to the bottom. Velvet smiles, standing before the open roll-up door of a shop in the Fashion District. Peter Huxton, next to her, mirrors her smile, his a tad too wide.

I lean in close, examining the material between my manicured thumb and index finger. "The burnt red. I can already see it taking the runway next month."

"My thoughts exactly." Velvet steps back and examines a fold-up table with various bolts of fabric in her preferred shades:

cerulean blue, cotton-candy pink, and seafoam green. The place she told me to meet at is a standby for this community—smaller than my first studio apartment but always offering the best fabric sourced at wholesale prices. Bolts of cotton occupy most of the tables that line the walls, but I also spy leather, pleather, satin, and polyester toward the back. A one-stop shop.

"Addison. So good to see you. How was your flight home?" Peter simpers.

"Long. But you know the drill—or maybe you don't? It must be ages since Ovid Blackwell sent you abroad. Probably better for everyone, though. No discomfort of first class on those old bones."

While Peter is not exactly to blame for the board barring me from our most important clients, he delivered the message. Sharing bad news with Addison Stern comes with backlash.

Peter purses his lips. "Ms. Eastman was just telling me how excited she is about our PR strategy to launch her line at Fashion Week."

"Oh yes. We discussed it on our flight together." Watching my VP squirm in front of a client is almost as delicious as the pound of siu mai I ate before leaving Hong Kong. But Peter has nothing to worry about. I'm always representing Ovid Blackwell in the best light possible.

"Wonderful. Just excellent." Peter turns a shade of red to match the faux-suede handbags displayed on the wall beside us. "I'm so glad you could join us this morning to go over details."

The Fashion District hums with vendors, shoppers, and designers, all preparing for the festivities of Fashion Week. A banner with a purple border hangs above the entrance to the city blocks with the dates: OCTOBER 9–13.

"Should we head inside and see the back room?" Velvet asks, oblivious to my pissing match with Peter. "My supplier said she just received a shipment of Lycra that could work for my accessories. I'm thinking ornate headbands to complement the pencil skirts."

Velvet follows a petite older woman who wears the kind of long, loose-knit sweaters seen on Asian grandmothers across the West Coast.

"Not so fast," Peter says, taking my arm.

"Oh no. Is that your hand on my person?"

He releases me with a huff. "We've got a problem."

"I'm listening."

A shopper pauses by the storefront. She examines the handbags behind us, then continues to the next store, which sells tulle in bulk. Around the corner, metal crashes in a fender bender as Velvet exclaims that the quality of something is "gorgeous" in the back room.

"You deliberately disobeyed me."

I laugh. "Peter, my father is absent from my life, but I know he's somewhere in Arizona, and definitely not you."

Peter swats the air. "Don't do that. Don't make a joke about this. I told you the board wanted you off big-name clients, then you go and woo the biggest of the season in Hong Kong. You don't want to offend the board."

"Oh, I should be scared?"

"Of course not. But these people are highly connected, with relationships across industries. They can influence your career at Ovid Blackwell—and elsewhere, if it comes to that. They employ all kinds of . . . professionals."

"Tell the board that I can't help it if Velvet was impressed by my work."

Peter folds his arms across his suit jacket. He sighs. "No. No, I suppose you can't. But they are not happy about this, Addison. You undermining the board, on top of the mess with Phinneas Redwood, does not paint you in an attractive light."

"I know my bone structure. I look just fine."

"I mean it, Addison. Make sure Velvet Eastman gets the white-glove treatment. Since you commandeered her interest, the board will allow you to take her on. But right now, you're not behaving very much like partner material."

He steps past me.

"There you are," Velvet says when Peter reaches the back room. "I thought you and Addison had gotten lost among the tables."

"We have GPS for that," he quips. "Tell me more about this piece." Plastic bags are jostled, drowning out the conversation from where I stand, still at the shop's entrance.

You're not behaving very much like partner material.

Irritation boils beneath my skin as Peter's words grind in my eardrums. I've done everything possible to merit the promotion—everything short of murder, as it were. Now, thanks to Phinneas's killer, all my progress has been waylaid. I had to travel literally across the world to score a single client worthy of my skills.

The media won't let go of him. Online and on air, commentators are declaring his loss "the greatest upset to the pharma industry" since Viagra. Now disability advocates are pointing out that the police don't seem to have any leads after over two weeks—or aren't making an effort to solve his murder.

Ovid Blackwell won't let me take on any other new clients, beyond Velvet. Not while the person who attacked Phinneas continues to roam LA, and the ensuing interest in me remains.

My phone vibrates with a text message. From Connor.

Meet me at the café across the street. Two
Girls One Cup of Joe. Now.

I turn toward the coffee shop on the corner of Figueroa, my
hackles already bristling after talking to Peter. The very last
person I desire to see watches me through the window.

All these men demanding something of me. Phinneas, at least,
knew not to push me. Although his cryptic final message to me
in card form has taken up more space in my head than I usually
allow for clients. For anyone.

I double-check that Velvet is well enamored with the Lycra
shipment, then slip over to the café.

"Addison," Connor Windell says when I reach his table.
The last I saw him, he looked like he was emerging from the
wild—wrinkled clothing, bloodshot eyes, smelling of dust and
body odor. Today, the plain black tee he wears is crisp beneath a
taupe bomber jacket, his jeans clean. With brown hair that waves
across blue-gray eyes and square features that remind me of an
attractive Lego head, he looks the way I remember him: enticing.

"Are you following me, Connor?" My tone is sharp. A warning.
"What can you want from me when I made it clear I would not
help you screw over my client?"

The telltale smirk that he always wore when he knew something I didn't appears. A bad sign.

"I don't think you want me to shout this, since I'm guessing
you're here for work. Can you imagine what your colleagues
would say if they knew you committed a felony?"

One big step takes me to the empty seat before him. "What
are you talking about?" I hiss.

"See, I have a friend," he says, toying with a sugar packet. "A guy who knows things. When my trip to Santa Barbara to track down Devon Lim didn't pan out, I asked him for help. But he did me one better."

I roll my eyes. Is every man this morning going to speak to me in riddles? "What's your point?"

"He told me you got into some trouble, Add. Two years ago, after we were together, you took a chunk of change from a client trust account."

"I . . . I don't know what you mean." Oh God.

"No?" He fakes confusion. Touches his finger to his chin. "Because there's more. After you stole money from a client account and made international purchases with said cash—therein lies the felony—you called in favors with some government contacts, one of whom eventually joined a policy think tank near my old place. Why? Was it because . . . bleeding-heart Addison Stern had a dear, dying uncle somewhere that she needed to extricate from a cell in the southern hemisphere?"

For once, I'm speechless. A pigeon saunters along the sidewalk outside, nipping at crumbs that line the cracks.

"Nope. This was all in order to make an ex-boyfriend safely disappear to Italy—to hide after a deadly hit-and-run. Tsk tsk, Addison. I thought you were a more original thinker than that. The Amalfi Coast? So passé."

Connor laughs. The smug has-been. Shock that seeped across my core gives way to anger.

I lean closer across the table, far closer than I would prefer, to keep this conversation as secret as possible. Velvet's squeals were still audible when I reached this side of the street, and I know I don't have long before she or Peter comes looking for me.

Yes, I did everything that Connor rattled off like a proud peacock. Symbiosis—not love—makes you do crazy things. Especially when you owe a year's worth of favors to the hit-and-run driver.

"Connor, sweetie. Jealousy isn't your color. These baseless accusations won't help you win me back."

He rolls his eyes. "I'm not jeal—"

"I only dated Farron for a minute," I say with an exaggerated pout. "We were each too dedicated to our careers, so no need to—"

"More importantly, you jeopardized your own career by committing a—"

"You don't have any proof."

"I do. I have the electronic paper trail—a receipt—that shows you took funds from a client and repurposed them for your ex's escape plan." Connor smiles.

My stomach turns as I recall the hoops I had to jump through to get Farron's new passport in time. "Show me."

"No. You'll have to take my word for it."

I pause. An espresso machine burbles somewhere behind me. "So what do you want, Connor? Hm? Devon Lim's location? I don't have it. You came here to harass me for nothing."

"Do you deny it?" Connor raises his voice. "That you embezzled funds and smuggled some guy out of the country?"

"Shh!" I slide into the chair beside him, closing the gap between us, and clap a hand to his mouth. "Shut up!"

His mouth presses warm and wet against my palm, and the smell of moss and pine enters my nose. My heart pounds against my ribs. Heat flushes my cheeks, then spreads down my body in a direction I haven't considered with Connor in literal years. He peers back at me with curiosity and . . . something else. Desire?

Ugh. I shove away from him, nearly knocking myself backward. "What do you want, Connor?"

He stares at me a moment longer than would feel adversarial. Sweeps his gaze across my chest, then back up to my face. "What do I want?" he asks with a smile.

I shoot him a look. *I fucking dare you.*

He clears his throat. "What do you think, Addison?"

"I wasn't lying to you when I said I don't know where Devon Lim is."

Connor scoffs. "You, not lie? A first."

"Look, I haven't done any work for him in at least a year—"

"Then I need you to help me find him," Connor interrupts. "This is it for me, my only shot to get my life back. I need to do this job for my client, and apparently I need your help to do it. If you don't, I'll blast what I know to everyone I ever spoke to in the media, in addition to your boss. I will ruin you, the way you ruined me. Are we clear?"

Splatter hits the pavement outside. The pigeon cocks its head innocently on a telephone wire above.

"All right, Connor. I'll help you. But know that I will find my own leverage over you. And when I do, you will immediately destroy that receipt. And you have to help me, too, just like you suggested back in my condo."

While I would rather kick him across state lines, Connor may prove to be more useful than he is a nuisance. He knows how to find information. Things. People. And I need to get back on top at Ovid Blackwell by solving a murder.

Come hell or high fashion, that partner title is mine.

"Do I now?" Connor grins, the tops of his cheeks hitting his eyes. "We'll see about that."

CHAPTER ELEVEN

PHINNEAS

BENEDICT CANYON | JULY 3

PHINNEAS REDWOOD: [Glass tinkling; gulping] *Captain's log: Well, that was a bust. Hong Kong was a whirlwind of playtime, meetings, and pining after a woman who no longer wants my heart. She wanted other parts of me* [laughter], *but not the heart.*

[Clears throat] *I'm back home, Future Editor. And you'll be grateful I didn't record during my week abroad. We went to the mainland a few times, but mostly Annalise and I stayed on the island. I did shoot my shot with her, again. I don't know if readers will care about that—I probably shouldn't— but maybe she'll prove to be some great muse of mine and this will all make sense. A few nights together didn't really solve anything. Not our original disagreements, or the fact that she cheated on me with what's-his-face.*

We hadn't seen each other in—oh, ten or fifteen years, since back when we both attended a Stanford reunion. Yet all the old hurts and longings resurfaced like not even ten minutes had passed.

[Pause]

Annalise was incredibly helpful, however. Enthusiastic, even, about getting me meetings with the right people to sell my new product in Asia this fall. I don't really know what I've done to deserve her kindness.

[Gulps] *Have I told you about the new pill? We're calling it Shapextrin. The marketing team thought Victration, which I liked, sounded too much like* castration. *I mean, castration is another way to lose weight, but only about a pound. We also considered Friendical, but then that seemed to appeal to a younger, teenage demographic, and we do not want that. No, sir. Not after the shit that happened in the nineties.*

I still remember the call in which my lawyer told me a bunch of fifteen-year-old girls were found providing welcome baggies of my drug to new recruits to the cheerleading team. Thanks to an embezzling pharmacist uncle. Several of them were hospitalized. I got so much flack for that personally. It didn't help that I was also dating a nineteen-year-old at the time—I was twenty-five, for the record—so it looked like I was endangering teenagers across the spectrum. In my defense, I was . . . she was . . . She was nineteen and made me feel like I was the smartest man in the world. Not a great reason, but I needed someone to build me up at that point, still wallowing from my breakup with Annalise.

I know, I know. [Gulp] *It's tacky to even discuss in today's climate. "Older man seduces younger woman. Teen." I didn't know how to act at the time. I didn't have a publicist to kick my ass into shape—thanks, A.S.—I only had mommy issues and self-esteem issues that caused me to make terrible choices and approve doomed marketing strategies. I was the original chemist behind it all, but I didn't know anything about leading a company, or the ethical questions related to telling women they should lose weight to be happy. Thrive, Inc. was my baby. My legacy on this earth that I concocted while still in college. How was I supposed to know someone would die from it?*

[Glass tinkling] *The first time I saw a photo of her, I was still in my one-bedroom apartment, at the kitchen dining table that I grabbed for free off La Cienega Boulevard. My lawyer brought the picture over—because I asked him to. I needed to see her.*

Her bright white teeth in her school photo looked like something out of a Colgate commercial. She was fifteen. Paola Hayward of Lincoln, Nebraska. Big, thick curls that went past her shoulders and nearly covered the acid-washed denim jacket she wore. She was barely a teenager, more like a little kid, with big chubby cheeks still. For years after, whenever I heard someone say my pill brought back their "girlish figure," I thought of her. Of the girl that died and the woman she never became, thanks to my drug.

I didn't try to create a new product for a long time. The idea of putting out another weight-loss pill that could harm more people made me anxious. So I started tinkering. I thought about what I still liked about the whole creating-something-for-public-consumption thing: helping people to improve their health—to feel better about themselves—and in a way that felt more attainable than your traditional diet-and-exercise approach. I'm happiest when I've had a solid night's sleep, so I started playing around with enzymes that would support that. After many, many failed attempts, I finally figured out Shapextrin—a pill that helps people metabolize food more efficiently, to sleep easier and more soundly. It's not another weight-loss drug, not exactly. It's a weight-loss wingman that proactively sets the groundwork for someone when they are ready to tackle diet and exercise.

It's still in the realm of transformation. But in a less aggressive way. A more holistic, balanced way. Kind of like Phinneas-in-his-twenties versus Phinneas-in-his-fifties. Anyway, I'm hoping that's how it comes across when Shapextrin launches later this year.

And I wouldn't have had the idea, or the impetus, I guess, if it hadn't been for Paola Hayward.

[Pause; gulps] *A pretty . . . pretty terrible thing to say aloud.*

It's a good thing Hashim Swartz came into my life way back when. He told me—no, he demanded that I do exactly what he said in order to ride out the scandal. To ensure that Thrive, Inc. survived when a young girl didn't.

Honestly? [Scoffs] *I don't know how I would have made it through without his sage, domineering, money-grubbing micromanagement.* [Glass tinkling]

CHAPTER TWELVE

CONNOR

BEL-AIR | SEPTEMBER 8

Squeals nearly burst my eardrums as the open-air tour bus creeps to a pause outside a copse of eucalyptus trees. The two-lane road in Beverly Hills is barely wide enough to accommodate our twenty-person ride, but the driver pauses anyway.

"1987's Sexiest Man Alive lives here. Any guesses who that is? Anyone?"

A woman with a purple visor sitting with two teenage daughters, deeply engrossed in their phones, flaps her hands. "Oh! It's—it's—"

"Harry Hamlin! I loved him growing up!" another woman, seated across the aisle from me, shouts. The driver tosses a fun-size

Snickers to her, then launches into gossip about Lisa Rinna. Visor, the woman who couldn't get her answer out, begins crying at being *this close* to the former heartthrob.

I check my Hollywood tour map again. Only two more stops before we reach my destination in Bel-Air. When I told Addison I had signed up for the morning drive, she nearly laughed herself hoarse. She said Devon Lim isn't going to emerge from his house just to greet a bunch of tourists with smartphones. Why would he?

I countered that she hasn't been able to get ahold of him—and she said all her colleagues at Ovid Blackwell swear he hasn't checked in for months—so what's the harm in trying?

It's been three days since Addison agreed to help me. I thought finding and following Devon Lim would be a slam dunk after that. I'd be able to track him as he canoodled with his lady friend, then report back to his fiancée's mother, Genevieve Aspen. Then again—surprise! Nothing is easy for me these days. I should have known.

Buoyed by Gen's wire of cash to my bank account, I've been driving all over town at the mere mention of Devon Lim. I went to his former assistant—and paid for breakfast—to question her about Devon's recent romances. Using information gleaned over pancakes, I stopped by Devon's dry cleaners to see if he's had any women's clothing laundered over the last few weeks. During the middle of Wednesday night, I tried to peek inside Devon's garbage bins, which were rolled to the curb for trash pickup the following morning, but all I found was a small bag of dirty paper towels, used tissues, sponges, and a Lean Cuisine microwavable meal. Cleaning supplies and dinner for some housekeeper. The guy isn't at his main residence in Bel-Air or his vacay home in

Santa Barbara. Addison doesn't think he's out of the country, but she's proving less in-the-know than I remembered.

The driver clutches a two-way radio, and the speakers crackle overhead. "Next stop, the Hills!"

The tour bus lurches into drive with a jolt. The women wave goodbye to Harry and Lisa as we creep forward beneath a canopy of trees. Climbing above the flat neighborhood of Beverly Hills, I recall the last time I went to a party down below. It was some talent agent's house, but he knew everyone who was anyone. And a long time ago, they all knew me.

We turn off Beverly Glen onto a side road and narrowly avoid a Smart car zipping past. Open to the public through the east gate, Bel-Air welcomes our tour bus without even a nod from the security booth.

"Coming up on your right, we have the mansion that belonged to Tony Curtis—"

"Oh my God, really?" Visor says, swiping to her phone's camera app. "I love *Some Like It Hot*!"

"Not only Tony," the driver resumes, "but Marilyn Monroe, Burt Reynolds, and Sonny and Cher. The alabaster courtyard fountain is just there, hiding behind the row of arborvitaes and wisteria. Everybody got a view?" The driver and all passengers on the bus lean to that side, while I face left.

Down a narrow street opposite, the blue hand-painted mailbox of Devon Lim stands at the end of the street, where a tunnel of Italian cypress begins. A mailman drops a handful of letters inside; then he waves to someone. He climbs back into his white truck as a woman emerges from between the hedges. The housekeeper who eats Lean Cuisines retrieves the mail, as she has done each day the last three times I've taken this tour at this time. When I tried to approach her directly, while she was cleaning out the lawn fountain, under the guise of just having moved into the neighborhood—integrity be damned—she told me Mr. Lim wasn't at the house. I then asked if he had gone on an errand and would return shortly, or if he was on vacation. She only glared.

Now the housekeeper flips through envelopes but doesn't lift her head to catch me watching. She heads indoors, the long hem of a white sweater fluttering. If Devon Lim is inside and cheating on his fiancée with another woman, his employee doesn't seem to mind.

The mail truck reaches the road on which the tour bus idles, and I turn away from it to peer at the Tony Curtis et al. house and hide my face. Alberto Rodriguez, devoted mailman, father of three, military veteran, and staunch Republican, was flattered when I struck up a conversation with him at his local deli yesterday and told him what a great job he was doing in "my" Bel-Air neighborhood. But when I asked him whether he knew if anyone had moved out recently—"I haven't seen this guy, Devon Lim, at 26618 Wilbever Court for a while"—I got iced out. Alberto said he kept his job and cushy mail route for two decades because he knows how to keep his mouth closed.

A puff of black exhaust is what's left as Alberto descends the hill out of sight.

"All right, everyone. We've got two minutes for photos in front of the multihyphenate house before security comes barreling around the corner. Who wants their pic?"

The driver descends first, with the entire bus filing out behind him. When I reach the asphalt, instead of lining up along the manicured lawn and a sign that reads TRESPASSERS WILL BE PROSECUTED,

I slip around the back. I don't look behind me until I am nearly hidden by a tall hedge at the bend in the road.

Despite casing this address, questioning neighbors and postal personnel—and, yes, rifling through more trash—I haven't had a clear read on whether Lim is home. Whether this is the spot where he's been entertaining a mistress and cheating on Genevieve's precious daughter. Although I tried confirming information the right way this time, Gen is getting more demanding for progress. Which means I'm out of options.

An ad for a luxury meal service peeks from a mailbox. I grab the stiff cardstock, tuck it under my arm, and continue my casual, totally casual, jaunt down the sidewalk. When I reach Lim's house, I slide behind the housekeeper's wagon in the driveway to cut across the lawn. I slip the card under the mat, hit the doorbell, then pivot and make my way along the three-car garage.

The door opens. "Hello?" the housekeeper calls. I stride up the side of the midcentury Colonial like I live here, pulling my hat low. There are security cameras nearby, there must be. Lim had them on his vacation beach house, so why wouldn't he set them up in his actual home? Doesn't really matter, not to me. All I need is to confirm whether the guy is here—and if he is, whether he's alone.

The back entrance, a California glass door the length of the entire wall that retracts and accesses the backyard, is wide open. I pass a bucket with a towel draped along the rim, beside a spray bottle. It must be window day.

Once inside Lim's cavernous megamansion, I scan the ground floor. Its layout was published on an *Architectural Digest* website eight years ago during renovations by the previous owner, and Lim seems to have kept things the same: four wide hallways that lead to the foyer where the housekeeper is, the butler pantry and the kitchen, the downstairs primary, and a staircase.

A door shuts. She's back inside. I choose the hallway leading right, then dip into the first closed room on my left. A den. Jackpot.

Inside, opposite a deep cushy couch buried in laundry facing a mounted flat-screen TV, a cherrywood desk is stacked with paper and filing trays. Devon probably forbids his housekeeper from cleaning in here. A laptop is missing from a dock, and the cable connecting to a widescreen computer monitor stands alone, as if bereft of its life partner. Briefly, I think of Addison and how poetic it might be, if I could rely on her like that.

I sift through the loose pages on top of the first tray. Halfway down the stack of receipts, a prescription for an inhaler brand I know from infomercials, and articles about tech, I find a page with an interesting letterhead. Devon Lim's.

I scan the top paragraph. Then read it again, to be sure.

Devon drew up a proposal—to create an app that monitors weight loss when paired with medication. A specific medication: Shapextrin. Wasn't that Phinneas Redwood's upcoming product? The proposal is printed on Devon's personal stationery and dated three weeks ago.

Phinneas's name is nowhere on this sheet, but it's definitely possible he read the proposal. Maybe he even chatted with Devon about it directly. Maybe he told someone about it the night that he died.

Phinneas and Devon could have been working together. And I'm going to rub Addison's nose in this information so hard, she'll think she's back in college doing lines.

Singing carries from the hallway, interrupting my thoughts— the housekeeper, bopping along to a pop tune as she makes her way through the house. The song is getting louder.

I snap a picture of the proposal on my phone, then turn, scattering the top few pages to the floor. A receipt for a luggage reservation lands face up. The date is from two days ago, with Air France. Son of a—

Have I been just missing Devon at each of his properties?

Grumbling to myself, I request an Uber. Set the pickup for the bend in the road at the Curtis house. When I slide into the hallway, the housekeeper's heavy footsteps stomp overhead on the second floor.

Once securely seated in a Kia Telluride, I scroll through notifications on my phone. Two messages from Genevieve came in while I was sneaking around Bel-Air.

Connor, my dear. Tell me you have
something juicy to report.

Then:

Rather, tell me I haven't been footing
the bill for you the last three weeks with
nothing to show for it.

I bite back a sigh. Nothing to show for it? That's a little strong, considering I've sent her updates and we've spoken on the phone each week—way more than I provided in reports to her in the past.

"Hey. Don't I know you?" My driver glares at me through the rearview. A man with brown eyes, pink skin, and a red Cardinals cap pulled low over his forehead.

"What?" I pause my placating text to Gen.

"Connor, right?"

I stiffen. I can't get a read on this guy's face from where I sit—trapped in his back seat. "No. I'm Terry. You must be confusing me with someone else."

The man pushes his cap up for a better look at me. "No, it's you, all right. Connor, the private eye. You told my boss that I was stealing from the company. You got me fired."

Sweat dots my forehead. I remember this guy. Ryan Fogerty, whose boss, Vijay, suspected him of siphoning off product—luxury handbags—when they arrived from the supplier, then passing them to a ring of buyers specializing in selling in-demand items online at a major price gouge. It's always online these days.

"Not only that," Ryan continues, "you got me fired, then got my wife fired, too."

Is the heater on? I glance to the front dashboard, but the A/C is pumping through the vents.

I shake my head. "I only told Vijay that you probably had a teammate in your scheme, and he reported your wife to her job on Rodeo—"

My driver brakes hard. He pulls over, knocking into the curb of the sidewalk, still a mile away from where I'm headed. "You thought that she was posing as a customer so I could pass her the extra bags—while you pretended to be searching for your lost child. When she came out of our store, holding a bag of my gym clothes, you were crying and a mess—remember that? She felt so bad for you that she asked you to watch her stuff while she went to go look for your 'kid.'"

Air quotes. And a snarl. "She wasn't any part of the game!

Just dropped by to give me my heart medicine that day and pick up my laundry. Now I'm driving for Uber and ferrying my neighbors' teenagers at all hours, just to pay my mortgage."

Realization cuffs me on the jaw. This guy had such a good scheme going, he was living in Bel-Air. A fact I completely forgot about until now. "I—I'm sorry, I had no—"

"Disgusting—abusing her compassion. Manipulating a kind woman. Get out of my car before I throw you out."

Without waiting for a nicer invite, I slink from the back seat.

Burned rubber rips into the air as the guy peels back into traffic on Hollywood Boulevard, nearly colliding with a thrill-seeking bicyclist.

The walk to the Hollywood Tours Buzz depot is hot, sticky, and long. Plenty of time to recall what a jerk I was. It's true, Ryan Fogerty was stealing from his boss, and I was paid a pretty penny to sniff out his crimes. But I didn't need to loop in his wife as collateral damage. And posing as a bereft parent is some next-level scumbaggery.

I finally reach my Land Rover rental, feeling as gross on the inside as I do on the outside. My plan was to head back to my Airbnb to regroup, but being alone in Silver Lake sounds pretty awful right now. Although I made progress this morning—gained new info without hurting anyone this time—a sour taste coats my mouth. I followed Devon Lim's trail in two cities and learned a lot—see, Genevieve?—but never his actual location.

Tourists crowd the lobby of the Hollywood Roosevelt Hotel, an old haunt of mine. I head straight toward the restaurant and bar, upbeat music blaring throughout the first floor. Front and center at the pool, my former favorite table is open, and

I slide into the seat. Way back when, I used to come here to conduct meetings or to gather my thoughts. Work on theories. Plan out next steps to hunt down targets.

Being here is grounding. I try to refocus, to push the syndicated reruns of my mistakes out of my head.

My newsfeed crawls with reports of the usual: violence, scandal, and a few social media influencers deliberately leaking nudes. Three articles further down question whether there is a conspiracy related to Phinneas Redwood's death. Redwood was a mainstay of the popular consciousness for his size as a little person, his larger-than-life personality, and being a CEO of a diet pill company. It's not surprising that Addison's name keeps popping up in relation to his. A publicist as feared and hated as she is doesn't usually allow herself to get that close to homicide, let alone be at the scene of the crime.

Over a Shirley Temple and a cheeseburger—my favorite meal—I continue scrolling.

Thumbnails of headlines offer more of the same, but I know what I'm after: anything that mentions a tech mogul or Devon Lim, or *Devon Lim and Phinneas Redwood*. What would Lim be doing in France—if the luggage reservation I found can be believed? Why leave the country right now when he's probably mid-grovel to his fiancée? Why would he not tell her his plans? If they broke up, Genevieve would have updated me.

I scan articles for any mention of the Aspen family while I'm at it. Genevieve prefers a low profile, and I need her to continue footing the bill for this investigation—and give me that bonus—more than I realized. Gianni called me last night in search of the money I owe, despite me already giving him 10 percent of it. He called from a blocked number, then left a brief voice message—"Hurry up, Connor"—while someone screamed in agony in the background. Who, I don't know. But I don't need to. The reminder was loud and clear to work harder—faster—if I value my health.

My finger pauses on an article's thumbnail image of a laptop. The text beneath it reads RISE OF DRUG USE AMONG SOFTWARE RICH. The platform is a two-bit player in mainstream media, and its readership amounts to peanuts. But the fact that it leads with the "software rich" has me intrigued.

I take a gulp of my Shirley Temple and dive in.

Scanning the article doesn't offer much: only that after the tech boom of the early aughts, then the Great Recession that followed, the software giants that remained continued to amass wealth—the obscene kind. Those who were successful in the industry as software engineers saw some of that money trickle down. Most of them had too much, more than they knew how to manage responsibly. Cue drugs.

"Either drugs, sex, or alcohol," I comment aloud. The burger is still warm, the cheese not yet stringy. The perfect comfort food. Poolside, two women in bikinis dive into the water, still warm in September in LA. One of them, a brunette, surfaces, then throws me a lusty smile.

I smile back but keep reading. The only woman I can think about lately is Addison Stern, against my better judgment.

I stop chewing. Reread the paragraph I just skimmed. Beneath an image of a famous engineer in Silicon Valley, the article mentions him. Devon Lim.

Clutching my phone closer, I slide the screen up.

>Months ago, another casualty of tech wealth, software genius Devon Lim was arrested for felony drug possession. The app that first brought him success, Irish Gbye, enables a user to remotely delete text messages from a recipient's mobile phone up to twenty-four hours after a message was sent, regardless of the recipient's security settings.

That's it. No additional context or consequences. The author moves on to discuss the general opioid crisis currently entrenched across America. I scan the article again, top to bottom, for another mention of Lim. Using my phone's spyglass function, I search the text for the key word *Lim*, but only the one sentence is found.

As I lean back in my chair, the cold metal shocks the exposed skin of my arms. The women in the swimming pool approach another man wearing a suit, seated on the opposite side. A new song by a singer I once did a keg stand with in Malibu while I was investigating his ties to traffickers at his father-in-law's request blasts overhead.

How was Devon Lim's name buried in the middle of an op-ed from last week when he's one of the richest app inventors of the decade? Why is this the only mention I've seen of him being arrested months ago—and for drugs?

"Ovid Blackwell," I mutter. "Of course."

I tap my call log, then smash Addison's name with my index finger. The phone rings. Although I read the spreadsheet file that I stole on my thumb drive, Addison's notes were hard to make sense of. I only understood Devon Lim's Santa Barbara address because she included it as a PNG file, copied into a cell.

"You again?" Her voice is velvety, as if she's in a crowded movie theater and she's sneaking away to answer.

"I found something."

"Oh?"

"Devon Lim. He was picked up for drug charges."

"That happened a year ago. How is that relevant now?"

I pause. Watch as a beach ball is slapped into the chlorinated water. Condensation forms a ring around my glass on the wooden table. "How has Ovid managed to keep the drug arrest quiet all this time? I just read about it online."

Addison scoffs through the phone. "Not possible. We locked down the media, the police, and his colleagues, keeping them all from uttering a peep. The only way that info would be leaked is if . . . Shit."

"What is it?"

A tapping noise emanates from the phone. "No one in the United States, definitely not in California, would have published that. What was the platform name?"

"*Big Time News*."

"I should have known," she growls. "*Big Time News* is owned by—"

"Das News, the German conglomerate. Why does that matter?"

She pauses, and I can almost hear the Cheshire Cat grin she wears. "Because. I know where Devon Lim is hiding."

"France?"

Another pause. "Why would you say that?"

The image of Devon Lim's luggage reservation returns to mind, but I see no reason to share more than what's necessary with this PR edition of ego personified. "Devon recently flew there. Look, more importantly, Phinneas Redwood and

Devon knew each other. Devon even wrote up a business proposal directed to Thrive, Inc. for an app to pair with the new pill that's launching this November."

"Phinneas never mentioned it to me. How did you find out about it?"

"I have my secrets."

An appreciative grunt carries through the phone. "Don't we all?"

I lean back against the chair. I've got Addison exactly where I want her. "Well, I think I have my marching orders, then. Au revoir."

"Nice try, Connor. But if Devon and Phinneas are somehow mired together in this debacle, I'm not letting you handle a visit to Devon alone." She exhales into the speaker. "Let's go to France."

CHAPTER THIRTEEN

ADDISON

THE FRENCH RIVIERA | SEPTEMBER 14

Seaside air cuts through my sweater, brushing my moisture-deprived skin. The red-eye from LA to Luxembourg was easy since I was asleep, then the flight from Luxembourg to the tiny spit of an airport in Toulon was racked with turbulence. Ugh. At one point, the route was so bumpy, I grabbed on to Connor's sleeve beside me. A flutter twirled inside my stomach as I realized that he still uses the same aftershave I always loved—the woodsy scents of pine and moss.

Luckily, Connor was passed out and slept right through my moment of terror. I hate flying. But I hate needing anyone more.

While Connor enjoyed a deep REM cycle, I couldn't stop thinking about the card I found on Phinneas's desk. The writing—A.S. 131023—wouldn't be a bank account, not with so few numbers. The letters *A.S.* could be my initials, but they could also stand for something else. It's been at the back of my mind—and hidden between my cell phone and its protective case—ever since I was released from the crime scene. Knowing Phinneas, it's probably a reminder to buy more Absolut Strawberry.

A black town car slows before me on the sidewalk. "Taxi's here," I call over my shoulder.

"Addison, come on. Check out the view, at least." Connor stretches a palm toward the two dozen sailboats lounging in a water inlet below, toward the horizon beyond, appearing to quench the fire of the setting sun.

"Connor, try to act like you've been here before. Get in the car." I slide into the black leather back seat and give an address to the driver.

"I haven't been here. And that's not our hotel address," Connor says, slipping in beside me.

"So you are paying attention."

Connor shuts the door harder than necessary. "We're going to Lim's house right now?"

The driver pulls away from the arrivals terminal. French rap hums from speakers along the dashboard. A bucket containing ice and two splits of champagne hangs from a crochet hook on the driver's headrest. The only way to toast reaching the Côte d'Azur.

Once Connor told me that a German platform published news of Devon Lim's arrest for drug possession in an article, it was clear that Devon was abroad. No one should have known outside the United States unless Devon was getting chatty here in Toulon at his other vacation home, which he remodeled recently and whose blueprints he sent to me as a humblebrag.

"Maybe you're not aware, but I'm a very busy woman," I reply. "And the sooner Phinneas's murder is resolved, the sooner I'm able to resume dominating. If Devon has details to share, I'll be the first to find out."

The Google Alert I set up pinged my inbox with a dozen search results once we landed. Each of them mentioned the most important details of Phinneas's murder: No suspects have yet been named; his publicist—me—found the body. Old news.

The driver lifts an eyebrow in the rearview mirror but doesn't show other signs of understanding English.

"Addison," Connor begins with a huff, "I need to watch Devon and see whether or not he's cheating on his fiancée. That's the first step here. Not rolling in, guns blazing."

The car slows, turning onto a narrow cobbled road up the hillside. A mailbox juts from a stone wall covered in vines and the driver turns left, past it, into the entrance of an impressive villa overlooking the bay.

"I can't go in with you like this, directly. Addison? Addison," Connor hisses. "Excuse me?" he says to the driver. "Can you drop me off back on the road behind us?"

The driver shakes his head. "Pas d'anglais."

Connor deflates against the black leather. "Shit. This is not how this is supposed to go, Addison. I didn't tell you about Devon's business proposal just so you can put my investigation on blast."

I nearly purr. "Keep that in mind next time you try to strong-arm me, Connor."

We roll to a stop in a concrete, circular driveway in front of two carved columns that might belong in the Hollywood Hills or Greece. The sun hits the white paint like a pink spotlight, casting the two-story house in a romantic glow—I glance at Connor—for another duo.

I step outside, grateful for the thick-heeled Prada Mary Janes I always take with me to Europe. The cold air that greeted us at the airport has dropped another few degrees, and I press my oversize clutch to my long-sleeve burgundy jumpsuit. Although I'm jet-lagged and would prefer pajamas after our multicountry flight path, no matter where I find myself, I know image is everything.

After asking the driver in French to wait for me, I take the curated pebble walkway toward the front door, leaving Connor to sulk in the car. When I reach a bench set against a lattice of climbing vines, I glance behind. Connor has slumped into the back seat, with only his mop of brown hair visible.

Along the south-facing side of the house, light emanates from behind metal shutters open toward the Mediterranean Sea.

Excitement tightens my chest. Someone is home. I was right. Addison Stern loves being right—and why shouldn't I? It happens so very often.

With an extra hop in my step, I approach the front entrance around the corner. Flanked by still-lush hanging baskets of rosemary, the front door is painted azure blue, matching the water below.

When I knock on the door, it swings inward. Pushing against the large knob planted in the center, I give it a nudge.

"Hello? Bonjour? Mr. Lim, it's Addison Stern."

Silence.

"Devon?" The car is nearly out of sight from where I stand, but I'll bet Connor is still moping on the back-seat floor. I step into the foyer. Although I haven't been here before, Devon proudly showed off photos of his vacation property during my visits to his Bel-Air home. Ostentatious but with a likeable dose of humility, Devon was always the first to point out the perks of being wildly successful and to celebrate others' achievements, as well. When my former client—heiress to a skin-care empire turned first female governor of California—was elected to office, Devon sent me a basket of oranges and Veuve Clicquot to celebrate the groundwork I'd laid for her the previous year.

"Mr. Lim? I've been trying to reach you by phone. I'm in France for a new client's campaign and I thought I would . . ." I let the story I crafted while flying at thirty thousand feet taper off. "I thought I would check in on you. Ovid Blackwell has a few exciting new developments to share with its most important clients. Hello?"

A dog barks somewhere down the road. The house is silent and appears to be empty, despite the illuminated chandelier above a pristine canary-yellow range and the fresh smell of lemon and pepper hanging in the air. A meal was cooked here recently. Beside the hidden refrigerator that masquerades as a large cabinet, a tied-off trash bag sits on the brown tile floor.

Heat emanates from the spotless oven. I peek inside and find a half-eaten pie on the top rack. Whoever enjoyed a late lunch was planning to return shortly—maybe imminently; that would explain why the door was left unlocked.

Unless there's someone still home. Someone gasping for air, or trying to stop the blood from pooling onto the—

I inhale a shaky breath. Pause, alone in the kitchen. "Devon? Mr. Lim? Are you here?"

Stifling the memory of wandering through Phinneas's home, I

take the carved wooden stairs that lead to the second floor of the villa. I grasp the polished marble handrail, new urgency driving me up each step. Gooseflesh breaks out across my neck, as I recognize the awful feeling tracing my spine: déja vu.

"Stop it, Addison," I whisper to myself. A mirror at the landing captures the anxiety wrinkling my brow, negating my recent fillers. "Knock that off, too."

I relax. Wait for my skin to unpleat.

Sparsely decorated with cavernous ceilings, the house amplifies the sound of my movements. Each step creaks, revealing my position as if it were a security alarm—the sole one at this address, it seems—notifying the inhabitants that an intruder has broken in.

"Mr. Lim?" I call again. France's strict gun laws make it difficult for civilians to possess a firearm at home, but there are other weapons that can damage a skull.

"Mr. Lim? It's Addison Stern with Ovid Blackwell. Your publicist." Damn Connor, looping me into another B and E.

With a twist of my wrist, I push open the door closest to me. I step into a reading room with bookcases covering one wall. Crossing a white sheepskin rug, I take care to avoid the pointed corners of a mahogany coffee table, then scan the wicker basket set in the middle. A few discarded items lie tossed within: a receipt, a coin, some pebbles from the beach. I glance at the unadorned walls, then the bookshelves, filled with colorful spines. Nothing unusual. I search for some trinket or note to confirm Devon is, in fact, here, or something to suggest how Phinneas and Devon knew each other, if they ever met, or if Devon was just another prospective investor in Thrive, Inc.

A peek into the remaining rooms on this level—a bedroom

with starched sheets, a spacious bathroom twice the size of the bedroom, and a game room with a flat-screen TV and VR headsets scattered across a leather sofa—reveals a recently used suitcase, complete with airline tags still on the handle, but no Devon Lim.

I circle back to the reading room for another glance at those spines. No pattern to their organization jumps out at me, as the books aren't slotted in by title, by author, or by color.

When no one barrels into the study wielding a candelabra, I turn to leave. Cut my losses. Relief mingles with disappointment that Connor and I can check into the hotel tonight and come back tomorrow morning.

Then an object in the wicker basket catches my eye: a black-and-white casino chip—not a coin—nearly covered by a receipt for landscaping, and a printout of a hotel confirmation. The words PLATINUM MEMBER and LE SALON ROSE are visible in small etched letters along the chip's border.

Victory tingles along my neck beneath my loose curls. Even if Devon Lim is in the French Riviera purely seeking downtime—a refuge away from his hectic, successful life at home—VIP habits endure across continents.

I tuck the chip into the slim pocket of my jumpsuit. "It's time we caught up in person, Devon."

CHAPTER FOURTEEN

PHINNEAS

BENEDICT CANYON | JULY 18

PHINNEAS REDWOOD: *Dear Future Editor. I probably need to have you sign an NDA before I let you listen to all of my ramblings. So stop whatever notes you're taking and make sure you signed in the little block at the bottom of the page. Did you do it? Okay, okay, take the time to read the fine print and what have you. [Pause] Now, let's continue.*

Hashim Swartz is a person I wouldn't normally call a friend. I thought he was at one point. Then my bank account got too large, with too many zeros, and he became something more of a . . . a hanger-on, if I'm being nice. A demanding killjoy if I'm not. I first met Hashim while he was doing lines off the backside of an Italian film actress at my house in Sorrento. When he sobered up, someone told him about my work, and he asked to see a formal pitch, stateside. Three months later I was staring at the same man who peed into my pool then shouted "I am Bacchus!" before he passed out in a hammock, only this time he was wearing a dress shirt buttoned all the way to his Adam's apple.

Trying to generate interest in Thrive, meeting with investors in the pharma industry who I thought might appreciate the compounds I'd created—the (oh, hell, what's a better way to term it?) the formula for my weight-loss magic drug, as the New York Times *and* Science Monthly *both called it, was frustrating. No one was offering what I knew I was worth. By the way, make sure you get a quote from the* Times *and Sci Mo about me. Terrence Fiske, an editor at the* Times *owes me one.*

Anyway, I needed someone to balk out loud, to challenge the product in real time. I needed Hashim. So, at one meeting, I did my spiel, offering up a certain percentage of stakes in the mix, and he spoke up. He said, "Make me believe you." [Noise] I mean, I almost laughed right there to his face. But I didn't. No, your boy Phinn didn't miss a beat. I replied, "Science doesn't require your subjective buy-in if you understand its concepts. Science just is."

Hashim Swartz replied, "Based on what we know at any given time, yes. We also thought the world was flat for a good many years."

I go, "Very true. But now that we've emerged from the Dark

Ages, it would behoove us to accept certain facts as they are. Namely, I can block a specific enzyme to shrink fat cells— and we're the only diet pill that's accomplished that. Ever."

Approving nods rippled across the long conference table then. I went over the data, the studies we ran, the tests, and the deck I made myself, to lock in interest. I was sweating like a primate but no one seemed to notice—with those dollar signs clouding their vision! [Laughter] You know? It was all a downhill ski after that, straight into the signed contract and marketing plans and a few intensive reports from the FDA.

While the other investors faded away over the months that followed, Hashim remained close. We would have lunch at least biweekly for a while before the first pill launched. He wanted to know more about the product, about the organic chemistry behind it, he said. But I knew the real reason behind his invitations to eat at some of the finest restaurants LA County has to offer: He meant to keep tabs on me. Wanted to keep me close in case his investment went south. Wanted to ensure I was doing business the way he thought I should.

How did I know that, you ask? At each eatery location, no matter where we were, I could always see a man hiding just out of sight. I'd have to search the periphery and scan across a stretching boulevard, but I'd find him. A hat pulled low, dark clothing, and a profile with a pug nose. Medium build, too. I always notice someone's height.

Did I find it strange that Hashim had a kind of bodyguard who may or may not do his bidding? Not really. If you live in LA long enough, and mingle with a certain tax bracket of individuals, you really do see it all.

Years and years ago, I was out with my ex, Annalise. We were leaving some bar when we saw that super-famous actor—you know, that one guy with the hair, in the end-of-the-world movie with the dog? Well, he was sitting on the patio of a five-star restaurant on Melrose, having a drink with a blow-up elephant seated in the chair across from him. He seemed completely himself, carrying on conversations with fans and the waitstaff. Annalise and me, we thought he might have lost a bet. We laughed about that moment for weeks. This actor was, like, the biggest, most hard-core symbol of masculinity at the time, and he was just sipping a cosmopolitan with his plastic safari companion.

She has the best laugh, Annalise. We didn't do too much laughing in Hong Kong together—something about her rejecting me again made things a little tense. But in the good times— man, her happiness sounded like a wind chime. Beautiful, cascading. Even better, the effect that it had on me translated to pure bliss. That's the real drug I should be selling. The Annalise Effect.

[Sniffs]

Oh, wow. I didn't realize it was getting so late. Nearly noon. [Weak laughter; footsteps; liquid pours into glass] *At least I'm not in a public place? One of these days, I'm going to have to cut back on my alcohol intake.*

But that's Future Phinn's problem.

Hashim was always on me about appearances in public. Maintaining a professional demeanor, tipping waitstaff, and being able to walk out on my own feet despite the number of drinks on my bill. He would have flipped if I ever had a dinner with a pachyderm. He yammered on and on about how my personal actions could either help or harm my company, his investment.

Hashim and his bodyguard got kind of intense at one point. I remember one week, when every time I hit my favorite bar on Sunset, the same man with the pug nose would post up about a block away. Watching. Waiting for me to make a mistake. Inevitably [gulps] I did.

CHAPTER FIFTEEN

CONNOR

THE FRENCH RIVIERA | SEPTEMBER 14

Addison comes stalking out of the two-story villa like a runway model—shit, no. Like Medusa, hair perfectly curled and twirling in the ocean breeze . . . ah, crap.

Get it together, Connor.

I slink across the back seat, as far away from the woman who ruined my life as possible. Try to insulate myself from the excitement of finally traveling again, after I traveled for business and pleasure for so many years. To not confuse that joyous feeling of being in France with feelings for Addison.

"Some space, please?" Addison stares me down from beside the open car door, gesturing to my cell phone lying on the middle seat. I grab it, and she slides inside across the black leather.

"Au casino de Monte-Carlo, s'il vous plaît," she says to the driver. He nods, pulling forward in the courtyard.

"Wait—what did you find inside?" I ask. "Was Devon Lim there?"

"No. But he *was* there today."

"So why the casino? That's—what—a two-hour drive? Neither of us is exactly dressed like James Bond. We just got off an international flight, we should go to our hotel." I stifle a yawn. Despite my protesting, I did sleep on the flight. A shower, though, that's pretty hard to accomplish at thirty thousand feet.

"It's eight in the morning back in LA. Wake up." Addison checks her lipstick in her cell phone's camera app. It's perfect, of course. Gag.

We descend the hill and turn back onto a main boulevard. The bay of floating vessels matches our progress, mile for mile, continuing with each bend in the road. I scan my trousers and gray knit sweater. Both are wrinkled, but at least I folded my jacket in the overhead bin during our flight. I might be allowed to enter the casino, approved by the members of security and the concierge stationed at the epic brass doors. Might.

"Was there any feminine clothing inside the house? Some hint that a woman is staying there with him?"

Addison locks her phone. "Not that I saw. But there was a suitcase open in the primary bedroom with his airline baggage tag still attached from three days ago, and the kitchen was still warm from a meal of some kind. We must be just missing him at each of his homes."

I scowl, hearing the analysis that's mine to do. Addison shouldn't have entered the place without me. She should have told me no one was there and then allowed me to go in and do my investigation. I'm the PI.

I open my news app on my phone, then hate-scroll through headlines. Don't want another public clue to Devon's whereabouts to slip past me. Not when Addison is hoarding information.

"Most importantly, I found this next to a printed hotel confirmation." Addison holds up a gambling chip. "There are only a handful of public, sexy attractions in the French Riviera open in the off-season, at least to American tourists."

"Le Salon Rose." I nod. "The casino's former reading salon. I know it."

A placating smile curves her lips. "Finally, someone's head is in the game."

The journey churns by in a seascape of crashing blue waves and rocking sailboats. Enough time for me to reflect on all the ways Addison Stern has undercut me, exploited me, or made me look the idiot: obviously, when she fast-tracked my retirement; more recently, when she allowed me to go all the way up to Santa Barbara, probably knowing Lim was at home in Bel-Air the whole time; when she withheld info on Lim's drug arrest, which she could have shared at the outset of our new partnership; how she surprised me by directing our taxi to Lim's home as soon as we got into this back seat, then insisted we go straight to Monte Carlo, without once asking for my own take.

By the time we glide to a stop along the manicured topiaries of the legendary casino and resort, I'm grinding my molars.

We step from our taxi onto a red carpet, then cross the paved courtyard flanked by burbling fountains and conversations in French—no, Italian. Passing beneath the Baroque-style entrance that's dripping in decadent gold motifs and wrought-iron décor, we pause to hand over our passports at reception. Once registered, we sweep through a vaulted foyer entrance decorated with chubby cherubs that gaze down on all who pass within. The concierge beside the cloakroom nods his approval of our attire as he accepts our suitcases to hold in coat check. I get an extra sniff from him—the tuxedo-wearing hall monitor—but I'm allowed to continue in. Addison follows brass plaques that indicate the Salon Rose can be found in the east wing.

Internally, I want to break away. To swing around to the salon from the other side and conduct my own search without having to follow in Addison's pointed footsteps. Any effort on my part to take the lead only elicits a smirk from her, probably sensing my irritation. Not that I'm great at hiding it. When Addison announces we are approaching the corridor that leads to hotel guest rooms, I snap, "Maybe you should go explore them." She laughs, harpy that she is.

A woman in a flared skirt and pearls greets us at the double doors inside the restaurant, one of several on the property, if those plaques can be trusted.

"Welcome to the Salon Rose," she says. "Reservation name?"

"Actually, we're looking for someone," I chime in, unwilling to be Addison's sidekick any longer. I'm the one with the leverage.

Addison throws me a steely glare. She lifts the casino coin she found in Devon's house. "Yes, we are. What does this chip mean?"

The woman brightens. "That's for our platinum member program, of course. Right this way."

We follow her into a spacious room decorated in gold and pink. Marble tabletops are distributed throughout, while Renaissance paintings decorate the walls and white crown molding lines the ceiling. Our footsteps clack along the polished wooden floor, then grow silent on thick decorative carpets that depict a stag hunt. A narrow door leads into the back of the restaurant, the VIP area. An empty VIP area.

"Where is everyone?" I ask. "It's dinnertime, and no one is here."

The woman smiles. "Dinnertime in the U.S., maybe. Here, local custom is to dine at nine o'clock. Can I provide you with menus or a complimentary glass of champagne?"

"No," both Addison and I say in unison.

The maître d' leaves us to return to the front entrance. Across the hardwood, flames dance in a massive fireplace so large it could be offered up as a guest room. Adjacent and beneath a panoramic painting of fornicating nymphs, a bartender polishes glass stemware.

"May I serve you something?" he asks in accented English.

"No," Addison and I say again.

"Stop that," she snaps at me. "If you had anyone else left to use as a source, I would be asleep at home in LA."

"Not flying around in bat form, seeking out your next victim?"

"A comedian. Did you finally decide to do something you're good at instead of wasting everyone's time as a—"

"I am good at PI work, and if you had let me do my job back at Devon's house, we wouldn't have had to come all the way out here for nothing."

"Right, because your suggestion of going straight to bed in Toulon was so brilliant. Something tells me you aren't so great at PI work when you have no one left that trusts you."

"Hey, my list of sources dwindled thanks to your selfish, self-serving instincts to get a leg up at Ovid when you stole my—"

"You're no innocent, Connor. Don't pretend like I started the backstabbing."

I pause before replying with another jab. The bartender chops a lime on the wooden counter while concert violins screech from the casino sound system. "What is that supposed to mean?"

Addison huffs. "You know exactly what it means."

"Do I? Look, you didn't have to come here. You insisted on joining me because *I* figured out that Devon and Phinneas may have been in business together. Besides, if you had any friends, you might know what it is to help someone simply because they asked."

Brushing long, dark hair out of her eyes, she hugs her elbows. "Well, I wasn't deadweight, Connor. I found the VIP chip, and Devon is probably somewhere close. But there are hundreds of rooms on the property with exclusive clubs and restaurants, gaming halls, and countless other opportunities for fun for someone like him. I'm not going to traipse around here all night. I'm going to the hotel."

"Which hotel? You're driving back to the one in Toulon without me?"

She rolls her eyes to the gilded ceiling. "I'll be in the lobby while I try calling Devon again. You have thirty minutes. Then I'm gone."

"Fine."

"Fine." She stalks back into the restaurant, her red jumpsuit swishing as she goes.

I'm not chasing after her. If she wants to get butt-hurt about her lack of friendships, she should act differently. Live differently. At the hotel, we have separate rooms. She can check into hers right now and leave me to finally work without her meddling.

Don't pretend like I started the backstabbing. Irritation spirals along my ears. As if I'm to blame for our falling-out after she stole information from my phone for a client. I'm pretty sure she gained a corner office after the crap she pulled.

Don't pretend like I started the backstabbing. What was

Addison talking about? Is she still hung up on what happened in my car, years ago? Or something else?

Back then, I did a lot of things I'm not proud of. Some of them were unethical, left a bad taste in even my mouth: blackmail, lying to people for weeks to gain their trust, and, yes, implicating a woman in her husband's luxury-handbag theft. Did those actions have unintended consequences that touched Addison's world—like what happened to the wife of my Uber driver from Bel-Air? If I'm being honest . . . it's possible. Though I would never have done anything to hurt Addison, not deliberately—not then, at least.

Regardless of my intentions—was I to blame for our breakup?

Still grumbling, I straighten my jacket, then step back into the restaurant. Try to shake off the guilt that's been needling me since I moved to Vegas.

When I reach the hallway that leads to the main entrance of the casino, I pause beneath an ornate light fixture—another cherub, this one holding a lyre. A plaque beside it offers directions to various on-site attractions.

The in-house florist might be worth a visit. If Devon Lim is here and he's cheating on Genevieve Aspen's daughter, he probably brought his mistress with him. Men like him—powerful, rich, and entitled—don't travel without someone to spoon. The florist in Santa Barbara said he's a regular customer whenever he is in town. I wonder if the same goes for him while he's abroad with a lady friend.

I cross the central rotunda. Violins swell from the overhead speaker system, but the din of playing cards, chips, and cheers from the gaming hall nearly overwhelms the music. As I walk down an embroidered runner designed with swirling vines, ocean animals, and geometric shapes, I'm reminded of just how much money has probably been made here. Like in Las Vegas.

Given the flush of cash I have from Genevieve, I could try my hand at these craps tables. Maybe I could win back more of the money I owe to my bookie.

No, no, no. Stay with it, Connor.

I give myself a hard pat on the cheek. Recall that this job is my shot to get my life back—gambling again will only add more problems to my plate.

Three men in dark suit jackets pause at an indoor fountain where I need to turn. One of them stands a foot above the rest, and I stop dead beside a painting of a Grimaldi, the ruling family of Monaco, in nineteenth-century clothing. Is that—Gianni?

But a loud crash—dishes breaking, followed by laughter—echoes from the rotunda, and all three heads turn. None of them is Gianni. Or Gianni's goon who ran after me in the Bellagio.

Exhaling, I continue forward. Tension hitches my shoulder blades as I pass the trio, stays until I reach a door around the corner that bears the words FLEURS DU CASINO.

Flowers of every color burst from the modest room. The florist, a stout woman with closely cropped brown hair, is happy to accommodate my English, then a bit of my poor Italian. When I ask if a gentleman has been in recently to purchase purple roses, she nods immediately. *Yesterday*. I describe Lim—tall, black hair, a mole on his chin, Asian American—and she nods faster. But Americans visit this place in droves all year round.

"Was he with a woman? Did he . . ." My voice trails off.

In Lim's Bel-Air home, I saw a prescription for an inhaler. Although I got the information while breaking and entering, it's the only detail I have that could be helpful.

"We had drinks together with other friends earlier, and he left his inhaler. I'm trying to return it to him. Would you know his room number? I don't want him to have an episode without his medication."

I shouldn't be exploiting Lim's private medical information to my advantage, I know. It's contrary to that new integrity vibe I had going for me back in the States. But is it wrong, really, if it confirms Lim is in his hotel, and gets me the upper hand over Addison?

Before I retired, I used to think the ends justified the means. My time in Vegas, in exile, confirmed the opposite, much in line with my granddad's way of thinking. And, man oh man, he'd be disappointed to learn reprogramming isn't going as great as it could.

"Of course, of course," the woman replies, dark eyebrows drawing together. She taps a few keys on her computer screen. "Room 1888. If he needs more fleurs, please tell him, call my shop directement and I'll have a fresh bouquet sent."

"Merci beaucoup." I exit the shop, my strides longer and more confident than they've been since I landed on this continent.

I take the elevator to the third floor. A housekeeping cart nearly blocks the narrow hallway built in the 1850s, and I glide my hands across a pile of luxury shampoo bottles as I pass.

Two watercolor tableaus frame a white door. Room 1888. I press the master key that I swiped from the maid's cart against the electronic keypad, ignoring the DO NOT DISTURB card dangling from the handle. Gears shift, and the door unlocks.

I step into the foyer of a spacious suite as the door shuts behind me. "Hello? Mr. Lim?"

Someone moves in the next room, the floorboards creaking,

out of sight. I creep into the suite, fully aware that I may be tackled at any second. But I need to confirm for myself whether this is his room.

The foyer leads into a plush sitting room decorated in purple and gold with satin pillows on pillows, velvet curved-back chairs, a glass coffee table, oil paintings hung on the walls, and a flat-screen television perched on a white entertainment center. The space evokes royalty, complementing a view of the sparkling waterfront of the Mediterranean Sea beneath the open balcony. A door to my right leads into a wine bar, brimming with stainless steel. To my left, past a love seat with a swirling purple-and-white pattern, double doors remain shut. The bedroom.

A tan jacket lies thrown on the back of an extended sofa, while dirty dishes from room service tower on a polished mahogany dining table. Purple and yellow roses gathered by a ribbon fill a slender vase beside them.

New noise comes from the bedroom. A dull sound—like a drawer closing. Choosing my steps carefully, along the baseboards, I hop to the thick rug beneath the sofa. Inside the tan jacket, I find a wallet and driver's license presenting Devon Lim's charismatic grin, charming even at the DMV. This is his room.

I clear my throat. "Mr. Lim, I'm here with . . ." Shit. I don't want to reveal who I am exactly, since I'm still investigating him.

"Mr. Lim, I'm with guest services. Can I clear away your dishes?"

Melted ice cream forms a puddle in a tall crystal glass. I hope he's not planning on dessert.

Some kind of sauce has hardened on a dinner plate with looping designs along the edge, the linguini appearing stiff. When did Lim order this meal? How long has it been sitting here?

Goose bumps sprout on the back of my neck. "Mr. Lim?"

"Yes," a muffled voice grunts from the bedroom.

A single-word reply. Kind of strange in its cadence, too. The tone seems off, somehow.

Grasping a curved mantel clock, I creep closer to the bedroom. "Okay, thank you. I'll leave now."

My muscles flex the farther I stalk, gearing up for whatever—whoever—waits behind the whitewashed oak. I reach for the golden knob in the center of the door. Sweat forms under my arms as waves crash below, violent in their decibels through the open balcony. I close my fist around the knob, then yank.

Devon Lim lies face up on the rumpled sheets of a king bed, his eyes staring vacantly at the ceiling. Blood seeps across the white sheets in a perverse tie-dye pattern, emanating not only from his body but from the body beside his—a woman's.

"Well, this is awkward."

I jump back, swinging the mantel clock in front of me, and find Addison Stern—skeptical eyebrow raised—in the corner of the bedroom. New horror washes down my chest. "Addison. What are you doing here?"

She glances at my weapon. "Before you do anything stupid, I should probably explain myself."

CHAPTER SIXTEEN

ADDISON

THE FRENCH RIVIERA | SEPTEMBER 14

The bedroom has taken on a disturbing smell, somewhere between musty and sour. Connor continues to stare at me like I might unhinge my jaw and swallow him whole. I smile, an action that causes him to flinch.

"Can we go back into the sitting room?" I glance at the two corpses, who were possibly in the middle of waking up or going to sleep when their assassin came. A jade necklace shaped like a heart peeks out from the top of the woman's pajama top. Tattoo ink covers the side of her arm: a dragon. "Let's give them some privacy."

Connor follows me, sputtering. "How— What did I just walk in on, Addison? Did you—? Are you—?"

"Connor," I interrupt, my tone sharp. "Are you actually asking if I murdered two people?"

He doesn't say anything. Only stays behind the console table that kisses the love seat. The clock piece is gripped tight in his fist. He's keeping his distance. He thinks I killed them.

"Got it," I murmur. "I'd be hurt if I wasn't so insulted."

Connor moves to the balcony doors, never taking his eyes from me. "Why are you here? How did you know to come here?"

"I could ask you the same questions."

"Addison. Tell me why you're here." He's moving to the landline telephone—which connects to the concierge by simply hitting the zero button.

"I came to see if Devon was in this hotel." A pillow and folded blanket are placed on the couch, next to a closed laptop. "I knew the room number he would choose because he told me he always chooses the room with the most eights. The security bar was blocking the lock when I got here, the door open."

"Why did you tell me you would wait for me in the lobby?"

"Because I wanted to see for myself if Devon was here, alone. And if he was with another woman. It's not in my client's best interest to have his indiscretions publicized."

"So you were trying to protect him from me. Thanks."

A pregnant pause stretches between us. He thought we could trust each other. How sweet.

I smooth back a strand of hair. "I agreed to help you find Devon. Not allow him to be trapped by you and your benefactor."

"Addison, look around you. If ever there was a time for you to level with me, it would be now." Connor angrily runs a hand through his thick brown hair, causing his sport jacket to strain at the shoulders. He leans against a dining chair, then stares at a painting of cypress trees that hangs on the wall, the desk below it with its landline phone, the breaking waves of the ocean beneath the balcony. Anywhere, it seems, but at me.

"Connor . . ." My voice trails off. He doesn't lift his head. "Listen, I'm still pretty jet-lagged. . . . Processing what I walked in on will take a few . . . I didn't plan on cutting you out entirely."

He doesn't move. Although I know I shouldn't regret anything about my choices—I was acting in my client's interest, my own, after all—watching Connor's belief in me splinter makes me question myself for the first time in years.

Does this man really have that effect on me? Does his refusal to make eye contact twist my stomach so acutely—or is that the post-traumatic stress from discovering yet another dead client and his companion?

"Housekeeping," a voice calls from the suite's door.

"Fuck," Connor whispers, panicked, snapping out of his funk. "What do we do?"

I train my gaze on him, undeterred. "Why did you come here, Connor? Or did you get here before me?"

Dark eyebrows knit together. "Are you accusing me of something?"

"Oh, I'm so sorry to disturb you." An older woman, rail thin and weathered, flutters her hands into the pockets of a blue apron tied across her midsection. "I came by this afternoon, but the 'do not disturb' card was present most of the day and—"

"It's good that you're here," I interrupt. "We need to call the police. Immediately."

Once a few tense phone calls are made, police officers in gray-and-black uniforms flood the hallway outside. Connor and I are each questioned separately, as well as the housekeeper.

A police officer with an extra-large patch on his shoulder, the captain, confiscates our passports from the reception desk in the lobby; we're not allowed to leave the Schengen Area, the EU countries that agree to waive passport checks at their borders, for seventy-two hours while the casino's surveillance footage is reviewed. Once we sign a witness statement—in English—we are escorted to the edge of the casino's property and into a waiting taxi that holds our luggage, which someone must have moved from the cloakroom. The two-hour drive to our hotel is made in silence. Our mutual accusations hang heavy between us.

When Connor and I arrive at our side-by-side hotel rooms, I am exhausted. Physically, yes, after traveling for close to thirty-six hours, but also emotionally, as I've now seen three dead bodies in just over three weeks. Addison Stern can take a surprise in stride, even a corpse in close quarters. But I'm off my game, after landing on a different continent and experiencing anew the scent of a body past its expiration date.

Devon's glassy gaze was too similar to Phinneas's empty stare. Too evocative of the same finite end to their respective hopes and dreams, their professional goals toward which they worked their whole damn lives, which now mean nothing.

I side-eye Connor as he jams the electronic hotel room key against the lock pad. We dated off and on for several months, and mostly had the time of our lives, three years ago; I did. He made me laugh more than anyone has, his smarts were the first to match mine, and his skills while naked had no rival. But did I ever really know Connor? Considering he appeared in Devon's hotel room barely sixty seconds after I entered, wearing his best shocked expression, and he was separated from me for approximately thirty minutes—during which time he could have surprised Devon and his companion, then circled back behind me—I'm not sure.

Connor knows the police are watching me back in LA. Would he do something this heinous, at the request of a client, and deliberately involve me? He hates me, we're all aware. But to what extent?

How much has exile changed him from the ambitious wonder boy I once almost loved?

"What is it?" Connor asks, returning my eye contact. He tenses, as if sensing my doubts.

"Nothing."

When I am safely behind the fireproof door, I engage the security latch. Silently, I count to ten, watching through the peephole.

At the number twelve, Connor steps into view. He peers at my door. His eyes drop to something—the door handle? Then he retreats to his room.

\\\\\////

"Velvet Eastman is an innovator and someone to keep on your radar." I sip my espresso in the nearly empty hotel restaurant. Adjust the Airpod in my ear. At four in the afternoon, the wicker chairs and granite tabletops are occupied by only myself and a British man who asked the server for tea.

Last night I hardly slept, jet lag be damned. Not because I was traumatized by finding yet another dead body—two of them; it is unfortunate, and I liked Devon well enough as a client. But my mind was already moving ahead to the next few days of events I was supposed to attend in LA for Velvet Eastman. I spoke with another police officer from Monaco this morning via phone, and she reiterated how I am to stay put in case they have further need of me. No flying home on my original flight. Not that I could without my passport.

When I asked whether they had questioned Connor again, there was a pause. She asked, "Why? Should we have?"

I answered, "Only for parity between us. Of course."

Once I shut my hotel room door last night, I couldn't get Connor's expression out of my mind when he entered Devon Lim's bedroom—a mix of shock and something else. Resolution. Confirmation. As if he expected the bloody scene before us and knew of it in advance.

A scoff interrupts my train of thought.

"Addison? It is seven in the morning here." The reporter from my long list of media contacts who might be interested, excited even, in Velvet Eastman's new line laughs. "Tell me you have something more specific than 'Velvet is an innovator.' Let's be real. She was the owner of a high-end whorehouse."

I roll my eyes, unseen. "Well, you and KTSC are the very first to learn that Velvet will be debuting her own fashion line at the upcoming LA Fashion Week. And you're right; Velvet is more than an innovator. She's an entrepreneur, originally from Chicago, who engaged with clientele that includes world leaders and icons in her luxury, members-only club, where certain individuals could mingle in a safe environment, then relocate elsewhere to continue their relationships. Velvet never owned a whorehouse, *obviously*," I drag out. "Prostitution is illegal in Chicago. But she is a force, and you should count yourself lucky to break this story in advance of her television interview that airs in two days."

My tone is sugar sweet with a hint of arsenic. "I'd suggest you make this news part of your entertainment-and-arts segment on this morning's show. There's another major development from one of my clients, but it's completely under wraps for now. And that will change very soon."

"Hm. All right, Addison. We'll add in Velvet. This other news better be juicy."

I hang up, not yet knowing what I'll tell KTSC when the time comes but confident I'll have an additional gem to share by then. I must be careful when the news of Devon's death does become public knowledge. One discovery of a body—Phinneas—is an accident. Three seems like a pattern.

I sip more of my espresso at a table overlooking the tranquil sea below. A server offered me a croissant chocolat earlier, then the menu in case I wanted an American lunch, but I declined both. I stepped out of my room to work with a view. The same sailboats I took note of yesterday continue to bob in the waves.

Years ago, I dated an automotive stylist for luxury cars, Farron Greystone, who moved to Italy—the ex-boyfriend with the hit-and-run record that Connor used to blackmail me. After things died down with the authorities, Farron promised me, he would take me on a tour of his yacht along the Amalfi Coast if I ever wanted to join. The work he does, designing and improving automobile appearances, also provided him with a second yacht, which he docks outside of Ibiza, and he said I could choose my holiday destination. So close, yet so very far away.

"Addison."

I look away from the schooners. Framed against two gilded light fixtures, Connor stands several feet back from my two-top. Wise choice.

"Can I help you?"

"Afternoon to you, too." Connor slides his hands into blue trousers that pleat across his hips.

"Have you called your client yet?"

Connor pulls out the chair opposite me, without my invitation. "To tell her my quarry is dead?" He winces. "Geez. That hasn't sunk in quite yet."

"Yes. She was offering you a bonus if you broke up the affair, wasn't she?" Before he passed out and drooled like an infant on our flight, Connor dished the details of this current job. Thank you, airplane libations.

"Right." Connor nods. "But I don't know if that was his girlfriend, *the* woman he was cheating on his fiancée with."

A server delivers an espresso he must have ordered at the bar. I peer at Connor over the rim of my own tiny cup.

"Or you don't want to implicate your client when you know these murders are an international crime and multiple law-enforcement agencies may subpoena our phone records later on. I wouldn't, at least. Especially if my client had actually offered me a bonus to kill someone."

Connor glares at me. "That's not what happened. And you might keep your voice down, Addison. The staff here will be questioned, too."

His tone is prickly, infused with anger, leaving me to wonder anew if I agreed to an overseas trip with a murderer. We don't know each other anymore. That's certain.

"Actually." Connor stands. "I just lived one of the most traumatic experiences of my life—yet again with you involved, somehow—and I don't have the bandwidth for this crap."

"You never did. You were drowning in the deep end, even before you left—"

"Before you double-crossed me."

I laugh. "Is that what losers call winning? I had no clue."

Connor turns to the window, to the hillside that reaches the inlet of the sea, mumbling obscenities. He downs his espresso in an angry gulp. Then he stops. Lowers his cup.

"What is it?" I ask. "You act like you've never seen a catamaran before."

Connor shakes his head. "No. A guy I know—no, I don't. I mean—he's here. From Santa Barbara—he's here."

"What?" I scan the boardwalk below, nearly hidden by a row of wild cypresses.

"I—I need to go."

The trees sway in the ocean breeze, and then the branches part. A lanky man in a black jacket, jeans, and boots searches for something, turning his head back and forth. He's tall, nearly level with a sign indicating the area is a pedestrian zone. A jogger in leggings passes him, and he watches as she climbs steps built into the hillside directly beneath us. He lifts his line of sight to the glass window of the restaurant, to exactly where Connor and I freeze in place.

"Shit," Connor whispers. The man stares at us a moment longer, then breaks into a sprint. His jacket flaps as he climbs the steps, revealing a handgun tucked into his jeans. "We have to go."

"What? I'm not going anywhere, Connor. I'm not involved with whatever you did to this person, or anyone else you pissed off in North America," I snap. Connor's panic is contagious, and I take a rattling breath. We're thousands of miles from home and I just discovered a new crime scene, thanks to him. I'm not getting more involved in his problems than he's already forced me to be.

Connor takes two steps backward. He glances at the front

entrance of the restaurant, the only one in view. "We need to leave, Addison. I don't know why he's here, but I think he followed me from Santa Barbara. He's going to count you as a witness, Addison. He saw you."

"I don't understand. Why would a hit man fly overseas to track you down? Why not wait for you in California?"

Connor shakes his head. "Honestly, I don't know. But these are questions you and I should be asking far away from this place."

"But where do we go? Our passports are with the Monegasque police."

Connor takes my elbow, making me stand. "Get your stuff. I'll knock on your door in five minutes."

We take the stairwell to our rooms, then disappear within. I throw my belongings back into my suitcase, then stick my head outside. Connor peers down the hallway, holding the handle to his own suitcase.

"Ready?" he asks.

We descend the same back stairwell, not daring to take the elevator, and have just reached the ground floor when a loud bang sounds overhead, where our rooms are located. Two more erupt. Gunshots.

I rip open the door to the lobby, where a shaken man behind the reception desk speaks to someone on the phone in quick, quiet French. A siren peals in the distance as Connor sweeps through the automatic glass doors to exit the hotel I found online whose reviews called it "serene to the point of boring." We slip into the back seat of one of the taxis waiting at the curb—luggage across our laps—and I tell the driver to go.

"Should we start driving to Paris? You were just there, right?"

Connor asks, his cheeks flushed.

"I was. And that's exactly where I would look for us, if I were your pursuer." On my phone, I pull up the website for Eurail tickets. "No, we're going to the Amalfi Coast."

CHAPTER SEVENTEEN

PHINNEAS

LOS ANGELES | JULY 20

PHINNEAS REDWOOD: *Look alive, Future Editor, I am outside and mingling with the one and only Hashim Swartz!*

HASHIM SWARTZ: *Are you recording me right now?*

PR: *Yes, obviously. Future Editor, we are at lunch to discuss possible celebrity endorsements for my new pill, and we've had a few lunch beverages and started talking about the good old days, just to bring you up to speed. Now, Hash, what were you just saying?*

[Silence]

HS: *My name is Hashim. If I want you to call me Hash, I'll tell you directly.*

PR: [Laughter] *Oho! Good to know, Hash-im. But really, though, say again what you just told me.*

HS: *Dude. I don't know what you mean.*

PR: *Really? C'mon, we were just saying how terrible the timing was for my diet pill to come out in the eighties, right after Jane Fonda was getting all that flak about her workouts and someone else died on that other pill, the one with the funky sounding name.* [Gulps] *C'mon.*

HS: *Phinneas, I really think you should drink some water.*

PR: *I'm good. I've only had one beer. Okay, three. But back to what you said—I don't know why you're being so weird about this now. It's a fair thing to say on the record that if my investors hadn't pushed my product to everyone as much as they did, I wouldn't have had the trouble with the teen girls.*

HS: *You're trying to get me to go on record that Thrive, Inc. was at fault for something that has been successfully litigated in your favor, Phinneas. Be careful here. Besides, wasn't the trouble with the teen girls rooted in your interest in them?*

PR: [Laughter] *There it is! Seriously, though, you were always the only one who I felt understood my product, and the life-changing benefits it could offer—the self-esteem, the health stuff. You were the only one to see it as more than just a diet pill. I'm working on my memoirs, and I think* *you could be a good resource to recall that time period. The hope of it all. And the sex.*

HS: *Right.*

PR: *Hash—I mean, Hashim? Come on, I know there was some trouble with it back then—*

HS: *Back then? Why don't we discuss the ways in which your company is currently generating interest in the latest product? Hmm? How about we discuss that?*

PR: *Okay. Okay, you made your point. Look, I'm wary of how the beginning of Thrive, Inc. has been characterized. I want to capture how hopeful I was—we were—about improving lives. It wasn't all about profit.*

HS: *Really? Why don't you ask me, then, instead of trying to trap me with a recording?*

PR: *I wasn't trying to trap you—*

HS: *Typical. You weren't trying to do something, ergo it shouldn't count against you. You weren't trying to offend the head of product design at Thrive, Inc., ergo it's not your fault she left when you suggested she be the first to try Shapextrin.*

PR: *She had just gotten done saying that she'd been so stressed, she felt like an insomniac. I thought she could benefit from the pill. For sleep purposes.*

HS: *Phinneas, let's be straightforward here. Leopards don't change their spots, and CEOs don't grow a conscience* overnight. *You want me to go on record that it wasn't your fault that Thrive's money tanked during the last few years. But you know what? I think it was.*

PR: *Hold on. Where do you get that?*

HS: *You've only ever taken your role as CEO as a joke. You never took it seriously.*

PR: *That's not true—*

HS: *When you first pitched your drug to investors in a conference room, you ended the presentation with a photo of strippers crossing a finish line in heels with the caption "thin to win."*

PR: *Yes, yes, okay, that's true. It was not my best deck. I think you'd agree I've gotten a lot more—uh—professional in my business affairs.*

HS: [Grunts]

PR: *And it was the eighties. The late eighties. Reagan was in office and the counterculture was a little much.*

HS: *Why don't you hand that to me? Your phone. Yeah, a bit closer. Answer my question, since you're feeling so transparent: How is Thrive, Inc. currently generating interest in Shapextrin? Hmm? The fact is you've only ever been interested in the profit, the sex. Your company hasn't changed any in decades, because even now it's taking money from—*

PR: [Overlapping] *All right! All right! Where's the red button on this piece of sh—*

CHAPTER EIGHTEEN

CONNOR
AMALFI COAST | SEPTEMBER 16

Tired doesn't describe the state I'm in. Exhausted, either. Maybe delirious. As I watch Addison dozing in the train seat across from mine, I know I must be delirious to not run in the opposite direction from her.

Italian countryside whizzes by the windows of our train car, blurring fields of olive trees and cubed two-story villas. I've never been to Italy, though my mother was part Italian, and the sheer absence of office buildings is exotic. If I wasn't fleeing from a gun-wielding hit man . . . I could get used to this.

Once we took our seats and the train started chugging through the urban streets of Nice and out of Monaco, the literal scene of the crime, I was able to relax. Get my bearings. Finally meet the stony glare that Addison had been leveling at me since we peeled out of the hotel porte cochère.

"I'm sorry," I told her. "For everything."

She ignored me all the way into Rome during the twelve hours that followed, even while she called her ex-boyfriend Farron, the hit-and-run driver who led her to commit a felony, and explained that we need a place to crash—she said, "Me and . . . someone else. Not a friend, definitely not." Thanks to the Schengen Area, we are able to move across the Mediterranean and three countries without our passports, but we still won't be allowed to board a plane until almost two days from now.

The rest of the route into Salerno is winding. When we exit the train, I'm grateful to stand immobile on the ground. Dark skies overhead could mean it is six in the morning or midnight, despite birds singing peppy tunes. Apart from the lights at the train station, the surrounding village appears asleep. Waves rumble, their foam just visible in the lamplight. The Amalfi Coast. I've traveled a lot, but I don't know that I ever thought I would arrive here. And with a pursuer en route.

"What are you smiling at?" Addison asks, an eyebrow cocked. "No, wait. Don't tell me. *It's so beautiful.* Is that right?"

I chuckle, grateful she's progressed from hating my guts to teasing me for being starry-eyed along the Mediterranean. "Actually, I was going to comment on what a dump this place is, but to each their own."

She scans the street for a passing taxi. The two that were waiting at the train depot already sped off with their fares.

"Addison." I clear my throat. "Do you remember when we took the Surfliner to San Diego that one weekend? You fell asleep with your head on my shoulder and were mumbling in Italian.

You said 'grazie mille,' or something—"

"Ugh, don't remind me. I was staying up late doing Rosetta Stone then, and I had that awful crick in my neck for the rest of the day."

I roll my weight onto my heels. "Uh, maybe you did, but I got tennis elbow working out that kink later on at the hotel."

"Kink at the hotel?"

I turn to Addison, at the wink in her voice, but she stares at the road straight ahead.

"Ah. Finally," she says.

Without waiting for my reply, Addison strides toward the cab that drifts to a stop at the train station exit, towing her carry-on suitcase behind her kitten heels. I follow her into the back seat, unsure of what just happened between us. Did something happen? Do I want it to?

The driver pulls away from the curb while I'm still second-guessing every thought that races through my head. Another hour goes by, during which we cover ten miles. The cliffside two-lane road is so narrow—the hairpin turns so dangerous, to my city mind—that we can't afford to hit the gas. I avert my eyes from the rocky coastline, now illuminated thanks to the pink horizon in the distance. Luxury homes built into the hill are dark. Only wayward gamblers and ice queens are dumb enough to be awake right now.

We climb a road above and pull into a neighborhood of sorts, although each compound easily takes up ten thousand square feet. The driver says something in Italian, to which Addison answers "Grazie" without missing a beat. Begrudgingly, I credit the way she carries herself, even under insanely stressful circumstances as ours; she's always in control, Addison Stern. To a fault.

A blue door opens beside a latticed fence that lines the property, opposite an apartment condo. Dressed in a gray bathrobe and pajama pants, no shirt, a man steps the few feet to our taxi. He opens Addison's door.

"There's my girl." Farron, I guess, grins like he just won the lottery and offers a hand to Addison, who actually takes it. She steps from the car.

They hug in an embrace that can only be described as sensual, leaving me, still trapped in the back seat of the cab, to gag. Farron moans.

I clear my throat. "Hi there. I'm Connor."

Addison and Farron move out of the way, then Farron retrieves our luggage from the trunk.

"Welcome to Positano," Farron says, another way-too-early smile on his chiseled features. Not only does the man sleep with no shirt, he also seems to have oiled up for the occasion. Baby sun rays have started to infiltrate the dark of night and spotlight the hairs of his chest.

"Coffee, anyone?" Farron waves us past the lattice gate and onto his property. We take a path of flat white rocks beneath a garden gazebo. Adirondack chairs are scattered to the side.

"Do you have Baileys?" I ask, my tone wry. Addison continues ignoring me, sashaying after the ex-boyfriend she said she dated for "only a minute" because they were both too dedicated to their careers.

As I step over the rough-hewn stone threshold of the home, it's clear just how dedicated this guy is to making money. Warmth emanates from the heated tiles, evident to my sore, cold feet through my oxfords. The open floor plan spills onto a spacious living room dressed in seafoam green, with direct views of the water beneath thanks to a trio of sliding glass doors bookended by polished whale bones hanging from the ceiling.

"Wow," I whisper, despite my immediate distaste for this whole situation. For the animal jawbone.

It is my fault that we essentially got chased out of France. During the journey here, in between restless naps, I tried to logic out how and why a stranger would come for me. The only thing that makes sense is that Gianni is behind it, that he sent someone to follow me to Santa Barbara, then to attack me here. Even with my 10 percent down payment, I do owe him a shit ton of money. A quarter-million dollars is no small sum—not to me or him. An obscene amount across a series of poorly placed bets. But why spend more bills on a plane ticket for an Olympic sprinter to wring the cash out of me along the French Riviera? And how in the world did he know to check the exact hotel where we were staying?

Genevieve knows that we're abroad, but that's it. There wasn't time to send her the trip logistics, and I'm paying for what's necessary with the cash she wired to my account.

Large seashells frame a mirror beside the kitchen pantry. I catch my worried reflection and spot Addison behind me sniffing coffee grounds about three inches from Farron's face. She whispers something to him, wearing a sly smile. Exactly the way she used to look at me in the morning over a plate of eggs. Quickly, my worry shifts to irritation, frustration that Addison whisked us here, and resentment that all my problems always lead back to this woman in the black linen jumpsuit.

Holy shit. I'm . . . jealous, watching the pair of them. Of no-neck expat there, and Addison Stern, the gorgeous bane of my life. What the hell is wrong with me?

"Connor? Are you all right?" Addison asks. Both she and Farron have stopped huffing beans.

"Yeah. Why?"

"You just swore three times. You're . . . talking to yourself."

"Oh. I'm tired. That's all." I gesture to the stool underneath a sprawling kitchen island. "Can I?"

"Sure, sure," Farron says. "Hey, swearing to high heaven seems normal to me after what you two went through."

On the train, while Addison was telling him most everything, I kept looking behind us, searching for a car that might be following. But none appeared. Later, when Addison fell asleep, I couldn't stop staring at the shadows of her collarbone, the curve of her cheek as it came to rest on her shoulder. I needed a distraction. I popped in my noise-canceling headphones and told Genevieve about Lim. She was duly shocked and saddened—but I think a bit relieved. It was clear from day one that she wasn't a fan of the guy for her daughter.

"Right," Farron continues. "How about that Baileys?"

I shake my head. "No, thanks. I was only kidding. I'd fall asleep on my feet if I had any."

"Addison?"

"I'll pass. But if you still make those delicious blueberry waffles, I'd be in for some breakfast." She practically moons at him, and I feel the same foreign irritation nipping at my shoulders.

"You got it, Addie." Farron breaks out the waffle iron, then shows us to our respective rooms. He tells us how he used to rent this out as an Airbnb before he got sick of "the man dipping into his pockets" back home in New York. Even though I'm aware that Farron is the fabled hit-and-run ex, I let him tell me how moving abroad was his own decision.

In Italy, Farron says, the taxes are "way, way less, bro," and he can conduct his global business more efficiently from here.

"Connor, you're in the Azure Room here. Addie, sweetheart, you'll be staying next door in the Teal Room."

Addie? Sweetheart? God, I've got to get out of here.

Farron sweeps a hand to showcase the desk nook built into a corner of the room, a taupe suede love seat beside it, and the bust of a woman carved from what seems to be driftwood on a nightstand. Retro headphones that fit around the ear hang from a hook above the love seat, a basket of records, and a suitcase that's been repurposed into a record player.

He pushes off from the doorframe, continuing down the hall. "Next, we have the first bathroom. You can use the jet tub if you'd like, but we also have the indoor lap pool in the other part of the house."

"You know what?" I interject. "Thanks so much for letting me stay here, Farron. I think I need to lie down, though. Long night of travel."

"Oh, for sure. Molto bene." Farron gives me a wink, then he slips an arm around Addison's waist. "I was so happy to hear from you. Wild that we meet again on this side of the world, huh?"

Addison seems to melt right into him—and I don't know if it's for my benefit or his. Can she sense how annoyed I am by this whole interaction? Is she still furious with me for dragging her into all this? Or does she genuinely like the guy?

As they continue into a second sitting room, decorated with what look like Warhol paintings, she peers at me over her shoulder. "Sleep tight, Connor."

Within thirty minutes, the whole place smells like sugary batter. Sultry voices carry down the hallway to where I lie on the king-size bed, with a fluffy body pillow and an azure-blue goose-down comforter.

Addison's voice drips with false interest: "Really? Land Rovers had a malfunction across the company? From what year to what year?"

I bite back a groan. When we were dating, Addison Stern couldn't give a shit about what car she was driving—let alone electronic features across the industry. I turn and smash a throw pillow across my ears, then close my eyes. Imagine I'm at any place but here.

\\\\\////

Laughter wakes me. For a second, I forget where I am. And I think that Addison is cracking up next to me in bed, watching me sleep with my mouth guard, the way she did the first time we actually slept full REM cycles while side by side. Strangely, it was the most intimate moment I'd ever shared with someone—so perfectly mundane, yet vulnerable when I failed to wake up early to remove the goofball orthotic. Then I remember that I'm in Europe—Italy, the Amalfi Coast—and her laughter isn't for me now.

I peer at the ceiling. Designs are carved into a recessed level—a deliberate Easter egg left by the architect. A trio of hearts stands out above the other seashell and ocean elements, just like my granddad had as a tattoo—one for each of us: him, my grandmother, and me.

A mirror on a dresser beside the bed reflects my sheepish expression. I'm on the Amalfi Coast and I've been sulking the whole while. Well, screw that. My granddad, who was a crossword-obsessed cop, always said the best days are ahead of you, so look up. I've been through so much worse than this.

And I'm letting go of my frustration with the last thirty-six hours right now.

I swing my feet to sit at the edge of the bed.

Following Addison's and Farron's voices, I navigate the hallway, noting the crisp white-and-green theme that swallows each room. The house looks different in the light of day, and after six hours of uninterrupted sleep. I pause at the edge of glass doors leading to a smooth stone patio overlooking the water. Steel railings descend from the edge in direct access to the Mediterranean Sea.

A framed photo on an end table catches my eye. In it, Farron stands with a few other men dressed in swim shorts and wearing top hats in front of a red lamppost.

"This looks like a fun time," I say, stepping onto the patio, the photo in hand. A show of peace—an interest in Farron and his world out here. Without the scowl I adopted upon leaving the taxi.

Cool air hits my skin, and the long jacket that Addison wears while standing beside Farron against the railing makes sense. They turn to me, Farron with a smile as the ocean breeze ruffles his longish hair, Addison with a blank stare. I've interrupted their conversation, and she's not happy about it.

"Oh yeah," Farron says, examining the frame. He takes a seat on one of the two cushioned chaise lounges on the deck. "This was maybe ten years ago, when I was only coming here during the summers. A total blast. These guys were my ride-or-dies then, but they've all moved back home."

"Are they American?"

Farron takes a sip from a tall glass. Ice clinks together, swimming in amber liquid. "No. An Englishman, a Frenchman, a German, and a Spaniard. Our own 'walked into a bar' joke."

Addison pauses mid-sip of her red drink, a cran-vodka, maybe. "I know that lamppost. Is there a giant slide that leads into a swimming pool just out of frame?"

"Yeah," Farron says with a smile. "Yeah, and a penguin with a tray that holds drinks by the pool. You been?"

"No. I just . . . I've seen it before. Where is it?" Addison swirls her glass in hand.

Farron leans back onto the cushioned wicker chair, still shirtless, but now wearing an unzipped cardigan and different sweatpants. "Over in Sorrento. It's the party spot whenever the owner comes into town. Then, Friday nights during the summer, people just know to show up, and there are plenty of . . . samples to play with."

"What does that mean?" I ask.

Farron gulps back a mouthful, ice cubes clinking. "Ah, you know. Drugs, alcohol. The legal and illicit kind. For a while, the parties were legendary across the Mediterranean, from the Riviera down to Syria."

Addison and I exchange a look.

Farron shakes his drink. "Nearly empty. Anyone want anything? Connor?"

"No, I'm good. Thanks."

Addison sips her cran-vodka as Farron heads indoors to the kitchen. She resumes leaning against the iron railing. "Did you recognize that lamppost?"

I shrug, joining her but not standing too close. The waves below coalesce, then disperse into white foam. "Never seen it before."

Addison downs her drink. She turns to me with sharp eyes. "Why were you really sneaking up to Devon's room without me? In Monaco."

A lone seabird glides on the ocean breeze along the beach. It dips toward the water, drags its feet, then flaps its wings to catch the next current. Something about the view and the proximity to the last great frontier on earth—the sea—makes my filter with Addison drop.

"I wanted to prove that I could still do my job. That I didn't lead us down a European rabbit hole for nothing. That I was capable of executing the work that I used to love."

She's silent for a while. The seabird does the same routine. Dive, drag, flap its wings to higher altitudes before diving again.

"I had a nice time with Farron while you napped."

I lift my hands to my ears. "Ugh. Please don't tell me anything."

"No—we talked. I asked Farron about a glitch in the computer system of my Benz, and he shared that those have been common the last few years, across the luxury-car industry."

"Fascinating pillow talk."

"Connor, stop. I'm trying to . . ."

"To what?" I turn away from the waves to face her.

She inhales through her nose. "Years ago, when I accused you of deliberately car-dialing an Ovid Blackwell client, the president of the AFL, while we were in your back seat, I was . . . well. It turns out that—you know, this is harder than I—"

I laugh. "Holy shit, is Addison Stern trying to apologize?"

Addison rolls her eyes. "Well, I don't have to."

"No, no, please."

"Farron said your Land Rover likely malfunctioned. That phantom car-dialing has been a common issue. Which means you didn't mean to humiliate me to a client."

A grin spreads across my face. "Well, well, well. At long last, the truth comes out. Despite me repeating it all these years. Without fail."

"Right. I . . . regret that—"

"Really?"

"Connor, the interrupting isn't—"

"All right. Go, go."

"I'm sorry," she forces through her teeth. "I stole info from your phone for my client because I thought you meant to hurt me."

"That's not a reason to ruin my reputation."

"No. You're not wrong." She purses her lips. "But no one gets the upper hand on me and walks away unscathed . . ."

Her voice trails off in a way that seems almost . . . sad. What is Addison Stern remembering in this moment? I know she didn't have a great upbringing, that both her parents disappointed her in lasting ways. Is she recalling a moment with her family or a professional letdown?

"Well, I never saw our relationship as getting one up on the other. It was a partnership."

A tight smile. "I've always been a team of one."

I pause. "You don't have to be."

The tide begins to recede, withdrawing then returning in seven-second intervals. The sound is tranquil—soothing as I process that much of my failed career is rooted in misunderstanding. Probably there's a poetic analogy about my life buried in there, but I can't sort through it right now.

Addison apologized. Finally.

A dolphin breaks through the surface for a moment. Then it returns to the aquamarine depths.

Addison grips the rusted iron railing. "So, since we're clearing the air . . . you didn't kill Devon and his girlfriend, because your client asked you to?"

"Are you serious? You think I would—I could—do that?"

Addison hesitates. "It doesn't seem on brand for you."

I lean onto my elbow, closer to where she stands. "No, Addison. I did not. I got back into PI work because my client—the only client still willing to work with me—wanted information on her . . . on Devon Lim. But I would never agree to act as a mercenary, no matter the paycheck. I have nonnegotiables."

"Okay." She sips her drink. "Okay, I believe you. Against my better judgment."

"Why your 'better judgment'?"

Addison sends me a smile, the first one meant for me in years. She traces my forearm with a pointed fingertip. I don't know if it's the alcohol, or that Addison has chosen to pretend she's on vacation, but she inches closer. "Because trust is for the naïve."

A screech pierces the early evening. The seabird shoots up from the water with a fish in its beak this time, a victory cry trailing behind.

"What if you're stuck on a deserted island with someone?" I let my gaze settle on Addison's glistening lip gloss. "What then? Is it okay to trust someone then?"

She pulls me to her, eyes bright despite the alcohol. Her lips connect with mine, sending jolts of lightning to my core. Instantly, my mind goes blank and all I can see or feel is this woman. The taste of her. The cran-vodka.

We step back indoors and confront Farron, passed out on the deep sofa facing the water. His new drink rests on the end table, forgotten.

Addison's fingers are in my hair, coaxing me to where I already want to go. We slip into the first bedroom we reach—mine—and fall onto the comforter of the king-size bed. She wraps two toned legs around my waist, strong and trembling at the same time, and I grasp her tight in my arms, desire overwhelming the logical part of my brain that wonders what I am doing. She flips me over and climbs on top, running practiced fingers along the buttons of my shirt. The setting sun through the window casts an alluring glow on the features I've alternately seen in my dreams and my nightmares.

"Addison," I whisper. "Are you sure you want to—"

She pulls my shirt from my arms. "Connor Windell, just because you only gave me lusty eyes on the deck doesn't mean I haven't been wanting this since you broke into my apartment."

"Sure, but you've been drinking, and we're both still exhausted from—"

Addison places her hands on my shoulders, locking eyes with me. Her expression is clear. Determined. And one that I've seen on her when she's about to bag her prize. A lock of hair falls from her braid to drape across her face; then she suddenly looks like she did before everything nose-dived between us: the version of this woman whose laughter was my favorite alarm clock. My Addison.

I trail my lips along her chest, undo the buttons of her jumpsuit until black lace is free, coarse yet soft against my tongue. She moans, sending a shiver through my groin, and I know all rational thought is completely screwed—as I hope to soon be. I sit up against the headboard, unzipping my trousers as she stands and shimmies out of her clothing. Hovering above me, Addison grasps my jaw in her hand, fixing me with her gaze.

She leans down over my ear. "I'm going to enjoy this."

Lowering onto my hips, she slides down until we connect and shoot stars across the sculpted ceiling above us. I can't think. I can't reason. All I know is that I've waited three years for this moment, and all the bullshit in between has only heightened my desire for her.

"Connor," she whimpers, grinding against me. "Connor, I need you."

The three hearts of the ceiling come into focus as I breathe deep Addison's floral perfume and clutch tight her soft, surging curves.

CHAPTER NINETEEN

ADDISON

LOS ANGELES | SEPTEMBER 18

So that was a fun surprise. Although it's true, I have been fighting the urge to tear off Connor's clothing since he popped back into my life, I didn't expect us to spend the night together. The whole night. And while Connor still snores like a train, he's just as sweet a sleeper as I remember. His skills between the sheets are even better after so much time apart, and I definitely enjoyed myself. Twice. Not that we had anywhere to be or anything to force us out of the bedroom. It seemed as if Farron was still into the wild drug parties he mentioned, as he'd added something to his drink that made him sleep until the next morning.

When Farron woke up, he seemed unsurprised to see Connor and me eating at the kitchen table together. That waffle iron really is excellent.

While Connor and Farron arranged for a taxi to return us to the train station, I checked my phone and found dozens of messages from my media contacts and Ovid Blackwell, all desperate for news of Devon Lim's death. The American embassy must have finally reached Devon's next of kin, his mother, during the night. The news outlets would have gotten wind soon thereafter. I called the Ovid attorneys, just as I did when Phinneas died, but I didn't let Aarin prattle on this time; I already knew the drill, and I had more platforms to personally contact. Rather than let the international media get too far ahead with the story, I decided to take back control by telling my contacts my version of the events. I'm dictating the narrative again.

Devon Lim was a genius in the app industry, I tell three major platforms. His work changed lives, and his thinking will continue to mold our world long after his death. Most importantly, I emphasize to everyone I speak with how he was discovered by a maid in the hotel—and that Connor and I learned of his death afterward. If the French or Monégasque police publicly state otherwise, it will be my word and all of the American internet's search results against theirs. If there's one thing I've learned, it's that an image or idea needs to be seen seven times before the consumer understands it. I'm planning for my average Jane to see this message a solid ten.

The journey to the airport took forever. First, another twelve hours by train back to Nice, where at least a police sergeant agreed to meet us and deliver our passports. Hotel surveillance footage at the Casino de Monte Carlo confirmed that someone else entered Devon's hotel room hours before I did, before Connor did, and the medical examiner confirmed both victims died early that morning. I asked the sergeant if a man was responsible—maybe one athletic enough to sprint up a hillside carrying a handgun. As I mentioned to the sergeant then, the person who chased us and fired shots in our hotel in Toulon could very well have followed us from the casino after first killing Devon.

The sergeant replied that law enforcement in Toulon hadn't been in touch. He hadn't heard much about a shooting in a hotel, but he would discuss the possibility of a link.

At that point, Connor announced it was time to head to the airport for our flight.

As we walked the jetway to our plane's open hatch, a tingle pricked my neck. I paused before stepping into the aircraft to stare back up the empty, narrow funnel into the terminal.

\\\\\////

"Here, let me get that." Connor reaches for my suitcase handle, then maneuvers our luggage to the curb in front of baggage claim. Los Angeles sunshine warms the crewneck sweater and wrinkle-free khakis I chose for our flight.

I tuck a curtain of black hair behind my ear. Relief spooled through my body at the jolt of our airplane's wheels connecting with the tarmac on American soil. We made it. Then Connor brushed my pant leg, reaching for a magazine he bought before the flight, and the relief was replaced with unease. We slept together in Italy, and it was objectively amazing. Or maybe it was fueled by stress, fatigue, and a little bit of alcohol—but the orgasms were amazing. All of them.

We flirted the whole plane ride—twelve hours—while I debated whether the playful interaction should end once we touched down at LAX. It felt strange and also like a rerun of your favorite show that you wish had never ended. Yes, Connor is the reason we were run out of Toulon. And I should ream him out every time I glance over my shoulder—especially if our attacker is only a stone's throw away in Las Vegas, as Connor suspects. But Connor has always felt like my equal, and in ways that no other man has. He's smart, driven, well connected, and he could make bike shorts seem sexy. He got me into this, and I'll be damn sure that he gets me out of it.

I'm a publicist. I make the news; I don't become the news.

"Addison Stern?"

A man in a black suit maintains his distance on the sidewalk. I glance at this stranger from the open back door of the town car I reserved mid-flight. My fists clench. A friend of the Vegas hit man?

"I'm Special Agent Jonas. We met a few weeks ago at the Ovid Blackwell office."

One of the twins, the FBI agents. This time he's wearing a green tie decorated with pumpkin pies that clashes with his light brown complexion. Someone get this man a mirror.

"You again? Is harassment part of the Bureau's protocol?" I ask, my tone cool.

"I need to speak with you and Mr. Windell." Agent Jonas nods to Connor behind me. "Now. Take your luggage."

"Agent Jonas," I begin. "We just completed a difficult several days in Europe. We'll meet with you la—"

"The government is highly aware that your 'difficulty' led to another death," Agent Jonas interrupts.

Travelers within earshot look up from their phones. A few move to the next concrete bench, several feet away.

Irritation flushes my skin. The last time anyone spoke that way to me, I destroyed their spouse's budding culinary career in New York and ensured their child was blacklisted from the private school they had been wooing. But this is a federal agent.

I muster a blank expression. "You have five minutes."

We follow Agent Jonas back inside the terminal. As the automated doors slide shut behind us, enclosing us within the airport and under federal jurisdiction, the air-conditioning engulfs me like in the deep end of a pool. Connor goes to hold my hand, but I shake off his touch.

Agent Jonas leads us to a door beside a baggage carousel, down a long hallway, and into a room the size of a shoe box.

"Take a seat," the agent says.

Connor pulls out a metal chair that scrapes against the tile. His hand pauses on the chair next to him, but I shake my head. "I'll stand."

Agent Jonas is impassive. "Ms. Stern, were you good at math in school?"

"Excuse me?"

"You're now linked to a second and third body within a month, despite swearing you had nothing to do with the first. You must know that equation doesn't add up."

I let his implication that I'm trapped slide off my back like an effleurage massage. "My strong suit in school was language arts, not math."

I peer at the corners of the white, undecorated room and note the camera positioned above the closed door. We're being recorded.

"More importantly, you paid a visit to yet another client who wound up dead. Why were you in Monaco?" Agent Jonas remains standing while Connor sits between us, watching our tennis match.

"To see the sights."

"And the inside of Lim's chest cavity?"

My stomach churns. The sweet perfume of the freshly cut roses in the hotel suite returns to mind, along with the ferrous smell of blood-soaked sheets. I swallow back bile.

"How boorish, Agent. There's a lady present," I deadpan.

"Honestly, I can see you traveling any distance to keep your secrets safe, Ms. Stern. Especially if Lim knew you were actually involved in Redwood's death. What I don't understand," Agent Jonas continues, "is why you need to loop in a disgraced private investigator?"

Connor grimaces. "That seems unnecessary."

"Disgraced, yes—as well as incredibly efficient."

"Also unnecessary." Connor shoots me a look.

"Anything else, Agent?" I ask. "Did you have a closing joke, or will you use the remaining minute?"

Agent Jonas shrugs. "You're not under arrest."

"Ticktock."

"But—you should know that while a few days ago we didn't have any suspects in Phinneas Redwood's death, we now have two."

"Why does the federal government care?" I ask, then recall the conversation we had in my office. "Was his death a hate crime, after all?"

Agent Jonas mock-pouts. "Feeling anxious, Ms. Stern? You should be. Know that we're watching you both. And if you make one wrong move—I'm talking you forget to recycle your paper coffee cup—I will personally slap handcuffs on your entitled wrists."

We leave the way that we came, maintaining a careful pace. Once we emerge into the sunshine again, it no longer feels like a warm welcome back to our home country but a threat. A preview. A warning that here, in this perpetually vibrant city, we might be boiled alive.

The drive back to my apartment goes fast, largely because I'm mentally reviewing recent events. I found Phinneas Redwood murdered, shot in the chest and head; Connor and I found Devon Lim and a friend fully expired, also shot in the chest and head; a man appeared to track us all the way to Europe and, according to French media reports online, took the trouble to fire a weapon as he pressed hotel staff to reveal our room numbers.

I'm sure Agent Jonas is up to speed on all of that. And a nameless track star is, perhaps, less intriguing an identification to his supervisors than a publicist and private investigator who have more dirt than Runyon Canyon on Southern California's drug-peddling, politics-dabbling elite. Once, I thought the FBI was above any political leanings. Around the time that I still believed in Santa Claus.

The driver rolls to a stop outside my West Hollywood condo. Connor exits first onto the sidewalk. He holds out a hand to help me from the deep seats, and I accept.

Once the driver has unloaded my suitcase to my stoop, he gets back in the car, leaving Connor and me alone. We'd been silent on the drive from LAX, each probably contemplating our escape route from this exact awkward goodbye.

Connor is a handsome man. Tall, though not tall enough that I hurt my neck looking at him—or kissing him, I recall with a squeeze in my stomach. His hands are strong yet uncalloused, and they gripped my body with endless passion only two nights ago.

Before we broke up, I thought he might have been someone I could stay with awhile—unpack the deep-seated fears of abandonment and rejection that make me so driven, efficient, and—according to naysayers—ruthless in my career. Connor admired my ambition. He matched it with his own. One night, he shared how a client of his got caught looking into his daughter's professor for academic misconduct, only to expose himself for bribing that same professor earlier in the year. We laughed about that client's misdeeds all night over a bottle of wine, and others on many a night, certain we would never be so gullible as to get trapped into similar foxholes.

I realize now I misread the situation years ago, when—after feeling humiliated in the back of Connor's car—I went snooping into his phone as my form of utilitarian revenge. Though Connor lunged to the dashboard of his Land Rover and hit the red bar to end the call, I was shattered that my trust had been toyed with—abused and discarded, by yet another person in my life. In spite of all the late-night talks we shared during the months we dated—the moments when I felt like Connor actually understood me as I opened up to him, when I had taken the gargantuan leap to extend the tiniest branch of trust his way—I believed he had wronged me.

The thick, protective layer returned over my heart then, and—although we reconnected in Positano—my armor hasn't budged. Nor should it, considering the FBI interrupted a normal return home from the bowels of LAX. The feelings for Connor that began to simmer in Italy, and before, are no longer relevant to the task at hand: survival.

Two of my clients have been murdered within close proximity to me, maybe by the same killer. Connor—with his gambling issues, easygoing grin, and charming, barely there hair-care routine—could be the target. But if I were to take a close look at all the people who might wish me harm, I'd need the zoom feature on my laptop to appreciate the size five font of a mile-long list.

Ovid Blackwell won't promote me to partner until this mess with Phinneas's case is resolved, the FBI is suspicious of Connor and me, and the man who attacked us in France will be stateside again soon, no doubt, hunting us down. This is bad.

Connor reaches for me, but I withdraw. Addison Stern puts herself before anything and anyone else when survival is in question.

His expression hardens. "It's like that, huh? We're finally on the same page again in Italy but return to the old hurts here?"

I shrug, internally reaching for the familiar indifference I wear like a shield. "We had an authentic moment that didn't last."

"'An authentic moment'? I'm not some gossip platform that you're giving a quote to, Addison. Look at me."

The sapling behind him on my portion of sidewalk has begun to shed its leaves. I continue to stare at the ground. "Connor, I don't trust you. How can I, with so much history behind us?"

He narrows his eyes. "Let's agree to move past it, then. You now realize that I didn't mean to hurt you, and I'm sick of complaining how you betrayed me."

I wave a hand. The matte, gunmetal-gray nail polish of my manicure has chipped on my index finger. A crack in my perfect routine. "The last thing I need is another distraction."

Connor winces. "That's what I am?"

"But—you are the only person I believe wants what I want at this moment."

"What does that mean?" he pushes. "Look, we're wrapped up in this together now, like it or not. You heard Agent Jonas back at LAX."

I scoff—will him to stop pouting and look at the possibilities straight on. "Yes. And I'm going to find whoever is doing this to me—to us—exactly the way that I decide is necessary. You threatened me with revealing how I helped Farron—"

"Ah, I think the actual term is *embezzlement*. Yep. Misconduct of some kind, for sure."

"And if you start scheming against me again . . . well. Every publicist knows a fixer."

"So we're back to threats? Addison, I thought we reached some kind of understanding back in Italy. I thought we were . . ."

His voice trails off while I struggle to make sense of my fight-or-flight instincts. "Look, I enjoyed myself—"

"Enjoyed yourself? I'm not a walking tour of the Vatican."

"But the bottom line is I can't do this right now." I wave a hand at his face, his chest that I could lean into for hours. "There's too much at stake, given Agent Jonas's surprise visit. You have to know that."

Connor shakes his head. "I don't. We can work together and see where this goes."

I take in his hopeful expression, the stubborn curl of his upper lip. "Yes, we'll continue to work together. But we're not spending the night together again. We can't make this any more complicated than it already is."

He's silent. A car door slams somewhere down the street behind him.

"Besides, you're from Las Vegas now," I add. "You should know better than anyone."

Connor drops his chin. "Ah. What happens in Europe stays in Europe. Got it."

"I'll be in touch." I climb the steps to my condo. When I reach the front door, I recall how Connor ambushed me here only a few weeks ago. "Hey, you didn't make any copies of that key you left in my condo. Did you?"

Connor musters a small smile. "If I need to give you a note of cutout magazine letters, I'll use the post office."

I scowl. From Connor, it's not a serial-killer missive I worry about. By the time I am safely inside my home, the town car's engine has roared back to life, and the car has pulled away from the curb.

In my kitchen, I pause while placing my pepper spray on the counter. Phinneas's note—the one I found in his office—didn't have magazine cutouts, but it did list a series of numbers, and my initials: *A.S. 131023*. It's the only clear piece of evidence that someone might be targeting me. Everything else—the coincidence of walking in on the bodies of Devon Lim and an unknown woman; a gun-wielding pursuer chasing Connor and me in the south of France—is murkier. And while I'm certain the digits aren't a bank account, I'm also sure that they aren't an item number for his favorite vacuum.

I slide onto one of the barstools at my kitchen counter. Pull open a new web browser tab on my phone and google the digits for a dozenth time. Thirteen. Ten. Twenty three. Are these ages at which significant events happened for Phinneas? Phinneas first launched his company when he was twenty-three years old. But the internet fails to spit out any details relating to his youth that might qualify as major moments in his life. And if the numbers are actually pairs—ages—why are they out of chronological order? Why are they not listed as ten, thirteen, then twenty-three?

Instead of viewing them in groupings of two, I split the

numbers down the middle: 131 and 023. A quick Google search of the digits presented this way still turns up empty, even when I include the initials A.S.

Connor should be back at his Airbnb by now, over in Silver Lake. Although the goodbye was hard, and more painful than I expected, boundaries needed to be set between us.

He was so crestfallen. The memory of the frustration in his voice fills my ears as if he were here, sitting on my other kitchen barstool. *What happens in Europe stays in Europe.*

I suck in a breath. "Connor, you genius."

"Thirteen. Ten. Twenty-three. October 13, 2023," I murmur, already typing new search terms. Google says that only one large-scale event is set on the West Coast that day, though it's not related to the pharma industry. The website at the top of the returned results is one I've already bookmarked.

"But why would Phinneas care about the closing ceremony of LA Fashion Week?"

I reach for the Côtes du Rhône on my counter. This bottle was personally recommended to Emilia Winthrop and me by the sommelier of a brasserie on the Champs-Élysées, and I was waiting for the right occasion to uncork it.

When I lift the glass to my lips—swirl the burgundy liquid to watch the legs cling to the sides—the memory of a stained UCLA sweatshirt flashes to mind.

CHAPTER TWENTY

CONNOR

LOS ANGELES | SEPTEMBER 21

My phone pings, nearly vibrating off the worn dining table of my Airbnb in Silver Lake. I lurch from the kitchen counter to grab it before it drops to the scratched hardwood. When I made a reservation for this place, I assumed I would be investigating Devon Lim for around a month; the one-bedroom bungalow would serve for the location, not the frills. Now, since Genevieve has been consumed with helping her daughter through her grief—and too busy to pay me for my work—it feels like the soonest I can get out of here with cash in hand for Gianni is Christmas.

Two messages from Addison:

> I know where I saw that lamppost. The one in the photo at Farron's.

A snapped image follows of the framed photo of Farron and his multinational friends standing beneath the red lamppost that caught Addison's attention back in Positano.

While I'm typing a reply—*And?*—she calls me.

"What's so exciting about it?" I answer, cutting out the pleasantries.

"I saw that red lamppost at Phinneas's house," she says, breathless. "It was in a panoramic image that spans three feet and hangs in his great room. The red lamppost is next to a pool with a slide, and behind this long one-story house with a pink-and-orange sky in the background—sunset, above some property he said he owned. I had no idea it was in Europe, I thought it was Cancún or somewhere."

"Okay, slow down. What of it? Why does it matter if Phinneas had a house in Italy?"

"Farron said that place was 'the spot' every Friday night during the summer. He and all his friends hung out there."

"Yeah." I return to the kitchen counter. Frown at my avocado toast with its perfectly scattered kosher salt, now barely lukewarm.

"Farron's friends are all millionaires. If they were hanging out at Phinneas's house, and enjoying lots of legal and illegal drugs from his stash, I wonder if that came back to bite him in some way."

The bread is definitely cold, bordering on soggy. "Like if his investors got wind of him behaving in a way that might blow back negatively on his company. Maybe. Have you done a reverse-image search of the guys in that pic?"

"You can do that with a pic of a pic?"

I throw my breakfast in the trash. The metal garbage bin under the kitchen sink slams shut with a bang. "I'll call you back."

After downloading the photo, then zooming in on the four men, I use an app to cut and enhance the image. It takes a few tries, but I manage to smooth out the uneven lighting for more even coloring across the multinational and multiracial features. I pinch in farther, then cut and save each man's face as its own PNG file. Adding them to the black hole of the internet, then searching their names using their faces, takes me the rest of the morning, but I track them all down.

Most of them are just what Farron described: millionaire Europeans, and one English transplant who comes from old ranch money in Montana. However, the German—a man named Hashim Swartz—is a well-known venture capitalist. When I cross-reference for search results that feature his name and Thrive, Inc., I hit pay dirt.

Relief mingles with excitement in my gut. I did it. I accomplished a tricky task without breaking and entering, blackmailing, or bulldozing a customer service employee. None of the three *B*s of private investigating that used to come second nature to me.

Is it possible—could I do this work and not embarrass my granddad's memory?

As I dial Addison, I can't help but smile.

"You know, it's considered rude to hang up on someone," she answers.

"Or is it expedient, when I just found out one of Phinneas's investors used to frequent his wild Mediterranean drug parties?"

Addison sucks in a breath. "Tell me more."

\\\\\////

The next day, Addison and I roll along Melrose Avenue. Traffic is light during midmorning, but I nearly rear-end a Tesla whose driver is snapping pictures of boutique shops, probably for the social media content. Hashim Swartz's office building is a somber gray two-story belonging entirely to him. Dedicated to venture capitalism and "ushering in the next great idea," according to a sparsely built though user-friendly website, Swartz is in the office on Thursdays, and by appointment only. The terra-cotta roof recalls the Amalfi Coast, reminding me of all that we learned while abroad. A sick feeling twists my stomach.

"Michelle Yeoh."

"What?" Addison says as I brake for a teacup dog that dashes into the crosswalk.

"Name the six degrees of separation between Michelle Yeoh and Kevin Bacon." When she only lifts an eyebrow in response, I add, "It's a game I play when I'm doing surveillance."

Another blank stare. "I only like the high-stakes career kind, where I steal clients from my competitors. The long game. Have you seen anything on our shooter?"

While on the phone yesterday, I shared with Addison that I've been watching for news of our hotel in Toulon—any clue to our pursuer's identity. We reviewed the trip to Europe in detail, searching for clues: why we were there, who knew about the trip, and what countries we visited where we have enemies. France, Monaco—a principality—and Italy. My list consisted of a friend-of-a-friend from college who is now a banking big shot and who lives in Nice; I "took" his unrequited crush back then, a girl I dated for two seconds, and he bad-mouthed me to anyone who would listen after that, saying I ruined his prospects for happiness. Plus a guy I did some work for about ten years ago who now resides in Spain, whose marriage fell apart after I accidentally unearthed his extramarital relationships—with his wife's cousins.

Addison, it turns out—surprise—has a lot of people who dislike her: an ex-colleague who was fired after Addison beat her in a performance review at Addison's first job who does PR in Rome now; an ex-client who ruined her own career as a Christian novelist by doing a nude photo spread for *Maxim*, now living in Corsica; a movie producer whose chief residence is located in Paris who employed Addison as an assistant in Beverly Hills but asked her to clean up dog poop, which she tidily left on the movie producer's front porch; and a Parisian marketing company that she most recently pissed off when she fired the entire staff from a perfume shoot about a month ago. And these were only the possibilities along the Mediterranean.

At one point, the connection cut out while we were talking. A windstorm was going nuts outside, and I offered my Airbnb as a spot to work from together, but she laughed through the phone. "You'd like that, wouldn't you?" she said. And it's true. I would have liked that very much.

I can still remember Addison naked and glistening, moving over me, the way she commanded the bedroom without uttering a word. A powerhouse, with or without her tailored jumpsuits.

Instead of merging our locations or hanging up, we spent the rest of the night on the phone, researching from our respective laptops. Around two in the morning, I woke up on the couch with my phone on my chest—Addison's steady breathing audible through the speaker.

The Tesla slows beside a Hermès pop-up shop, and I hit the brakes. "According to Reuters, there was a gun fired in a Toulon hotel, but the shooter managed to hide in one of the rooms until the police moved on to the next floor. It wasn't until later when the security cameras were being reviewed that everyone came to the conclusion that he likely stole a suit from a guest's room and walked out of the building wearing a sun hat."

"Tricky. Any word from Agent Jonas?"

"The FBI Asshole has not contacted me."

"Me neither."

"Good. You ever see *Crouching Tiger, Hidden Dragon*?"

Addison raises an eyebrow.

"Fine. I'll do this Bacon alone." I park on the street, and then we walk a buffed concrete path to the building's front door. While Addison tells the receptionist, a young blond woman, that we have an appointment to see Mr. Swartz—a fact we could only swing this week by using the Ovid Blackwell name to snag a meeting—I focus in. Since I'm one of the few who never saw *Crouching Tiger* . . . Michelle Yeoh was in *Mechanic: Resurrection* with Tommy Lee Jones.

Tommy has been in so many movies, I hardly know where to start. *Men in Black. The Fugitive. No Country for Old Men.* But when did TLJ appear on film with my guy?

The receptionist leads us down a hallway. She gestures toward the final open door on the left, and it hits me: Tommy Lee Jones was in Oliver Stone's *JFK* with Kevin Bacon. "Boom. A Bacon number of two."

Addison and a middle-aged man wearing a graphic tee and ripped jeans stop talking to stare at me.

"Sorry. Uh. Could you repeat what you were saying, please?"

Addison looks like steam might come from her ears, but she adopts a smile. "Mr. Swartz, please excuse my . . . colleague. He's a little jet-lagged."

Swartz laughs. "I've been there. So what do you want to know about Phinneas? I was so sorry to hear of his passing."

"Brutal murder," Addison corrects him. "I imagine that, as an investor of Thrive, Inc., you must be more than *sorry*."

"Certainly," he replies without pause. "It's devastating, personally and professionally, that Phinneas was killed."

Addison nods. "We were hoping to learn more about your experiences with Phinneas. We know he was a big fan of throwing parties in Europe and that you went to a few. You must have been close."

"And you're not with the police?" Swartz's German accent seems heightened.

"No. Just grieving friends." Addison is deadpan.

Swartz raises a skeptical eyebrow. "Is that so?"

"What Addison means is," I pipe up, "she worked with Phinneas and now we're looking for answers, at a personal level. Phinneas meant a lot to us, as we're sure he did to you."

"Ah." Swartz invites us to sit in two curve-backed chairs with a sweep of his hand. Addison throws me a look, not quite grateful for my assist, but takes a seat anyway.

"Well, he was the life of any get-together," Swartz says. "All the best and most dramatic ideas were his. And alcohol's. I first met him through my buddy Farron"—Addison and I exchange a look, but she doesn't interrupt him—"then decided to invest in Thrive, Inc. after that. Although Phinneas was all smiles usually, I came to learn a lot of that was to mask deep-seated pain."

This guy sounds like a Hallmark special. He's full of it. But this is Addison's show.

"Any idea who might want to harm him? Someone who he upset abroad, or to whom he might owe money?"

"Money is usually the cause of all problems." Swartz lowers his gaze, as if saddened by the idea. "But I don't have a name for you. I'm sorry."

Addison pauses. "Really? You're unwilling to point us in a specific direction? Perhaps a friend-of-a-friend with whom Phinneas had . . . let's call them . . . shady dealings? We know he had access to all kinds of drugs, as a pharmaceutical industry leader. And that you did, as well."

Swartz narrows his eyes. "Are you implying something?"

"Not implying. Merely stating the facts."

"Well, thank you for dropping by." He stands, straightening the hem of his graphic tee. "But I'm going to ask you to leave now."

"Wasn't there a drug charge in Germany a few years back?" Addison continues. "I'm sure the companies in which you're an investor would be interested to learn that."

"Excuse me? Do you have any idea who you're speaking—"

"Mr. Swartz, please." I lift both hands, still seated. Addison is stone-faced in the chair beside me. "All we want is answers about Phinneas. Justice for him. Isn't there anything you could tell us, or the name of a person you think we should talk to? Please."

Swartz remains standing, but he looks down and to the left. He's hiding something. "Phinneas had a good heart. And I want justice for him. I would suggest you check with the staff at Seven Wells."

"The rehab center?" I ask.

He nods again, faster this time. "That's the one. You never know what staff overhear during those group therapy sessions."

"Wouldn't that be confidential?" I ask.

Swartz breaks the impassive expression with a half smile. "Money can be the cause of all problems. But it can also be the solution."

My phone buzzes in my pocket. Genevieve Aspen. My benefactor and current boss. I excuse myself, then step outside into the lobby. "Gen."

"Connor," she says. "I was worried you'd forgotten about me."

"Clearly no." The receptionist ignores me—probably trained to see and hear nothing outside of appointment check-ins. "What can I do for you?"

"I need an update, Connor. We know that Devon, God rest him, is dead and gone. My Hyacinth is beside herself with grief, and my contemporaries are beside themselves with laughter that Devon made such a fool of my family." Genevieve huffs into the receiver. "Who killed Devon, Connor? Although he was not yet my son-in-law, he was clearly associated with me. I want answers."

"I understand. I've been a little busy with some adjacent developments—"

"Whose developments, Connor? Your initial task has been concluded—finding Devon? Check. Breaking up a possible affair through whatever means necessary? Also . . . check."

Genevieve is silent, and I wonder if my heavy breathing has put her off. "Gen?"

"I'm thinking, Connor."

I step outside for privacy, despite the receptionist's trained discretion. A car door slams on the corner of Melrose and a side street—a brown pickup truck with a white stripe parked about a half block down. The engine sputters to life.

The driver stares at me in the rearview mirror. Something about him is familiar—his outline, the dark brown, almost black of his buzz cut. When he realizes I'm watching right back, he ducks his head in the front seat. The truck pulls away, narrowly missing a car that turns into his lane, and I take note of the first part of its California license plate—GTOEY.

"Connor?" Genevieve speaks again. "Has the woman who Devon was found with been identified?"

"No, not yet. No passport, ID card, or similar was on her body, according to local police." I type out the plate's letters and number in my notes app. A description of the vehicle.

"Right," Genevieve draws out. "It's just . . ."

"Yes?"

"You see, Connor. I'm having trouble understanding something. I told you to break up the affair through any means necessary and that I didn't want to know how you did it."

My heart hitches. A car honks right beside me, speeding through a light, and I jump. "Yeah."

"Well, I'm wondering . . . No, never mind."

"What is it?"

Genevieve takes a drag from her cigarette, and I can picture her red lipstick leaving smudges along the paper. "I'm wondering if you took that literally, Connor. Did you . . . end the affair . . . through any means necessary?"

I turn my body away from the building's entrance. "Are you asking me if I killed the female companion? Killed them both?"

Her silence is a gut punch. I nearly reel against a city bench. Holy shit. She thinks I did it.

Genevieve takes another drag. "I would never say anything to that effect over a phone call, Connor. You never know who might be listening—who might have invited a third party to be a fly on the wall."

A public transit bus stops and starts at the intersection, eliciting more honking, buying me some time. When the noise dies down, I reach for a nonchalant reply to Genevieve's murder accusation. "Right. Yeah. Listen, I think I'm onto a new lead here. I'm sure I'll have information for you on Lim's killer soon."

"Of course, my dear. We'll be in touch. In the meantime, I would suggest you hurry. We know too much about each other, Connor."

I hang up in a daze.

"Genevieve thinks you killed Devon and his girlfriend?" Addison startles me, standing at my elbow like she's been here since the truck peeled out. Her hand closes around something in her jacket pocket. Pepper spray that she threatened me with back in her apartment during our reunion, likely. The space between her eyebrows pinches.

Flustered, I reply, "She's openly wondering about it, at least. Can you believe it?"

Addison glances at a blue delivery van that passes. "Strange."

"Yeah." I start toward my Land Rover, with Addison following. "Anything else of interest in there with Swartz?"

"If you count that he once bought Madonna a drink at Knott's Scary Farm 'interesting,' then yes. Anything of note out here? Besides your murder accusation."

I stare in the direction the truck pulled away. "Maybe. I have a friend at the DMV, so I'll get back to you."

"It's impressive, Connor. Sneaking around, spying on people, digging up information while leveraging people's hard-earned careers."

I turn and find her eyes are narrowed.

It wasn't a compliment. More of an observation. Or concerned commentary that I've surpassed her lackluster expectations of me.

"Hey, someone's gotta be the bad guy. You wouldn't know anything about that, though, given the love fest between you and Swartz."

Addison smirks. "He was very cordial once you left. You probably misread the situation."

"Oh? Does 'I'm going to ask you to leave now' really mean 'Please stay and enjoy some caviar'?"

She ignores me, chin lifted high but smiling, as we reach my rental. I sneak an appraising glance at Addison. Her thick black hair is styled in waves today, and the sun highlights her pink lipstick.

"Hashim Swartz seemed pretty chummy with Phinneas," she says as we slide into the front seats. "If only you had met Phinneas at one point. It'd be so helpful for us both to know his personality, who he might have offended. Who might have wanted to kill him."

"Yeah. Shame our paths never crossed."

Addison hits one of the preset stations, and mariachi music blares from the speakers as I pull forward into traffic. I sneak a glance at her and find her wearing her usual RBF. Someone else might be concerned that she was upset, but her default impassivity only means she's alive. Paying attention to the mistakes I keep making.

Pretty soon, I'm going to have to stop lying to Addison and tell her exactly how I knew Phinneas Redwood.

CHAPTER TWENTY-ONE

PHINNEAS

BENEDICT CANYON | JULY 25

PHINNEAS REDWOOD: *Yup, it's recording. Okay! So what am I supposed to be doing, exactly?*

[Muffled speech]

Speak into my phone if you can, there you go. Yeah, a little closer. Lean down. Farther.

ADDISON STERN: *Phinneas, sweetie, I didn't wear a V-neck blouse today. You're not going to get a better look at the girls, no matter how far I'm hunched over.*

PR: *You know me too well, Stern. So repeat the instructions* *for me again. Now that I have my phone going and I can reference the details later on.*

AS: *You could just call me if you have questions.*

PR: *No, no, recording. I'm recording. What were you saying about the Boom Chicka Downtown app?* [Sips liquid]

AS: [Sighs] *Boom Boom, the video social media app. It's the latest craze among Gen Z, and even millennials are reluctantly moving to it from the older, more established apps. Boom Boom users and their videos are moving mass quantities of product these days, and for anyone who is selling anything, it's important to have a presence there.*

PR: *Right. That's right, you said that. But what kind of videos are we talking about? I mean, what am I supposed to be posting, considering I have a whole marketing department that's promoting Shapextrin to our targeted demos? Like, why am I doubling up the effort?*

AS: *Because, Phinneas. You're the star. If you got your head out of the bottle every so often, you'd be more aware of your power and potential to take the whole industry by storm.*

[Silence]

PR: *Ouch, Addison. You wound me . . . with a compliment. That's a strange feeling.*

AS: *Let me rephrase.*

PR: *No, don't. I haven't always . . . no, I haven't ever really zoned in on my role here. I kind of wasted it last time around.*

My ex always told me that. We fell in love right before my first pill really took off, and she broke up with me afterward because of my . . . ethics, I guess.

AS: *And what were those?*

PR: *Uh. I didn't have any?*

AS: *And that upset her?*

PR: *Well, yeah. She was an idealist who wrote for nonprofits, even though she came from money. She believed in big love, big dreams, doing big things to change the world. I wore my own pair of rose-colored glasses for a while. Then she cheated on me. And I got distracted to cope.*

AS: *Distracted?*

PR: *Don't make me say it. You've got Google for resurfacing all my mistakes. Especially the ones who were putting themselves through "medical school" with "performance art."*

AS: *You don't have to make air quotes, Phinneas.*

PR: *Anyway, what I'm getting at here is that I'm ready. I'm ready to do what it takes to turn this ship around and be a better CEO—face of the brand, or whatever that's needed.*

[Pause]

AS: *Are you? Do you genuinely want this, or is this all related to her—to your ex? If we successfully launch this next product, but she still doesn't approve of your efforts, will you spiral, Phinneas? Or maintain the hard work you—and I—will be drilling into over the next few months?*

PR: *I want this. In 100 percent sincerity, I do.*

AS: *Good, because—*

PR: *And . . . it is all for her. I can't help that. It's the truth. Probably always will be. So you'll have to work with me at the risk of watching me implode somewhere later down the line.*

AS: *A Phinn-plosion?*

PR: *Now, see—you are listening. So tell me, again, about this Boom Chicka—sorry. This Boom Boom app. I'm dialed in now.*

AS: *[Sighs] Phinneas, I have to admit: I don't believe you. I don't think you're actually committed to change. [Sniffs] Phinneas, have you—goddammit, have you been drinking?*

PR: *Only a little, and in the comfort of my own home.*

AS: *I know for a fact you were at a business meeting not thirty minutes ago, and that you just came back. I could smell the fresh exhaust from your car in the driveway. [Rustling]*

PR: *Hey. Hey, what are you doing? [Laughs] C'mon, it was just a little mimosa with my product team. You can't leave yet, you haven't even told me what videos to upload.*

AS: *Mr. Redwood, although you hired Ovid Blackwell and they provided you with the best of the best—*

PR: *Mr. Redwood? Stern, are you breaking up with me? [Scoffs] No, c'mon, sit down. Please.*

AS: *No. [Huffs] I have defended you to everyone who will* listen: to my VP, the president of Ovid Blackwell, CNN, MSNBC, and Pharmaceutical Weekly. Even Science Bros, the website for young scientists who deadlift at the gym, laughed when I said you would be ready for in-person interviews in three weeks' time. You're proving me wrong this instant.

PR: [Groans] *Look, I couldn't care less about Science Bros— or any other self-aggrandizing platform whose leadership can't spell "enzyme."*

AS: *That's clear. Abundantly. But I care, and you're making me look like an idiot.*

PR: *Let's not exaggerate, Stern. Don't get so emotion—*

AS: *Don't. Patronize. Me. I care about whether you can pull off this transformation, and I wish you would, too. But the only thing that gives you pause is whether some ex-girlfriend, who dropped you like a Redbox subscription decades ago, gives a shit about your charitable donations. Wake up, Phinneas! What she thinks doesn't matter. You matter. Your health matters. Your professional reputation matters.*

[Pause]

PR: *Okay.*

AS: *Okay what?*

PR: *Okay, you're right. I'll . . . stop drinking. Out in public. And I'll make a real effort to drink less at home.*

AS: *I don't believe you.*

PR: *I'm serious. This time, I am. What you're saying is absolutely true: I need to do better for myself and stop pining over a woman who has washed her hands of me. I deserve a better life than drinking my daylight hours away and alienating colleagues at mimosa meetings. Thrive deserves better, and so does my next pill—that's where I think you're right. I think Shapextrin can really help people, and I . . . want to be one of them. I . . . I see all of that now.*

[Pause]

AS: *Okay.*

PR: *Okay what?*

AS: *Let's continue.*

CHAPTER TWENTY-TWO

ADDISON

HOLLYWOOD | SEPTEMBER 25

V elvet Eastman looks every bit the fashion designer, seated across from me in the private corner of the patio at the Chateau Marmont, where I arranged for her interview to be held. An onyx fisherman's-net sweater from her own line drapes across her shoulders, revealing patches underneath of a cream satin tank top. Black hair is set in a loose French braid down her back, complementing the gold eyeliner she wears that ends in a cat eye, while distressed jeans that I know cost more than a flight to New York hug her long legs. Tendrils of ivy hang overhead from the lattice pergola flanked by lush palm fronds, adding to the secluded atmosphere of this iconic Hollywood spot.

The reporter, a mainstay in gossip news, approaches our table. She swings long straight hair behind the shoulder pads of her periwinkle blazer. "Well, my team is all packed up. Scintillating, Velvet. Thanks so much again for chatting with me. I'll be sure to tell Addison the go-live date for your piece. I can't wait to see your designs on the runway."

Velvet beams. "My pleasure."

Once the reporter has safely departed from the patio, I lean across the table. "You were brilliant."

"It went well, didn't it?" my client squeals. "I've always wanted to be featured on Starling Lewks."

We spend an hour discussing Velvet's upcoming television appearances and the angles we'll continue to hit regarding Velvet's new turn as a designer. Although much of the country is familiar with her headlines as a high-end madam, certain platforms will amplify that controversy for ratings. We know this. We are prepared for this. Once the media finds an idea that engages an audience, they are loath to let it go.

Peter shared that the police remain in touch with our attorneys, that Phinneas's murder continues to drive clicks and viewership. He says the board is still salty about me taking such a prominent client and downright incensed that I've been linked to yet another murder—three of them in total; he says that my heightened visibility on Velvet's campaign only fuels further speculation by police, by the public. As the uncle I never had, I gift Peter with a maximum of one message per day in which he offers his unsolicited perspective. Then I remind him that the customer is always right, even in public relations.

Velvet personally requested me. Once I deliver the publicity campaign of the year for her fashion debut, the only words the board will have for me are *Should we serve Dom or Moët to celebrate your promotion to partner?*

Velvet leans over the stack of talking points I've written for her and organized according to calendar date and urgency. "This is good. I feel good. Ready."

"You're a natural at these interviews," I reply. "It's a wonder you didn't permit them for so long."

She exhales. "I mean, I loved my career in Chicago, but it had its complications. That's part of why I am so excited to begin this next chapter. To begin again, in a way, and pick up where I left off a long time ago. I applied to art school in Illinois. Did you know that?"

Of course I did. But I sense she wants to tell her story in her own way. "No."

Velvet is wistful, centering her attention on a trailing vine of arrow-shaped leaves. "I've been sketching designs since I was a child, but I never had the opportunity to pursue anything, for lack of money."

Similar to my own story, growing up in trailers. The shared background is probably another reason I've been so energized working on her campaign. Well, that and the push to discover just what Phinneas wanted me to know about Fashion Week. So far, I've learned the closing day's agenda will feature a number of designers, and most notably that Velvet's line will debut last—the closing runway show of the whole week. An interesting coincidence, if I could call it that. I asked the nonprofit behind the week of style, LA Artists in Fashion, about the schedule. The party line was that the most anticipated show is always the one chosen to close out the week. A vote is taken, and no one person decides its outcome. Although most of the fashion industry continues to ice out Velvet on a personal level, at least we're making headway.

"Go on," I prompt now.

"Well, when I finally did have enough cash after working about a thousand jobs, and delaying college for forever, I applied to the Chicago Institute of Design and Art."

"And you were accepted?" She wasn't.

"Nope." Velvet shakes her head. Gold eyeliner smears in the crease of her eyes. "I would have died from delight, I swear to you. I loved fashion, but I was also into all the Impressionism paintings and watercolors of Monet and all that stuff. It was after I got rejected that I started walking the streets myself, off and on, then later formed my club for the protection of women and my community. I liked sex, most of the time. But I liked the money more."

I lean across my untouched strawberry tart. "Sweetie, don't we all?"

She smiles. "Now, after so many years of wishing and working at it, I'm finally going to unveil my debut line at LA Fashion Week, of all places. It really is a dream come true. And"—Velvet taps the stack of papers before her—"it's all thanks to you."

"In large part, yes." I smile, allowing myself the credit I deserve. "But we've also got all the major news outlets and their affiliates in the biggest fashion markets across the country interested in you and your story, Velvet. The next two weeks are going to fly by, thanks to the brilliant way you've played your debut so far."

Velvet beams. "I hope so. If this goes well, I might even move back to the States for good, if the prudes will allow me to grab groceries without blowing a fuse."

I pay for lunch; then we walk out to the Chateau Marmont valet. My phone pings with a new text from Peter that contains a link to an article—probably questioning Phinneas's death and the continued lack of answers. The posts, memes, and op-eds wondering what happened to the Thrive CEO have been numerous, and Peter has sent them all to me in a thinly veiled reminder of his concern.

At the foot of the steep hill that leads onto Sunset Boulevard—an icon unto itself, known for its trendy hedonism—protestors wave signs. HONK IF YOU HATE BROTHELS! is stark in thick black marker.

I turn to Velvet, inspiration striking like a rattlesnake in the canyon. "Be sure to save any sketches you make this year. When I'm through rebranding your image, LACMA is going to be asking to feature your paint-by-number tableaus right next to your original clothing designs."

\\\\\////

The stop-and-go traffic is brutal this time of day, and I step inside my condo grateful for the reprieve. A framed Steinlen print of a cat that hangs beside a wall calendar in my kitchen seems downright cuddly today after the nonsense with Velvet's haters. Animals, especially the fake kind, are always preferable to people.

Connor called on my way home from the office, suggesting we leave in an hour to check out the Seven Wells rehab facility. I laughed until I got a cramp in my side. "You want to leave at four thirty to sit in traffic—in this city?"

"All the better reason to meet earlier, if you can," he said before hanging up. "I got news from the DMV."

I slide onto a barstool at my kitchen island, then check my phone's notifications. My assistant, Malina, sent me a link and the message *Check this out.* When I tap the URL, a home page appears for the Hong Kong marketing firm we hired to work Reed Song's architectural unveiling.

Beneath a banner sits an embedded video from the local news, showing Reed stepping from the roomy Escalade we arrived in. He waves like the regional star he is, then the camera follows him a few steps up the red carpet. In the corner of the frame, I'm visible exiting the car, waiting for photographers to get their close-up of my client.

"That outfit was a great choice," I note to myself. An unseen commentator mentions Reed's achievement in bringing such a unique design to life in Wan Chai, one of the most densely populated urban areas in the world.

"No one can dismiss Reed's contributions to Hong Kong," the announcer continues in Cantonese, "and to amplifying Chinese innovation globally."

I smile, saving the link on my phone. "Very kind. And exactly as I suggested coverage should go during my in-person meetings on the ground."

To Malina, I write out:

Send a basket of oranges and a special bottle of whisky to Walter Ng at the newspaper Hong Kong Economic. The copper themed Blue Label edition. Expense it from Ovid's Achievements account.

The camera follows Reed until he disappears inside the lobby, then circles back to where a reporter stands before the Escalade. A woman in jeans and a crop top watches at the edge of the crowd of onlookers, media personnel, and guests of the event. She appears anxious and not at all celebratory—or judgy—as the rest of the crowd does.

"Now, where have I seen you before?" I scroll back through the footage with my finger, resuming at where Reed disappears indoors. As he turns to throw a glance to his mistress, the frame cuts to the reporter and the woman in the background again, only now I see that the woman is speaking to a reporter from another network—a man who bows slightly when addressing her. The crowd around the woman withdraws to give her, and the camera's spotlight, enough space. Her dyed blond hair is curled, her makeup heavy, and her jeans low rise. She waves to someone, and her shirtsleeve lifts a few inches. A tattooed dragon twines around her arm. The Chinese mystical protector.

The same tattoo I saw on the woman wearing pajamas beside Devon Lim—dead in Monaco.

Chills twirl down my spine. What was Devon Lim's girlfriend—or new love interest—doing in Hong Kong at Reed Song's event? Was Devon there, hiding from his fiancée, Hyacinth Aspen? What are the odds that this girlfriend was there at the exact same time I, Devon's publicist, had flown there as well?

I scroll back through the video to the first frame, in which this woman is visible between the shoulders of two tall reporters I recognize from meetings with the *Hong Kong Journal*. She's young, judging from the Hello Kitty mini backpack she wears, though women in their twenties and beyond love the franchise.

Dyed blond hair contrasts with dark roots, while big brown eyes are nearly covered by blunt bangs.

I stare at my phone's screen, doubting my own eyes. The woman is Annalise Meier, Phinneas Redwood's ex-girlfriend. She lived in Hong Kong, I knew that. I recognize her from a framed photo he kept on the highest level of his sparse bookshelf in his office. In the picture, the pair of them press their cheeks together over a plate of spaghetti. What are the odds of Annalise being in Wan Chai on this exact day?

While the reporter speaks, Annalise shifts her weight to try to see past the swath of bodies outside the building's entrance. She laughs at something, though the sound is inaudible.

"Annalise was Phinneas's first love. She was killed while with Devon Lim." I start the recording over from the beginning, when Reed steps from the Escalade. The woman is there in the background, visible in fits and starts as the crowd jostles forward.

The proposal that Connor found on Devon's desk in Bel-Air was clearly meant for Phinneas's company, Thrive, Inc. Though I wasn't convinced until now, Devon and Phinneas did know each other.

Someone knocks at my door—Connor with his updates. I set my phone on the counter, then rise to unlock the dead bolt.

"Come in, I need you to see something."

"Hi to you, too," he says, wearing a bomber jacket that every elder millennial owned at one point or another. He scans my empty counter. "No wine?"

"Just got home." I show Connor the video, and he confirms that the woman with the tattoo, Annalise Meier, was definitely the corpse in Devon's bed.

"Strange to see her alive here. Eerie." Connor slides onto the barstool at my counter.

"Even stranger, she's Phinneas Redwood's ex-girlfriend."

"He had relationships? I thought they were all one-night stands."

"Don't be cute. It's too much of a coincidence that she would attend the event I just did in Hong Kong."

Connor crosses his arms. The faded leather of the bomber jacket smells greasy, like he picked up fast food on his way here. "Do you think she knew about the business proposal that Devon planned to pitch to Phinneas? I wonder if she was the go-between."

I stare him down. "Possibly. That still doesn't explain what she was doing at the unveiling."

"Maybe she was tailing you." Connor sticks out his lower lip. "Speaking of stalkers, remember that pickup truck on Melrose? I saw it parked on your street out front."

"What?" I cross to the front window. "Is it still there?"

"No, it drove off when I was walking up. But my guy at the Hollywood DMV got the rest of the license plate, based on my description of the truck and my estimate of the year. He says the truck is owned by someone named Fernando Castillo."

I glance at my phone again. Annalise Meier is frozen in a conspiratorial giggle with someone beside her. "Never heard of him."

Connor shakes his head. "Castillo is into politics, as far as I can tell from his social media accounts. Was he a client of yours?"

"Definitely not." I pause, absorbing the fact that I might have a secret admirer—more likely hater—on wheels. "Could this Castillo be with Swartz?"

Connor shared his suspicions about the venture capitalist after the awkward way Swartz pointed us toward the rehab facility. A little too hastily, too eagerly, in Connor's opinion.

"Maybe. Hedge funds and politics go hand in hand."

I growl, locking my phone. "Well, Fashion Week will be here in two weeks. I need all eyes to be on my client—the live one. The internet sound bites on Phinneas's murder have not let up, and if that truck driver is linked to this whole debacle, we need to learn more."

Connor retrieves a key fob from his pocket. "Let's take a quick detour on the way to Seven Wells. See what we see."

Nearly an hour later, we arrive in Los Feliz, just east of the 101 freeway. There is no such thing as a "quick detour" in a city that has five times as many cars as people. Connor slows at the edge of a neighborhood mural. In the painting, children dance in a circle, wearing traditional Mexican dresses. A salute to local culture.

"What are we doing here? I'm not a fan of the *Blade Runner* house," I add, knowing the Frank Lloyd Wright creation lies just beyond the next corner.

"There's the pickup truck. Beside the barber shop. And that door next to it is the address listed on the truck's registration." Connor rests both arms atop the steering wheel. He shuts off the radio, interrupting a song about second chances.

As if in sync with Connor's words, the driver's-side door opens, and a portly man steps out. He looks right then left across the busy street. He sprints through traffic like a human version of Frogger, pausing in the middle passing lane, then running the final two lanes to the sidewalk's safety. He disappears inside another building beneath an unlit sign that extends over the road to catch hungry drivers' eyes on their morning commute. Donuts.

"So that's Fernando Castillo, I'm guessing."

Connor doesn't take his eyes from the donut shop. "He's coming back out."

The same man—Castillo—exits. This time he has a new individual behind him. A man whose thick black hair is gelled straight back, the sides of his head shaved. The gray sleeves of his button-up shirt are rolled to the elbow.

"You recognize that guy?" Connor asks as the pair does another Frogger dance back across the street.

"No. Not at all. But he doesn't look like he eats many donuts."

Connor shifts the car into drive, and then we pull forward past the address registered to the pickup. Tall windows are covered with black construction paper.

"Maybe he does escape rooms," Connor says. "Or scared-straight intervention programs for troubled teens."

"I doubt it. He's got too much free time to be an entrepreneur if he's following us with Castillo," I growl. "Whoever he is, find out."

CHAPTER TWENTY-THREE

ADDISON

CALABASAS | SEPTEMBER 25

On the 101 freeway, as we drive toward the rehab facility that Hashim Swartz told us about, we are silent. Traffic hums and honks with the monotony of any other day, but inside the car my thoughts are racing to connect Phinneas with a random pickup truck. How does Devon relate? How do I?

We approach a domed building that broadcasts serenity and a costly price tag atop the cliffs of Calabasas. I try to focus on the here and now. On Seven Wells, a shining beacon of health, according to its brochure. We park in a small lot between two black Hummers. A man all in spandex walks his tiny white Maltese along a stretch of the sidewalk beside us.

"Maybe they were in a throuple," I say.

"What?" Connor cuts the engine.

"If Phinneas and Devon each slept with the same woman, then they all end up dead—were they in some kind of business arrangement, or romance?"

"That's a stretch. Devon was also engaged to a society woman, Hyacinth Aspen, and had an amazing career in tech. What in his background makes you think he'd have this totally alternate life that threatens all of that?"

"Oh, my mistake, I thought you were a certified PI," I drawl. "Let's not be naïve. Examples of double lives abound in your industry."

"Based on what I know about Lim, which is a lot"—Connor shrugs—"that would be wildly out of character."

"Wildly—you don't have to emphasize how dumb you think my idea is."

"I didn't say that—"

"Look, at least I'm thinking of all the possibilities here. You're not adding anything to the investigation the way that you said you would."

"Really, Addison? You'd just dismiss all the work I've put into the last several weeks? Not to mention I'm doing the legwork with the DMV for this pickup-truck stalker—"

"Okay, okay." I wave off his rant. "But I think we should find out if Phinneas and Devon met to discuss business at some point. Then determine how Annalise Meier plays a role here, or if she was only caught up in the middle."

I huff, thoroughly annoyed that I'm having to do Connor's work for him. Aren't I supposed to be reaping the rewards of our partnership? I brought Connor to Devon, albeit after Devon had already died. Connor said he would help me figure out what happened to Phinneas since his benefactor still wants answers about Devon, apparently. The meeting we had with

Hashim Swartz gave us the name of Phinneas's rehab facility, but Connor wasn't able to find anything else interesting about the guy. Not legally, he said.

Insert eye roll.

"You're right," Connor says. He takes a deep breath. "You're totally right. I'm still noodling on these new developments, and not doing a good job of communicating that to you. Sorry."

He shifts toward me to touch my hand across the center console. For a moment, he leaves it there, our skin connected. The memory of the rest of our bodies pressed together surges forward in my mind, my chest, my stomach—before I push it down.

Connor's reaction is placating. I see right through it. "You're the private investigator. And we're running out of time."

I exit his car, then stalk up the path to the glass doors of the facility. We shared a night together. A single night. I can't let that distract from whatever nonsense is afoot here, trying to trip me up. The business card that I found in Phinneas's office—a tailor shop in Beverly Hills—says we only have two weeks and change until my balance comes due.

Inside the facility, a woman smiles from behind the front desk. Her pearls and blue sweater scream yacht club, or Vineyard Vines. "Welcome. Are you visiting or checking in?"

I suppress a smirk. As if. "A friend of mine recently passed away, and I know he stayed with you in the past. Three times, actually. I was hoping to speak to someone who might remember him as a guest."

If the vibe here is to pretend this is a luxury hotel, I'm game.

She purses her lips. "I'm sorry, I wouldn't be able to confirm any details about the stay of one of our guests, living or deceased."

I crook a finger, urging her closer. "Your manager. Now."

"I assure you, there's no way we can—"

"And I assure you that I am two seconds away from calling my friend at the *Beverly Hills Gazette* and reporting the hideous bedbug infestation at this facility."

The woman's eyes widen. "We have no such thing."

"Honey, if I waited for interesting truth tidbits to surface, I wouldn't be in PR. Your manager. Now."

"That's me. How can I help?" A woman who wears all her stress in pleats across her forehead nearly fills the doorway beneath a plaque that reads GUESTS ONLY.

Thick black hair is styled in curls around a face with no makeup. Although this woman is easily five feet ten inches or taller, she slouches into her high-waisted trousers. "Posey Delacruz, director of the Seven Wells Wellness Resort. How can I help you?"

"I'd love to elaborate," I begin, then shoot the receptionist a look. "In private."

Posey ushers us through the opaque glass door into a sitting room with deep armchairs. "What can I do for you—?"

"Addison Stern, publicist with Ovid Blackwell, and this is Connor Windell. A client of mine was a guest here at one point, Phinneas Redwood. Three times. He passed away recently."

Posey blinks twice. "As I overheard my receptionist explaining, I would never confirm someone stayed here. HIPAA and all that."

"Right. Sure."

Connor sits in the armchair to my left. He peers into the ceiling corners as if searching for something. Probably still "noodling on these new developments."

"But I'm not interested in Phinneas's official diagnoses or recommendations for treatment. I'm looking for notes from group therapy, visitation records, or the names of anyone he might have befriended while a guest here."

"Everything you're describing is protected under privacy laws."

"Ms. Delacruz—Posey—Phinneas was killed. Murdered. And I'm hoping to serve his killer the justice they deserve."

Both Connor and Posey lift their eyebrows. I'm laying it on a little thick. Dial it back, Addison.

"I guess I'm confused," Posey says. "The police are investigating the case, aren't they?"

"Of course. But my clients are my world. I owe it to him to find out what happened."

The eyebrows lower. I'm getting warmer.

"And you think I have those answers?"

"I think Phinneas spent three seasons with you and your staff when he was at his most vulnerable. A person doesn't complete treatment at one of these facilities without divulging certain information."

"Speak plainly, Addison. I have a tour to give to an Oscar winner in ten minutes."

"Did Phinneas suggest he was in trouble with his investors? Or that he misused company funds?"

Hashim Swartz was quick to point us toward Phinneas's rehab stints, possibly trying to distract us with something shinier than his own misdeeds. But if Phinneas was throwing lavish drug parties in the Mediterranean, and that's where Hashim first met our troubled CEO before becoming an investor in Thrive, Inc. himself, other investors could have been up to speed. Maybe they frowned on Phinneas's antics. Maybe Phinneas wasn't meticulous with how he paid for said illicit drugs. Company funds could have been redirected by him, jeopardizing a profitable enterprise with the federal government. And that would infuriate people with a lot of zeros in their checking accounts.

Posey shakes her head. "Honestly, I would love to ensure all our guests find peace. One way or another. But I can't think of anyone who Mr. Redwood might have mentioned as bothering him—during any alleged stay. We try to check in with guests after they leave Seven Wells, but it can be hard to keep up with the myriad of vices these days."

"Oh? In what sense?"

"Prescription drug use has exploded, most commonly. There's been an uptick in diazepam abuse."

"Which, for non-pharmacists, is . . . ?"

Connor clears his throat. "Valium. Valium is the brand name of one kind of diazepam pill."

"That's right," Posey says. "It was uppers for a long time, then downers, then chemically modified super uppers, and now the classics once again. Our facility is as busy as ever, and it has become untenable for us to keep tabs on our former guests. Any other questions, Addison?"

Although she is cordial, I get the sense that a gossip sesh won't do it for Posey Delacruz—not when an actor with an addiction is waiting. "Anything unusual that you can recall while Phinneas was a guest here?"

Posey twists her mouth to the side. "We did receive several large donations from an anonymous donor while . . . a high-profile guest stayed with us. Each time."

"Anonymous?" Connor asks.

"Through an attorney. That's all I can say."

We thank her, and she shows us to the main entrance. As we

take the concrete path to Connor's gas guzzler in the parking lot, a man emerges from a still-running Escalade. Wearing dark sunglasses and a zipped hooded sweater, the man nearly bowls us off the walkway as he stumbles into the lobby.

\\\\\////

"Velvet, you look stunning." I air-kiss my client on the steps of City Hall in Downtown LA. Today, overcast gray clouds contrast with Velvet's purple puffed sleeves and silver buttons that reach all the way up to her neck. Sleek matte Lycra pants hug Velvet's jaw-dropping curves.

She squeezes my hand. "I'm ready for this."

"You are." We reach the entrance of City Hall together as I scan the extensive walkway and the manicured lawns on either side. The property encompasses a city block and provides a beautiful place for LA residents to have lunch, mingle, take meetings, or relieve themselves on one of the dozen public benches. We pass beneath looping designs carved in the stone overhead.

Turning left down a tiled hallway, every other square painted with a detailed motif, I lead Velvet toward a conference room I secured with the council member's secretary's help. High ceilings decorated in painted gold designs and blue felt cloth that hangs along the foyer's second-floor balcony could belong in a palace or old-money mansion on the East Coast. My kitten heels clack against the polished floor, energizing my steps. Despite the chaos surrounding my search for Phinneas's killer, and the suspicion landing on me regarding Devon's murder, business is rolling. Velvet is making progress among the fashion industry's snobs. And she's about to lock in a powerful partnership.

Meredith Gaines, the incumbent in next year's midterms, was desperate for an edgy endorsement when I reached out. I suggested she meet with my client to discuss Velvet's new fashion line. The two women could mutually benefit each other. Councilor Gaines will wear one of Velvet's designs in a photo op for her upcoming campaign in exchange for Velvet's public support as a formerly notorious woman with a new career—Gaines is a die-hard supporter of women-owned businesses and second chances. Velvet will gain legitimacy and acceptance as an entrepreneur peddling legal wares that are coveted by all. Even local officials.

Introductions are made. The two women smile, posing for photos. Tony Hopkins, a publicist I once saw at big-screen red carpet functions before he became a government fawn, whirls about his client, adjusting a hair here, smoothing a suit lapel there. He's been practically living in this building for years, moving from one government insider to the next like a bribe tucked inside a handshake.

While the leaders spend a moment chatting about mundane topics—"How do you like the LA weather?" "The traffic here, my God!"—I approach Tony.

"Good to see you, Tony. It's been ages."

He glares at me. "Addison Stern. The last time we met you were telling *TMZ* that I was high on the job at the SAG Awards."

I let a hand fly to my chest. "Was I? That doesn't sound like me."

"No, no, it was you. You wanted my client to move to Ovid Blackwell before her next big movie came out. She had just finished community service for stealing money from that orphanage, and everyone wanted her. The stunt you pulled that night made no one in the film industry want to work with me, so I had to move over here to City Hall." Tony leans closer. "To these people, government officials. They're even worse than actors."

"Well, from what I hear, you've been very successful in these parts. So I guess you can thank me." Tony does not mirror my smile.

"What do you want, Addison?" His tone turns annoyed. "I know you never give out a compliment for free."

Councilor Gaines and Velvet are still enjoying themselves, laughing now about how petty people can be. "So astute, Tony, exactly as I recall. I was wondering if you've heard anything about the upcoming Fashion Week. Will the councilor be attending? She seems to be a fan."

After I decoded the dates on Phinneas's card, my power move that secured Velvet as a client was even sweeter. I'd be working in the LA fashion scene and attacking both goals without a dewdrop of sweat. But each meeting, photo op, and interview has only confirmed that Velvet has a tough hill to climb for acceptance in the industry she so admires—providing zero insight into what Phinneas could want me to know about the final night of Fashion Week. As far as I know he never met Velvet, unless he visited her gentlemen's club at some point, all the way over in Chicago, and there's no way he would have known I'd be working with her for the event. The Google Alert I set up has kept my inbox steadily pinging with news articles and op-eds wondering what happened to the small-statured CEO. Until October 13 arrives, I'll be examining the business-card clue for answers. Even if it means playing nice with competitors.

Tony rolls his eyes. "Not if I can help it. The last thing she needs is to be seen as frivolous or spending taxpayer dollars on designer clothing."

Behind Tony, framed photos line the white plaster walls at eye level: elected city officials from the last ten years. In the center of one, a man stands heads and shoulders above the rest of the group like the apex of a pyramid. Graying black hair is long on top and shaved on the sides. The same Frogger jogger who crossed the street with Fernando Castillo, whose truck was following Connor and me.

"Who is that? The tall one," I ask, careful to keep my voice low.

"In the middle? That's Jamie Mendez. A former city official, now seeking election in Congress. Why? Did he get in your way once, too?"

"Tell me more about him."

Tony sighs, but our charges are now discussing climate change and its effect on the supply chain. He's stuck with me. "I don't know. Jamie Mendez, he was over in the seventh district but got booted out by voters a few years back. There was a scandal with a rival that didn't land well for him."

I recall the black construction paper covering the windows of the business he disappeared within. "What kind of scandal?"

Tony surveys the room behind me. "I know a few things. But why would I share them with you?"

"Oh, honey." I bat my eyes. "You must know what happens to people who cross me or, worse, withhold information from me?"

Tony scowls. "I'm a publicist who works exclusively with the LA city government. You think I'm hiding anything that hasn't already been outed?"

"I think I once saw you exiting the Garage in WeHo a little over a year ago."

Tony shifts his weight. He steps closer. "What of it? It's not a crime to visit a place with good food and drink, no matter the neighborhood."

"No, of course not. But I think your wife would be interested to know you were sampling the local fare. Is Charlie still the bouncer there? Or did he get fired after you were caught checking his dipstick in the palm fronds?"

Tony's face loses its color. After a moment he picks his jaw up from the hardwood. "Jamie Mendez is blacklisted from most government circles. After his rival Greg Sistine, another former city official, died from a prescription cocktail four years ago, no one wanted to work with Mendez. They had each ranted in public about how the other guy would get 'what's coming to him'—very on brand for two Ovid clients."

"They're not ours. I'm sure of that. I've never heard of either of them before today."

Tony lifts a haughty eyebrow. "The great and powerful Addison Stern is not all-seeing, all-knowing?"

"Don't test me, Tony. You'll fail that exam. Why was Mendez not arrested, if he threatened Sistine before Sistine died?"

Tony huffs. "No proof. But that didn't stop the blowback. Even though Mendez was literally in a hospital visiting pediatric cancer patients when Sistine's death occurred, Mendez had zero traction for a few years; everyone suspected him. Now I guess he's running for election, though, to the House of Representatives this time."

"Intriguing. Does he have a publicist?" Maybe I can strong-arm another PR colleague into dishing the goods.

Tony sneers. "I would have thought it was you for the way Mendez managed to escape the negative press. Addison Stern. The Teflon publi-bitch."

I smile and press my palm to his cheek, stepping into his

personal space. He flinches backward. "I'm going to have to update my LinkedIn with that. Thanks for the content."

"I wouldn't get involved with him, Teflon coating or no." Tony shrugs off the discomfort of my touch. "Mendez has family rumored to be in with the mob all the way back to their heyday during the seventies. Half the bodies turning up in Lake Mead outside of Vegas are probably from the Mendez-mob collab."

Velvet laughs, too loudly, signaling that her conversation is almost at an end. I whip out my phone to check the time. "Well, much obliged for the information. See you at the next red carpet eve— Oh. Silly me."

"How did you know? About me and Charlie?" Tony asks, still fuming.

"Oh, sweetie. I keep notes on everyone I've ever met, just in case something comes in handy."

"Wow. Does it ever get tiring, not trusting a single soul? Always poised to rip people apart?" Big brown eyes glisten.

"Does a bird tire of feeling wind beneath its wings? No, Tony. It doesn't."

Velvet and I leave a few minutes later. A council member's time is precious, after all, and I walk Velvet to where her Tesla is parked in the adjacent guarded lot. I get to my own Mercedes and unlock my phone to call Connor when a new thought stops me: What if Jamie Mendez did have something to do with his rival's death? If his associate is following Connor and me in his pickup, he could be watching us for reasons unrelated to Phinneas. As someone with ties to Las Vegas, Mendez could be keeping tabs on another desert flower: Connor.

When I make a left onto Spring Street, I check my rearview. A man stands on the stone steps leading up to City Hall closest to the busy road. His characteristic button-up shirt, paired with a garish necktie, is obvious from where I coast in traffic. FBI Agent Jonas lifts a hand in a wave, as if he saw me—or knows the dark blue custom shade of my Benz.

The stoplight at the upcoming intersection turns yellow, but I step on the gas and floor it toward the freeway.

CHAPTER TWENTY-FOUR

PHINNEAS

LOS FELIZ | JULY 27

PHINNEAS REDWOOD: *Can I get a coffee? Yup, me over here. Thanks.*

Two sugars. [Muffled] *No real sugar? What do you mean, this is a GD donut shop, isn't it?* [Laughs] *Oh, but it's a donut shop in LA? All right, I'll take Stevia.*

[Clinking] *Thanks.*

MAN: *Hey, how are you, Mr. Redwood?*

PR: *Fine, doing well. I've got a bear claw, a glazed, an old-fashioned, and a cream-filled glaze here. What could be better in life?* [Sips] *Call me Phinneas, by the way.*

MAN: *And likewise, I'll be Jamie.*

PR: *Nice to see you again, Jamie. Wasn't it back in—?*

JAMIE MENDEZ: *The Beverly Hilton, that's right.*

PR: *This is some operation you have here. Campaign head-quarters across the street, and your pick of the day's freshly fried treats. Who do you have to fluff to get that kind of service?* [Laughs]

JM: [Clears throat] *It's my, uh, cousin's shop. Been in the family for a long time.*

PR: *You're from LA, then?*

JM: *You got it. Born and raised. Gardena.*

PR: *Hey, Inglewood for me. Neighbors.*

JM: [Slaps table] *How about that? Well, I'm so pleased you made the time to come down here, Phinneas. You're an icon in your industry and, I think, a huge influencer for your generation, and future generations to come, no doubt. I want to share what we're doing here in our little donut-shop block.*

PR: *Sounds good. You don't serve liquor here, do you?*

JM: *Ah, no. No, we don't.*

PR: *All the better. I'm— Never mind. You were saying—?*

JM: *Yeah, I'm really energized to get elected to Congress in order to better serve this community. I know your district* *is helmed by the mediocre Maya Sheridan, with her lack-luster support of a free market, but I hope to win your vote, Phinneas. We want to emphasize more awareness around accessibility in all public places throughout California and the country.*

PR: *Uh-huh. Go on.*

JM: *My grandfather lost his leg in World War II, and the prosthetic he wore was never great on stairs. I vowed to him that my work in politics would benefit every American but would highlight those with special needs.*

[Pause]

PR: *Did you ask me here hoping for an endorsement—*

JM: *Or a check.* [Laughs] *We're not averse to either.*

PR: *Did you ask me here because you want me to be your mascot for the Little Person community?*

JM: [Pause] *I thought you might appreciate the work I'm doing. My goal is to amplify inclusivity for all Americans, regardless of their disability or size.*

PR: *Oooh, that's going to be a hard pass for me.*

JM: *Phinneas—*

PR: *Mr. Redwood.*

JM: [Clears throat] *Ah, Mr. Redwood. I asked you here because I'm looking for votes. And you appeal to a broad cross section of society: Anyone who watched* *your commercials in the eighties and nineties, Gen X, millennials, and—yes—the Little Person community.*

PR: *Don't forget—anyone who likes a redemption arc. Although it remains to be seen how successful that detail might be.*

JM: *I think, with your help, we could really reach Californians. We could make a difference in people's lives.*

PR: *Okay, well . . . I'm not down with being anyone's token anything. But I appreciate the effort to amplify inclusivity, especially from a disability standpoint. I'm working on improving people's lives with my next pill.*

JM: *That's great. I want to learn more about it.*

PR: *Yeah, it'll be out in a few months. My team is already gearing up more infomercials and Boom Booms to flood the feeds.*

JM: *Boom Booms? Is that . . . [Pause] adult content?*

PR: *It should be, right?*

JM: *No, no, that's the . . . the video app, right? So, what do you say? Do I have your support?*

PR: *My personal support—yeah, you can have that. Whether I can promote you in public depends on my publicist's take.*

JM: *Your publicist? I imagine whatever you decide to do, that person will follow.*

PR: *Well, more specifically, she'll tell me if I can afford to publicly link myself to another troubled figure.*

JM: *Troubled? Me? I'm sure you're mistaken. I haven't had a speeding ticket in decades—*

PR: *No, nothing as pedestrian as a moving violation. The shady past. The violent dealings. The friends you keep.*

JM: [Pause] *I'm afraid I don't know what you're talking about.*

PR: *Really? You see, I know your reasons for inviting me here. But I had my own, in agreeing to join you.*

JM: *You'll have to enlighten me.*

PR: *I want the dirt, of course!* [Laughs] *Did you really have . . . anything . . . to do with that politician's death a few years back? Wasn't he a rival of yours?*

JM: *Goodness, uh . . . You know, I'm afraid I'm going to have to end our meeting. I've got a busy morning ahead.*

PR: *No, no! I don't mean like you did anything. No, definitely not. Just, like, did you . . . know . . . anything? I'm purely curious. From one ne'er-do-well to another.*

JM: [Pause] *I'm . . . I'm sorry. This was an awkward foot to get off on. If you'll allow me—*[muffled] *Carol! Grab us another bear claw here.* [Clearly] *I'd like to get your vote and maybe your endorsement, but we don't have to work more closely together. Or maybe you can simply keep quiet about this meeting. What is that?*

PR: *Hmm? What is what?*

JM: *By your leg on the booth. Is that your phone, recording? Are you recording this conversation?*

PR: *Well, yes. But not for anything weird. For my personal use. And maybe my memoirs.*

JM: *That's not— Wait a minute. I need you to stop recording and delete the file.*

PR: *I'm not going to do that.*

JM: [Louder] *Delete the file. Goddammit, I knew I should have vetted you harder. She said you would be an asset to my campaign, but that's what I get for cutting corners. Here.* [Something drops] *Take your donut, and please leave.*

PR: *She? Who's "she"? Who suggested me? And hey, I have more than one. A larger bag would be appropriate if you're kicking me out. I guess I don't have to tell you I won't be voting for you.*

JM: *Take all of them, then. Please leave.*

PR: *Moreover—you know what? I'm gonna be campaigning for other people. Yeah, against you!*

JM: *For the love of God, please stop recor—*

CHAPTER TWENTY-FIVE

CONNOR

SILVER LAKE | SEPTEMBER 26

"Where are you?" Addison practically shouts into the phone.

"I'm at my Airbnb. Why?"

"Drop me a pin. We need to talk." A car honks in the background. "Silver Lake?"

"Yeah."

Her blinker clicks on. "See you soon."

Thirty minutes later, Addison Stern marches up the brick walkway of the Airbnb I rented. Hidden perks of the one-story bungalow include late-night parties thrown by the neighbors that rage until four in the morning and an apple tree that produces only sour fruit. But I'm a night owl and I prefer oranges anyway, so this place has been a winner.

Addison sways on my doorstep, her fist ready to rap the knocker, but she pauses. She lifts red-painted fingertips and brushes the hair back from her face. Smooths the ruffled sweater edge along her belt. Reapplies lip gloss—of all things. If I weren't watching her through the peephole, I'd ask if she is expecting someone else at this address, other than me.

She knocks. She scans the front porch impatiently, no doubt taking note of the old-fashioned rocking chair next to the NO SOLICITORS sign that hangs in the window. She knocks again.

"Connor Windell, answer the door!"

I open the door, faster than I should, and she cocks an eyebrow in response.

Without the barrier of the fish-eye view, Addison is gorgeous. Sleek everything, from her jet-black hair to the smooth red jacket that lands mid-thigh on black jeans. She's a vision—and, I remind myself, so were the sirens in those Greek tales before they lured sailors to their deaths.

"There you are," she says, entering the house, strolling right on in. "I called and gave you my ETA, where were you?"

"I'm sorry, milady. Mayhap I should have been curbside to help you alight from your carriage."

Addison turns on her heel, a sharp pop of color against the owner's Pier 1 decorative scheme. "I know who that guy is, the man who likes donuts and knows Castillo. Jamie Mendez. Ever heard of him?"

"Wasn't he in politics? I think I voted for him a few years ago when I was still a resident here."

Addison nods. "A local council member, before he began his current campaign for the House of Representatives. I was at City Hall and talked to another publicist who says that Jamie Mendez has family ties to Vegas and the mob."

I lift both eyebrows. "And he's friends with a guy who owns the pickup that's been following us. Now that's interesting."

"Connor, are you listening? He knows people in Vegas. You live in Vegas. Is there someone you pissed off back there who you're not telling me about?"

I stride to the bar that separates the kitchen from the sitting room, a vestige of the swinging sixties when this house was built. "Ah, well. Yeah. There is."

"Who?" Addison slams her hands on her hips.

"Gianni. My bookie." I rub the back of my neck. "But the guy has no affiliation with any mafia org. He's just an Italian American who launders dirty money and takes unsupported bets from naïve but extremely good-looking men."

Addison does me the compliment of a smirk. "So you're saying that your bookie, to whom you owe—I'm guessing—a bucket of money, has nothing to do with Castillo supposedly tracking you down?"

"Well, you too. The pickup was parked on your street. Are you sure Jamie Mendez was never a client of yours?"

Addison scoffs. "Yes, I'm damn sure, Connor. So where does that leave our investigation? Jamie Mendez was implicated in the death of his political rival a few years back. He's got enough skeletons to fill the Hollywood Forever Cemetery, and I'd bet sending a lackey to tail a nosy publicist-and-PI duo would be an easy undertaking."

"But who's the guy who attacked us in France? The most distinctive things about him were the gun in his belt and the nose that looked broken about eight times."

Addison shakes her head. "He's not Fernando Castillo or Jamie Mendez. I'd never seen him before, or since."

I cough into my elbow. "Ah, that's not exactly true for me. I told you that I saw him in Santa Barbara. Or I think I did. But he must have been looking into Devon Lim, the same way that I was, because he was standing outside a florist that Devon had visited recently. Then he found us near Devon's French Riviera home."

Addison gapes at me. "And you're just catching me up now?"

"We haven't seen him since. And I got a brief look at him in Santa Barbara, then two seconds of watching him hurdle stairs in Toulon."

Addison pulls a barstool from under the counter, then takes a seat. "You didn't think someone would travel across the world to track you down, so you kept the info to yourself. How humble."

I don't reply. She's right. I should have been up-front with Addison—about a few things. God knows the woman already doubts me. But to confide in her is to be vulnerable with Addison Stern, and anyone with half a brain knows that's a bad idea. One half of my brain still has enough blood flow to function properly, at least.

"We still don't know that guy's identity," I continue. "But the French police finally came out with more info. Because Devon Lim is American and the woman he was found with, Annalise Meier, has Chinese and German citizenship, apparently the police were slow to release details of the crime scene. Trying to appease all the intergovernmental agencies and whatnot."

"I'm watching paint dry here," Addison grumbles. "What's your point?"

"By searching the French news platforms online, I found out that police said something unusual was found at the crime scene."

Addison stiffens. "What was it, Connor? Was it a card?"

I shake my head. Allow myself a smile. I'm probably enjoying withholding from her a little too much. But it's either torturing Addison Stern or blackjack, right?

"The police haven't released that yet. But we already know that surveillance footage showed a man entered Devon Lim's room before you did, over twelve hours before. Likely, right when Devon and the woman—Annalise Meier—were going to sleep. Devon on the couch and Annalise in the bedroom."

"Connor, we saw them in bed together."

"We saw two individuals fully clothed in pajamas sprawled on a bed, dead. Devon and Annalise could have been platonic. They could have been hiding in the same room, or corralled there by the attacker."

"Sure. If you believe David Blaine actually levitates."

"Well, I don't think Devon was cheating on his fiancée with Annalise. My gut says he didn't. The French news also said police are looking for a man, someone standing at least five feet ten inches tall."

"That's your height, Connor."

"Six feet, thank you very much."

"How did you find all this out? You don't speak French."

I step into the kitchen, where I left a full can of Diet Coke. "Mais oui. Or at least un petit peu. And Google Translate speaks beaucoup français."

"Look, the FBI agent followed me to City Hall today. We need to work faster. Smarter." Addison huffs. She paces across the worn hardwood flooring, between a brown leather couch and a dining table in the street-facing nook.

I purse my lips. Aim for casual. "What do you think was there?" I ask. "In Devon's hotel room. What was the unusual item?"

She pauses. Children play down the street, screaming joyful cries that pierce the neighborhood's daytime quiet. Addison shifts toward me. Slips her hands ever so casually into her pants pockets.

"What do you know, Connor?" Her voice is sweet. Dangerous.

I lick my lips. "Nothing. Just a hunch, is all. I wondered if maybe you had found something offbeat before. Recently. Maybe at Phinneas's crime scene. You mentioned a card."

Addison shrugs, but her shoulders barely move. A tight, constrained gesture. "No."

"No, 'course not. That would be strange, and something you'd want to report to the police. Unless, that is, the item—the card—implicated you somehow."

She tilts her head. I have the wherewithal to be glad I hid the sharp objects in the kitchen before she arrived. "You know, Connor. I wouldn't have called you a great PI before we resumed our . . . friendship. I'd have said good. Above average. But now you're impressing me."

I remain standing behind the counter in the kitchen. My Diet Coke glistens on the Formica, highlighted by sun rays filtering through the window beside me. I search for something to distract her before she completely shuts down. "My dad said I wasn't very good, actually. He did a bunch of PI jobs for the city, then for some really wealthy clientele. He didn't approve when I started doing my own investigations at fourteen."

Addison hasn't slouched from her defensive posture. "His mistake."

"It was. My first job convinced him otherwise when my client—my mother—suggested that he might be doing some illegal work after hours down by the LA River. We thought some white-collar crimes for someone. Turns out, he wasn't doing anything illegal. Just cheating on my mom."

She softens. An inch. "I'm sorry."

"Ah, you know. It is what it is. He stopped talking to me then. Said I would only hurt people as a PI. Then my mom died a year after that, and my grandparents took me in."

In hindsight, that first time investigating my dad was when the morals and ethics my mom instilled in me started to loosen—to slide, depending on the situation and the importance of making money. In order to find out where my dad might be meeting his mistress, I turned on the waterworks and told a community service worker that he was missing—that he needed his heart medication. A small manhunt for him went off, and ended in catching my dad with his pants at his ankles, him listening to Barry White in a glamping tent with another woman.

"Wow. What an asshole."

My throat closes, thinking about all that. The first time in a long time. I cough to regain my focus. "Yeah, it's disappointing. Still is."

"No, I mean it. What a self-centered loser to lay such a judgment on a kid, on his own son. You didn't deserve that," she growls.

"Thanks. Did I miss something? I've never seen you get worked up over anyone who wasn't a client."

She smooths back a loose hair. "Oh? I guess I have some maternal instincts after all."

I raise an eyebrow.

Addison scoffs, then scans the floorboards. "All right, maybe not. But it . . . it hurts me to think of you that way. Exposed and discarded." She lifts her gaze to mine, the hint of a smile on her face. "I'm the only one who can do that to you."

"Oh yeah? Thanks, I think." I go to join her in the front sitting room, hugging the edges of the kitchen like I might spook a stray animal. My heart beats in my throat while Addison shifts her weight to the other foot—as if she, too, is aware that something just passed between us. An "authentic moment," she might term it to her media contacts.

"So, the item," I say. "What did you find at Phinneas Redwood's house the night that he died?"

Addison purses her lips. "A business card. For a tailor. With a series of letters and numbers written on it that I think refer to the final night of Fashion Week. The letters are A and S."

"Your initials."

She nods.

I cross to the dining table. "I'll get my laptop. Search on your phone for the Monaco news outlets and see if there's any mention of a note or something similar. I'll search in Italian, since Monégasques speak that, too. Let's see how much you should be worried."

We're at it for an hour. Two hours, while I sneak glances at Addison across the table, above the air plant I got in Santa Barbara. Is this what Stockholm syndrome is like? My nearly atrophied PI muscles are warming up—just as when I sat outside Devon Lim's Santa Barbara home playing Six Degrees of Kevin Bacon—along with other organs that come alive when I stare at my antagonist's face.

The smooth skin of her neck. Her palm, pressed against her cheek.

Twice, her foot brushes up against mine underneath the table. The second time I swear she does it deliberately, before apologizing and moving away.

We break for dinner, after getting lost in European Reddit threads that suggest surveillance systems are "hyper easy" to hack and could be modified to remove someone's image from a late-night recording.

Over pizza—thin crust at Addison's insistence—the conversation again turns to Phinneas's death note. "Why would Phinneas want you to pay attention to the last night of Fashion Week?" I ask.

"I don't know, honestly. I've done browser searches using the sequence forward and backward. It comes up as a flight number, serial numbers for industrial ventilation fans, and some product related to molecular engineering. The only thing that makes sense is that Friday. Maybe Phinneas was planning on attending as part of some cross-promotional scheme and wanted to tell me, before he got murdered."

"What about that tailor from the card? I can't find anything online that would link Phinneas to the owner. Did Phinneas ever mention him to you before?"

Addison shakes her head. "Never."

"Well, we should check it out. Ask some questions in person."

"Ugh. Probably." Addison stretches her arms behind her head, arching her back. She took off her red jacket an hour ago, revealing a tight black sleeveless sweater underneath. Soft curves seem more pronounced against the knit fabric, pushing against her clothing. She moans.

"God, I'm so over this. I thought we were done when we found Devon. I thought finding his corpse would seal the deal on my innocence, as the surveillance footage would have to show someone sneaking in before me. Now I feel like that was just the depressing start to a greater pupu platter."

"Have you ever seen *Footloose*?"

"Excuse me?"

"The movie. With Kevin Bacon."

She stares at me, totally blank.

"It was his big break into movies as a struggling actor. But afterward, he spent his entire paycheck over, like, a week and was broke again and waiting tables. It wasn't until he filmed a cameo in the movie *JFK* that he really hit it big."

Addison yawns. "What's the point of story time, Connor?"

"Sometimes the big break isn't actually what it looks like. The important thing is to keep going."

She's thoughtful a moment. Soaking in the wisdom I have to offer. Or that Kevin Bacon has to offer. "Well, I would never want to be an actor. I've got too many dead bodies in my past for that." Addison rises from her chair. "Figuratively, of course. I'm getting a drink."

Her words linger in my head. *Too many dead bodies.* I looked into Addison's history—a long time ago. She is being facetious about dead bodies. And yet, familiar suspicion of her returns at the mention that she could be hiding something I didn't uncover. Addison had a tough upbringing in Lancaster, north of LA, living on food stamps in a trailer park with her mother. Her father left when she was a baby but was in and out of her life during her childhood. For the first time, I wonder how all of that affected her.

"You only have Two Buck Chuck? What kind of home is this?" Addison shouts from the pantry.

Someone knocks at the front door. Addison stops rifling through bottles and peeks her head out over the bar counter. We aren't expecting anyone. Without a word, she steps to the bar counter. Her hand drifts to hover above a knife we used earlier to slice up the pizza.

I cross to the front door, the floorboards announcing my

approach. I reach for Addison's coat on a bench beneath the window, then withdraw the pepper spray she carries in her pocket. Armed with only the possibility of inflicting a painful thirty seconds, I pause at the peephole. A woman stares back at me. Blond and petite.

"Who is it?" I ask.

"Hyacinth Aspen."

Addison grunts behind me. "Who?"

I open the door. "Can I help you?"

Hyacinth, the picture of a younger version of her mother, Genevieve, trembles on the porch. "Can I come in?"

Alarm bells wail in my head at the idea of letting this person, this stranger, inside. But I've worked with her mother over the years and dug up many of their family secrets at Genevieve's direction, including that she was born *Jenna* Miller, though she didn't share that with me. I know that Hyacinth is twenty-six, a little naïve for her age—the result of an affluent and sheltered upbringing—and will put hot sauce on anything. Like, literally, she throws Red Hot Rooster on salads.

"Ah yes. Sure." I step back and let her enter.

Addison narrows her eyes at us from where she stands in the kitchen. "Hello," she says, now wielding the knife.

"I'm sorry to barge in like this. But I had to come in person," Hyacinth says to me, her voice thick with emotion.

"What can I do for you?" I cross my arms. Hyacinth is more beautiful than I remember. Thick blond hair is thrown up in a messy bun, while crisp blue eyes that shine with unshed tears are stark on her makeup-less face. She clutches her elbows in the floral blouse she wears, and a Bob the Builder cell phone cover pokes out from the front pocket of her baggy jeans.

"I—I've been a wreck ever since . . ." Hyacinth trails off. "My mother has a security detail on me at all times these days—she's so paranoid since Devon's—" A sob escapes her as her hand flies to her mouth.

"Do you want to sit?" I offer.

"No, no. Really. I don't have much time. I just managed to slip out of a restaurant while the bodyguard grabbed a burger. I got into an Uber. He'll be here any second."

"How did you know where I'm staying? Why did you come looking for me?"

Hyacinth purses her lips. "My mom told me. I'm here to . . . I need to ask. Did you see Devon cheating on me with another woman? Tell me the truth."

Her voice breaks at the end, but she straightens. I shake my head. "I didn't. I'm not sure what you know—"

"Mom said he was on camera sneaking a woman into my house—her guesthouse—while I was on a wine-tasting trip. Then I heard Devon talking to a woman on the phone, telling her he was going to France. He told me it was for business, but it was for pleasure. Romance. He was . . . he was cheating on me. Wasn't he?"

Genevieve shared the security footage with me. Devon led a woman wearing a teal mid-length coat into the guesthouse after midnight but I couldn't see her face, and their interaction did not appear overtly sexual. Their relationship was ambiguous via grainy night vision. The woman left an hour later appearing unhurried, walking across the grass in loafers, then disappearing past the camera's field of view.

"Please," Hyacinth says, taking my hand. "I need answers. And I think you're the only one who can give them to me."

I lick my lips. Search for a way to soften the blow. "He did sneak a woman in, but I don't know if anything transpired between them. There's no evidence that he was cheating. Only that he invited a woman into your home while you were gone."

Genevieve's staff all confirmed what I saw on camera, but of course, the only people who knew what happened after the door shut are Devon and the mystery woman. I had Genevieve's house manager search the property's other camera angles for a possible sighting of the woman's car or license plate. No dice.

Hyacinth takes a small step away from me. Tears spill down the apples of her cheeks. "Then my mother was right. If it walks like a duck and talks like a duck . . . Devon cheated on me."

I stiffen, feeling Addison's heavy gaze on us both. The knife glints in my peripheral vision. "I'm sorry, Miss Aspen. I wish I had more specifics for you."

A car door slams out front. She flinches at the sound. "Call me Hy. And thank you."

She pulls me into a hug, wrapping her arms around my waist. She lingers a second longer than I was ready for. Then the would-be widow reaches for the door and slips outside. A minute goes by. Neither Addison nor I move while a car engine fades into the distance.

"So . . . strawberry vodka, then?" Glass clinks in the kitchen as Addison finds what she wants. She brings me a pint glass with two inches of liquid. I raise an eyebrow at her.

"No proper cups." She lifts her coffee mug in a toast. "I gather her mother is your client. Genevieve Aspen."

I run my hand across my jaw. "Yeah. No way to keep confidentiality about her identity now."

"I've seen Genevieve at hedge-fund events." She nods.

"Hyacinth seemed into you."

"Yeah. She did." I take a sip of the fruity liquid. Lock the front door. "That was weird."

When I turn back, Addison is inches from my face. I jump. She smiles, as if she enjoys my surprise. My fear.

She traces a finger along my jaw, then draws it across my lips. She sucks her own finger a moment, never breaking eye contact. "You splashed some vodka there. Don't worry. I got it."

"Addison Stern. Are you jealous?"

She laughs, raising her chin. "I'm competitive. And we've made some good progress tonight. I feel like celebrating."

"Oh, and being held in my arms would be a good thing, then. Not a distraction?"

Addison peers up at me from beneath dark lashes. "It would be the bubbles in freshly poured champagne. The best part."

I pull her close, too eager to hold her to question her logic. Our mouths connect, and she tastes of pizza and alcohol and conquest.

We tumble into the bedroom, a small space with only a queen bed, bumping into wall fixtures as we land on the comforter. She takes off her knit tank, then shimmies out of her jeans, and I do likewise, too confused by the last fifteen minutes to second-guess myself. We climb into bed as I hitch her knee up to my chest.

"Hey, Addison, we're not in Italy this time. Should we—?"

Addison responds by pulling me to her—to the red lace bra she either wears all the time or chose this morning because she intended for this to happen. "Quiet now," she whispers.

Then she arches her back and leads me inside with a moan.

CHAPTER TWENTY-SIX

ADDISON

SILVER LAKE | SEPTEMBER 27

Bloodcurdling screams pierce my sleep, and I am wide-awake in the gray hospital room, clutching at the paper gown I wear and fumbling for my phone on Connor's nightstand. Wait.

"Hello?" I mumble into my cell, the half dream dissipating fully. Judging from the headache I have now, the alcohol that Connor and I imbibed all night might not have been top shelf.

The dream was a nightmare, actually. In it, whoever killed Phinneas had been following me since the night I discovered his body. They attacked me, sending me to Cedars-Sinai. A woman had just entered my room when my cell phone's chiming ringtone interrupted the scene.

"Addison. It's Velvet. I need you to catch the first plane to Chicago. Like, now."

I sit up in bed. Throw off the white comforter. Connor stirs beside me, shirtless. And distracting. I swing my feet over the side, away from him.

"What happened?" I find my jeans and my top thrown across the accent bench along the wall; both clothing items are wrinkled. I sigh, yanking them on.

"It's my ex-husband. He's threatening to reveal the identities of my biggest patrons."

I pause. Velvet's ex, Mike Wadsworth, cut off contact ages ago, according to her—he works in law enforcement as the deputy chief of Chicago Police. I would never guess he'd risk harming their respective careers and reputations by even hinting at knowledge of Velvet's business. Anything that Velvet did—or didn't do, if I'm asked—reflects badly on him. "That's concerning. But why do I need to be in Chicago today?"

Velvet sucks in a breath. "Because he's threatening to do it on live television this afternoon. If he blabs about who has visited my club, this could be a disaster for my new career. I need your help, Addison."

"I'm on the next flight out."

"Who was that?" Connor yawns as I end the call.

"Velvet Eastman. I'm needed in Chicago. Keep looking for how Jamie Mendez might relate to Phinneas's death—and to Devon's."

Connor sits up against the headboard. Sunlight trails into the bedroom through the window blinds, casting a patchy pattern on his tan skin. Thick hair falls across his eyes, and I have a flash of when we first slept together three years ago. He traced circles on my arm until I fell asleep. Then I woke to daylight and him sitting upright like he is now, not moving, not wanting to disturb my dreams. He still likes to cuddle, the polar opposite of me.

"Good morning to you, too."

I zip up my jeans, then pause. "Don't let orgasms cloud your vision, Connor. We have work to do, especially if Mendez is actually targeting you."

He smirks. "You know you can just set me loose, right? No micromanagement needed?"

I sit beside him, the mattress dipping beneath our weight. His hand snakes its way around my waist, and I lean into him like he never moved to Nevada.

"Lesser men have lost everything for speaking to me that way."

Connor smiles. His touch is cool against my neck. "Good thing I don't have anything left." He kisses me, the warmth of his lips spiraling to my stomach and below. I curl my fingers into soft brown waves, pulling him closer for a deeper kiss. When he pushes my sweater from my shoulder—begins trailing his mouth across my collarbone—I break the moment, short of breath.

"I'll be back tomorrow. You can convince me what a rebel you are then."

"I'll practice my brooding stare." Connor repositions my sweater. "Hey. What changed last night?"

"What do you mean?" I check my cell phone's clock. I still need to go home and pack a bag before leaping over to LAX.

Connor shifts so that he sits straighter against the pillows. "I mean, why did we . . . why did you—"

"Decide on champagne?"

"Yeah. After saying you thought that . . . champagne would be a distraction."

I soak up the image of Connor Windell, my onetime boyfriend and longtime nemesis, shirtless with only a sheet covering the bottom half of his body. Then envision a younger, more innocent, teen version of him seeking out his dad along the LA River. A version not unlike myself at that age—a little lost, with a chip on my shoulder and a hunger for what I thought was due to me.

"I think I just felt more connected to you," I reply. "You felt—this all felt—safe."

Connor warms me with his gaze. "Well, it will all be here for you when you get back."

\\\\\////

Thanks to a miracle of light traffic, and mobile apps that allow me to book my flight and a town car while I pack, I'm up in the air before rush hour ends. Chicago smells like deep-dish and exhaust the moment I step from O'Hare International into my taxi, but I maintain a straight face. The real antagonist today is time.

On the four-hour flight here, I sought out every internet tidbit on Mike Wadsworth across the last thirty years—the time span of his career spent in service to the greater Chicago area. Messaged my contacts within Illinois state lines, each of whom returned zilch on the man. The majority of my findings were, sadly, positive: awards, accolades, and community events that recognized Mike for his contributions to the city as a police officer. Only a few negative reviews popped up, mostly of Chicago law enforcement in general, one of which mentioned Mike by name. Still, there was nothing compelling enough to suit my need: straight leverage. An online neighborhood bulletin board even included a post from a woman who announced she named her baby boy after Mike.

Without concrete information to use against him, and time dwindling before my plane landed, I wrote down all the arguments in favor of Mike Wadsworth keeping his mouth shut. Ultimately, I settled on the simplest message: karma. Never do to others what you don't want to come back around to you in a cosmic sucker punch.

At the polished birch reception desk, a young man with peach fuzz shoots me a smile. "Welcome to the Dynemax Tower, home of Chicago's CNBW-7. How can I help you?"

"I'm Mike Wadsworth's publicist. He's being interviewed on *Today in Chi-Town* in twenty-two minutes, and I needed to be upstairs"—I lift my phone to eye level—"thirty minutes ago."

The receptionist hesitates. "I'm sorry, what was your name again?"

"Addison Stern."

"You're not on any list."

I glare at him, funneling my fatigue and irritation at Mike's idiocy—his audacity in threatening to reveal Velvet's leverage over half the important men in the country—into my narrowed gaze. "I'm also his wife, and he hasn't taken his medication today. Do you want him to have an epileptic fit live on camera?"

The receptionist shows me to a pair of gold-plated elevators. "Take the one on the left to the seventeenth floor," he says, then retreats behind his desk, safely out of my reach. Or so he thinks.

Mirrored doors slide shut. Then I'm whisked through one of the tallest buildings in the city. The woman who stares back at me is calm, not even a smidge of red lipstick out of place. She smiles.

"Smug much?" I murmur. Connor seems to like her, though—despite everything. On the flight here, I took a break from writing strategies for managing Velvet's ex and thought about everything

Connor and I have experienced since he broke into my apartment a month ago. While not the reunion I would have envisioned, having Connor back in my life has been . . . nice. Fun. Sexy, and even a little romantic. The thick layer of ice around my heart has begun to thaw recently, like a glacier in July.

Once, a long time ago, I thought I might have been in love with him. Possibly. Prior to the dialing malfunction of his Land Rover. He was arrogant, ambitious, and driven in all the ways I prized about myself then. He's still those things, but at a lower volume, for some reason. A dialed-down version of himself that, happily, allows my light to shine at stadium-level wattage.

The elevator slows to a halt. With a ding, the doors open onto a bustling scene of pantsuits, pointed heels, and loafers scurrying across the shining tile. I turn right onto a long hallway that I know leads to the greenrooms, thanks to Google images and Velvet's recollection. Although I've never been in this building before, Velvet gave me the layout and said to check Greenroom 1 first, which is where she's stayed each of the three times she's been interviewed on camera here. I find Mike noshing on a giant bowl of M&M's.

"Mr. Wadsworth," I say, shutting the door behind me. "We need to talk."

Mike is alone in a room painted blue, ironically, with framed photos of some of the biggest celebrities to grace the soundstage of CNBW-7. Thinning hair probably normally hidden by a police cap is styled to the side, strands alternating between brown and gray. A shiny maroon dress shirt is unbuttoned too low, revealing chest hairs playing a game of peekaboo. I would fix it for him, but he's not my client. He's the opposite, in fact. In this moment, he's my client's enemy.

"Who are you?"

"Addison Stern. Velvet Eastman's publicist."

Mike straightens. He dusts his hands over the candy bowl. "Then you'll know I'm deputy chief, and I don't care for being harassed."

"Mr. Wadsworth—"

"Deputy Chief."

"Deputy Chief, your ex-wife shared with me that you plan to divulge her former patrons' names on live television, in the name of your planned run for mayor next year. Something about bolstering public trust in you, despite your history with a female entrepreneur."

He barks a laugh. "Is that what you call the two-bit handler of an illegal whorehouse?"

"Gentlemen's club of consenting adults that centered sex work and women's safety. Velvet is an innovator. And I'm here to remind you that sharing her hard-earned secrets would be a very bad idea."

Only one side of Mike's thick mustache slides up. "Is that a threat?"

A male voice shouts in the hall beyond the door. "The cat segment goes in two minutes!"

"Of course not, Deputy Chief." I slide both hands into the pockets of my white peacoat. The picture of innocence. "Harassment of a law enforcement officer wouldn't be very wise. It's a fact. To share Velvet's professional data that was gained while you were married to her would only be used by your critics to show that you are a fair-weather seeker of justice. You only pursue it when it suits you. Isn't that right?"

"Absolutely not. I was married to Velvet back when she was only called Ashley, when we were both in our late teens, while I was still in high school. We separated for a few years but didn't divorce until later. It was during that time that she started her business—" He uses air quotes around the word. "And way before I got into law enforcement."

I drag my index finger along the soft back of an upholstered armchair. "Still. You did join law enforcement, then kept mum about your knowledge of Velvet's undertaking during the last—oh, thirty years. Do you really think voters will forgive the omission simply because you provide a laundry list of Dirty Harrys? I doubt it. Especially when I tell everyone it was a family business and you enjoyed the profits of Velvet's hard work."

Mike drops his gaze to the carpet—itself a shade of blue. "I'll have to think about it. I promised the network a big announcement today."

"Tell them you're running for mayor next year."

He shoots me a look. "I already announced. Last month."

Sloppy, Addison. Too many orgasms are making me sloppy. "Then tell them . . ."

The news circuit hasn't yet moved on from Phinneas's unsolved murder. Google Alerts has been sending me articles that mention Phinneas on all the major national platforms. This morning's from CNN ran alongside the headline WHY IS JUSTICE SO ELUSIVE FOR PEOPLE OF SHORT STATURE?

"Tell them you're close to uncovering who killed Phinneas Redwood."

Mike pauses. "The diet pill guy?"

"The unsolved murder victim who's gracing every home page across social media and browser pages nationally. You could be the altruistic—"

"Overreaching—"

"—candidate for mayor who wants to extend help wherever it's needed. No matter the zip code. As you would do for the broad and diverse neighborhoods of Chicago."

Mike stares at me, as if seeing me for the first time since I entered the blue greenroom. "And how exactly am I supposed to be close to uncovering the killer's identity?"

I pluck a red M&M from the pile. "An anonymous source."

"You?"

"Someone who always comes through when they say they will."

The door opens behind me. A young woman with a headset and a clipboard pops her head in. "Mr. Wadsworth? You're on in one minute. We need to start walking."

"Think about it," I say to Mike. "Make the right decision for both you and Velvet."

"You really don't know, do you?"

I pause at the door, past the anxious production assistant checking her cell phone's clock, and stifle a sigh. I hate any suggestion that I'm not up to speed on the latest. "Do tell."

Mike shakes his head. "You have no idea who you're working with."

"Yet somehow I'll sleep just fine tonight."

I continue down the hall to the elevator without a backward glance. Seventeen floors later, as I walk through the lobby, I catch Mike's segment on an oversize television mounted next to reception. The camera closes in on his face, which boasts the kind of wrinkles you only get from caring about others seven days a week. The banner beneath him, which cuts off the errant chest hairs, reads: A BIG ANNOUNCEMENT FROM CHICAGO'S DEPUTY CHIEF MIKE WADSWORTH.

The news anchor laughs, too earnest, too chipper. "That's right, we are all dying to hear this revelation from you, Deputy

Chief. Is it the truth about what's really in the Chicago River?"

Dry chuckles all around. Sweat glistens along Mike's hairline as he clears his throat. "Yes. Uh, yeah—I mean, no, nothing about the river."

Awkward silence. Mike smiles, sweet but not too effusive, and I know his decision.

I exit through the glass doors of the tower to the tune of Deputy Chief Mike Wadsworth saying, "Phinneas Redwood. CEO of Thrive, Inc. You heard of him? I'm working on uncovering who murdered the poor guy."

CHAPTER TWENTY-SEVEN

ADDISON

WEST HOLLYWOOD | SEPTEMBER 28

T he flight home is quick and relatively painless, thanks to the first-class ticket on Ovid Blackwell's dime. I would have taken the company jet, but Mr. Griffin insisted it stay with him in the Bahamas. Something about reducing our carbon footprint by a flight or two.

Peter nearly pitched a fit when he heard I traveled to Illinois for a thirty-six-hour trip, but he got on board when I told him the context: It was do or die for Velvet Eastman; go there or allow all the goodwill we'd been—*I'd* been—building for her debut to tank before Fashion Week. There was no way we could let Velvet's trade secrets slip through her fingers and earn her new powerful public enemies before this next chapter even began. Especially when

243

Phinneas's note directed me to the final night of the weeklong event.

Dusk sets in through the blinds of my apartment. I'm not jet-lagged, but I am exhausted when I cross the threshold. A neighbor's dog yips erratically, then falls silent. The only outside noise audible from where I lean against my counter is the gentle hum of traffic that soaks the Los Angeles terrain.

I pour myself a glass. Bordeaux. The spiced flavor of currant washes down my throat as if the liquid were an actual massage. I relax. Take a breath after the craziness of the last day and a half. Despite a number of obstacles lately, I'm still managing to do my job—and damn well, at that.

Of course, I did promise a high-ranking police officer that I would find Phinneas's killer. At the time, my instinct was to promise a scandal-adjacent revelation. I figured that I was already working to get back on top at Ovid Blackwell by uncovering his attacker; why not offer the identity to Mike Wadsworth sometime in the future—when my client needed his silence today? With any luck, the killer will catch wind of Mike's announcement, too, and start to feel my breath down their neck. Nothing like a little added pressure to make someone fumble their next move.

My phone lights up with a text message. Connor.

Are you home?

We've been trading texts since I left his Airbnb yesterday morning. When my plane hit the tarmac at LAX, my phone lit up with five new messages, each more urgent than the last. I tried calling him when I got into a town car, but he insisted via text that he couldn't tell me anything over the phone—that he needed to tell me in person.

I reply:

> Just got back. I'll come over in a
> couple hours.

Although my hotel was first-rate in Chicago and I treated myself to a nice dinner for a successful trip, I'm beat. I deserve a little apéritif.

My phone vibrates with another text. This time from Tony Hopkins, the government fawn:

> Against my better judgment, I wanted to
> give you a heads up.

Three dots blink in a quick pattern as I wait for Tony to type out his next message. I take another sip of my Bordeaux. Then:

> Councilmember Gaines got clued in this
> afternoon that Variety is doing a piece on
> you, and other industry leaders who have
> had recent scandals – she's withdrawing
> her public support of Velvet's new line.
> Sorry. The piece should hit tomorrow.
> Apparently, an anonymous source says
> you're more involved in that Redwood
> murder than anyone has reported.
> And they shared that you once illegally
> obtained info for work, which then net you
> a new corner office. Must be nice.

"Seriously?" I growl. Just what I need—more public scrutiny of me, this time with the added bonus of another setback to

Velvet's integration into the fashion world. Terrific.

A new text from Tony appears at the bottom of my screen:

> Don't say I never did anything for you. And forget you ever saw me at the Garage in WeHo.

Footsteps climb my porch, followed by a knock at my door. "Addison, it's me."

"Connor?"

Cracking his knuckles, then shifting his weight to the other foot, Connor peers into the peephole, shaping his head into a strange oblong. Déjà vu washes over me as the wine spools through my core. He looks the same way he did in the hotel hallway in the French Riviera. Anxious. Nervous, like he's got some bomb to drop on me. As if he's hiding something.

Is he the anonymous source dishing to *Variety*? He's the only person who would care that, years ago, I was awarded an office with a view at his expense. I open the door. "You couldn't wait?"

He shakes his head, then beckons me onto the porch. "No. I need to show you something."

Connor drives us down Sunset Boulevard into Beverly Hills. When he valets the Land Rover in the circular driveway of one of the most well-known hotels in the country, I turn to him. "I thought you were more practical than this. You rented a room at the Beverly Hilton?"

He shakes his head. "It's something else."

A sense of foreboding comes over me as I step onto the buffed curb. This is where the Pharma for Female Gala took place, weeks ago. The event that was meant to be Phinneas's debut back into society, and instead coincided with his murder.

We enter through a glass door held open by a bellhop like it's the most natural thing in the world—it is for me, at least— then Connor directs us right, past the deep-red reception and concierge desks through the bustling lobby. Beneath vaulted ceilings, we continue down a sprawling hallway illuminated by teardrop crystal chandeliers, our footsteps rapping a brisk rhythm against dark polished floor that reflects the hem of my jumpsuit. Crowds of tourists and guests that we pass admire the thick, sky-blue drapes framing floor-to-ceiling windows that overlook Wilshire Boulevard and conduct amateur photo shoots while posing on the luxury wraparound settees in the middle of the hall.

Connor turns into an empty conference room—no, ballroom. According to the plaque beside the entrance, the Verdant Glen ballroom features a max capacity of three hundred.

Instead of leading us farther into the rectangular space or to examine one of the paintings on the walls, Connor pauses beside an open book on a lectern. Signatures and brief messages are written across the unlined pages. A guest book.

"Connor, why are we here? The Golden Globes don't happen until January." I want to shine a flashlight above his face and interrogate him about his contacts at *Variety* magazine—but I'm also intrigued by the darty way he keeps stealing glances at me. What is he driving toward?

"Yes, and what other events are held here?"

"All kinds." I pan a hand across the empty room and its birch hardwood floor. "Anything one wants, probably, with the right number of zeros as payment."

"Small conferences. Team-building seminars. What else?"

"Galas. Connor, get to the point. I've had a busy thirty-six hours."

"Shareholders meetings. Profitability votes. Investor presentations."

I scan the signatures along the nearest page. "Whose, exactly?"

Connor lifts a finger, then begins flipping backward in the book. One page. Two. Three. "Back when his company was first formed, Phinneas attended a meeting of venture capitalists right here in this very room and discussed it in an early *GQ* interview. It was here that he convinced his investors to take a chance on him as a freshly graduated pharmaceutical engineer. It was here that board meetings were held for the first five years of the company's formation while Phinneas was searching for a permanent office space befitting what he thought was his groundbreaking product."

"Wow. How did you think to look at his *GQ* interview?"

He continues to flip backward, as if ignoring me. The tome is larger than I realized, its pages thinner than I first thought. "Addison, I searched different European news outlets for any mention of a note at Devon's hotel crime scene or some object left behind that might incriminate you—but I didn't find anything. Instead, I went back to Jamie Mendez and thought about why a pickup truck from his entourage might have followed us to Hashim Swartz's building."

"I'm listening."

"What if Hashim was downplaying his true opinion of Phinneas, knowing that Phinneas was murdered? He wouldn't want word getting around that he actually thought Phinneas was an idiot, draining Thrive, Inc. of its profitability. That's not a good look for an investor with a potential motive."

Right. We talked about this. Pop music from the Top 100 blares across this room, not dampened by guests checking in or taking selfies.

"But Hashim's record stands pretty clean. He's just a rich expat splitting time between LA and Frankfurt. Mendez, however—he's got a colorful past. And according to public disclosures of his own campaign contributions during his first and second runs for office, he's pretty loaded."

"With possible mob ties," I note. "So you knew Thrive, Inc. held meetings here and thought you'd ask management if Jamie Mendez and Hashim Swartz ever met."

Connor shakes his head. He flips almost to the very front of the book, then points to a signature beneath a date. The year 1987 is written in block letters. "Better. I know they have."

I step to the lectern and recognize Hashim Swartz's name at the top corner, then a list of other names underneath. Jamie Mendez features near the bottom, above Phinneas's name.

"So they were both early investors in Thrive?"

Connor stands straighter in the glow of the hotel's ornate light fixtures. "This puts all three of them in the same room at the same time. Hashim Swartz sits on the board of directors of Thrive, Inc., and Jamie Mendez publicly disclosed that Swartz was among the largest donors to support his run for the House of Representatives. The storefront we drove past with the black construction paper on the windows is the business address registered as his campaign headquarters."

"Wait a minute, wait." I step back from the lectern. "Mendez has the shady background, I'll give you that. But would he really kill Phinneas or have him killed if he's running for a spot in the House? What would be so dire that he'd ruin his political career to get Phinneas murdered?"

A group of housewives in Chanel tweed march down the hall, complaining about lumber cost increases. Connor leans closer to me. "It would make sense if Mendez was bleeding money into a company that he thought Phinneas was tanking. If Phinneas was more of a liability than an asset at this point."

"And Devon, and Annalise Meier?"

Connor pouts his lower lip. "Collateral damage, maybe. Devon and Annalise were privy to a business meeting or transaction gone wrong, before Devon hightailed it to Europe to hide out. I also learned that Annalise Meier was a double major at Stanford: English and human rights. She worked for the Human Rights Commission in Hong Kong, in the Wan Chai district. If Phinneas was working with Devon Lim on some kind of app for his new product, and Annalise consulted for Devon, or for them both, to ensure international labor standards were followed, she could have been a direct target of the killer—more than a bystander with bad luck. Or maybe Phinneas confided something to Annalise. After all, she was important enough to frame."

The group of women doubles back the way they came, laughing. One of them sloshes a drink that stains another woman's cream skirt. More laughter.

"What does that mean?" I ask.

Connor takes a photo of the guest book pages with his phone. "What's that?"

"Important enough to *frame*. No one framed her for anything. And we discussed that Phinneas dated Annalise, but not how important she was or wasn't to him."

In Phinneas's office, he had a single framed photo on his bookshelf. An image from college of Phinneas and Annalise. Her cheek, pressed close to Phinneas's sparse facial hair, as if they were good friends, possibly romantic. Black undyed hair was swept up in a ponytail, while dark brown eyes framed a strong aquiline nose. How could Connor have seen this picture?

Connor shrugs. "It's just an expression. I'm sure she was significant to Phinneas."

"She was his girlfriend, a long time ago, though not a business partner," I continue, focused. "Phinneas made it clear to me how much she meant to him."

"Someone confessed their more vulnerable feelings to you? That's a surprise." Connor's tone turns acidic. "If Annalise Meier was an old friend—or ex, or whatever—of Phinneas, then she could have introduced Phinneas to Devon, just like you said. Important enough."

"What is your deal? Why are you getting upset?"

Connor huffs. "Did you ever do PR for Annalise?"

"No. I would have told you."

"Really?" He lurches forward. "You lied to me. Two nights ago, Hyacinth Aspen came over to the Airbnb and said she heard Devon telling a woman over the phone that he would be in France. Then you seduced me. You wanted me to forget those details before I connected the dots."

I narrow my gaze. "What dots are those?"

"You knew exactly where Devon was, the whole time. You let me bust my ass all over Southern California—up to Santa Barbara, then Bel-Air—all the while knowing he was headed to France. You only copped to the information about his French Riviera home when I figured out that his drug arrest was published by the German news outlet."

"Okay, all true. But it doesn't mean—"

"You were the woman on the phone call with Devon that

Hyacinth overheard. You've been lying to me for weeks. What else are you lying about?"

"Look, I may have been the person that Devon called, but—"

"Does that make you the only living person, beside his fiancée, who knew Devon's location, and where to find him?" Connor glares at me, the accusation flung out in the open. As if he already knows the answer to his question.

I draw a shallow breath. "Devon called to tell me he was going to France, it's true. He wanted to know if he should stay stateside, to vouch for me. There was so much attention and suspicion swirling around me then."

"Oh, really? Devon Lim was a billionaire altruist?"

"He was a nice person, yes."

"Who would do anything for . . . his publicist?" Connor shakes his head. "Nope, doesn't sound right to me, either."

I level him with a stare. "I was acting in my client's best interest at the time. And you said that Annalise Meier was important enough to frame."

Connor pauses. "You said she was . . ."

"I said she was Phinneas's girlfriend," I interrupt. "I never mentioned the fact that she was the only framed photo in his office. Only someone who has been there would know that. Not even the media has had access to that part of the crime scene, so there's no way of knowing without visiting the site. You did work for Phinneas at one point. Did you hold some grudge against him?"

Connor scans the hall of clustered tourists and cushioned benches along the wall.

"Addison, no. I didn't hold any grudge against Phinneas. You—"

"That's right, *you* have been cursing my name ever since you left Los Angeles."

"What does that mean?"

"*Variety*. I just learned I'm being included in a takedown piece by *Variety* magazine on entertainment industry professionals who have been hit by scandals. You're the anonymous source for it, who complained I stole info from you for profit. Isn't that right?"

"No—that's not—" Connor sputters.

I've got him. Cornered him, after he had the nerve to suggest, yet again, that I might have harmed a client. And still, a sticky feeling of remorse taints the usual glow of winning. Connor was my partner in all this—my lover and my first friend in ages. I don't usually have friends, not when it comes to my line of work. There's no loyalty in true ambition.

Connor shakes his head. "I didn't act as a source against you. To anyone, although I could make my own Wiki page of all the ways you've wronged people by this point. No, I'm just another casualty on the long list of people you stepped on to advance."

"Don't do that—don't pretend you're some victim." The words I used to scream at my mother tumble from my mouth with ease. New nausea pinches my stomach, but I push on: "You knew Phinneas before any of this happened. You lied to me, Connor. You broke my trust, too. Again."

I don't need him. I don't need anyone. Growing up in poverty and with a neglectful single mother who cared more about garnering sympathy from the neighbors for her ailment of the week than her daughter, I learned that I am truly the only person I can count on. And I am the very best to have in my corner.

"You're right," Connor starts. "I didn't tell you about doing work for Phinneas, because I knew you would jump to this conclusion, that I could be to blame somehow—"

"Oh, I'm not being fair to you? Really? Let me guess. Phinneas owed you money for a job. Sounds like motive for murder to me."

"Addison, cut that shit out! You can't just say whatever comes to mind during a homicide investigation—"

"If you're frustrated with how it's gone, maybe you only have your terrible professional record to blame!"

He flinches, and I know the cut landed. "Keep singing the same tune, Addison. Your wit is showing."

I search for the words to twist the knife and be done with this whole charade of parity. Of mutual respect—emotional connection. "Well, you're just a loose-lipped PI, and now you're linked to a murder, as far as anyone's concerned."

Color drains from his face. "At least I know what it's like to have people trust me. You'll never experience that burden because you're an unlovable opportunist, Addison. No one could ever care for you. You're only out for yourself. I see that now."

Laughter carries from the bar past the lobby, contrasting with the sickly tension of the ballroom. I don't reply. Connor is spot-on about me, yet again. A flush climbs my neck—embarrassment at seeing the only person I've cared for in years, on more than a utilitarian level, describe me in such heartless terms.

Am I heartless? I always considered myself pragmatic. But hearing Connor's ruthless assessment of me, I'm not so sure.

Connor lied to me—for weeks—probably waiting until the right time to strike with this *Variety* piece. And while it's not like I opened myself up and tucked the key to my heart in his back pocket, I gave him more of me this time around than I ever thought possible. Only to learn our recent relationship was steeped in dishonesty. On both sides.

Without a backward glance, Connor snakes a path between tourists down the embroidered carpet runner. He takes the corner, toward the main entrance, as my mother's voice comes to mind: *Addison, you spoiled brat. You don't care about me. You don't care about anyone but yourself.*

I spot a large-brimmed pink sun hat up ahead at the restaurant's bar. The housewives will have asked the bartender to pop a white wine from a good year. One that will taste crisp and clear. Not the same as the bubbles of victory. But I'll accept any filter that dulls this sour taste in my mouth.

CHAPTER TWENTY-EIGHT

PHINNEAS

BENEDICT CANYON | AUGUST 2

PHINNEAS REDWOOD: *It's been a fun ride, hasn't it? Today is Wednesday, and I just realized it's thirty-five years to the day that Thrive, my miracle pill, went on the market. I was twenty-three years old, fresh out of graduate school, just having completed the accelerated PhD program and wielding more money than I knew what to do with. Enter a few questionable choices—women, mostly—and you've got the next decade of my life. It was a good time, though. The only people who say money doesn't buy happiness are those who have never gone without it.*

[Old-fashioned ringtone]

Oho! Wow. I did not expect to see this name again. That can't be good. Hello?

MAN: *Mr. Redwood?*

PR: *Speaking.*

MAN: *It's Connor Windell. The private investigator you worked with a few years ago.*

PR: *I recall. To what do I owe this pleasure?*

CONNOR WINDELL: *Listen, I'm sorry to bother you. Do you remember when I was investigating Zenith Puglia for you?*

PR: *That sounds right.*

CW: *Yeah, well, then I hope you also recall I offered you a discount. Because, uh . . . you were experiencing . . . difficulties.*

PR: *I think you mean rehab, but okay.*

CW: *So I gave you a discount at the time, with the under-standing that you would pay back the full price once you landed on your feet. And I just learned that you have a new product coming out this fall—*

PR: *Oh, wow. That's what this is about? You hear that I've got some hot new shit and you've come to claim your share?*

CW: *Mr. Redwood, that's not at all what I'm saying.*

PR: *I barely remember what job you're talking about. Why should I pay you extra for an unmemorable job?*

CW: *I tracked Zenith Puglia's executives as they courted your investors in Europe and Hong Kong, with the understanding that you wanted to know if your investors were . . . two-timing you, essentially.*

PR: *Ohhh. Yes. Yes, that's correct. And you found—*

CW: *That no one had officially partnered with your competitor. But there was growing consensus then that you weren't fit to be CEO. That your business decisions were damaging the company, and the fact that you were reluctant to approve new product ideas was stymieing Thrive's growth.*

PR: *Sounds about right. If I was still in rehab when you were doing this recon, then my investors were more than up-front with their criticisms. Some more than others . . .*

[Pause]

CW: *Well, the job you gave me outlasted your entry into rehab. It was ongoing when you exited the facility ninety days later. You said at the time that your company lost significant value when news of your alcohol addiction surfaced—*

PR: *Alcohol addiction, drug addiction, sex addiction, life addict—*

CW: *Right, and you suggested that you pay me the full sum later when you had the money. Well, I'm guessing you have it now.*

PR: *Didn't you retire? I heard that somewhere.*

CW: *I did.*

PR: *But you need the money now?*

CW: *Pretty badly, actually.* [Slot machine bells ringing]

PR: *Where are you? Are you in Vegas?*

CW: *Look, Mr. Redwood. It would be really helpful if you sent me a Venmo or Zelle or wire with the cash. I'll accept it however is convenient.*

PR: *Carrier pigeon?*

CW: [Sighs] *Yes, yeah. I really need the money.*

PR: *What's the amount? The bill I owe you.*

CW: *Thirty-one thousand dollars.*

PR: [Sputters; coughs] *Seriously? You expect me to Venmo you that? Just so you can gamble it away in Sin City?*

CW: *Or Zelle, or a check. I know you're good for it, Mr. Redwood. And I'm not planning to gamble anymore.*

PR: *Ha! That's rich. I heard that from other rehab guests. "I'll never do it again, just give me one more hit." No. No, I am not good for it. I don't have that much liquid lying around. Hey, you know what? I'm kind of in the middle of something. I gotta go.*

CW: *Mr. Redwood, wait.* [Pause] *I'm not— This isn't some kind of extortion, I just want what's owed to me. Fast. I need the cash.*

PR: *And I need to get back to my work.*

CW: *Mr. Redwood! I—* [Muffled laughter; screaming; slot machine bells ringing] *I learn a lot of things through my work. I know things my clients would probably prefer I don't, but it's all in due course of tracking down information. I'm normally very discreet, but . . .*

PR: *But? . . . You'll use something against me unless I pay thirty-one grand for a job I don't remember asking you to obsess over for months? Who the fuck are you?*

CW: *I'm just . . . an ex-PI, trying to settle up. You have my number. Tell me when you're ready to pay what I'm owed. Or you'll force my hand.*

PR: *And I wouldn't want to do that?*

CW: *No, Mr. Redwood. I'm positive you wouldn't.*

CHAPTER TWENTY-NINE

ADDISON

LOS ANGELES | OCTOBER 9

A small, white-haired woman wearing a floor-length navy dress perches on the edge of a cushy armchair. Knobby fingers twirl the pearls that dangle to her lap.

"And that, my dear, is when I knew that Connor Windell was behind the murder of Devon Lim." Genevieve Aspen leans forward, crossing bony elbows on her knee. Her bright blue eyes are hypnotizing, her speech persuasive.

The interviewer gasps. "Genevieve, that is quite the accusation."

The widow Aspen scoffs. "Only to those without the temerity to speak the truth. The police will sort out the details in due time. I'm just cutting to the chase in advance."

"Wow. Connor should really use her PI." With a quick tap, I turn off the TV in the corner of my office. My reflection in my hard-earned window view offers a mirthless smile. Connor has crossed a few lines in my book. But he doesn't deserve to be smeared across the national daytime circuit. And while Genevieve Aspen has made only one appearance so far, on this afternoon's news segment, I saw that she's slated to be featured on two other talk shows next week. It's only a matter of time before public opinion begins to question Connor's innocence, regardless of the facts.

It might be his comeuppance, considering his contributions to that *Variety* article. Though I'm used to the heat at this point, Peter was not pleased when the edition published over a week ago. He's taken to calling me daily now, to "check in" and see how Velvet's campaign is coming along. Micromanagement that I don't need.

The internet has likewise continued providing screenshots and links to articles naming Phinneas and Ovid Blackwell in the same sentence. Despite their variations on the same information, the police still have no leads. Or none that they're sharing. Which means that after Fashion Week concludes in mere days and my work with Velvet is complete, I'll still be on the equivalent of PR bedrest. A fate worse than not making partner, being restricted from doing my job with existing and new clients means I'm off the radar—which means, if I'm gone long enough, clients could stop requesting me, stop trusting me. I could lose my job if this continues. And starting over at another firm—to begin my career anew—is not an option.

Since Connor left me to Uber home from the Beverly Hilton— we haven't spoken. Not that I had the time to set Connor straight, with a packed schedule the last week and a half doing final prep with Velvet. The live interview she did on *Good Morning LA* went exactly as I planned, along with the three recorded interviews for national news segments.

The flurry of activity has been exactly what I needed. I've only gone to bed before midnight once this week, and then I stared at my phone too long before climbing beneath my thousand-count Egyptian cotton. Debating. Forming the text message in my head: *How could you, Connor? After everything that's happened between us, knowing how hard it is for me to—*

But I didn't send it. Didn't even type it out. And, instead, I chose sleep, recharging and waking up the next day to dominate. No sidekick necessary.

Tonight, Fashion Week begins at the Art Ex, a massive warehouse amphitheater on Sunset Boulevard, where Velvet will make her red carpet debut in approximately one hour. I need to get moving.

A quick pout in the mirror beside my office door affirms my makeup could be featured on the runway later—smoky eye, glossy lips, contouring. After a few meetings with colleagues, but mostly confirming with media representatives that they would feature Velvet's line according to my messaging, I draw the blinds and change into my designer ensemble. Black satin blouse with black trousers. Velvet will arrive at the opening ceremony of Fashion Week in the luxury Escalade I arranged to pick her up from her home, where a team of individuals has been whipping her eau de mid-fifties brothel madam into Chanel No. 55.

"Showtime."

With my cell phone in my roomy front pocket and my usual red carpet emergency supply tote in hand, I stride into the lobby.

Ovid Blackwell's signature entry music, low jazz, is replaced with an upbeat party mix; everyone will be in the Sunset Boulevard exhibition building for the Fashion Week kickoff shortly. I ignore the receptionist who says hello to me, then stop short on the polished tile. A man blocks the elevator doors—FBI Agent Jonas, wearing a black suit and a tie bearing the image of a writing quill. Peter stands beside him wearing an unknowable expression.

"Agent. How nice to see you in my place of business again," I say, simpering. "You look different here than under the airport's fluorescent lighting. Even less astute, somehow."

"Addison, we need to talk," Peter says, ever the Tin Man. "This way, please."

I follow the pair of them to a conference room midway down this floor. It's nearly empty; most of the finance drones have disappeared to a red carpet party. Ovid Blackwell boasts a grand number of designers in this year's display of creativity, and an internal memo this week reminded employees to show up in force.

Peter stands at the head of the table but doesn't sit. I stand next to him, opposite Agent Jonas.

"What is this all about?" I ask. "If you haven't heard, there's an important event tonight, for the company and for my client."

Peter fidgets with a pen. He clicks the top in and out. *Click-click. Click-click.* "We're just waiting on— Ah. Here she is."

Aarin Williams slides into the room, her natural dark curls bouncing at her shoulders. Ovid Blackwell's general counsel. "Am I late?"

"What's going on?" I ask again.

"Thanks, everyone." Agent Jonas scans our PR trio. "As you know, the FBI has been working with the Los Angeles Sheriff's office, as well as cross-referencing information with the French and Monégasque police abroad, as we try to nail down who is behind Phinneas Redwood's death—and now Devon Lim's death."

My skin prickles. "You told this to me at LAX."

"Right. Only now we've examined both crime scenes, reviewed security footage where available, and come to a conclusion."

"Which is?"

Agent Jonas smiles, and a sinking feeling squeezes my gut. "We had to talk to a few people first, though. And you've been busy since you returned stateside. But Hashim Swartz and his venture capitalist firm were accommodating, and so was Posey Delacruz over at Seven Wells Wellness Resort. Even Deputy Chief Mike Wadsworth was happy to chat with a federal agent over in Chicago and tell us how you claimed to know who killed Mr. Redwood."

"I never claimed that. I said I was—"

"That you had an anonymous source who was going to reveal all soon. How miraculous, if you yourself aren't the killer."

Agent Jonas pauses long enough for reality to sink its taloned claws into me, eliciting my fight-or-flight response. I shoot Aarin a look, trying to gauge how bad all this is. She shakes her head an inch, and I have my answer: banished-to-Anaheim bad.

"Addison Stern," he resumes. "We are formally naming you a person of interest in the deaths of Redwood and Lim. All that stands between you and a new title of 'suspect' is the analysis we're running on Mr. Redwood's computer files. Although that's probably not the promotion you'd hope for."

I reach for bravado. "You want to throw in the kitchen sink there, too? Why limit yourself to my clients—why not Annalise Meier's death as well?"

Jonas lifts one eyebrow. "We never publicly named Meier.

Interesting that you know the victim's full name."

Damn. A misstep.

"Is it?" I ask. "Or is it more interesting that you've been eyeing me as a suspect for weeks, yet have only succeeded in calling me a person of interest?"

"We would have named you for the death of Meier, but she's not an American citizen and is out of our jurisdiction. The Monaco police, however, may be contacting you soon."

"So I'm not under arrest."

"No, not yet. The sheriff will provide updates later today on our progress in a press conference. Then it will be public knowledge that you are being investigated as part of these homicides."

"Which means one thing for us, Addison," Peter begins. "You're on unpaid leave, effective immediately." He casts me an apologetic look as the proverbial ax lands across my neck. "I'm sorry. This is not the outcome anyone wanted, and definitely not during Fashion Week."

I turn to Aarin. "Is this—all of this—legal? Isn't there something we can do to stop me from being publicly identified?"

Aarin's eyebrows plunge together. "It's all aboveboard. But"—she glances at Agent Jonas—"if you're named an official suspect in these deaths, then I'll have more to say. For now, my counsel is to sit tight."

I scowl at my sad sack of a VP. "Peter, I have done everything possible to get Velvet Eastman ready for her Fashion Week debut. Do not sideline me here."

Enough emotion fuels my words that my eyes glisten for a moment in a convincing crescendo. I worked my ass off to launch this chapter of Velvet's career, all while trying to find Phinness's killer—the only one-two punch I had to convince

Ovid Blackwell I was ready to resume care of my elite clientele. But I wasn't—Connor wasn't—successful. And now I know Connor was never on my side, either.

Peter's eyebrows pinch together. "Addison, I wish there was another way. But it's company policy that any formal involvement in a criminal investigation by an employee will result in suspension until further notice. We all want to find out what happened to one of our oldest clients."

Peter shifts his attention to Agent Jonas. "I sincerely hope this is the right way to do it. And not another means of sabotaging my innocent employee. Because harassment is not something we take lightly."

"Neither does the FBI take dual murders, Mr. Huxton." Agent Jonas nods to me. "We sent a notice to your Lancaster address, requesting that you come into the FBI office in Downtown LA. I'll see you then."

"Lancaster? That's my mother's house. I haven't lived there in over fifteen years."

Agent Jonas shrugs. "Then you might provide an accurate address on your taxes this year. The notice has all the information you need. We'll be in touch."

"Addison," Peter calls out as I storm from the conference room. But I don't answer.

Rippling with anger, I march back through the lobby with its grating pop music and into the elevator. Someone says, "See you at Art Ex, Addison?" and I bite back the urge to scream.

Five floors down, I reach my Benz in a fury. My car door echoes in the garage as I yank it shut. Pulling onto Sunset and away from the opening night of Fashion Week.

After the last six weeks and all my efforts to get Velvet's talking points perfected—her interviews engaging but deflecting—I can't believe I would allow this to happen. I knew Phinneas better than most, and I thought I would uncover The Clue to find his murderer well before this date arrived. Mike Wadsworth, the turncoat, also reaches out to me via text asking for an update from my "anonymous source," but I mute him.

When I awoke this morning, I had the whole week planned out. My client has events and interviews each day requiring my attention and expertise. But I didn't anticipate the FBI declaring open season on me this afternoon. I should have, considering the desperation Agent Jonas has projected each time I've seen his weathered mien—but didn't.

Traffic is light on my way into West Hollywood. I pass my condo, unwilling to relegate myself to its professionally designed interior, and continue onto Santa Monica Boulevard. The usual bumper-to-bumper traffic at three o'clock has diminished, barely a soul on the road in this part of the city. Everyone who's anyone is getting ready for opening night.

An oversize donut teeters dangerously above an intersection I pass. My thoughts flash to Connor and his theories that Jamie Mendez is behind my professional chokehold. Why are the police not looking into that guy? If Mendez was angry with Phinneas— that the money he invested in Thrive, Inc. was taking a slow nosedive—why are the police not naming the seedy politician as a person of interest?

Is that why I'm being followed—targeted by these deaths? Mendez holds me responsible, too, as the publicist that didn't rein Phinneas in?

Irritation makes my foot heavy, and I accelerate the car. Agent Jonas didn't share when the news conference would take place, but I'd bet my gifted MAC makeup collection that he wouldn't provide a large buffer of time. The update will be broadcast soon.

A sharp pang of frustration—no, regret?—hits me at the thought of Connor storming away from me at the hotel. We each said things that were hurtful—that crossed a line. I would never deign to chase after him, of course, but I wonder if there is something I could have or should have done differently—whether I was making a mistake, allowing a PI to set me loose when suspicion continued to linger on me like on a department store perfume sample stick.

Whoever killed Phinneas, then Devon, would have known that I would be eyed in some degree as their publicist, or that it was a happy possibility. Who could want that blame to land on my toned shoulders?

To my left, the Hollywood sign is visible, jutting from the mountainside that separates Tinseltown from the San Fernando Valley . . . and my childhood home.

I hit my blinker, then turn onto the 101 freeway. A dark blue two-seater darts past a string of cars to coast in the middle lane behind me. Forty-five minutes elapse, during which I drive in near silence. Horns and squeaky brakes are the only soundtrack to my route to Lancaster.

When I spot the weathered green freeway sign announcing I made it to the city center, for the first time in ten years, the dark blue car appears in my rearview. I exit at the off-ramp. A streak of color zips forward, continuing on the freeway, faster than it has moved in nearly an hour. Was that car following me all this time? Or am I teetering toward paranoia now?

Shopping centers and boutique shops from the eighties line the main road and bring with them a rush of memories, most of them bad: the trailer park where I spent the first two years of my life until my mom's then-boyfriend bought us a modest two-bedroom house; the free lunches I received at my elementary school, then my high school; getting caught shoplifting at Maia's Threads when I was fourteen, and subsequently convincing the owner to gift me the ripped jeans so that I could be Maia's very own walking billboard at school and beyond. I smile to myself as I turn down Hartwood Street. Not all the memories are bad.

Cramped one-story houses fill the block, with desert-friendly plants and wildflowers decorating the walkways. Set apart from the rich neighborhood across town, front yards, though small, seem nonetheless curated by caring hands, the small patches of green grass vibrant and the rock gardens raked with precision. I note a thriving cactus beside a front door painted yellow. Lots of people know that image, presentation, and reputation count.

Just not Dinah Stern.

As I pause at the intersection before my mother's house, the beater car from my adolescence backs out of her driveway. A jolt passes through me as I recognize my mother at the wheel.

Although I drove an hour to my childhood home and haven't seen or spoken to her in a decade, the FBI's erroneously delivered notice was calling me—not any desire to see Dinah. I idle at the empty intersection until the faded red sedan disappears in the opposite direction. Then I park at the curb of a square one-story with a dilapidated porch and exit my Benz.

Two quick raps on the door, beneath the peekaboo window, go unanswered.

I reach under a ceramic angel that rests on a dirt-covered wooden table, then grasp a familiar pointed shape: the house key, same place as always. "Dinah, Dinah. What if someone wanted to break in?"

Feeling the acute irony after Connor's B and E of my condo, I step inside. The front room is exactly as I last saw it. Dusty afghans cover a worn sofa, magazines piled high atop the two end tables, and the unmistakable sting of antibacterial sanitizer lingers in the air. Ghosts surface with each step forward, reminding me why I avoided this place as long as I did. Echoes of my mother's drunken tirades return as clearly as if she were still sitting on the couch in her pajamas at four in the afternoon. Always, always, with what a victim she is. How bad her feet—no, her back—no, her sciatica aches. With zero desire to change the narrative.

I head straight to my room, although it no longer belongs to me after fifteen years away. And especially not in a two-bedroom, where each square foot counts. Dinah turned it into a shrine to herself. Images of her from when she was a star cheerleader and then gymnast while in high school are framed and hung along the wall. Interviews she gave to the Idaho newspaper in the town where she grew up are highlighted and cut to form a collage of her name in headlines: DINAH STERN CINCHES FIRST PLACE; LOCAL TALENT DINAH STERN SCOUTED BY COLLEGES; DINAH STERN PERFORMS AT HOMECOMING.

On the writing desk that occupies the corner, an official-looking letter on a pile of mail displays my name. TIME SENSITIVE is stamped across the front. The FBI's notice that I've been labeled a person of interest and a summons to visit their office.

Plucking the letter between two fingers, I turn to leave. If Dinah remembers to look for this envelope later, she'll probably assume she lost it in the pile of magazines and mail stifling the front room. No sense in lingering in this graveyard.

What would have happened to Dinah Stern, had she not broken her foot her senior year of high school? Would she have excelled in her sport to keep her college scholarships and never known the cutting joy of receiving others' sympathy? Would she have thrived on achievement rather than developing acute, diagnosed hypochondria and Munchausen syndrome? Who knows. As easily as I can envision a life where Dinah Stern was a functioning member of society, I picture a young Addison reaching out for a hug from her mother and having her five-year-old hands smacked away and called dirty.

No matter. I learned at a tender age that trusting others only leaves you vulnerable—and underachieving. It was the shortcut I needed. No gap year necessary to "find myself." That lesson got me through school, out of Lancaster, and into a big pond where I could more fully prey upon smaller fish to reach the apex of the public relations pyramid.

I pass into the hallway, nearly skipping along the worn carpet. Being here, noting the framed photos of me that were put up for show, I feel strangely confident. Certain. At peace. I've moved past this shithole and the woman my mother wanted me to be—her mini me. Her assistant and first sympathizer. Instead, I've taken life by the balls and turned her failures into my successes.

On my way back to Highway 14, I pass the main street of downtown Lancaster. Sandwich boards along the sidewalk advertise upcoming holiday sales, requisite for this time of year. Above limp efforts to attract new customers, one sign visually towers above the rest: a large high-heeled shoe illuminated by vanity bulbs that flicker in a bouncing cadence. Maia's Threads has gotten a facelift.

Curiosity—though definitely not nostalgia—gets the better of my desire to hightail it home to a bottle of '94 Bordeaux. After all, now there's nothing for me to do there except scroll. Though I had planned to be out until the early-morning hours—first accompanying Velvet at this evening's kickoff event, then to the after-parties and the after-after parties—I called Velvet during the drive and shared that my assistant would be handling things in my absence. Rather than admit the FBI is investigating me and that I got suspended from Ovid Blackwell, I said I was fighting the flu that's going around. Livid is an understatement of Velvet's reaction, but I assured her that I wasn't done. Just because I wouldn't physically be present tonight didn't mean the debut of her line this Friday, the last day of Fashion Week, wouldn't be a raging success. I won't be on the red carpet, but I'm not finished pulling the strings.

Nineties grunge music plays from a speaker outside the record store that I park beside, the soundtrack of my birth year. A bookstore advertising an all-secondhand inventory, a vegan grocery store, a hardware store, and a custom bridal shop are the only brick-and-mortar survivors on this block, standing strong against the online marketplace.

As a teen living in a borrowed house owned by yet another boyfriend of my mother's, I got out of there whenever I could—and went five-finger shopping in each of these storefronts. Once or twice I was caught—reprimanded by a store owner or sales clerk—but the police were never called, nor my mother. Every time, my crime was written off as an innocent mistake—because I insisted it was, and the person in charge agreed. Rather than instill in me the self-assurance that I could continue to swipe retail goods, to maybe amplify my habit at a department store with a bigger payoff, I became enthralled with persuading people to believe what I wanted, what I decided was the truth.

The street is empty as I cross the two lanes to Maia's Threads. From the single-level corner space it used to occupy when I was in the ninth grade, Maia relocated to the middle of the block, to the two-level property that was once a hotel.

"Seems we've both done well for ourselves." I tug on the heavy glass door, then step inside. Designer labels cover the floor on artfully dressed mannequins, while the upstairs level promises an expensive, brand-name assortment of women's luxury shoes.

"Addison?" A woman whose childlike voice I would recognize anywhere straightens where she speaks to a young sales associate. Maia Weller smiles but her expression leaves me cold. "To what do I owe this surprise?"

"How are you, Maia?" I shift my hand onto my hip, accentuating the black ensemble I planned to wear to a red carpet tonight. Without a doubt, I look incredible. "I was just in the area, and I thought I would pay a visit to my very first client."

Renovations turned the hotel into a first-rate retail experience not evident from the outside. Natural light filters in through long glass windows facing the street, illuminating tablets stored on easel stands so customers can shop designer inventories directly. In the back along a row of espadrilles, a different sales associate in a red floor-length dress models a pair of heels I just saw in Paris to an interested customer sipping a glass of champagne. Midway down the store, beside a sweeping white oak counter and a register, a computer screen the size of a full-length mirror waits to virtually dress shoppers who would prefer a bot do the work for them.

Maia clucks her tongue. "Is that what I am? From what I recall, you were my first criminal to take advantage of my open storefront."

I bare my teeth. "Memory is so unreliable. It must be quite difficult to afford the rent of this space. Especially with only two customers. Is this the evening rush?"

"Oh, I own it," Maia says. "Along with several other locations. Santa Monica. San Diego. Temecula. It's been a good two decades since we last met, Addison. But I suppose I have you to thank for that."

She steps closer to me with each word. Slowly. Deliberately.

"Why is that?" I ask, standing my ground. Nobody cows me into a retreat. And I'm intrigued—confused—by this woman's attitude.

"Well, after I caught you stealing those awful bedazzled jeans that were everywhere then, I realized you'd been taking from me whenever you came to shop. Security cameras didn't see it. You were too practiced at such a young age."

I hold her stare. Has she been waiting to tell me off all these years?

"Allegedly," I reply. "If you're looking for an apology, I'll have to disappoint you."

"No, no. No apology. I didn't ask you for one then, and I won't now." Maia brushes the fabric of a pleated skirt worn by a mannequin. Removes some imaginary lint. "As I said, I should thank you. When you suggested that you act as my 'walking billboard,' advertising my clothing across your high school campus and elsewhere, I thought it was brilliant. I was grateful to your scheming little mind."

Story time is getting old, even if what Maia is recounting is accurate. "Well, it's been nice catching up, but I have somewhere very exclusive to be. Excuse me."

"I could have turned you in, Addison. Filed a report with the police, but I didn't. Do you know why?"

I pause while turning back to the entrance.

"Because you were right. I needed a more captivating way to draw customers into my store, and your adolescent pitch was smart. Effective. Sales went up, even as I wrestled with telling you off, to never return."

"So you kept my . . . activity a secret because you knew I was right."

Maia gives me a self-satisfied smile. "You weren't taking advantage of me. I knew something that you didn't, even though you correctly said I needed to change my marketing strategy. By allowing myself to lose my inventory to you, and not pressing charges so we could work together—" She waves a hand around the showroom, at framed photos on the wall of what must be the other locations of Maia's Threads. "I actually won."

I dip my chin. This woman has obviously waited a long time to give her speech. I respect her promoting her version of the events, however she's told herself they went down. It's what I would do.

"My congratulations. It's good to see I'm not the only Lancaster native thriving—"

"Excuse me." Maia turns on her heel, back to her sales associate.

The arrogance. The audacity. Reeling from the unfamiliar—to me—dismissal, I move to the exit. As I pass a display of satin blouses, my mind jumps to the myriad ways I can professionally embarrass her and ostracize Maia's Threads from local economy leaders.

Then I recall that Ovid Blackwell has relegated me to unpaid leave. And the FBI has its poorly paid resources watching me.

Damn.

With nothing left to do or say, I lightly touch the clothes hanger bearing the nearest satin blouse. The fabric shifts, though remains upright, as I exit the designer fashion store. After the day I had, if I must start losing to win—like Maia, apparently—I'm off to a successful start.

CHAPTER THIRTY

PHINNEAS

LOS ANGELES | AUGUST 7

PHINNEAS REDWOOD: *Sorry about that. My housekeeper just started, and she didn't know where to find the towels. She's been calling me all morning. Can you state your name and what bureau you're with again?*

WOMAN: *Special Agent Cacciotti with the Federal Bureau of Investigation. I'll just take a few minutes of your time.*

PR: *Sure, sure. Did you want a water? Emma, can you grab a Topo Chico for the agent, please?*

AGENT CACCIOTTI: *No, that's all right. Thank you.*

PR: *Cool.* [Muffled] *Never mind, Emma! I said, never mind!* [Clearly] *What can I do for you?*

AC: *I was interested in learning more about your latest product.*

PR: *It's not launching for another few months.*

AC: *Right, I'm aware. What interests me is the advertisements that I've already seen.*

PR: *Yeah, it's kind of a prelaunch campaign that the marketing department thought would be helpful in drumming up more interest.*

AC: *Do you need that?*

PR: *Yes and no. We have the financial backing that we needed to create the product, support it through testing, federal approvals, and endorsements from the scientific community. Now we're hoping for a final influx of investor activity to push for . . . civilian endorsements.*

AC: *You mean celebrities.*

PR: *Not necessarily.* [Pause] *Okay, yes, celebrities are always nice.*

AC: *Like the model, Billie something, and how she was the spokesperson for that diet pill in the early aughts.*

PR: *Ah, no, not like Billie Trixie, not at all.* [Laughs] *Her death was probably related to the sham pill she was taking for weight loss, which— Actually . . . it was more likely driven* *by her starving herself due to the external pressures she so acutely felt. [Pause] So no.*

AC: *Mr. Redwood, are you familiar with the Lanham Act? It's a federal law that prohibits false advertising or claims that otherwise harm the consumer. You know it?*

PR: *This isn't my first drug campaign. Yeah, I do. But that's regulated by the Federal Trade Commission.*

AC: *Yes, that's correct. The FBI investigates mass-marketing fraud. And what concerns me, you see are, those early advertisements that have been floating around at three in the morning. The ones that claim Shapextrin is currently available for wholesale preorders and if you "act now you can get the body you've always deserved." Are you aware that your company has already begun accepting preorder payments from those three a.m. consumers?*

PR: *I'm not. But I know my legal department would research whether it's okay to accept those at this point.*

AC: *You sure? Because that kind of language—the body you've always deserved—may be defrauding your consumer already. And the FBI has received several anonymous tips that point to you as the person behind this prelaunch campaign, that it's a strategy from the top.*

PR: *Whoa. Look, I'm not in charge of marketing, okay? I don't have granular oversight of every tactic that gets approved by the ad guys on my team. The infomercials don't say you'll get a great body—just the one you deserve. And I'm no finance* whiz, but I pay lots of people who have degrees to manage that stuff—who all said it was fine to accept preorders. [Pause] *Am I under arrest?*

AC: *No, Mr. Redwood. Not yet. But you'd make my job a hell of a lot easier if you'd pony up the facts and tell the truth.*

PR: [Laughs] *The truth, huh? When I figure out whose version of it you want, I'll be glad to share.*

CHAPTER THIRTY-ONE

CONNOR

SILVER LAKE | OCTOBER 13

Hyacinth Aspen is eye-popping in her movie star's gown, a splash of glamour standing on my front porch between a potted cactus and a rocking chair. Honey-blond hair tumbles around the thin straps on her shoulders, while bright blue eyes seem to laugh, although she's silent. The body-hugging dress she wears shimmers with the slightest movement.

"Connor," she says. "It's nice to see you again."

"You look incredible," I say, leaning in for an awkward kiss on her cheek.

"Thanks. So do you."

I confirm the gold satin pocket square is peeking out from my black suit the way it should, then take Hyacinth's hand and escort her to my rented Land Rover. Considering Genevieve, Hyacinth's mother, bankrolled my transportation—before she accused me of murder on national television—it seems fitting to drive her daughter in it to the closing ceremony of Fashion Week tonight.

I open the passenger door for her, feeling like a high school junior. Hyacinth is a beautiful woman, and sheltered, but kind, as far as I found while researching her relationship with Devon. I should be glad—excited, even—that she accepted my invite to accompany me and on such short notice. Instead, every time we make eye contact, I see Addison.

Addison Stern, the only person who was ever on my level, who could fire back a quip or retort—sometimes faster than I could. Whose jet-black hair and eyes that kiss at the corners, as she used to say, always led me to foolish, idiotic decisions, but also made me feel alive—reckless in a way that I never behaved because I thought a low profile would benefit my business. Addison loves being at the forefront of whatever main event or trend is at hand. Although she says she dislikes being the center of attention, she occupies its orbit with flair. Hyacinth, with her innocence, her fair complexion and pixie-like features, doesn't hold a candle to my scandal queen.

"Mr. Windell? Is now a bad time?"

Agent Jonas pauses on the cracked sidewalk in front of my Airbnb's lawn. The orange tie he wears, with actual oranges on it, matches the setting sun behind him. Hyacinth throws me a curious glance from the passenger seat, but she pulls out her phone and takes a selfie.

"Agent. Uh, yeah, we're heading out. Can I help you?"

He looks from me to my passenger seat. "Aren't you and Addison Stern an item?"

"No. We're not. What can I do for you?" Although there's still an hour until the closing ceremony of Fashion Week starts, I'd rather not dawdle with this guy. I caught the sheriff's televised update on Phinneas's case. The entire country knows that Addison Stern has been named a person of interest in his death.

"Huh," Agent Jonas grunts. "I like my women on the spicy side, but to each his own."

"Great. How can I—"

"Mr. Windell, the FBI has some questions for you regarding Devon Lim. You're probably up to date on Genevieve Aspen's accusations against you?"

I grimace, then sneak a glance at Hyacinth. Still on her phone. "Yeah, I am."

"Right. While we're not looking at you for Phinneas Redwood's death—not yet—we are noticing some disturbing connections between Mr. Redwood and Mr. Lim."

I force my face into a blank expression. "Really?"

Agent Jonas nods. "Any chance you can come into our offices tomorrow?"

"Saturday? That might be difficult." Sweat begins to dot my forehead. *Evade, evade, evade, Connor.*

"Oh, Mr. Windell. There are no weekends for those of us wanting answers about your former client's murder."

"My . . . ?"

Agent Jonas's smile twists my stomach. "Your client. You did some work for Mr. Redwood a while back, didn't you? A relationship that you failed to disclose to us for—what? Over a month now?"

He stares at me. Watches as my eyebrow involuntarily twitches. "We don't have a maximum number of suspects,

Mr. Windell. And anyone can be named a person of interest at any time. I'll see you tomorrow afternoon. Let's say three o'clock?"

Without waiting for my choked reply, he saunters away, turning the corner out of sight.

I get into the driver's side of my rented Rover.

"Ready?" Hyacinth asks. Her lipstick is freshly reapplied. "I always love Fashion Week here. New York and Miami are such long flights."

"Yeah. The very best. So convenient."

As we drive in Griffith Park's shadow on our way to the Art Ex hall, streetlights bathe Hyacinth's face in yellow, giving her a sickly glow.

"Who was that man?" she asks.

I swallow the bile rising to the back of my mouth. In all my investigations as a PI, I've never come this close to being at the center of one myself.

"Just a colleague. Wanted an update on a project." A green sign overhead directs us to the center lane of the road that continues toward Hollywood. Hopefully to answers. "You know, I'm surprised you agreed to join me tonight."

"You won't tell my mother, will you?" she asks, with a hint of a smile. "I sound like I'm twelve."

"No, I won't. We're not exactly on . . . speaking terms right now."

"I'm aware. My mother loves controlling people, and if they don't get in line, they should expect the backlash that follows." Hyacinth stares straight ahead, her voice bitter. "Though I do hope a photo of us lands in *Vogue*. We got into a fight when I told her I was done having a bodyguard and she blew up at me, saying she knows better than I do, and—no offense—going out with you is entirely meant to piss her off. She is going to freak when she learns I came with you. Sorry—"

"No, no problem. I get it. I'm glad you said yes."

"Oh yeah?" Hyacinth turns to look at me while I brake at a red light. She darts her tongue between glossy lips. "Why is that?"

"I mean, you're the perfect date for an event like this."

Hyacinth beams. "Aren't you sweet? Thank you."

She lays a hand on the center console, but I don't reach for her. I'm not interested like that—though she is the perfect companion tonight. These days, sneaking in as a lone male would attract too much attention. But walking in with my head held high and a beautiful woman on my arm, I'll look like any other studio exec come to ogle the models.

Ten more minutes pass before we roll into the roped-off valet area, where a young guy in a pink vest waits. Whatever Hyacinth's reasons are for rebelling against Genevieve, it's not my place to judge. Right now, the only thing I care about is uncovering the connection between Phinneas's death note and the closing ceremony. There are no other events today in the city of this size. If the sequence of numbers is today's date and Phinneas's killer was planning to attend tonight, or Phinneas wanted Addison to attend this event, then the Art Ex exhibition hall is where I should be.

The valet opens my passenger door and helps Hyacinth out. I toss him my keys with all the douchebaggery of my early twenties, then take Hyacinth's hand to approach the flashing lights. Photographers crouch, lift their cameras high above the crowd, and elbow to the front for a better view of whatever passing celebrity poses for pictures. "Who are you wearing?" is shouted more times than I can count while Hyacinth and I navigate the edge of the pulsing crowd.

The red carpet extends for a full city block. Reporters and well-dressed attendees mingle together, all while keeping a watchful eye for anyone looking to snap their picture. A young man bends at the waist for a shot of Hyacinth's white sparkly gown while two women beside him hold up their cell phones, livestreaming on the carpet. "Who are you wearing?" the photographer asks.

"Dior," Hyacinth purrs, flinging open a slit in the dress that reaches her hip. We continue walking in tiny steps to accommodate her stilettos.

Music throbs from an entrance covered by thick navy curtains that draw open, then close each time someone goes inside the hall. Once we walk through the crowded antechamber, past the coat check that no one uses in LA, into the main hall, house music bumps from a speaker system and pounds my chest plate. Chairs upon chairs face an extended runway beneath a dazzling strobe show.

Hyacinth squeals. She waves to a young woman seated within a roped-off lounge beside the stage. She strides toward the enclosed love seats and two security guards who bar the entrance, then pauses. "Connor, are you coming?"

Catering staff scurry past while carrying trays of gray mousse in porcelain cups. Guests cluster at two full-service bars on opposite ends of the room, with heads turning toward one man standing at a cocktail table, posing for photos. Former and future politician Jamie Mendez.

"Let's catch up later."

Hyacinth lifts both eyebrows. Her red-painted mouth closes into a tight line. "Well. We'll see."

Standing just shy of Mendez's orbit, a small, familiar woman gazes adoringly up at him. Black hair is swept into a tight bun, and a pointed nose and broad smile make the resemblance between them strong, though I know I didn't see her outside of his campaign headquarters, playing Frogger with Fernando Castillo.

Deafening music makes overhearing Mendez impossible while he glad-hands attendees, even as I stride right past him toward the bar. The closing night of Fashion Week was bound to be well attended, but is it an opportunity to win over the art base of LA? A new thought hits me square on the jaw: Did Phinneas know that Jamie Mendez would be here tonight?

Chills skim my neck. He must have. Tonight must hold the answer to why Phinneas was killed—and I think I know by whom.

A woman sidles in front of me, jumping to the counter and shouting for a glass of Chablis.

Addison should be here, and not barred from doing her job. After the sheriff's press conference, she texted me, telling me she was suspended from work—forced to lie low by her boss's choice—but that's it. Since then, it's been a symphony of crickets from Addison Stern. Which is just fine by me. I've also kept a low profile, knowing the FBI and the police are actively watching me, waiting to see if I'll make a mistake.

Laughter erupts from where Jamie Mendez was standing. I turn as someone collides with my elbow.

"Oh, excuse me." The woman smiles, as though I said something funny. The older woman with Mendez. "Is this the line for the bar?"

A crowd jostles along the counter, harassing the three mixologists hired for the gig. "I'm not sure there is one, but you're welcome to take my place."

I step aside for her to squeeze past me; then I stop short. The wool of the woman's coat scratches my fingertips. The teal color of the fabric is familiar—more than that, the jade necklace she wears, a simple rock on a gold chain, is eerily similar to the one Annalise Meier was found wearing while in bed with Devon Lim.

"Your necklace is beautiful. Where did you get it?" I ask.

Her hand, unadorned but for a gold wedding band with a simple blue stone, flies to her collar. "Thank you. I made it."

"You're a jewelry designer?"

She nods, beaming. "I am. A few of my pieces will be on the runway tonight. Everyone thinks my son"—the woman lifts her chin to Mendez, still glad-handing—"is here tonight for voters, but he came along to support me."

"He must be very proud of you."

The strobe lights change to shapes that cascade across the room. Stars wash along the woman's face, Jamie Mendez's mother. "He's a good boy. He came with me to a recent gala, too."

"If I wanted to have a piece custom made, do you do that kind of thing?"

The woman smiles, lifting her chin. She straightens her shoulders, and a twinge of remorse hits me for getting her hopes up. "Of course. I like to get a sense of the recipient, though, whoever the piece is for. I always suggest that I come to the person's residence to sit in their spirituality. The kids might say 'their vibe' these days. It's a little unconventional, but it works for me."

I stare at Mendez's mother. At her small outline, the dark features that pop against the lighting installed along the runway. Genevieve provided footage stills of her property that I analyzed for hours. Images that were originally captured with night vision, but which I had a specialist enhance to determine their true coloring. This woman visited Devon Lim at the Aspen guesthouse in the middle of the night.

"Sure, sure. I get that." And that would explain why Devon needed her to visit the guesthouse belonging to Genevieve—a notoriously meddlesome mother who hires private investigators to snoop into her family's lives—at night to avoid notice. Devon secretly commissioned a custom piece for his fiancée. Did he commission a separate piece for his mistress?

House beats reverberating through the walls suddenly shift, morphing into trumpets and fanfare. The final runway show— Velvet Eastman's—is beginning.

"I better get my drink," Mrs. Mendez says, handing me a square of paper. "Here's my card. How many pieces were you thinking?"

"Oh, two. Three?" I'm distracted, watching the show attendees scatter to their seats. "At least three."

"Really? I have to say, that would be amazing. I could use the work, if I can be so honest. My son has a birthday coming up, and I'd like to get him something nice."

"Oh. Uh, yeah. That sounds good." I make eye contact with Mrs. Mendez again. Excitement brightens her dark features, highlighting small teeth.

"Well, Mr. . . . ?"

"Gucci." *What*—?

"Mr. Gucci, I'm available whenever you want to discuss designs." She beams brighter than a vanity bulb at the Pantages Theatre. A pang of guilt needles my side, as she continues on to the bar for that drink. I didn't have to lie. Didn't have to get her hopes up. But I'm off my game, after falling out with Addison. Resuming the old ways of business comes more naturally to me than I'd like.

A purple hue falls across the exhibition hall. Strobe lights pulse outward from the empty stage as a voice announces that the next and final runway presentation will begin in five minutes. Well-dressed attendees stride to their seats, the masses eager for a good view. I search for Hyacinth's stark-white dress among the various patterns, somewhere toward the front, and instead find her seated behind the red rope of the VIP area.

Malina, Addison's assistant, is front row and showstopping in light blue—I read that cerulean would be featured in Velvet's color wheel.

The president of Los Angeles Artists in Fashion, the brain trust and moneybags behind this week's clothing display, already welcomed the crowd. The "warm-up act, before the main event," I heard an older man sniff outside. Before Velvet Eastman's line.

Many attendees settle into their seats, but a few dozen remain standing. A camera crew grabs live shots beside a reporter dressed in sequins. The sticker across the camera reads CHERIETV, a gossip channel I used to watch at three a.m. Scanning the backs of heads and profiles, I search for Jamie Mendez or his mother, but another figure catches my eye. Along the back wall, a woman in a black, form-fitting dress that hits at the knees, with black thick-rimmed sunglasses to match, accepts a drink from a passing server. She grimaces, then forms the words "You call this Chardonnay? Take it back."

Forcing the glass back onto the tray, the woman lifts her chin a haughty inch. She scans the room, making eye contact with me. She startles. Then she breaks into a speed walk toward the restroom.

I step into her path just before she reaches the push doors. "I thought that was you."

Addison Stern glares at me from behind Jackie O sunnies.

Blunt bangs of a brown wig land askew when she shakes her head. "Excuse me, this is the ladies' room."

"Do you want me to say it? Shout your name for the world and the police and your *boss* to hear? Where is he? I thought I saw Peter out in the crowd, near your assistant. Peter! Hey, Peter!"

Bass pummels the speaker system, drowning out my words to anyone more than five feet away, but Addison-in-disguise hisses anyway. "Connor, stop it! How did you know it was me?"

I smirk. "Call it a sixth sense for entitlement."

"I think you mean empowerment."

We move to the side of the bathrooms, to a corner alcove. "You've been attending events all week, haven't you?"

Addison deadpans, "I wasn't about to let things go to the wayside after all my hard work."

"But you couldn't let any blowback land on your client."

"Of course not." She takes a moment to scan my suit jacket, my slacks, and, probably, the gel in my hair. "You dressed the part."

"I tried, at least." A trombone solo charges in. "Listen. I know we aren't each other's favorite people right now—"

"Understatement of the year."

"But we need each other. You're a person of interest, and I'm not far away from an official announcement, either."

Addison twists her lips to the side. "What did you learn?"

I take the moment to lean in and update Addison on my conversation with Agent Jonas, then Mrs. Mendez. Violins rip into the song, turning the melody head over heels. The strings section of whatever band is playing goes nuts on the DJ-run track, amping the room and the excitement. Violins give way to vocalization that crescendos, builds into a note that could break glass.

Addison meets my eye, standing closer than she has in over a week. Heat emanates from her body, and I'm aware that only three layers of clothing separate my skin from touching hers. She cocks an eyebrow. "Show's starting."

Models cascade down the runway. Each of them pauses at the end to allow a whole view of Velvet's creations. The color wheel ranges from blue—the cerulean I read about—to green, then purple, then red. Several models wear jewelry, some understated, some ornate, and I'd guess a few belong to Mendez's mother.

Nearly forty-five minutes elapse, at the end of which the crowd erupts in applause. I continue watching and analyzing the audience, taking note of who among the attendees appears bored (a few, including Jamie Mendez) or downright angry (more than I would have guessed). Velvet herself emerges from the wings to walk beside two models, all three of them wearing different versions of the same fisherman's-net sweater. A broad smile illuminates the designer's face. Then shouting interrupts the moment.

Words get lost in the music as a man in a jean jacket yells, surging from the crowd. He rears backward, then unleashes a white cloud onto Velvet and her creations.

Cries pour from the audience, shock and outrage rising above the speaker system. The man takes off. He leaps onto the stage, slipping behind curtains as chaos explodes in the exhibition hall. People swarm the runway, swallowing the models, as Velvet gasps. She claws her throat, then she collapses, disappearing underfoot.

"What just happened?" I turn to Addison, but she is as white as the powder bomb that was lobbed at her client. I scan the mass of bodies, searching for a teal wool coat—a pressed suit beside it.

Someone shouts for help—"Is there a doctor?"—and police run through the entrance, followed by EMTs. The crowd recedes like the tide among the scattered Chiavari chairs.

Addison steps backward, behind my shoulder. She whispers, "I can't be here. We can't be here."

Without another word, we slip down the hallway toward the service entrance. Emerging into the alleyway behind Art Ex, Addison trips, her shoe caught in the cracked concrete. We hobble past a boba shop, casually, slowly. Like we didn't just exit another disaster, like we haven't a care in the world.

Once we reach Addison's car where she parked two blocks away, I sneak a glance at her profile. Sweat beads at her hairline, dots her upper lip.

She pauses just before ducking into the driver's seat. "What is it?" she asks, seeing my face.

An ambulance races past, in the direction of the exhibition hall, its siren nearly overwhelming my words. "Jamie Mendez. He was missing from the crowd."

CHAPTER THIRTY-TWO

ADDISON

WEST HOLLYWOOD | OCTOBER 14

A green glow pulses beside me. My phone. I fumble for it on my nightstand, then squint at the time above a photo of me during my very first trip to Paris, standing beside that bridge with the "forever love locks" and making scissors with my hand. It's midnight. And an unknown number is calling me.

I roll over in my expensive sheets. Connor and I parted ways at my car, knowing he had already been seen at Fashion Week. He left a date there. He'd need to return to the scene for questioning or it would appear suspicious.

Later, when I got back to my condo, I scrolled my feed. I saw that he had arrived with Hyacinth Aspen on the red carpet. She appeared much more polished than when she showed up at Connor's Airbnb under the guise of rebelling against her controlling mother. I saw the way she looked at him, how she hung on his every word and blushed with just the right virginal sigh.

Normally, I try to be fast asleep this time of night, well aware of how important a good night's rest is to one's beauty regime. Not tonight. Over thirty missed calls and text messages have come in, most of which I have ignored. Many are from Connor, but the rest are from Ovid Blackwell colleagues.

Social media says that Velvet Eastman was attacked, and whatever was thrown at her sent her to the hospital. But I know better, since I was the one to orchestrate the whole spectacle.

It was my idea to plant a flour bomb at the end of Velvet's runway show. The guy I got to chuck a fistful of the mundane baking ingredient was an actor I found on Craigslist who I assured would not be identified or experience any legal repercussions. It was a publicity stunt, and one of my better ideas, I thought—until Velvet collapsed onstage.

Something else is at play. Something I'm not in on, and that may have gravely injured—though not killed, not yet—another of my clients.

Shock rippled through my body as I drove away from the exhibition hall: Whoever killed Phinneas, Devon, and Annalise Meier—if they were killed by the same person—must be behind this attack on Velvet.

Although I have deliberately waited until hours after the news broke to take any action myself, now feels like the right time. I scroll through my phone to dial the only person I trust in this situation. Who has as much to lose as I do.

Peter's voice is hoarse when he answers. "Addison. Did you hear?"

I nod, although we're only on audio call. "I did."

Peter grunts. "I left early from the show, but most all of Ovid Blackwell was there. Malina watched from where the social media team was seated, as chaos—I mean, complete madness—broke out. People ran for cover, though the police say it was only flour. More complete forensic testing is underway to confirm. The police interviewed Malina for hours."

I turn on the TV. Footage of the aftermath is featured on late-night local news. "Did they say who did this?"

Peter waits too long to reply. "You, Addison. I'm sorry, but they think it was you. That's what my source with LAPD says."

"But I was home all night. You put me on leave." Velvet knew the opposite, as I had reassured her I would be present at all events to make sure things ran smoothly. But she's the only person who knew in advance that I had sneaked in tonight.

"Right. I know that," Peter says. "The police will figure out who really did this, and soon."

"Have you heard anything about Velvet? Why she collapsed? Has she been released from the hospital yet?"

"No, I don't have any of those answers. But I'll tell you if that changes."

We hang up. Although I know calling Peter was the right thing to do, discussing the situation aloud makes everything feel more real. Dire. The sticky sheen of fear hugs my shoulders.

An unknown number pops up on my screen, again. Some instinct twists in me to answer. "Hello?"

"Addison Stern? This is Helga Humphries, I'm a nurse at Cedars-Sinai Hospital. Velvet Eastman listed you as her 'in case of emergency' contact."

"She did? Is she okay?" I ask, my heart racing.

"Ms. Stern, she's been hospitalized after nearly overdosing on diazepam. We need you here immediately."

My feet slide into the faux-fur slippers beside my bed. "Give me thirty minutes."

\\\\\////

Several tubes wind from Velvet's body as she sleeps in the hospital bed. Instead of the house music she selected to accompany her designs on the runway tonight, the steady beep of a monitor is the room's only melody. I follow the nurse who called me to Velvet's side.

"She hasn't opened her eyes since her stomach was pumped, but she's doing okay," Nurse Humphries says, a crease in her forehead deepening. "It's a good thing so many police were at that fashion thing. She was brought in unconscious and frothing at the mouth."

"How did this happen? Wasn't she walking a runway when she collapsed?"

"Well, the paramedics who treated her in the ambulance said she appeared to have been poisoned by something. Then we pumped her stomach upon arrival here and found she'd ingested pills. Tests show that they were Valium."

I shake my head. "That's not possible. Velvet Eastman would not try to overdose during the night of her fashion debut. She's worked years for this moment."

Nurse Humphries shrugs in maroon scrubs. "Well, she didn't OD, exactly. Only a handful of pills were in her system, so it's possible she was allergic to them—had an adverse reaction. But we never know what's going on in someone's head, do we?"

"That is literally my job to know."

She turns to leave. "I'll leave you to your friend."

"Client. Not friend. Thank you."

At the door, Nurse Humphries pauses. "How are you, this woman's publicist, her only emergency contact?"

I regard her coolly. "I'm a people person."

With new skepticism showing in the lift of her eyebrows, she nods. "I'll be right outside if the patient needs me."

When Velvet and I are alone, I search the room for her clothing. Hidden beneath fresh bedsheets folded on a stiff sofa, Velvet's flour-covered fisherman's-net sweater is stuffed unceremoniously in a cardboard box on top of white slacks and her stilettos, Jimmy Choo's design. Her pants pockets are empty—but something small and firm presses against the fabric. I dip into the tiny, often-overlooked watch pocket beneath a belt loop and retrieve a crumpled receipt from a boba shop around the corner from the exhibition hall—Sunny Sips. The date and time shows the drink was purchased right before the closing ceremony began. Beneath the store's name and address, the cashier also input the customer's name: Addison. Someone gave my name when they ordered a drink for Velvet.

I wasn't with Velvet at the show—couldn't risk being seen with my client when I was placed on leave—but I did call her before she went onstage to wish her good luck. She said she was so nervous that she hadn't eaten anything all day. The only thing she consumed: a boba.

I glance at the empty doorway behind me. Nurse Humphries said there was a handful of pills in Velvet's system. Could Velvet have taken diazepam without knowing she was allergic to the drug—maybe just trying to relax during a stressful evening? Or did someone poison the boba that Velvet drank, the night of her big debut, then try to make it look as if I'm responsible?

Velvet's heart monitor pulses away, mundane as ever, as if I hadn't just found the smoking Sunny Sips receipt.

I cast an eye at Velvet's beleaguered face where she lies in bed, her mouth slack and mascara smeared. The updo she chose is now loose, scattered across the shoulders of her paper gown.

"Sweetie, you look a mess."

Using a wet paper towel, I gingerly wipe the black makeup from the creases of Velvet's eyes and the tops of her cheeks. Avoid pressing too hard on the delicate under-eye skin.

Velvet's excitement while we sat at the Chateau Marmont was contagious. I felt as hopeful for her then as I might for my own goals and dreams of making partner at the firm—not that that's happening anytime soon. Not now.

Never, in a million years, would I have predicted the way things have gone. Given the casual way Velvet pitched her line to the councilor at City Hall, the ease with which Velvet delivered our fine-tuned interview answers during live broadcasts, and the confidence she exuded as she opened tonight's runway show, I felt certain Velvet's rising star would be unstoppable at Fashion Week.

"Look at us now," I say to my client. My . . . friend?

I smile. All this talk with Connor about feelings, and needing each other, is making me soft.

My phone pings with a notification from my security app. My front door. I pull open the livestream, fully expecting the neighborhood cat to be sleeping on my doormat, and find a man on my steps. He bends down, searching for something underneath the mat. Lifts the potted, dehydrated aloe vera plant beside my doorbell. He's trying to find a house key.

"Son of a bitch." I zoom in on the man just as he turns halfway toward the corner of the portico. It's dark and nearly three in the morning, but the app's night vision shows this person wearing a loose hoodie and a baseball cap that he's got pulled low over his forehead. Something about him is familiar.

After instructing the nurse to call me if Velvet wakes up, I drive home following every traffic law, wary of heaping more complications onto tonight. A text message that I sent to Velvet's assistant, Camille, before I left the hospital goes unanswered. She should be awake, searching out answers or ways to help. She should be at Velvet's bedside.

I pull into my covered parking spot. Approach my door on high alert. Nothing on the porch appears disturbed. Even the ring of dirt that encircles my aloe vera plant remains unbroken.

My framed cat gleams, reflecting the nightlight above my counter, as I toss my keys on the granite. On my news app, related headlines begin to saturate my feed: ATTACK CONCLUDES FASHION WEEK. SHOCKING DEBUT OF FORMER MADAM'S FASHION DESIGNS.

Certain heartless critics deem Velvet's show a disaster. Despite the obvious audience approval, her designs are rejected by fashion critics as blasé.

"Unbelievable," I mutter. "The woman has to recover from an overdose, and her life's work is getting panned."

I brew a pot of tea on my stove. Settle onto a barstool and scroll for concurrent scandals of the night. My favorite ways to relax. Whenever a crisis calls for countermeasures, I wrangle the headlines until the press has no choice but to amplify the compelling gossip I hand select. Anything will do now to distract from Velvet's overnight stay in starched linens.

The offensive starts strong. I scroll the hashtag *FashionWeek* on my phone, past several posts that suggest more than one scandal occurred at the closing ceremony before the flour bomb went off: a trio of young actresses possibly snorting drugs in the bathroom; a singer known for her conservative upbringing wearing only a see-through dress and a thong. In the background of one photo, Hyacinth Aspen smiles pertly at the camera, her long manicured nails possessively clutching Connor's elbow.

Another hashtag, *LAFWnetworking*, provides my first bull's-eye: a photo of a married executive of a certain iconic New York magazine, showing him canoodling with a model that was recently named to *Sports Illustrated*'s Sexiest Bodies.

"But that's not enough. My client deserves to recover in peace."

Sipping my oolong, I check the profiles of the more notorious playboys in men's footwear—of a designer who created the patent for the sole that's on every basketball lover's foot today, who's a sensational sex addict. A photo that includes his very uniquely tattooed hand across a woman's body, covered in cocaine—"baby powder" his publicist will say, or maybe flour—surfaces under a different hashtag, and I know I'm in business.

After I send these two juicy finds to my contacts at all the major pop culture websites, competing fashion magazines, and a federal agent I once flirted with at the DEA, I lock my phone. It's nearly five in the morning. The last time I pulled an all-nighter, I was trying to convince the editorial staff at *Der Spiegel* during the German workday to do a sizzle piece on Phinneas's upcoming product.

Birdsong twirls in a three-note melody outside. Two nests are mainstays at the very top of the imposing oak tree whose roots have lifted and cracked the sidewalk. The world in West Hollywood is beginning to wake up.

On the LAFW hashtag, CherieTV uploaded a video that pans the room at Art Ex, right before Velvet's show began. I was standing beside the reporter and almost approached her in my disguise—forgetting myself, in an uncharacteristic move—to thank her.

Once one of Phinneas's most vocal critics, the women-first conservative news network suddenly went silent on Phinneas's questionable business and personal decisions over a month ago. Gone were the takedown pieces that clustered him with other notorious CEOs in the country, many convicted of fraud, sexual harassment, and worse. CherieTV, which is part of a larger group of female-driven platforms, simply stopped overnight. I meant to send a gift to the execs, before.

But there were no other interesting events to take Phinneas's place—no plane crash, mass casualty event, or otherwise. So why did they lose interest in Phinneas?

Was CherieTV paid off? By whom? Phinneas is an obvious answer. But his expertise lay in chemistry and embarrassing his company's board of directors. He wouldn't have thought to bribe a whole television conglomerate. Maybe he sent payments to a high-powered individual at CherieTV.

I write out a text message to Connor. Regardless of how we left things at the Beverly Hilton, if anyone can get the information, and quickly, it's him.

Before my thumb drops to send the message, I catch the string of texts that he sent in the aftermath of the runway show.

Did you get home okay?

Tell me you're okay, Addison.

This is all so crazy.

Look, I know we've had our problems but
I have to tell you something. You're the
only woman I've ever—

I set my phone down. Wait for the tension in my stomach—the anticipation clenching my heart—to relax. I can't go there right now. I can't—it's too—

Sudden tears well in my eyes, thinking about all the times I yearned for the love and support that Connor has shown me in recent months. My throat closes.

I haven't allowed myself to need anyone in . . . years.

My reflection returns my stare with glassy eyes in my phone's darkened screen. Do I still need the protection of that rabid independence?

Without reading the rest of his text, I send my message with a quick tap.

CHAPTER THIRTY-THREE

PHINNEAS

BENEDICT CANYON | AUGUST 15

PHINNEAS REDWOOD: *Captain's log: The year is 2023, and I'm about to return to a pharma gala for the first time in ten years. Five of those years when I didn't merit an invite stung, but those five were also spent drunk on another plane of consciousness, so they didn't sting as bad as they might have. But here I am, mentally and emotionally prepping to put myself back out there—and without alcohol. Yes, you heard right, memoirs, I have been on the wagon for about three weeks while in public, per Addison Stern's pushing—and, get this, I haven't taken a drink, while alone, in thirteen days.*

I know. I can't believe it, either.

It's been eye-opening. At first, I didn't notice anything, because I was gradually weaning myself off the juice. After three days of nothing, no alcohol—liquor, wine, nothing—I started to get the headaches. And the sweats. I probably soaked through four rounds of bedsheets in a week. And I didn't sleep for days, not fully—but I wonder how much of that was related to the obscene sweating. Once, around three a.m., I got into an emergency stash of vodka that I put in the freezer underneath a box of Costco orange chicken. Opened it up and everything—but then I poured it down the drain.

RIGHT? I immediately hated myself for removing the last temptation, but in the morning felt . . . good. Better and more clearheaded than I had since college. Anxiety levels are down, and tentative confidence that I can do this— maintain sobriety and attend public functions to promote my new drug—is up.

I've kind of entertained the idea before, of quitting drinking. But it was always with the intention of impressing some- one else, or something external to me—a girlfriend, or a possible collaboration between Thrive and a leader in another industry. Never in all my time did I think I wanted to get sober. Knowing what I do about myself, I just didn't seem worth all that trouble.

Then I started thinking deep about this next pill, Shapextrin, and the ways it could really help people get healthy—not just for bikini season, but for retirement. All the marketing ideas my team was pitching to me about how to position this drug as the next generation of Thrive, Inc. products got to me—the idea that if we're telling nameless consumers they deserve a leg up in improving their physical state, don't I deserve the same?

My suspicion is . . . yes. So here we are, thirteen days into the longest period of my life. Physically, things have been looking up—that was the first thing I noticed about myself. But the emotional changes were a surprise.

I hope this voice memo makes it into my made-for-TV movie later.

Last week, I went to a fitting for a suit to wear to the pharma gala. My assistant hooked me up with a great tailor in Beverly Hills, who doubles as a menswear retailer, but he doesn't have many customers of my stature. Meaning: I'm about two feet too short for the getup and light-years too sexy, but it's still a nice look. Suave in the shimmery dark blue lapels that bring out the blue in my blue eyes, and sleek in that it highlights the four pounds I've lost since embarking on sobriety. Or the semblance of it, back in July.

I'm there, looking like James Bond in a muumuu, about to karate chop the axis of evil, when in walks none other than Devon Lim. The rat bastard who stole my girl—kind of, not really—and whose app I personally use at least weekly. It's been forever since I last saw him fishing off the coast of Baja California on his yacht, dumping one-dollar bills into the ocean to test the direction of the air current so he could take out his kiteboard—and do a few lines of cocaine in the middle of the ocean for the "divine experience." I mean, come on. "Rat bastard," am I right?

Well, we get to talking. Catching up while I wait for the tailor to get his measuring tape. Devon says to me, "Did you ever think about writing your memoirs? You've lived a pretty interesting life." I go, "Yeah, actually. I am right now." Or I mean, not writing, but recording. Working on them. He got it. He said that he was considering the same thing, actually, and was working with a ghostwriter. Doing edits on his basic outline now before beginning interviews with the writer. I go, "That's awesome, man. Good for you." And he offers to hook me up with his guy. "At the very least," he says, "you know Annalise got into editing a few years back? Maybe she'd be willing to listen to your voice notes. Offer some critiques."

I nearly choked on my own spittle at that. Can you imagine, Future Editor? Annalise, the object of my long unrequited love, hearing how I still moon over her—how much I used to drink? No, definitely not gonna happen. I would rather die than have Annalise Meier listen in and learn I'm forever hopelessly in love with her. Devon moved on, at least, as he shared he was in love and engaged to some young thing over in Calabasas. For me, no woman compares to Annalise. Never has.

Although maybe Annalise wouldn't be so repulsed by the thought. Maybe it could be the nudge that she needs to reveal her own feelings? Once, I gave her a jade necklace, and the jade was shaped into a wonky little heart—deliberately. Kind of a symbol of how love doesn't always come in the form you expect it, or in congruent shapes. I wonder if she still has it.

I was, admittedly, a little bummed that during my last trip to Hong Kong in June, during which Annalise played tour guide, she didn't confide in me this new venture of hers. The editing stuff. She was always sharp with the written word, so that's not breaking news. But it would have been nice to—I don't know—confirm that she considers me a safe space. We left things a little weird on the island, and I haven't been able to stop thinking of her since.

Anyway, me and Devon were having such a nice time, standing around like we're at an open bar at a wedding instead of a high-class hole-in-the-wall that smells like cardamom. I can see why Annalise is still friends with him, despite their breakup a while back. Devon said she's over in Monaco a lot for work right now, near where his French Riviera home is—la-di-da. He was flying there soon to meet with some young app engineers, and he suggested they could build an add-on to my new pill coming out. An app to monitor the body's metabolism, or sleep cycles, or something. Although I didn't fully get the concept he was describing, I was surprised at how much I enjoyed the chat, and he said he'd send me a full proposal later.

Memoirs, this is a guy I once almost paid someone to attack. Almost. Allegedly. My girlfriend, the love of my life, cheated on me with his sharp jawline—a fact that basically sent me spiraling for decades, if I'm being honest. I never thought I would be ready—stable enough—to lean against a dusty table and discuss a collab with Devon Lim. Never. And yet it all feels . . . I don't know, like . . . this is a long time in the making. Like it was meant to be.

[Laughs] *How saccharine.*

Anyway, when the tailor came back with the measuring tape and new pants for me to try on, Devon paid for his hat that needed repairing "after rescuing baby swans from the sewer with an old lacrosse net"—I'm not even fucking joking, and yes, I am using air quotes. He said if I wanted to share a cloud link to all these voice recordings with him, he would pass it on to Annalise for high-level notes. Get her to check them out, to save me the trouble of asking her directly.

I know I spent a portion of these memoirs bitching about Devon Lim. But the guy's actually a class act. The tailor ended up doing good work, too. I grabbed a handful of business cards on my way out, for future reference.

All lovey-dovey conversation aside, when I left the shop, I had zero intentions of sharing a link with Devon. But it's been a week since then, and I needed that time to process what it all signaled about myself. If anyone is going to absorb my initial ramblings before they're polished up for public consumption, why not Annalise? She's known me a long time, even if we haven't spoken for two months—and before then, for a couple of years. I could do worse than to get her insight. And it's not exactly a secret that I'm still interested in her.

But I'll have to include a big fat caps-lock message to Devon in the email that reads "DO NOT LISTEN, DEVON LIM. NOTHING FOR YOU TO LEARN HERE. PLEASE FORWARD ON TO EDITOR." You know. Just to maintain the subtlety I'm known for.

CHAPTER THIRTY-FOUR

CONNOR

BEVERLY HILLS | OCTOBER 14

Addison peers at her phone outside of a cupcake shop, a large Tory Burch bag hanging from her arm. Dressed in a blue monochrome jumpsuit, she could be one of the celebrities that tourists follow along this city's small-town grid. Black hair cascades down her back in a high ponytail, and she wears the same dark sunglasses that she hid behind at fashion shows, apparently all week.

She looks up when I reach her side. "Hey."

"Hey. You get a sweet treat?" I nod to the window behind her, to the cupcake vending machine at the entrance of the shop.

"Does this jumpsuit seem like it accommodates cupcakes?"

I shake my head. "Not really."

An awkward moment passes between us as a tour bus guns its engine through the stoplight at the corner. Although we shared an emotional moment at the closing ceremony last night, it was out of a need for survival. Addison still carries more secrets than a priest in a confessional—but then, considering I hid my past with Phinneas, I do, too.

"What are we doing here?" I ask, leaving the question open on purpose.

Addison hesitates. She pulls a business card with numbers on it out of her pocket and brings it to my eye level, presenting the official printed information. Handwriting on the side facing Addison glows in the sun through the white cardstock. "We're getting my shoes cobbled."

Ah, the easy answer. A visit to the tailor. The plan we made before everything imploded between us at the Beverly Hilton.

She turns to the shop door beside us, but I plant my feet. "Wait," I say, my palms sweating. "There's something I need to tell you first."

I confess my prior history with Phinneas to Addison, watching her expression run the gamut from disinterest to anger to resignation. I tell her everything: the original job Phinneas sent me, of spying on his competitors in Europe; his surprise entry to rehab and the promise he made to pay me in full "later"; then the awkward but necessary call I made to him just a few months ago requesting that we settle up.

Finally, it's over. Addison purses her lips. "You hurt me. Again. I haven't allowed that to happen in a long time."

"I know. And I'm sorry I lied."

She hesitates. "And . . . you weren't the anonymous source to *Variety*?"

"No. I would never do that to you. I swear." I pause. Peer into the black sunglasses that only reflect my own nervousness. "But . . . you withheld information from me, too. Is there anything you want to say?"

The hint of a smile begins. "Yes. Let's go."

Then she tosses her hair behind her shoulder, as if we didn't get into an explosive fight about this two weeks ago. Familiar irritation with Addison begins to crawl up my back, before it stalls.

We're both liars. But I think, moving forward, we'll be telling each other the truth. "After you."

Next to the cupcake shop, this tailor and shoe cobbler has been in business since 1977, according to the painted sign on the glass door. Addison passes inside first, and the thick scent of leather and shoe polish hits my nose. An older man bends over a table behind a flip-up counter, pins poking from between his lips. He looks up from a pair of slacks.

"Picking up or dropping off?"

"Dropping off." Addison withdraws the pumps she wore to the closing ceremony last night. One heel has lost its pointy end. "I need this cobbled. Do you work with tweed?"

Photos of this man—the owner—and various movie stars and politicians from decades past cover the walls. Newspaper articles are framed or in shadow boxes alongside trinkets he must have collected over time.

"Do palm trees like sun?" he answers. "Give it here."

Addison passes the shoe for inspection. He nods. "Mmm."

"A friend of mine—he's of short stature—recommended me to you. Phinneas Redwood?"

"I get all kinds of customers. You'll have to describe him further."

"Sharp-tongued, in pharmaceuticals, blue eyes, brownish hair."

"Ah, Phinneas. He hasn't picked up his last order. It's been a couple of months since it was ready. Will you be seeing him soon?"

Before Addison or I can figure out the best reply, the man disappears into a back room. Cardboard is opened and plastic moved around. He pops back into the shop with a royal blue suit on a hanger and covered by a clear bag. "Can you give him this? I need the room in the back."

I lift a hand. "No, sir. We can't—"

"We'll let him know." Addison accepts the bag, then shoots me a look. "How much do we owe you?"

The tailor shakes his head. "He already paid. Wasn't sure if he'd have his assistant or someone else grab it. He was in such a good mood when he was here, talking to his friend."

"Friend?" Addison prods.

He narrows his eyes. "Can't remember a name. He was a new face. As for you, young miss, your shoes will be ready in a week."

I follow Addison out to the sidewalk, feeling uneasy. "Well, that was a bust. I didn't see anything interesting on the walls in there. Or that would suggest why Phinneas wanted you at Fashion Week."

Addison stares at me. "We hit the jackpot, Connor. As a reformed gambler, I would hope you can appreciate that."

"What do you mean?"

She holds up the blue suit on its hanger. "Phinneas meant to wear this to the pharma gala the night that he died. The tailor would have been one of the last people to see him alive in the preceding days when he came in. We know now that Phinneas was unhurried and unbothered at least"—Addison checks the receipt pinned to the bag—"six days before his death."

"And the fact that he missed the pickup time narrows the window of his attack."

Addison cocks her head. "The police thought that he died right before I got there."

"Right. But he could have been detained for hours prior to then, causing him to miss grabbing his suit."

Addison side-eyes me as a trio of girls in matching leggings runs giggling down the street. "My text message. Did you figure out whether Phinneas made payments to CherieTV?"

"Sort of."

She scoffs. "It's been seven hours since I asked for your help. You haven't figured it out yet?"

"In case you're forgetting, there are a few other situations at play. I've got an invite to speak to Agent Jonas in three hours—"

"And I've got a client holed up in a hospital recovering from an overdose she didn't choose."

I pause. "That's right. I saw on my newsfeed that she was still in the hospital. How did she end up there if you only gave a flour bomb to that actor?"

Addison scowls. "Her collapse didn't have anything to do with that. Someone planted a lot of Valium, I think in her boba, and Velvet's allergic to the drug. The damage was worse than it should have been. Regardless of the details, now everyone will think she has some kind of pill addiction."

I run my hand along my jaw. "She was poisoned at an event that Jamie Mendez, a one-time investor in Thrive, Inc., also attended. The commonalities keep adding up there. But about your text—Phinneas Redwood never made payments to CherieTV that I can find."

"What about to one of their affiliates?"

"Nope. Phinneas's financial history lines up with what we'd expect: lots of extravagant gifts to women, expensive vacations, techy gadgets for his home, and bottles of booze. But nothing like large monetary transactions to companies or employees associated with them. Debt or anything related to it doesn't seem to be a motivating factor in his death."

Rex Montag, the defense attorney I know with a Rolodex of connections, has been supremely handy since I came out of retirement. He owed me big-time after I helped his daughter get into UCLA, but I think we may be even after all the times I've called over the last month.

"Money is always a factor, Connor."

"Phinneas didn't make any large payments to CherieTV, but someone else did."

"Who?"

"An LLC. Go 1973. Did he ever mention that phrase to you? Go 1973 was founded around ten years ago, and the owner is listed as an attorney."

"Meaning?"

"Whoever actually owns Go 1973 LLC didn't want to disclose their name in public records, so they got an attorney to be the middleman. Some business affairs firm called Schweitzer & Harmon."

Addison huffs. The sidewalks begin to crowd with Beverly Hills shoppers and diners typical of a lunchtime on Saturday. We press back against the cupcake shop window. "Never heard of them."

"I doubt you would have. They act as go-betweens for companies that don't want to be known. According to my legal source, this LLC provided payments to CherieTV and other networks pretty regularly. Since it's been in business, Go 1973 LLC has sent money to nearly every major media outlet in the country."

"You think that's actually Phinneas's company, hiding behind an attorney?"

"It's possible. But if that's the case, his investors could know about it—company funds being repurposed or shuffled to non-pharma industry recipients."

"Which brings us back to Jamie Mendez," Addison says. "He supposedly has the friends for murder. He was never formally accused of his rival's death, but let's assume he slipped through the cracks of the justice system."

A teenage girl and her mom exit the cupcake shop. Each clutches her treat and a wooden spoon as they walk toward Rodeo Drive.

"Jamie Mendez was . . ." I draw it out. ". . . dollars to donuts, an investor at Thrive, Inc. early on, based on that guest book at the Beverly Hilton. We have no way of knowing if he was an investor when Phinneas was killed, but a pickup truck registered to his campaign manager, Fernando Castillo, has been following us."

On cue, both Addison and I scan the busy street of Little Santa Monica Boulevard. No banged-up relics from the nineties prowl into view.

"What about Hashim Swartz?" Addison asks. "We did see the truck outside his office on Melrose."

I nod, recalling his bland Hallmark answer about Phinneas's drinking and it masking his issues. "Swartz has his skeletons. Last night, after I started researching his inner circle back home, I found out that an old roommate of his died in Austria, after a fight over rent."

"Oh no. Not money—his favorite way to problem-solve . . . ?"

I smirk. Hashim Swartz's false concern in his office deserved a Razzie award.

"Very troubling, I know. But no charges were ever brought against Swartz. Why would he go after Velvet Eastman last night? How does she relate?"

Addison folds the suit of her former client into the large Tory Burch shoulder bag. "I don't think Phinneas and Velvet ever met, so I can't imagine Swartz would hold her responsible for Phinneas messing with his investment."

"Velvet was your most recent high-profile client," I continue. "Then Phinneas, and Devon Lim about a year earlier, right?"

She nods. "No, wait. Emilia Winthrop was before Devon. I was working with her at the same time I was polishing up Phinneas. I just did a commercial with her in Paris."

"Do you think she could be targeted next?"

Addison shoots me a look. "That would mean I'm the connection between all the victims. And we're back to the sheriff's press conference making me a PR pariah."

"Are you sure Phinneas never knew Velvet? Could he have visited her, uh . . . office . . . in Chicago?"

"It's called a gentlemen's club. And no, they didn't know each other."

"They're connected by fewer degrees than Jordan Peele to Kevin Bacon."

"What?"

I break away from watching a meter maid cruising down the street. She pauses beside a Porsche. "You said 'money is always a factor' earlier. We need to know if Phinneas owed anyone money, and if they tried to cash in the debt."

Addison cocks an eyebrow. "Sounds familiar."

A hard laugh pushes through my teeth. "Yeah, I know how quickly a few bad decisions can spiral."

"Actually, there might be a way to find out about Phinneas's financial history," Addison says, slowly. "But I need a laptop."

"I have mine locked in my trunk."

We grab it from the Land Rover, I re-up my parking meter, then we walk half a block to the only sit-down café on this street. Wi-Fi is free—at least something is in Beverly Hills—and Addison wastes no time clicking open a new browser tab.

She types in the website for Phinneas's cloud, then enters Phinneas's email address and a combination of letters and numbers for the password.

"Phinneas kept a super-detailed spreadsheet of figures and payments to donors and charities that would net him a tax break and good public opinion. I saw it myself. He saved it in his cloud every time he made an edit. Maybe there's something to link Velvet and Phinneas, and tie the last eight weeks together."

"Addison." I hesitate beside her at a raised table overlooking the sidewalk. "This is not a good idea. The FBI is definitely monitoring Phinneas's accounts, and you're logging in from my IP address."

"I want the truth," Addison says, typing a new guess into the password field.

"Truth is all about context." I shake my head. "We can't really know what this all means without Phinneas himself to provide it."

"Wrong again. Truth is whatever tagline is shouted loud enough and long enough by the best publicist in the room: me." She pauses, then a Cheshire Cat grin spreads across her lips. "I know what his password is."

CHAPTER THIRTY-FIVE

ADDISON

BEVERLY HILLS | OCTOBER 14

Breaking into Phinneas's cloud should be easier than valet. After months of spending time with him, learning as much about him as I could to help position him just right in the media landscape, I know he's too proud to use his ex as his password and he's old-school enough that he might have used his first pet's name—like Connor did. He was a good guy, Phinneas, though he made plenty of mistakes. He didn't deserve all this.

Phinneas's Boom Boom profile on my phone displays the three videos I strong-armed him into posting. Nothing more. When we began his account at the beginning of summer, I insisted that he choose a password that he would remember. One that was easy. Maybe even one that he used elsewhere. The fact that I would also have access to his page and his security settings didn't bother him, as he wanted me to help monitor the account. He wanted nothing to do with the new social media platform, protesting he was "too old" for it. The password that he chose for his Boom Boom log-in? *Nirv@na2*. A member of Gen X through and through.

Connor volunteers to grab us coffees from the barista counter, as if the extra ten feet between us will protect him against the federal crime I'm close to committing. Only I'm not going to tamper with evidence. Just sift through it.

When he returns with light blue mugs, I take a sip of the scalding liquid—just the way I like it. "No one has more than a handful of variations on the same basic password. So let's make this a one." I type in *Nirv@na1* on the cloud home page open on Connor's laptop. When that doesn't work, I change the at sign to the letter *a*. A white background with folders appears. "We're in."

Phinneas stored dozens of documents in his cloud. Folders for everything from monthly expenses to shoe sizes of his previous assistants cover the screen. Halfway down the page, a title catches my eye: *Gifts and Donations*.

"Is that it?" Connor asks over my shoulder.

Names of individuals, companies, and nonprofits occupy the first column, with dates showing from up to a decade ago.

"Wow, he was really generous," Connor says. "Didn't he write a check out to a children's hospital in his last moments?"

I smile, recalling my quick thinking as I stood on the sidewalk outside the crime scene. "Something like that."

A search of the recipients using the key word *Velvet* turns up empty. Then I try *Chicago* and *Hong Kong* in case Phinneas donated to a nonprofit that Velvet supported; zero results.

Phinneas and Velvet don't seem to have had a financial link, based on this file.

I click the tabs along the bottom of the Excel file. The first is labeled *G&D*; the second reads *Contacts* and contains a fifty-cell list of attorneys and the states in which they practice law. The third tab is blank, but I click on it anyway. A single phrase is entered midway down the spreadsheet: *Wash cycle*.

"What does that mean?" I ask. "Connor?"

He scrunches his eyebrows. "Go back. Return to the main page of his cloud."

I click back.

"Scroll down."

"So demanding," I mutter, but glide the mouse down the screen. Nearly at the bottom, a file titled *Dry cleaning* appears. With a double click, the spreadsheet expands to present dozens of entries—names of people, LLCs, dates, and dollar amounts. There's no title in the header, and, curiously, no dry-cleaning businesses.

"Whoa. What is this?" Connor asks.

"My guess is the noncharitable donations."

I search for the term *Cherie* and get back zero results. When I input the name of the conglomerate's CEO, Caius Birdbaum, that, too, comes up short.

"I don't think Phinneas made any shady payments," I say. "Although someone must have. Phinneas was no angel before he started working with me, yet the media stopped raking over his mistakes."

"Go back to the home page." Connor leans closer as I hit the back button. His breath tickles my ear, sending a shiver beneath my collar. "How about that?"

"Hmm?"

"That folder. The 'Memoirs' file."

I click on the icon in the bottom right corner. "I didn't know he was writing anything."

Several mp4 files pop up. Twelve in total.

"That's because he wasn't," Connor says. "He recorded voice notes."

"Well, let's see how much he enjoyed working with me." I move the cursor to click the play button, but Connor lifts a hand.

"Addison, I'm already sunk as a private investigator, thanks to Genevieve. And I'd rather not go to jail if I can avoid it. Let's call it good and hand over what we know to the FBI."

I shake my head. "Agent Jonas has been clear in his suspicion of both of us. Don't you want to go to your meeting with him today with something that proves we're innocent? You really want to pin your hopes on someone in the federal government looking beyond the easy option? That's us, if you're not following."

"I'm following. Look, I just—"

"I've made my share of mistakes, Connor. But not enough to warrant prison." I hit play, and Phinneas's smooth voice rises from the computer's speakers. I told him several times that radio interviews would be great for him.

My voice mingles with Phinneas's deep timbre. I raise an eyebrow at Connor. "He recorded me. I remember that meeting. He was drunk, and swore up and down that he wasn't."

I click the next file. Then the next. A few customers enter the shop, grabbing coffees to go, and leave, but it's otherwise just me, Connor, and the barista, who pops in Airpods and opens a biology textbook between drinks. An hour goes by as we listen to Phinneas's inner thoughts, heartbreaks, and ambitions. I know most of it—including what a dedicated drinker he was. Connor, on the other hand, seems riveted by each mention of a new person in Phinneas's life. When his own voice appears during the notorious call he made to Phinneas, asking to finally get paid, Connor purses his mouth and then watches the meter maid through the glass while she tickets a BMW.

Once that file ends, and Phinneas offers some random FBI agent a Topo Chico in the next one, Connor whips out a pad of paper I didn't know anyone still carried. He makes notes.

"You know we can access the files again, right? Writing down names isn't necessary."

"It is when these recordings feature Phinneas's friends who were killed," Connor replies, not looking up. "Devon Lim and Annalise Meier both had cameos. Both of them died after Phinneas. This is the missing link, Addison."

Devon and Phinneas reunited at the tailor's shop, according to the current voice note. Devon was the friend that the tailor couldn't recall. A sharp gust of air-conditioning seems to spiral down my back as I listen to the moment that would send me on this craptastic journey, when Phinneas grabbed several business cards, same as the one in his office that I pocketed.

Connor pauses the recording. "Is it possible someone else accessed these files, too? Before Phinneas's death. The killer could be another person who made an appearance."

"Let's see if they show up in the dry-cleaner spreadsheet." I enter each person's name, thanks to Connor's written notes. Although none appear, entries for *Thrive, Inc.* pop up several times. At least a dozen.

"Connor, are you seeing this? Why would Phinneas make a gift to his own company?"

"Seems odd to pay . . . himself, in a way. Which I don't think anyone would do, unless the reverse happened at some point."

"What? Make more sense, Connor."

"I wonder if Phinneas took money from the company earlier, and this was his way of rectifying his books before anyone realized the cash was missing. It's possible that as CEO he had access to—well—too many parts of the company."

I lift both eyebrows. "Wouldn't surprise me. Thrive was not exactly known as a goody-goody entity. Few corporations are."

"And look here," Connor says. He points to the bottom of the spreadsheet. "He made a donation to Ovid Blackwell."

"That must be a payment for services rendered. Not a donation or gift." I click right on the notes column for more detail. The recipient is listed as Ovid Blackwell, but the notes call out a limited liability company. "Go 1973."

"Whoa. That's it. That's who made a payment to CherieTV. Are you seeing this?" Connor taps the screen with his finger. "Phinneas links Ovid Blackwell to Go 1973 LLC."

We stare at the spreadsheet. I rest my fingers along the tracker pad, absorbing the three words.

"So the LLC is actually with Ovid Blackwell," I say. "Ovid Blackwell paid off CherieTV. Why wasn't I told about this?"

"I don't know," Connor begins. "It's not something a board of directors would publicize, but whether or not it's illegal depends on the details."

"Companies accept gifts all the time. Ovid Blackwell receives hundreds of thousands of dollars in trips and dinners from clients and their affiliates each year. What's the problem if Ovid sends a money gift to CherieTV?"

"Accepting little tokens of appreciation is probably fine, if that's all they are." Connor leans back in the metal café chair. "But if Phinneas gave a chunk of change to Ovid, and Ovid paid off the media companies that normally covered Phinneas in a negative light, maybe there's some kind of cover-up. Have you ever seen anything weird at the office? Secret meetings?"

"Secret meetings? Like a cult?"

"Addison. I'm serious." He folds his arms across his chest in his taupe bomber jacket. "Anything that only a select few individuals were allowed to know about. A dinner in a private room where decisions were made by Ovid and another company. A trash day when lots of old folders were thrown out, separately and securely."

I scoff. "I'm involved in all important decisions at the firm. The only oddball cover-up I've witnessed was when the FBI came to visit and the office threw me a party—"

The taste of my favorite strawberry tart with its shortbread crust floods across my tongue. The dry bubbles of champagne. Peter's subtle cologne that smells like sandalwood as I peered over his shoulder to halfway down the office via several glass-walled conference rooms. Individuals who I assumed were mail clerks were taking bags of white paper downstairs to where the shredder is housed. Records of some sort. Transcripts. Evidence.

"Oh my God." I meet Connor's intent gaze. "I think—I was there at the last cover-up."

"What? Really?"

"We need to get to my office. Like, now. I think we're closer than we realize to justice for Phinneas."

A smile warms his face, like I just said something funny. "Justice? Hi, I'm Connor. I don't believe we've met before."

I lift my chin. "If there's one thing I can't stomach, it's my work going unrecognized. And Phinneas died before he could put all my tutelage on display."

Connor squints, as if assessing my flawless pores. "You've got a good heart, Addison. It's buried way, way in, underneath a lot of accolades. But it's there."

He reaches across the chrome tabletop to rest his hand on mine. The instinct to pull back rises in me, to cover my discomfort at feeling so close to him again with a quip or a criticism. I push it down. Choke it back like I would a wheatgrass shot.

Connor lied to me for weeks about previously working with Phinneas. But he's also been the only person I can count on this last month and a half. As I meet his hopeful gaze, I know we're close to the end of this shitstorm. And I could use a passenger for the carpool lane.

"It's almost two o'clock. Are you going to make your meeting with Agent Jonas?"

Connor checks the time on his phone. "It's going to be tight."

"Wait," I say as he stands. "There's another voice note. Maybe two more."

"Bring them."

\\\\\////

A chime dings as the elevator doors open onto the fifth floor's vacant lobby. Opposite the reception desk and where I took that photo with Peter, the waterfall continues to trickle down a glass wall into a reservoir filled with pebbles. The sound is at once calming and eerie in a place usually bustling with machinations.

We made the drive in record time, despite me peering in my rearview for flashing lights the entire twenty minutes.

"This way." I motion to Connor to follow me, then I hear

them: voices. Laughter and glasses clinking from the operations side of the building. There's a party going on to celebrate the end of Fashion Week. Only Ovid would celebrate a week that culminated in someone's hospitalization.

I move along the polished tile, my rubber heels muting the noise. Connor follows like my shadow, making even less sound. He's done this before. No one should wander toward this side of the floor, but anyone could be crouched over a phone at a generic desk in the open plan. Clients in this town require handholding every day of the week.

I lead Connor past the research team's desks, toward the south stairwell. "The men I saw were hauling trash bags of paper down to the basement. An incinerator service comes and does disposal every other month."

Nameplates on desks blur past until we reach the corner of the building. As we descend the six flights to the level beneath the parking garage, our shoes echo on the concrete steps.

I fling open a door marked STORAGE, then fumble for the light switch to my right. It doesn't work. "Shit."

Connor lets the door swing shut to close us into darkness. I hit the flashlight on my phone. A massive water heater, pipes extending from the low ceiling, and a dozen white trash bags fill the space. Scanning the bags with my sphere of light, I find two that contain whole pages, not yet shredded.

"Help me." I hand Connor my phone, then untie the knot of the plastic drawstring.

The first bag contains pages of printed directions, like relics from 1999. The second bag presents dozens of reams of expenses. Money transfers within the Ovid Blackwell bank accounts. And wire transfers to media companies from Go 1973 LLC, spanning

CherieTV and most of the major networks on cable, along with a smattering of payments to streaming networks.

"Connor. Ovid Blackwell has been sending money to everyone who's ever covered our clients in their news segments. And look—a payment made to Seven Wells Wellness Resort late last year. That's when Phinneas was a guest there."

"What do you think the money is for?" Connor grabs a bag of shredded paper. He rips it open and starts pawing through it.

I scan the sums of cash and the dates around which they were sent. Each transaction is large, several thousand dollars' worth, with some in the five figures. The bulk of them are sent around the fall, aka election season, and February and March, aka pilot season, but there are also two entries for Zenith Puglia, a major pharma company, at the start of the year. Last summer, summer-reading season, six thousand dollars was sent to Volatile Entertainment, a news network known for targeting the angry-youth demographic, right at the time our office was launching the writing career of a former satanic rock star turned Buddhist monk.

"Guiding the narrative."

"Addison. Check this." Connor shines his own cell phone light on an empty white pill bottle that he pulls from the bottom of the bag. On the label, the word DIAZEPAM is clear in bold letters, alongside smaller text regarding the tablets.

A shiver skates between my shoulder blades. "Are there any others like it?"

Connor holds up two more empty pill bottles. "A lot—all in this bag that's meant to be burned to ashes."

"These pages show Ovid Blackwell sent money to a pharma giant. Then Velvet Eastman took Valium. When she's allergic to it," I add, still working through the puzzle pieces. "Why would she have ingested any at all if she knew she was allergic? And put some in her boba?"

Connor licks his lips. "A better question: How many Ovid Blackwell clients have OD'd on Valium?"

Chills sweep down my neck as I recall that Greg Sistine, the political rival of Jamie Mendez—former Ovid clients—died from a "prescription cocktail" four years ago; everyone thought Mendez might be involved since they had made public threats to one another, but Mendez had an airtight alibi. Another client passed away with Valium in her system three years ago, right before I joined the firm. Each death was ruled accidental, or suspicious but never solved.

I open Connor's laptop. Light from the screen floods the corner I stand in. The final voice note begins loading.

"Come on. Come on." Connor bounces, clutching strips of paper in hand.

Phinneas's voice comes alive through the speakers. He's at some kind of red carpet event. The audio goes in and out, probably due to poor Wi-Fi signal in the basement of the building, but I catch a few phrases at a time. I try skipping forward to a spot that's better downloaded and land on a woman's voice. She's crying. Then a man speaks to her.

I look at Connor, my skin shrinking along my bones. "We need to get to Emilia Winthrop."

CHAPTER THIRTY-SIX

CONNOR

THE HOLLYWOOD HILLS | OCTOBER 14

L aurel Canyon winds through darkness at twilight in Los Angeles. Branches with orange leaves still clutching on in October hunch across the road as my GPS directs us higher, in the opposite direction of my meeting with the FBI. This morning, I thought I would be there, begrudgingly. But plans change.

We turn onto Mulholland Drive. When the British woman of my settings tells me to turn left, I swerve across traffic, not wasting a second.

As Addison explained while we raced down Sunset Boulevard, Emilia Winthrop is her only recent client of the last two years who hasn't been attacked in some way. If someone is targeting

Addison by way of her clients, or people linked to Phinneas's voice notes, Emilia is definitely on that list.

Addison hasn't spoken to her since she was taken off high-profile clients. Before we hit the canyon, a phone call to Emilia goes unanswered.

Up an impossibly steep hill, a tiny driveway splits off from the main road. We creep forward, aware that the rev of our engine has likely alerted Emilia that we're close by—if she's there. If she's conscious and able to hear us. If, if, if.

Passing beneath palm fronds that part like a curtain, we pull into the dead-end brick driveway of a bone-white, single-story farmhouse. Wide stone steps lead up a hill to the front porch, a veranda that wraps around three-quarters of the house. A black roadster is parked at the garage.

"That's Velvet Eastman's car," Addison says. "What the hell is it doing here?"

A curtain flutters from inside the house. A flash of blue. We exit my rental, then take the steps to the front porch without speaking. My skin tingles—intuition that someone is watching.

Addison gives a quick knock, and the whitewashed door opens. Emilia Winthrop gapes at us. Slim leggings and a gray oversize sweatshirt could mean we interrupted a lazy Saturday evening or that she dresses with movement in mind. Muscular trapezii are evident at the wide neck of her sweatshirt.

"Addison? What are you doing here?" Emilia asks.

"Can we come in?"

Emilia nods, blond hair bobbing in a messy top knot. "Yeah, sure. I was actually—"

"There's no time." Addison steps indoors, and I follow behind. "I'm sorry, but I need to ask you a few questions."

We enter a foyer laid with bricks from the floor to the walls and ceiling. Everything is in red brick, before the house cedes to brown wooden floorboards leading to a sitting room and a mounted flat-screen TV.

Emilia raises an eyebrow. "Sure?"

"Why is Velvet Eastman's car in your driveway?" Addison asks. "She's in the hospital. So did you take her car from the closing ceremony of Fashion Week?"

"Velvet left her car here. Because she's staying here."

"What?" Addison narrows her eyes. "She said she was staying at a friend's house."

Emilia nods slowly, as if perturbed by the frenzied questioning. "I'm that friend."

Addison shoots me a look. "Velvet and I exclusively met at my office and restaurants to work together. She said she didn't want to abuse her friend's generosity by hanging out at her house all day."

"We met in Chicago, ages ago." Emilia waves a hand toward the sitting room. "I let her stay while I was in Paris. I just got back yesterday. Why don't we grab a drink? You actually came at a funny time because—"

Addison grabs Emilia's hand. The two women glance down at the intimate gesture, as though neither of them understands it. "We came here to warn you. I don't know why or how, but I think someone is going to come for you. My clients have all been targeted or attacked, including Velvet."

I don't like this—none of it. The red brick, the feeling that we're in a pizza oven, is making me sweat.

"Why wouldn't I be safe here? This is my home. The paparazzi even know not to bother me here." Emilia smiles, bemused by

Addison's urgency. She toys with the hem of her sweatshirt at her hip. I scan her frame—the oversize sweatshirt where someone could easily hide several weapons.

"Addison," I whisper. "She's wearing gray. She's in all gray, but I saw someone else."

"Who?" Addison growls.

"There was someone wearing blue in the window above the garage." The curtain moved as we climbed the steps to the front door. There's another person in the house.

Emilia shakes her head. "That's what I've been trying to tell you."

"Now is probably a good time to come clean." A voice rings from the sitting room, out of sight. Leaden footsteps cross to the foyer, where we still stand beside the front door.

Genevieve Aspen greets us with concern. "I came here to try to help."

CHAPTER THIRTY-SEVEN

PHINNEAS

HOLLYWOOD | AUGUST 17

PHINNEAS REDWOOD: *Hoo boy! The hustle and bustle of a Hollywood Walk of Fame star unveiling is not for the fainthearted, or the sober, Future Editor. I'm on day fifteen and clutching on to that wagon, though, and I'm betting on myself. It does help that the greenroom I'm currently in is full of seltzer waters. No hard seltzers, just plain water with bubbles. Pity.*

Grauman's Chinese Theatre. Me, I have no business being here unattended, but because my publicist is off catering to another client in Paris this week, I was invited here by her PR firm for a little red carpet fun. I think it was Addison's idea, to ease me back into the maelstrom from the sidelines before the gala tomorrow. Malina, Addison's assistant, has been my concierge for the day, and I'd give her a five-star Yelp rating if she hadn't reprimanded me for trying to sneak into the real greenroom. The one assigned to the actress getting a star. I've seen all of this woman's work, so I'm dying to say hello and fanboy a bit. Apparently she's pretty anxious about public appearances, however, so I've been barred from bothering her before the unveiling on Hollywood Boulevard.

Can't say I blame her. Since I arrived, there has been a flurry of people going in and out of her room, food trays, drink trays, aromatherapy oils and incense, and lots of people with headsets speaking to unseen cogs in this gigantic Hollywood wheel. Coming from the pharma industry, it's pretty neat to watch. I feel like a kid again, heading to the movies for one of her films during opening weekend. God, I loved this woman. Aimee Adeoye. Even her name sounds like royalty. She is just this absolute icon of class, smarts, and beauty—and, apparently, stage fright.

Anyway, I thought I would continue working on my memoirs since I'm stuck in this room for another thirty minutes until Malina comes to get me. But—what if I can get Aimee Adeoye to be part of them? What if this is our chance encounter that finally allows us to fall in love, as my teenage heart always dreamed we would? God, wouldn't that be a trip? I record our very first face-to-face meeting, the precursor to our life of love and exotic adventures together? Eat your heart out, Annalise.

Better yet, I could finally snag one of those celebrity endorsements that marketing is on me about.

[Door opens; muffled conversations; shouting]

[Muffled] *Excuse me? Where are the restrooms? Gotcha.*
Thanks.

Oh hey, Memoirs. The bathrooms happen to be just down
the hallway past Aimee's room? Lovely. Let's go.

[Muffled] *No, no, I'm good. Just heading to the bathrooms.*
Thanks, Malina. I'll head back to the greenroom for you to
trap me—treat me—to some good red carpet tips. [Muffled]
Yeah, I am a little rusty here.

[Muffled]

Okay, keep it moving, Phinn. Let's go, let's go. Almost there.

We're passing a wall of framed photos. This will come as a
surprise to you, Memoirs, but a lot of famous people have
been through here.

We're passing the kitchen. [Muffled shouting] *Heading past*
the carpet-lined staircase that leads into the theater. And
slipping underneath the stairs where another hallway begins.

[Silence]

Wow—make that a "sound-insulated hallway." Everything
is dead quiet back here, so we better be likewise.

[Muffled conversation]

I'm close to the actual VIP greenroom. I think I hear
Aimee Adeoye. Oh shit. She's crying.

AIMEE ADEOYE: [Muffled] *I don't think I can do it. There*
are too many people out there.

MAN: *I know, Aimee. It's a big group that's come to see you and applaud your hard work over the years. You deserve this. Let yourself enjoy it.*

AA: *I know, I know. You're right. Though, just between you and me, I recently got a concerning diagnosis. My shrink says I have agoraphobia . . . [Sobs] I can't go out there, I can't.*

MAN: *Aimee, listen—*

AA: *No, I can't. I won't. [Sobs]*

MAN: *Okay. Okay, let's think about happier things, hmm? Calming things. Are you binging anything good lately? Seen any new movies? I know you love to talk about work.*

AA: *I do. I can get lost in a character and not think about how frightening it is, being among large groups of people. My last director was so nice. He kicked out my costar, that bitch Emilia Winthrop, and cleared the set so I could focus on a really pivotal monologue. Emilia is always partying late and coming to set hungover. It's so tacky.*

MAN: *Very unprofessional. Someone might have to chat with her at the next big event.*

AA: *Yes, exactly. At LA Fashion Week? That's coming up.*

MAN: *All you can do is focus on you, Aimee. Here, have some tea. There are some small bits of ginger in there. Just swallow them whole.*

AA: *Mmm, thank you. My nerves are shot.*

MAN: *Best to drink it all.*

AA: *Yes, of course . . . Hang on. Is there someone in the hall?*

[Footsteps]

MAN: *Mr. Redwood. This is a private space for Ms. Adeoye to prepare for the star ceremony. Let me escort you back to your greenroom.* [Muffled] *I'll be right back.*

[Footsteps; conversations]

PR: *What the hell was that?*

MAN: *What was what, Mr. Redwood? Please, we really should return to your greenroom. The ceremony is going to begin in five minutes.*

PR: *No, I'm not going anywhere. What did you put in her tea?*

MAN: [Pause] *I don't know what you're talking about.*

PR: *I fucking well think you do.*

MAN: *Mr. Redwood . . .* [Sniff] *Have you been drinking?*

PR: *Excuse me. I actually haven't. I've been sober for the last two weeks.*

MAN: [Pause] *Mr. Redwood, if we can keep moving—*

PR: *Oh, I'm not going anywhere with you. You put something in her drink.*

MAN: *Her vitamins, Mr. Redwood.*

PR: *Oh yeah? Do you put vitamins in young women's drinks at bars, too? Oh, hey! Look at this everybody, we got a Good Samaritan who hands out roofies to the needy!*

MAN: *Mr. Redwood, I'm going to have to escort you back to your room—*

PR: [Scuffling] *Get your fucking hands off me! You think you can get me to cooperate the way you got Aimee to?*

MAN: [Overlapping; shouting] *Mr. Redwood, please! Have you been drinking? You're drunk! We need to go—*

PR: *What the fuck? Don't touch me! Hey!*

MAN: [Overlapping] *—back to where we can get you some much-needed hydration. Excuse me—Malina! Mr. Redwood here found the complimentary bar inside Greenroom 4.* [Muffled] *Yes, he's gone a little overboard. I need a water bottle in Greenroom 1. No, straight water, not seltzer. A mint and a coffee. Thank you.*

[Scuffling; door slams]

MAN: *Mr. Redwood, I apologize for the way I handled myself back there. Really. But I think it's time for you to leave.*

PR: *Oh, should I sleep it off? You're going to tell everyone that I was drunk and didn't see you slip something into a movie star's tea, is that right?*

[Silence]

You can't do that to others—people who trust you. You don't know what their chemical makeup is, what their allergies are, what their drug use is. I had a teenage girl overdose on my pill back in the nineties because someone slipped her several without checking her medical history. You can't do this.

MAN: *I hear the pharma gala is on Friday night, and I know it's going to be a huge success for you. I look forward to hearing all about it.*

PR: *Like hell you will.*

MAN: *Is that—are you recording me? You know it's rude to record people without their consent.*

PR: *What, this? Oh yeah. Well, it's just a voice memo, you know, nothing fancy. But once I hit "save," the file automatically uploads to my cloud. See? Just fucking did i—*

CHAPTER THIRTY-EIGHT

ADDISON

HOLLYWOOD HILLS | OCTOBER 14

Genevieve Aspen clutches her pearls, scanning our faces. Brushing back white-blond hair into her French twist hairstyle, the septuagenarian offers a morose smile.

"Addison Stern, I don't believe we've had the chance to meet," she says, her voice smoky.

"We haven't."

"What are you doing here, Gen?" Connor asks.

Genevieve glances to Emilia. "I'm here on an errand for poor Velvet. As I was telling Emilia, Velvet asked me to bring her the eye mask she always sleeps with to the hospital."

"She's awake?" I ask. "No one called me, and I'm her emergency contact."

Genevieve purses lips coated in soft pink. "No, well, they wouldn't have, dear. Velvet only just woke up around an hour ago, and right when I came to visit her. She passed out again after around five minutes, but she did ask me for this creature comfort. It's the least I can do for an old friend."

Connor side-eyes me, but neither of us moves. "You know Velvet?"

"My dear boy, powerful women must stick together."

He sneers at her. He darts his gaze between his former benefactor, who threw him under a whole proverbial fleet of buses, and Emilia Winthrop, celebrated actress who remains living and unharmed, apparently.

Well, if he's not going to say it, I will. "You shouldn't be here, Genevieve. None of us should."

"What?" Emilia laughs. "What are you talking about?"

"Have you been contacted by Jamie Mendez—or Ovid Blackwell?" I turn to her. "I still don't know exactly how Mendez plays into this, but he could be dangerous. Velvet's overdose wasn't accidental, and she was staying here, at your place. We think you are doubly at risk."

Emilia shakes her head. "At risk of what? You're not making— I mean, *you're* from Ovid Blackwell, Addison."

"Goodness. It seems I interrupted more than your evening, Emilia." Genevieve holds up a black eye mask with red trim. "I'll be going now. Thank you for the chat."

"Gen, I didn't see your car parked out front. Can I give you a ride?" Connor asks.

"No, thank you. I'm right around the corner where the turn isn't so tight."

"Emilia, who else from Ovid Blackwell has been in touch?" I ask.

Connor steps in front of Genevieve. "Let me walk you."

"Connor Windell, I don't know what you think you're doing—"

A knock at the door cuts off Genevieve's gravelly voice. Silence falls across our group. Emilia stares at me with wide eyes. "Addison? What is going on?" she whispers.

"You're being targeted, Emilia. By Ovid Blackwell and by Jamie Mendez, a former investor in Thrive, Inc."

"The diet pill company? I have never been on—"

"Emilia, that doesn't matter. Listen to me. I need you to go upstairs and don't come down until I tell you. Take Genevieve with you."

"Where would I be going?" Aspen hisses.

Another knock. Louder this time.

"Goddammit." I surge back to the front door to lock it, but before I can the knob turns and it pushes inward. Peter Huxton steps inside.

"Well, hello. Am I interrupting a party?" The Ovid Blackwell vice president gazes at us, curiosity creasing his forehead in a picture of innocence. Graying black hair and a wrinkled suit jacket give him the air of a frazzled grandfather rather than a PR executive who drugs people without their knowledge.

Peter's voice on Phinneas's recording, speaking to Aimee Adeoye, was clear to my ears. Unmistakable, despite the poor audio.

"Peter," I manage. "You're here."

"As are you. Everything okay?" He lifts both eyebrows, seeking reassurance from Emilia.

"It's fine," she manages. "Addison, I was trying to tell you. Mr. Huxton reached out earlier today, to come by for a visit. But right now I'm feeling a little crowded. And I need to leave for yoga soon."

"Of course. Of course." Peter frowns. "Everyone at Ovid is distraught at Ms. Eastman's situation. We were hoping you had some answers, Ms. Winthrop."

"Me?"

"That's why I called, since Ms. Eastman has been staying with you. I'm assuming that's why Addison is here. Is that not right, Addison?"

Sweat breaks across my chest. "Yes, it is," I reply. Because it's true. Because, what else do I say?

Peter invited himself to Emilia Winthrop's home. Peter medicated a different actress without that person's knowledge, then argued with a client of mine who was killed a day later.

Emilia gives me a wide-eyed stare. I'm the only person she knows properly in this group, yet she shrugs. "I guess we can go into the sitting room?"

Everyone moves from the foyer toward the crackling fire that's contained by heat-resistant glass. Exposed wooden beams in the ceiling add to my feeling of being unmoored—let loose in the world without direction or protection. Emilia trails behind, unsure of what we're all doing in her home. Rightfully so.

"Did you know that Velvet was having suicidal ideation?" Peter asks when we're barely assembled around a creamy marble coffee table, an ivory love seat, and matching deep armchairs. Genevieve is the only one who sits.

"Do you know that your firm has been threatening this young woman?" she huffs from the love seat.

Emilia breaks into high-pitched laughter. "What? No, I'm fine, really—"

"Ovid Blackwell would never suggest harm to our clients." Peter pauses, searching my face. "Did you say that to Ms. Winthrop? Is that why you're here—to turn your former clients against the firm?"

"Excuse me, I would never betray Ovid, but you force my hand when—"

"Ms. Winthrop. I'm sorry you got dragged into this. Addison here had to be placed on administrative leave, then she was asked to exit the building and not return. I'm afraid she didn't handle it well."

Emilia shrinks away from me. "Is that true, Addison?"

"No. Yes, but because there's more to it—"

"Ms. Winthrop, I'd like to suggest we meet another time. I'm so sorry we disturbed your evening. And please excuse Addison. She's a disgruntled, recently terminated employee who is now raking Ovid Blackwell's good name—"

"Recently terminated employee?" Out of all the bullshit that I just witnessed spewing from Peter's mouth, the audacity to suggest I was fired snaps me out of the daze I fell into upon opening the door to his hangdog mien.

"But what about allowing harm to come?" I ask Peter, my teeth set on edge. "You said 'Ovid Blackwell would never suggest harm to our clients.' Then why did Ovid Blackwell invest in diazepam?"

"Addison," he begins. "I'm not sure what you mean."

"Are you having a blackout, Peter?" I haven't moved, and neither has he; he's blocking one of the sitting room exits. "Why did Ovid Blackwell pay companies who manufacture diazepam, like Zenith Puglia? Why did we find dozens of empty bottles labeled 'diazepam'? You must know, you're on the board."

"Wait, what is going on?" Emilia asks. For the first time since she opened her door to us, fear skitters across her small features. "Why did you all come here?"

"Because Ovid Blackwell has it in for you, Emilia." I glare at Peter. "Ovid has been drugging clients without their knowledge or consent, and Connor and I think Velvet was attacked, too. She didn't OD. Since she was staying with you and you're my client, you might be targeted next."

Peter's eyebrows go sky high. "Addison, I'm sorry, but this is bordering on paranoid. Never in all my time with Ovid Blackwell have I seen any indicators of clients being drugged."

I scowl. "Excluding Velvet, of course."

"As I said," he draws out, "the idea that Ovid could be poisoning anyone is absolutely shocking."

I step toward him. "Something was done to Velvet. Why are you really here, visiting *my* client, Emilia—"

"You guys, you guys!" Emilia shouts. "Enough! Please leave my home. Now."

"I would love to." Genevieve rises.

"Gen, let me walk you to your—"

"I said, you have to go. Get out, all of you!"

"Ms. Winthrop, you'll have to excuse Addison—"

"Peter, tell us the truth. Why is Ovid paying off drug manufacturers and—"

"Stop it!" Emilia shrieks. "Everyone get the fuck out of my house before I call the police!"

"Oh, for the love of—" Peter growls. "Will someone shut her up?"

A noise cuts through the house. Emilia whimpers, then collapses against the back of an armchair, sliding to the hardwood. Red smears against the ivory headrest. I whirl to her side, where blood pours from the hole in her chest. She's been shot. She sucks in a perfunctory breath, stuck between a wheeze and a cough. Then her expression of disbelief freezes in a death mask.

My breath lodges in my throat. I can't move, can't do anything. Wetness pools in my eyes, then—before I can raise a hand—drips down my cheek. I stare at the woman who I visited in Paris not two months ago. We downed expensive champagne and caviar together in a sixteenth-century manor.

"Peter . . ." I manage to say. "What the fuck!"

He sighs. There's no gun in his hand. The neighbors wouldn't have heard the silencer shot. The only proof I have that a weapon was fired is Emilia's fading warmth beside me.

Then a man appears in the doorway from an entrance to the kitchen. Lanky but muscular, wearing a blue shirt that Connor must have seen in the window above the garage, with a nose that's been broken several times and dark eyes that glower. I recognize him. The assassin from the French Riviera. The person who chased us out of our hotel in Toulon. The night owl who snooped around my front porch.

"You. You followed me to Santa Barbara, then France," Connor says. "Who are you?"

"I had hoped it wouldn't come to this," Peter says. "But you had to go into such detail, Addison."

"This is my fault?" I whisper. Anger pulses through me, and I'm grateful to focus on something besides Emilia. Blood flows from the wound and onto the hardwood, undeniable even in my peripheral vision.

Genevieve is frozen on the love seat.

"Enzo, I think it's time for the second part of our plan. You have enough gas to get to the border?"

The man—hit man—called Enzo smiles a chipped grin. "I'll be long gone by the time the police catch up to the truck."

"You've been driving the pickup that belongs to Fernando Castillo," Connor says.

Enzo shrugs, indifferent to our confusion. "Nando and I go way back. When Mr. Huxton said he had new work for me I called up my buddy, and he loaned me the wheels whenever I needed them. He's been around the concrete circuit. He'll understand things got dicey."

Peter nods appreciatively. "Your bonus for the added—er, deliverable—will be en route soon. Make sure to wipe the security footage of the house before you leave."

Without even a *goodbye* or *I'll be in touch*, Enzo turns and exits through the kitchen at the back of the house.

Peter nods behind him. "I sent him to Monaco to deal with Mr. Lim and his friend, but your arrival complicated things. If he had caught up to you two in Toulon, none of us would be in the position we're in now."

Shock draws my face long. "Meaning we'd be dead. And you'd still be doing—whatever it is you're doing. Peter . . . you've been behind this the whole time."

Peter's warning to me outside of a shop in the Fashion District returns, as loud as a horn in LA traffic: *You don't want to offend the board. They employ all kinds of . . . professionals.*

It was never the board of directors who wanted me gone.

"The diazepam." Connor stands beside Genevieve, opposite where Emilia lies. A fur throw blanket draped across the backrest resembles another casualty. "All of this is due to drugging your clients?"

"Well, I wouldn't— It's unlikely to seem . . ."

"Emilia is dead, Peter." I interrupt his hemming and hawing. "You don't have to lie to us. We're all aware Connor and I know too much already. I knew it was your voice on Phinneas's memoirs within seconds. I didn't know you were capable of killing."

Genevieve popping in for a visit couldn't have been predicted, and I try not to look her way now. No sense in compounding what is already her likely death sentence—what may be ours.

Moments when Peter had my back over the years flood my mind—how he defended my unorthodox tactics to achieve the right publicity for a client or congratulated me on my hard work in the name of the firm. Peter Huxton was like the uncle I never asked for: rough around the edges, a little awkward, but supportive of my dreams. It was all an act.

Connor inches behind me as he speaks, positioning himself near a heavy potted plant. "Are you part of some cartel?"

A smile tips Peter's mouth upward; then he shrugs. "Drugs are never a first resort. But, sometimes, they help present the best possible image of clients who refuse to play ball. For the unruliest, a pill or three will make their way into a drink before a big event to get them to relax. To play by the rules. Use the carefully written script that we provide."

"Wow. Peter, I never thought you were lazy, but I stand corrected." I sneer, the gloves yanked all the way off. "A client can be coerced in other ways that will allow us to reach the goal that everyone wants. How long has this been going on?"

Connor clears his throat. "I'd guess longer than last month's trash bag took to fill up."

Peter peers at him, as if seeing Connor for the first time. "Mr. Windell. You're the PI that Genevieve Aspen accused of murder."

"Erroneously."

Genevieve coughs from the love seat. "That much is clear."

"I saw Aspen on CNN talking about you." Peter smiles again, indulgent. "Although you all may know the truth, no one will believe you. Not after the case I built up against Addison and

Connor. Nor will they believe a senile geriatric." He tips his head to Genevieve. "Like it or not, society ignores women when they become old. Especially the waffling kind who can't make up their minds."

A siren peals in the canyon. Red and blue lights flashing in the darkness somewhere. Is the siren for us? Agent Jonas could have realized by now that we broke into Phinneas's cloud, since the FBI was actively monitoring his accounts. He could have upgraded my person-of-interest title to full-blown "suspect," and searched the nearby CCTV cameras at traffic lights for Connor's license plate. Probably, the police are a mile away along a winding road, and it will take far longer for them to reach us than I'd like.

Then again, once the police or the FBI arrive, Connor's car will be searched. They'll find all the bags of evidence that we just lifted from the incinerator bin in the basement of the Ovid offices. Emilia's dead body will only appear as another victim— mine and Connor's—given the last eight weeks of carnage and our very public pursuit of the truth.

The truth. I have to laugh. I've been doing my damnedest this whole while to try to wrangle the storyline to fit my objective while learning who killed my clients. But somewhere along the way, this version of Peter and his definition of truth won out. Truth is only what the winners call it. Truth is whatever it is according to those in power.

"Seems we have more uninvited guests coming fast." Peter holds up a hand. He digs in his jacket's inner pocket as if he's got an incoming call, then withdraws a handgun. He releases the safety with a click. "Upstairs. Now."

"Peter, stop this," I say. "You're not a killer. Enzo did that part of the work. You've never even so much as fired a secretary."

"Is that right?" Peter's upper lip curls. "Or maybe you saw what I wanted you to see while you tried pushing me, along with the tried-and-true tactics that made Ovid Blackwell an icon in our industry, to the sidelines."

"What tactics are those?" I scoff. "Backroom deals, network TV, and working exclusively with entitled old white men? Because no one does that anymore. Not in the twenty-first century."

"I'm all for modernity," Peter snaps. "But not at the expense of our esteemed core, our longtime values."

"The only thing longtime about Ovid Blackwell is the board of directors, which hasn't had a vacancy for partner since . . ." I allow my gaze to settle on the lit fireplace. What was it that Peter mentioned during the party that Ovid threw for me? Hiram Benson was finally retiring from the board, and it was a huge deal. There has never been a woman among those seats.

"Since 1990, when the board was established," I continue. "You only supported my idea to move Ovid into social media, and my staged PR spectacles, to my face. Behind closed doors, you blocked me at every turn. Didn't you? That's why you told me to take a step down from work after Phinneas was killed. It wasn't for my 'own good,' like you said. It was for yours, because I was becoming too successful. It was for the preservation of the old guard."

Connor stiffens beside me. He steps closer to the potted plant and a sailboat paperweight that could cause a concussion from the right angle.

"You're right." Peter clicks his tongue. "But the old guard isn't only mine. It belongs to everyone on whose shoulders you're standing now. The people who built this city—the publicity industry—and those who first formed the essential teams that created the studio stars, pushed the politicians to greater heights, and cleaned up every public faux pas made by bumbling business leaders. And yes"—Peter levels me with a stare—"it even belongs to you."

"How inclusive."

"I've survived this long in Hollywood, after putting in more than my share of long nights and early mornings working with the most disagreeable public figures. It wasn't fair that I was about to be pushed out by a young—"

"Woman?" I growl. "Don't be shy. We can add misogyny to your list of embarrassing traits."

Peter scans his audience, ever conscious of image. "I wasn't going to be pushed out by anyone. Especially not some up-and-comer who arrived on Sunset Boulevard not five years ago. Do you have any idea how many interns and mentees I've personally coached over the years on how to make it as a professional publicist? Hundreds. Thousands. Each of those mentees relies on us and our reputation when they list our agency as a reference. I've built up the good name of Ovid Blackwell while giving back to my community—and you would waltz in and destroy all of that."

"How? By appealing to a younger, wider demographic?"

"By ruining what works."

Connor clears his throat. "I fail to see how murder—and attempted murder—of multiple clients works."

"Death was not what I wanted. This is . . . I'm not . . . We were only supposed to drug the individuals who couldn't stay out of their own way. It was a revival of some of the old tactics used back when Ovid Blackwell was first making a name for itself. Use of substances and payments to media outlets were the means to an end I desired very much."

"My undoing?" I ask.

A moment passes while I scrutinize his weathered brow for actual remorse, a moment during which Peter appears lost. Anxious and alone without his hired gun. His gaze lands on the spot where Emilia slid from the back of the armchair. Then it hardens.

"I wanted my legacy intact. But things took a turn. Phinneas forced my hand when Enzo went over to his house—only to scare him the afternoon of the gala, to get him good and drunk enough that he couldn't attend the gala and spread his nasty accusations about the firm. To buy us some time. But it turned into a standoff between the two, with Phinneas locking himself in his office, swearing he would tell the world about Ovid Blackwell's . . . activity . . . no matter the payout or our promise of reform. We had to improvise from there."

"And Phinneas figured it all out when you slipped that actress pills in her tea during her Walk of Fame event," Connor adds. "Did you ever try to give him a pill?"

"I never drugged Phinneas. I didn't get the chance," Peter says, candor back in place. "He was always too drunk to give him diazepam on top of the liquor."

"How considerate," I sneer. "Except Phinneas wasn't drinking when he died. He was sober—or trying to be. So is that another lie?"

"Probably," Connor says. "And when patience runs thin, Valium has been Peter's answer."

Peter lifts a bushy eyebrow. "That, or money. Money is usually all that it takes."

The trash bags and their semi-shredded records. "Hence the massive payments across the country to media outlets," I add. "Under the LLC Go 1973."

"G.O.," Peter corrects me. "Gerald Ovid, 1973."

The year Gerald Ovid began his first PR agency. Before going into business with Samuel Blackwell. Of course.

"We paid various individuals to ignore certain antics—the media, sometimes law enforcement, and certain malleable public officials," Peter adds. "Bribes worked for Ovid in the past. They worked very well. But when the firm is called to perform and provide miracles again and again to undeserving clients who don't pull their own weight—that's when other tactics come into play."

"But how does any of that relate to Devon Lim?" I ask. "He had a bump or two in the road"—more like the occasional bump of cocaine—"but he was upstanding."

Peter hesitates, still guarding something. Still hedging. "Well . . . some clients cost us in terms of payments, while others knew more than they should about Ovid Blackwell operations."

"Devon and Phinneas," Connor says. "They reconnected recently. Did Phinneas share what he knew about you with Devon and Annalise?"

"We should get you on our crack research team, Mr. Windell."

"And Velvet Eastman?" Connor continues. "I didn't see you at the closing ceremony, and everyone said you left Fashion Week early. You could have hung around. Used that extra time to grab the boba drink at the shop around the corner, with chipped ice the way Velvet prefers, poison it with diazepam pills, then place it in Velvet's greenroom. Right before the chaos of Addison's flour bomb."

Peter weighs his response. "The young woman I paid to buy the drink, who gave the name Addison to write on the cup, was more than happy to. Young hopefuls in this town are so eager."

My stomach churns. "And Jamie Mendez? How does he play into your game?"

"And Hashim Swartz?" Connor adds.

"They don't. But it was entertaining watching the pair of you circle Mendez and the bread crumbs of his world," Peter continues. "Enzo kept me up to speed on every new theory you tracked—even when you visited that tailor today. Mendez was a convenient distraction, while Swartz *was* seeking a way to oust Phinneas as CEO of Thrive—he was quite vocal about it during Phinneas's last rehab stay—but he never got the support from Thrive's stakeholders.

"For a while, it looked like things would go to plan. Agent Jonas would make the right decision and save us this final confrontation, and Emilia would be dealt with later in a way that would work out best for us all. Then Jonas followed the money from Phinneas's records—payments to us that we used to buy the silence of his critics—and realized the LLC belonged to Ovid Blackwell. He served a subpoena for Ovid's finances after I told you to avoid Fashion Week, Addison."

"Good thing I don't listen well."

Peter shrugs. "Come any financial faux pas that Agent Jonas decides Ovid Blackwell committed, the front-page headline will still be murder. Your horrific actions."

I suck in a breath, picturing the newsfeeds. He's not wrong. "Peter . . ."

He purses thin lips. "You could have been a part of it, Addison. Still can. Although I loathe the way you ascended in the firm— when you target a goal, your efforts are formidable. You're an asset to Ovid Blackwell."

"Provided that I know my place, you mean."

Peter hesitates. "I'm acknowledging reality. While the facts point to you as the culprit, as the true mastermind of these recent difficulties, they don't have to." He dips his head to Connor. "There are other options."

I lift a single threaded eyebrow. "Are you suggesting that I side with you and name Connor as the killer?"

"Now wait a minute," Connor pipes up. "How would that make any—"

"You think I have such little loyalty, Peter?"

Peter draws his lips into an uneven smile, as if it pains him— as if the true monster within is beginning to claw its way out. "I think you'll do what you've always done: choose what's best for Addison."

Connor casts me a nervous glance, but I can't reassure him there. A high-pitched horn peals outside, tearing through the air, ever-closer.

"Regardless," my boss continues, turning toward the sound. "What matters now is you've gone and led your pursuers, the authorities, straight to us. Exactly as I hoped you would."

CHAPTER THIRTY-NINE

CONNOR

HOLLYWOOD HILLS | OCTOBER 14

Sirens cry out in the canyons, nonstop. The FBI, pursuing me after I failed to show for my appointment with Agent Jonas? Does that mean they've been tracking me somehow? Panic tightens my chest. I should leave before they arrive—skip town with Addison. We could go somewhere in Central America. Although she seems to be entertaining the idea of selling me out—again.

The same thought keeps running through my head with this woman: Addison Stern always puts herself first, so I should stop pretending otherwise.

I scan the room. Search for a way out of this mess. Peter has the back hallway to the kitchen blocked, and the gun he wields keeps us all captive, anyway. Genevieve is so still on the love seat she might be having a stroke.

Placing a tentative foot behind me, testing the floorboards, I move toward the front door.

Addison's face lit up while we were listening to Phinneas's memoirs. Said we had to hightail it to her client's house right that instant—but this is not how I thought things would go down. Emilia Winthrop, celebrated actress, shot dead in her own home—a new victim in our proximity—complicates everything.

Peter cocks the gun and points it toward Addison. "What's your decision? Or will you let the police make it for you?"

She glowers at him. "You targeted me from day one. Why Connor?"

"Collateral damage, I'm afraid," Peter says. "Phinneas made such a scene at the Hollywood Walk of Fame event, and made it clear his ethics—or whatever CEOs of drug companies have—wouldn't allow him to keep quiet. When Enzo visited Phinneas the day of the pharma gala to fix our problem and found his laptop open to his memoir recordings, and a sent email to Devon Lim containing a link to them, we realized we'd need to cast a wider net to resolve things. Mr. Windell's investigation of Devon made him fall under that net."

I take another step toward the door. Then another. Lift a sailboat tchotchke from an end table.

"Devon and Annalise Meier were found together in Monaco," Addison takes up. "Did she also hear how you'd been dosing clients?"

"Most likely," Peter replies. He casts an eye at me but doesn't object to my change in location, the gun always lifted. Always watching. "Ovid Blackwell's IT analysts hacked into Phinneas's cloud. They confirmed that other IP addresses accessed the voice notes. Annalise Meier's was one of them. You really must have more confidence in your colleagues, Addison. Being a lone wolf these days is not very appealing in a partner."

"Oh, and I so desire to be appealing to a murderer," she snaps.

"But why Velvet Eastman? She did nothing wrong." I move closer to the armchairs, less than three feet from Peter. Almost in range. I rest my hand casually behind my back.

"Ask the conservative news networks if that's true."

Addison toys with something in the deep pocket of her jacket. Car doors slam shut outside in the driveway below. Footsteps fan out near where I parked the rental.

"Addison," Peter says, simpering. "Whoever will you coerce and abuse in federal prison, I wonder?"

I step wide, then dive to Genevieve on the love seat and yank her to a standing position. Jerk the sailboat paperweight high above her white bun, like an anvil ready to drop. "Peter! You don't care about this woman. You barely knew she existed until now, but she's ruined my life a thousand times over. Let me have my revenge, then we can get back to you pinning murders on us."

"Connor, what the hell are you doing?" Addison shouts.

I tighten my grip on Genevieve's shoulders. "If we're going down, Addison, I want it to be for something I deserved."

"Are you mad?" Genevieve whimpers. "Get off me, boy!"

"Peter!" I bark again. I slide a foot behind, dragging Genevieve with me away from the love seat. My elbow hitches up and under her jaw. "It's now or never, isn't it?"

More voices shout outside. Peter narrows his gaze, raking over Genevieve's terror with cool indifference. "She's not my problem."

"What?" Genevieve yelps as I force her, lug her small, kicking frame, toward the hallway beside the front door. "You'd like that, wouldn't you, Mr. Huxton? I'm just another old woman to be discarded?"

I grunt. "Genevieve Aspen, I'm not your only victim. But you will be mine."

I rear back, wielding the three pounds of aluminum above her head, then bring it crashing down to the floor. Twisting the knob, I rip the door open, then shove a screaming Genevieve outside to the whitewashed porch.

"Freeze! Hands in the air!"

Genevieve's cries erupt as more voices rush to her aid. I slam the door shut and turn back to face Peter and Addison where they stand alone in the sitting room.

My chest rises then falls, triumph pulsing through my limbs. "She didn't deserve to be caught up in this mess. Even if she deserves a whole lot else."

Peter glowers. "You realize I could shoot you right now and the police wouldn't bat an eye. You all but confirmed that you *are* the aggressor I made you out to be."

"Connor Windell, we've got you surrounded!" someone shouts on the porch. More footsteps sprint along the perimeter of the property. The same route that Enzo chose when he left.

"See?" Peter smiles.

I shake my head, though I don't break eye contact with Addison's former boss. "It was a risk. But it was the right thing to do."

Despite the adrenaline still flooding my veins, I feel a certain peace. At last, I took action in a way I know my granddad could get behind.

"Huh. I didn't realize you associated with Boy Scouts, Addison."

"I doubt I'd be allowed anywhere near a den meeting, honestly. Too many dead bodies in my past for that"—I shoot Addison a look, using her words from a few weeks ago—"but I'm not that person anymore."

She returns my steady gaze with a tight smile. One hand remains deep inside her pocket.

More knocks on the door, louder and heavier. Peter presses his mouth into a line. "Whoever you are doesn't matter to me, Mr. Windell. But it will to the police."

Addison's got a glazed-over look on her face that says she's only partly listening. She wore the same expression when I asked her to noodle through a Six Degrees of Kevin Bacon question.

We need to distract Peter. At least until the police come indoors.

Lingering at the threshold of the sitting room, I try to channel a movie star's charisma. Stage presence. Expert-level bullshitting. "You think you have everything figured out, don't you? But it's not just about a dance. Not anymore."

More shouting that cuts into my *Footloose* reference: "Addison Stern! If you're in there, come out now!"

Feet pound behind us, where the backyard must be located. I grab the sailboat paperweight from where I dropped it on the hardwood, then reenter the sitting room with slow steps, luring Peter's attention toward me.

Peter glares at me. "Be careful, Mr. Windell. You might get what you're asking for."

Addison clears her throat. "Peter, the FBI already has everything. They're currently ransacking Phinneas's computer files. Your deeds will be broadcast across the legal system any day now."

Peter narrows his gaze. "That could be true. But truth is

362

relative. Truth is power. And right now, I hold all of it."

"Do you? The truth is, I've worked for you for three years," Addison says. "Done everything that was asked of me and more. Why target me in your grand takedown of people who mistreated the Ovid Blackwell name?"

Another order is barked behind the house. The FBI agents are almost ready.

I take a step forward to reach the love seat. Peter shifts the barrel of his gun to me, no longer content to let me roam. "Because, Addison. You have burned more bridges in this industry than an on-air tirade against Hello Kitty. Although we never issued hush money on your behalf, the damage you caused to Ovid didn't go ignored. You'll take the fall for the deaths—then we'll start fresh, catering to the youth demo in a new chapter."

"Exactly as I have been pushing for the last year?" She scoffs. "How brilliant."

The police are outside. Genevieve is safe. Addison and I are probably going to jail, but we'll get out of here alive. All we have to do is wait. Keep Peter off-balance until the police break in. I shoot Addison a smile. A fringe of brown hair falls across my eyes as I reach for just the right Kevin Bacon quote: "I thought this was a party. Let's dance."

"You're right, Peter." Addison lifts an eyebrow to me, but she stays focused. "I should be applauding everything you've done in the name of the firm I love so much."

"Obviously."

"Thank you for having the clarity to protect Ovid Blackwell at all costs."

A loud bang hits the door. "FBI!"

My heart races in my chest, so close to freedom. Or to incarceration.

"I was brash—arrogant to not follow your directions." Addison speaks faster, lowering her voice, her eyes. Like some strange, cowed version of herself.

"Peter, I don't know why I didn't see it before," she continues. "But the way you planned the . . . deaths of Phinneas, Devon, and Annalise is almost too perfect. I get it—you asked me to step back from my job, knowing I wouldn't be able to resist investigating on my own. I would be seen asking questions about Phinneas, meeting with questionable investors, visiting rehab, having Connor look up old acquaintances, and acting as suspiciously as if I were Phinneas's killer, when in fact it was Enzo who attacked each of them. You painted me into a corner, Peter, and I have to admit . . ." She hesitates, as if steeling herself.

"Peter." She swallows. "You bested me."

Iron floods my taste buds. What is she doing? We want him off-balance, not feeling so smug and powerful that he can dispose of us like Costco samples.

Peter clears his throat. "I did. I meant what I said earlier, Addison. You are an asset to Ovid Blackwell. It'd be a shame to waste all that talent in prison—especially when there's a clear culprit right beside you. Connor was seen on camera breaking into Devon Lim's house in Bel-Air. He knew each victim, or he was at the scene of each crime. Are you sure he hasn't been working against you all this time?"

Hold up.

"That's deluded," I say. "You think that would really stick in court, that I attacked—"

"I could see it." Addison tucks a strand of hair behind her ear.

"The part of me that has always chosen myself over others—in the name of survival, just like you said, Peter—would be a fool not to consider your offer. With the FBI at our literal doorstep, it'd be stupid not to."

"Exactly."

"What?" I try to catch her eye, but she ignores me.

Where the hell is the FBI? Why aren't they in here already?

"It could work if we both confirm that Connor was behind everything," she continues. "Especially if you then made me partner."

"Addison." I wave a hand in her direction. Try to break the spell. "You can't be considering this."

The memory of Addison's horror, when she discovered me in her condo weeks ago, flashes to my mind. Followed by a different memory—the mortifying shock in my car when I realized a client of hers could hear Addison and me in the throes of passion.

Her fury when she realized I stole information from her laptop, and more recently the disgust she wore when I outright accused her of involvement in Devon Lim's death.

The sensation of her body pressed against my chest in the Amalfi Coast, warm and comforting as we lay in bed together.

Her hand in mine during the closing ceremony of Fashion Week as I led her out of the exhibition hall to the safety of the adjoining alleyway.

The light puff of her breath against my neck as we worked to uncover the secrets of Phinneas's computer files.

More sharp knocking pummels the door, searing through my masochism. I jump, anxiety twisting my gut. "Addison? Addison, look at me."

"Clock is ticking, Addison." Peter grins. "Ready to join the elite circle of Ovid Blackwell?"

She finally tears her gaze from the fireplace to meet my eye. "Connor is many things to me: enemy, colleague, source, lover. He's betrayed me, lied to me, and hurt me deeper than I've allowed anyone to in years."

"Addison," I plead. "You know I've apologized for every—"

"But the most important role he holds in my life is partner." She pauses. "The only kind that I want in this moment."

"Really? You'd prefer prison to a spot on the board?"

Addison simpers at her former boss, "Peter, if I want someone to gaslight me, then dangle a carrot in my face, I'll call my mother."

He lifts a skeptical eyebrow. "Does that mean—"

"No. My answer is categorically no."

Relief courses through my body as new shouts carry from the porch. "Three . . . two . . . one!"

The door bursts open, and federal agents descend through the front entry. "Drop your weapons!"

I throw my hands sky high, the sailboat long forgotten.

"You can't arrest me," Peter says, struggling with a federal agent, who places handcuffs on his wrists.

"I really wasn't planning on it," the agent says. "But my boss just radioed in to say otherwise."

"Who's your boss?" I ask.

"Agent Jonas. He said something about a social media thread?"

Peter stares at Addison with wide eyes. "What did you do?"

She withdraws her cell from her deep jacket pocket. "Come now, Peter. Anything near a phone is fair game these days. If you're dumb enough to allow yourself to be livestreamed without your knowledge—well, that's your problem."

"Holy shit!" I laugh, punching my fists at the ceiling.

"Addison, listen to me." Peter turns over his shoulder as two federal agents begin to drag him to the door. "My offer still stands—you can have everything you ever wanted at Ovid."

She eyes him skeptically. "What's done is done, Peter. Gen Z already tuned in to your confession—all 1.2 million of them that follow Phinnea's Boom Boom account—and everyone knows your dark secrets now. It's just as you always feared: The youth have arrived, and they'll be taking your job away."

His jaw drops as agents push him through the doorway to the front porch. Someone outside shouts for a paramedic. Genevieve's voice carries into the foyer: "My God, that was terrifying."

New uniformed men and women wearing jackets emblazoned with "LAPD" enter the sitting room from the kitchen, while I soak in the moment. We did it—Addison did it—the right way. With only a few bent rules, and a lot less morally gray area. A granddad-approved win.

A man in a suit jacket whose name I don't catch peppers me with questions, until Addison crosses the room toward me. I step forward, meet her in the middle. Brush the hair from her neck as if to kiss the sensitive skin on her body—my favorite place. Instead, I lean in close. "Addison Stern, you just made a big mistake."

"Oh?"

"You had the opportunity to wear the latest in iron accessories and to place a concrete wall between us." I smile. "But now you're never getting rid of me."

Police officers shout orders above the noise of feet and protocol to secure evidence while the FBI barks about the crime scene being in its jurisdiction. In the maelstrom, I focus on the heat emanating from Addison's frame, so close to mine. The sensual touch of her fingertips on my arm.

"You know I don't like to be threatened, Connor."

I nod, holding her tighter, removing any space between us.

"But you know what?" she adds.

"Hmm."

"That may be the first threat I actually enjoy."

CHAPTER FORTY

ADDISON

LOS ANGELES | ONE MONTH LATER

The fourth-floor waiting area of Cedars-Sinai seems reserved for Agent Jonas and me. Aside from a nurse who chats with a receptionist at the front desk, no one loiters among the gray upholstered chairs. Instead of elevator music playing from the ceiling speakers, rain taps against the window in the first of this season's much-needed showers.

Agent Jonas stands to greet me. Though his pants are wrinkled, he appears properly lint-rolled and rested. The promotion I heard he got for resolving Peter's murder spree seems like it came with a spray tan and a round of Botox, too.

Well, I solved it for him, but I try not to sweat the small stuff these days. And anyway, Connor solved it, too. His newly adopted mantra, that doing the right thing when no one's watching counts more than public perception, is starting to rub off on me. Like cat hair.

To be clear, I'm allergic to cat hair. But I digress.

I sent Maia's Threads a check for the clothing I pocketed years ago, quietly remedying an old wrong. And instead of announcing that I landed a very flashy French client for my new public relations agency in a big party or media blitz to kick things off, I simply livestreamed with her from a local patisserie while we grabbed espressos and discussed her goals for the year ahead. See, I told Connor. We're doing things for the client's benefit, which also happens to promote our firm, Six Degrees Public Relations. He only gave me a kiss, then let out his deep sigh that says he's indulging me.

"Ms. Stern. Have a seat." Agent Jonas offers me the well-worn upholstered chair next to him. He adjusts the blue tie with white roses that he wears.

I plaster on a smile. "I'll stand."

Agent Jonas nods. "I expected nothing less."

I check my cell phone. "So, how can I help now? I have a flight to catch."

"The Bureau has one outstanding question we were hoping you could answer."

"Good. Because I have one for you."

"Oh?" Agent Jonas stands with me. Thick, gray-flecked hair shines in the fluorescent lighting.

"What was the purpose of the business card that I found in Phinneas's office? Why were my initials and the closing date of Fashion Week written on it?"

"Yeah, that was for you. The voice notes we found on his computer confirmed Mr. Redwood suspected Mr. Huxton was planning to hurt someone else. Possibly at the closing ceremony. He wanted to warn you. Thought you had it in you to stop the additional violence."

"Really?" I lift my chin.

"I know, I was extremely surprised too."

I arch my eyebrow. "Well, Phinneas knew me much better than you do."

Although I meant to listen to the final voice note in Phinneas's cloud, Connor's careful tutelage in toeing the line won out. I haven't touched the files since Beverly Hills. I knew the FBI would notice. Well, that, and Connor finally changed his password on his laptop, and I knew accessing the cloud from my own computer was out of the question.

Agent Jonas folds thick arms across his chest. "And no one, it seems, knew Mr. Huxton. Not really. There's a lot that Mr. Huxton planned out over several months. Before Mr. Redwood was killed, Mr. Huxton actually sent in an anonymous tip to the Bureau to investigate Thrive's marketing, suggesting consumer fraud was at play."

"That may have been true, at least," I reply. "Connor discovered that himself, but he didn't think Phinneas was totally up to speed about it. Phinneas wasn't the most hands-on CEO."

Agent Jonas narrows his eyes. "Connor Windell knew about the late-night commercials and didn't think to report them?"

"Sweetie, if Connor did all the work, where would that leave you? Besides, Connor had a busy year. He didn't get a chance to tell anyone." Largely because Connor was waiting to get paid by Phinneas for previously completed work—and Connor felt bad for the guy. A bleeding heart, that one.

Agent Jonas purses his mouth. "Lucky for my job security,

then. It also seems that Mr. Huxton acted as an anonymous source to *Variety* magazine recently. We subpoenaed his phone records and dug into all the late-night calls as due diligence. An editor there explained Mr. Huxton refused to provide a name, blocked his number, and disguised his voice while he provided details on certain ruthless tactics of yours."

"I'll bet Peter was getting nervous. Anxious that Connor and I were getting too close to the truth and he meant to force a rift between us." It worked temporarily, but I won't tell this federal agent that.

I check my cell again. I really must be going. "I'd say that this is all quite fascinating, but that would be a lie. And my business partner is insistent on integrity these days."

"Then I'll give you my question: Why was Genevieve Aspen at Emilia Winthrop's house that day?"

"She was getting something for Velvet Eastman. They're friends."

Agent Jonas tilts his head down in thought. "Interesting. Since Aspen's first husband was Gerald Ovid, I wondered if maybe there was something else there. Did you know that?"

Slowly, I shake my head. Connor mentioned that Genevieve was a widow—not that she held that title twice over. "No."

"That doesn't surprise me. Aspen never legally changed her name to Ovid—she was known as Jenna Miller throughout their five years of marriage. Then Gerald Ovid died and Jenna met her second husband, to become Gene*vieve* Aspen within six months."

"A quick turnaround."

"The heart wants what the heart wants." Agent Jonas snorts. "Much like Mr. Windell might say these days—I gather you two are together now."

"We work together, yes. And, play together, too."

Agent Jonas frowns. "Well, if I find anything else unusual and related to you and him—don't worry. I'll be in touch."

I shake his hand, immediately regretting putting my hand in his limp, moist grasp. "I hope not."

Without another look at my former pursuer, I stride down the tile hallway to the final patient room on the right. Agent Jonas, and the drama he represents, is behind me now.

The last time I was here I only had to march past the reception desk of the ICU to my destination, but I welcome the extra steps. All the donuts Connor and I have been eating, since Jamie Mendez hired us for the last few weeks of his pre-election PR, are starting to show. On Connor, that is. Not me.

Mendez has been an interesting client. Lots of enemies, some backroom deals, and the kind of two-faced conversations I would expect of a man in politics with ties to organized crime in Vegas. What I did not anticipate was the pull he still exerted in the desert: Thanks to Connor and me publicly clearing Mendez of responsibility for his rival's death, he made some calls and got Connor's bookie Gianni to forgive his debts. Now, Connor only looks over his shoulder to check whether I'm following him or I stopped to take videos for our social media accounts, again.

Velvet Eastman nearly drops her pudding cup when I enter her room. Black hair is tied back in a smooth ponytail, and she appears only a shade or two tanner than the white paper gown she wears. This woman needs some sun.

"Addison," she cries. "What are you doing here?"

"I was here a few times, actually. But you were still out of it, so I doubt you'd remember."

I adjust the jade pendant I wear that Connor had custom-made by Mendez's mother. Although it's beautiful and exactly my style, I told him that a gift was unnecessary. If I want a bauble, I'll buy it myself. For some reason, he insisted.

A cushioned chair lies at the foot of her bed. I take a seat. "How are you feeling?"

Velvet winces. "Lots of aches and pains. The infection that set in after the overdose nearly reached sepsis. I knew that I was allergic to Valium, but I had no clue it was to such a crazy extent."

"I'm sure that was a shock."

"Emilia, though. She's been so sweet." Velvet smiles. "She's still recovering, but she's out of the ICU, too, at least. She rolled over in a wheelchair on Monday."

When the EMTs arrived at Emilia's house and declared her still alive, my small heart grew three sizes. There was a chance, at least, that I wouldn't have her death on my conscience. Plus, I genuinely liked her work. A sequel for the erotic thriller she starred in last summer was just announced.

"The doctors said you've been improving steadily, too." I nod. "You ready to go home soon?"

Velvet frowns. "To what, though? I've been too afraid to look at reviews of my fashion line, but my assistant said they weren't good. I didn't even get any sympathy praise since I collapsed on the runway. I mean, come on."

I offer my most compassionate sigh. "Velvet, sweetie. Would you want *sympathy* praise after all the hard work and creativity you poured into your designs and the stage production of Fashion Week?"

She lowers her eyes, clean of any makeup, nearly pouting. "No. I guess not."

"Good. Because I'm going to help you get the positive reception you deserve."

"Really? But how? They told me everything that happened with Peter. Ovid Blackwell must be in total chaos."

"All true. The FBI found voice note recordings that showed Peter targeted you for being . . . unruly."

She laughs. "Me? The slander."

I adopt a wry smile. "We'll sue him in civil court for every penny—after his lawyers wring him dry during the criminal trial."

"I'm going to count on it," she replies, almost appearing her usual lively self.

"And you're spot-on about Ovid being a mess. Which is why, for our relaunch of your line, you'll be working with my very own new PR firm."

Velvet's dark brown eyes widen. "It's about time you got your own house. Congrats. But are you sure you want to take me on? I'm pretty sure my image is beyond help. 'Former madam turned fashion designer overdoses on Valium due to nerves,' or whatever people are saying."

"Sweetie, we are going to overhaul your whole brand. Leave it to me."

Color flushes Velvet's cheeks. "Where do I sign?"

"Plenty of time for paperwork later. Right now, I have a plane to catch." I slide from the chair and get to my feet.

On a metal tray beside the bed, a pink eye mask nearly covers Velvet's phone. "Did you lose your other eye mask? The black one with red trim?"

"What do you mean?"

"Where is your other one?"

Velvet smiles. "Addison, this is the only eye mask I have. My assistant, Camille, brought it a week ago when I woke up. Usually I only wear it on airplanes, but the lights from the machines at night can be so annoying."

After promising to be in touch next week with a calendar of events and interviews, I slip from Velvet's room, eager to reach LAX.

Yet something about our conversation doesn't sit right. As I reach this floor's waiting area, realization slithers between my shoulder blades. When I catch up to Agent Jonas, who stands at the parting elevator doors, I lift my phone to my ear.

"Hello?" a gravelly voice answers.

"Genevieve Aspen, how are you?"

Agent Jonas doesn't flinch at my grip on his arm. He leans in closer as the chrome doors whisper shut without us.

"Well, in fact. Who is this?"

"Addison Stern. I just visited Velvet Eastman, your good friend to whom you delivered her favorite eye mask."

Pause. "Interesting. I hope you gave her my best. She was so out of it when I came to visit. Both times."

"See, that's the thing, Gen. I don't think you did. In fact, when I went to Emilia's house and found you already inside, you weren't there to retrieve an item for your friend Velvet. You had never met her before. You brought along an eye mask in your pocket as an excuse to enter Emilia's home and question her. To see if Emilia knew anything damning."

She scoffs through the line. Bravado. I can appreciate that. "About what, exactly?"

"You're Gerald Ovid's widow. You've lost two husbands."

"A terrible fact. Both philanderers."

"A motive, to make you share Peter's fervor to take out anyone detracting from Ovid Blackwell's good name, of which—I'm sure—you still own a percentage. Especially since Peter Huxton . . ." I trail off, piecing information together in real time.

A detail from my conversation with Peter before the fake party at the office resurfaces: *Everyone used different names in the eighties.*

In Emilia Winthrop's house, when Peter was deflecting from the murders, he said he wanted to keep his legacy intact.

"Peter Olivier Huxton isn't his real name, is it? The O stands for Ovid. Peter Ovid Huxton. He must have switched his surname with his middle name when he joined the firm."

Genevieve is silent.

"Peter is your former stepson. And he never wanted Velvet Eastman as a client, did he?"

When Malina discovered Peter had invited Velvet to our offices during the week I was in Hong Kong, she remarked that there were no follow-up meetings on the calendar—no plans to pursue Velvet with gifts or additional events to court her, something Ovid did for all high-profile clients as a rule.

"Peter didn't actually plan to sign her," I continue, "since he suspected Velvet's reputation would be too difficult to overcome—that she would be rebellious and he would be forced to drug her into compliance, as he did other challenging clients. He only meant to show an effort since our competitors were jockeying for her."

More silence comes from the phone while Agent Jonas nods.

"Then, when I went behind his back and courted Velvet directly, his hands were tied. Is that why Peter poisoned her in public at her runway show, to make it look like she was unstable and to damage her credibility since our PR campaign was less effective than we planned—rather than attacking her in private?"

I turn back to the hallway that leads to Velvet's room, half expecting her to appear in the doorframe with a thumbs-up. "It was luck that you weren't found out at Emilia's house and that Peter covered for you, his former stepmother."

Papers rustle in the background over the phone. The sound cuts off abruptly, and I know Genevieve has hit the mute button. Easier to search out a passport, pack a bag, and escape to your safe house in the Seychelles that way.

"But credit must be given where it's due, Gen. And I have to hand it to you and Peter. You purposefully brought Connor out of retirement to help you locate Devon Lim, who you knew accessed Phinneas's memoirs, because Peter used his 'crack research team' to hack into Phinneas's cloud. You always planned for Connor to reach out to me for help in tracking down the would-be son-in-law that you never liked, tidily ensuring I was tied to another murder. Annalise Meier really was in the wrong place at the wrong time. She should have stayed in Hong Kong, instead of traveling to Monaco to mourn with Devon."

I catch Agent Jonas's eye. He hits the elevator button, and the steel doors slide open once again. "Don't worry, Genevieve. The FBI is on its way to your home. And I'm on my way to an international flight, living my best life. Enjoy the rest of yours in monochrome orange."

\\\\\////

Sun scatters across the waves in green and pink jewels, rising along the coast of Cannes. The air is crisp, though not quite cold, hovering around sixty degrees. My navy lambswool coat provides the perfect amount of warmth while still blending in fashionably among the spectators to this morning's feat. Footsteps thunder toward the ribbon strung across the finish line, meters from where I stand, and I lift my phone as the first runner crests the hill.

Famous for its film festival, Cannes is also host to the French Riviera Marathon—a favorite tradition of one of my new clients. Despite boasting dual American and French citizenship, and being a globally recognized actor, Noémie Balzac appears as any other local athlete, sporting a sweat-soaked final layer of clothing—a tank top—after shedding the others along the twenty-six-mile route. She's not first in line to reach the ribbon, but she's close. Damn close. She'll be pissed about not quite reaching her goal of placing on the podium.

If she sees me, she doesn't let on. Noémie grunts as she passes me, pushing herself to outpace the woman next to her. Faster and faster she pumps her limbs, arms and legs flying as if no longer connected to her muscular frame. She sticks out a chin, then inch by inch pulls ahead of the runner. Only one more runner to pass to secure a bronze placement among the women. Two men battle it out ahead of the pack, another hundred feet farther ahead, but Noémie only focuses on her next moving target.

I unlock my phone to snap several photos. These shots are going to look great on my agency's new social media accounts. Sliding over to Instagram, I start livestreaming as Noémie pulls ahead of the next athlete. Ten people automatically pop in to start watching. Then fifty. Now one hundred.

Someone cries out. Thirty yards ahead, the woman running in first place trips, crashing to horrible road rash on the asphalt. The woman directly behind her is unable to course correct in time, and she follows suit, toppling to the ground.

Noémie can't believe it. She turns her head side to side, checking her peripheral vision, then guns it the remaining yards, all the way to a first-place finish among the women—third overall. She strides across the finish line, arms in the air in the most dramatic marathon victory this side of the Atlantic.

Ten thousand people are watching. Twenty. I hashtag *FrenchRivieraMarathon* and *NoémieBalzac*, then pan to the sparkling water glistening below as the sun continues its arc to the middle of the sky.

Not bad.

An hour later I find Noémie blissed out, wearing her medal and drinking straight from a bottle of Moët & Chandon while a woman from a beachfront hotel drapes a towel across Noémie's shoulders. Words in embroidered English read WHEN IN CANNES YOU CAN.

"Some more than others." I smile to myself as the party moves to the nearby five-star luxury hotel. Noémie excuses herself for a shower and a rest, and I do likewise before our planned apéritif later in the day.

My livestreams of the ornate, Baroque-style hotel foyer designed by a former princess of Prussia—the indoor gilded restaurant whose plats du jour are created by a Michelin-starred chef, and the first- and second-place race winners wearing their shiny medals (whom I run into on my way to my hotel room)— all seem to drive even more viewer engagement. I take a break from social media to refresh alone and don the black button-up, off-the-shoulder designer dress I bought to celebrate all the recent exciting news. The 360-degree mirrors in my hotel room confirm I look sensational. By the time I'm dressed for cocktails and hors d'oeuvres, descending a carpeted staircase fit for the *Titanic*, I've logged back into my livestream. Over fifty thousand people join me.

When I slide next to Noémie in a chartered car that whisks us off to dinner, she shares with me that she's also gained another five thousand followers since this morning. "Whatever you're doing," she adds, "keep it up."

The livestream of our arrival to dinner is punctuated with smiley faces, heart emojis, and exclamation marks in the comments. Everyone wants details on Noémie's next film and whether she will continue the hit middle-grade series she wrote for French children about being an athlete and a girl. The story itself was abused for promoting unrealistic body standards for prepubescents, but it was a best seller anyway.

As the owner of the restaurant escorts us to a private patio lit with fairy lights and presenting a gorgeous view of the ocean at twilight, I feel content. At first, I wonder if I should have eaten more today, the feeling a mere hunger pang. Then Connor's face returns to mind, from during our FaceTime in my hotel room, as he shared updates on Velvet's schedule and the research he did into the fashion critics who responded favorably to her line's debut.

"I miss you," he said before hanging up. Within seconds, he sent me a photo of his face edited onto Kevin Bacon's body in *Footloose*.

I cringed. Then double-tapped for a heart reaction to the image. Everyone makes sacrifices in relationships.

"Great choice for dinner, Addison." Noémie pats the chair beside her at a polished oak table that was brought outside especially for her. Small plates of galettes and dried sausage are already set across a gold-embroidered tablecloth. I take a seat to admire the view of twinkling waves, brilliant in the sun's diminishing reach.

"How are you, Addison? The jet lag must be fierce. You only got in—what, two days ago? It always takes me a week to adjust." Noémie rips into the loaf of house-made baguette on the table.

"I'm good. Definitely have jet lag, but I'm more excited about you conquering the marathon. All of Paris watched our livestream."

Noémie laughs. Then she launches into a play-by-play of her thoughts, sharing how adrenaline and sheer will pulsed through her body—propelling her to the finish line.

I'm only half listening. The livestreams have been so successful today, and the Boom Boom account I set up for Noémie last week has already surpassed one million followers, given the content I told her team to film and upload. Each of the tactics that I pushed for so long at Ovid Blackwell but were always rejected for a lack of interest—or concerns about time management and long-term maintenance, or safety reasons—are already proving their tangible benefits. As I glance around me, surrounded by a beloved client, excellent wine, and amazing sights, I know this is where I belong. At the forefront of PR strategy, serving the most innovative, if at times controversial, figures in the global marketplace.

Stars begin to dot the blue-gray sky overhead, like little place-holders for each of my business coups to come.

"You bitch." A voice growls behind me. "Salope. Espèce de merde."

Noémie gasps. I turn over my shoulder and find a figure in shadows by the restaurant's interior, beneath an arch trellis covered in ivy. Curse words have come at me in many languages, but not usually during an intimate patio dinner.

"This is a private table," I announce. "Gabriel?" I yell for the owner.

Shouts fly inside among the staff, followed by quick footsteps.

"You cost me my job. My friends. My girlfriend. My life as I knew it." A young man steps forward, revealing a long nose and full lips. Tension radiates from his frame, but I recognize him. The production assistant from the shoot back in Paris with Emilia Winthrop—the one I saw canoodling with the director of the perfume campaign.

"Your girlfriend? Or do you mean your boss?"

"Addison, who is this?" Noémie whispers.

"I'll handle him," I reply. Without bothering to stand—this peon doesn't deserve the effort—I lean over my chair. "I seem to recall you being part of the crew that attempted to ruin my client's life by taking humiliating photos of her."

The old me would have made a credible threat to ensure this person never approached me again, but I've been to hell and back over the last three months. I've learned a few things. Namely, that winning isn't everything, not really. As Connor reminds me, sometimes what happens behind closed doors is more important than pursuing public accolades. And that fear is not always the most effective tool; acting from love—or the semblance of it—can be just as persuasive, and with less blowback.

Noémie sucks in an audible breath, gauging the scene. She's got an impressive network of Francophile producers back home. I wouldn't want to fall out of her good graces.

"Look, monsieur. I'm terribly sorry for whatever difficulty you've faced since we last met. Now, if you'll excuse us, we are in the middle of—"

"That's not good enough." His arm cuts through the air to pull a pistol from his jacket and point it directly at our table. A shot fires. Pain explodes in my back, reverberating through my bones, as I fall out of my chair.

Cries, shouts, and screams pierce the night. Another body is tackled to the ground.

"Addison! Addison!" Hands grip my arm, my head.

Sirens wail on the street below. Closer. Closer now.

Wetness snakes down my cheek and into my ear.

My mother's voice returns to mind, as clear as if she were the person hovering over me with a towel. Dinah must have caught my livestreams, heard I was here. I reach for her, just as I used to as a five-year-old. She extends a hand, then brushes a crumb from her mom jeans. *I have a headache, Addison. So be a good girl. And clean up this mess.*

A man leans over me. Connor? No, that can't be right. He's at home in LA.

As this person—Gabriel, the restaurateur—shouts something, my vision blurs. Black, close-cut hair becomes brown, long and wavy across square features. Like an attractive LEGO head. It is Connor, come to hold me. He touches my forehead. His tense expression breaks into a smile. *Hey, Add,* he says.

Connor knew I needed him. He must have grabbed the first flight out.

A cool sheet spools through my body, leaving me dizzy. Relief? Happiness? Although I have fought against it all my adult life, the feeling of needing someone, and being cared for in return, surges in my chest. It's pleasing—in a way that truly makes losing to win the twist ending I never wanted. But, also kind of did.

"Addison, hang on. The ambulance is pulling up right now," Noémie says. Or is that Velvet?—Emilia?

"Addison? Addison!" Someone sobs.

More voices shout above me. Then they fade into the heavy, French accordion music—no, the nineties grunge music—that seems to be getting louder, swelling from a nearby speaker system. The sound of my childhood.

One thing is certain as I lie dying. The phrase *smells like teen spirit* still doesn't make a damn bit of sense.

CHAPTER FORTY-ONE

PHINNEAS

BENEDICT CANYON | AUGUST 18

PHINNEAS REDWOOD: *Look alive, memoirs. I'm afraid I have some bad news.*

Someone knocked on my front door tonight . . . a tall dude— aren't they all? Never seen him before. Said he was here on behalf of Addison Stern. Her new assistant . . . Lorenzo.

So I let him in. He was on the phone with Addison when he arrived . . . or someone who sounded like Addison . . . Sent by her to prep me for the gala tonight since she's flying back from Paris. [Slurring] . . . Something about Malina had the night off.

We went over talking points. . . . Then he brought out a tray of wheatgrass shots.

Wheatgrass shots? I hate those fuckers . . . I said. [Pause] *But Lorenzo said Addison's pre-event ritual required them.*

So he lined them up and I took them . . . one after the other . . . after the other. Three. [Pause] *It was only on the third one that I smelled the vodka.*

I said . . . the fuck? And the guy . . . Lorenzo . . . just smiled.

The shots hit me . . . hard. [Pause] *So hard. I haven't touched alcohol in weeks, let alone . . . three back-to-back . . . shots that smell like goddamned wheatgrass . . . and something else.*

So I knew. I stumbled down the hall to my office . . . locked the door. [Pause] *Shouted how I was going to tell everyone about Peter . . . Called 911. Twice. Four times . . . Busy signals. Every time. Stupid LA . . . always full of people in need.*

I feel terrible. I can't move. Can't hide. [Pause] *There must have been something else in those shots beside vodka.* [Slurring] *. . . in my chair like a loser behind my desk. Waiting. Waiting.*

Peter has come for me, as I thought he might. . . . I didn't know he'd send Gumby's uglier cousin to do the job.

[Banging noise]

Shit. Shiiiiiiiiit. [Banging] *He's at the door. Peter must be hiding some . . . next-level criminal shit.* [Pause] *Just how many people has he drugged before?*

Okay, I just hit the panic button on my home security

app. . . . Someone—anyone—better come along soon.

Fuck. But if they don't . . .

Okay . . . [Scratching] *In case this reaches you, Addison Stern . . . in case you're not working with Peter . . . I am writing down the only date you're going to need in the near future—but in the Euro format of day, month, year . . . October 13.* [Slurring] *Zero doubt that Peter is going to drug another client who jeopardizes Ovid's rep . . . probably Emilia Winthrop. . . . The police should know you're the only A.S. in my life . . . and you should figure out that Emilia Winthrop and everyone who is anyone . . . will be at the closing night of Fashion Week.*

[Pause] *Granted, Addison Stern is usually the one busting knees . . . rather than trying to save them. But Peter has gotten sloppy. Flippant about the damage he's doing.* [Pause] *Addison will be pissed to know he's entangling her beloved firm. And if this turns out to be one stupid scare tactic by Peter . . . I'm going to ream his ass out . . . and air all his dirty laundry in public. He can't just manipulate and force substance abuse on . . . innocent clients—real people with families . . . and plans for their futures. I can't let another tragedy go on, like what happened to those teen girls . . . Not without at least trying to do something.*

[Loud banging noise]

C'mon, c'mon cops . . . Where are they?

Ironically, Annalise always said she loved me . . . when we were together—but she worried that I loved money more than I cared for people in this world . . . and she was right. That's why we broke up even after I said we could still be together . . . despite her cheating on me with Devon Lim. She couldn't stomach being with someone who didn't share her humanitarian ideals. Well. [scoffs] *Look at me now, Annalise . . . I'm preparing to fight—maybe to the death . . . to hold Peter accountable for his* [slurring] *megalomania.*

I always thought alcohol would get me in the end. [Pause] *Just not in the guise of wheatgrass.*

If anything happens to me . . . [Louder banging] *tell Annalise I love her. I've always loved her. And . . . maybe more importantly, I forgive her. For everything.*

ACKNOWLEDGMENTS

Firstly, my heartfelt thanks go to you, the reader, for joining me on this romp through Los Angeles and beyond. I had so much fun writing this story and I hope you equally enjoyed the journey. Thank you for reading!

Gratitude must also go to my editor Cassidy Leyendecker and to Augusta Harris, and to the entire team at Hyperion Avenue. Your collaboration and editorial insights made this experience better than I could have hoped. Thank you, team!

Likewise, so much appreciation goes to copy editor Karen Krumpak for her work on this novel.

Thank you to Mark Povinelli, whose brilliant notes on an early draft of this story helped Phinneas to shine.

To Jill Marr, my literary agent and the entire team at Sandra Dijkstra Literary Agency, thank you. Your hard work, persistence, and good humor were always a light during this process. I am forever indebted to you.

Thanks must also be given to the 2020 Debuts Facebook group, for sharing with me a website that does all the work involved in the Six Degrees of Kevin Bacon game. When this writer's brain was fried, this website (and the 2020 Debuts group's friendship) meant everything.

Lots of thankys are directed to Michelle Lema, for sharing her descriptions of the Amalfi Coast with such depth and patience. I'm so lucky to call you a friend for going on wow!-a-lot-of-years!

I have so much appreciation for my friends and family members who allowed me the space to return messages and calls long after I should have. Your patience with me when I am deep in the writing process is enviable. I love you all.

Finally, to my husband and our kiddos: Thank you for granting me so much grace this year, and also being as invested in this story as I was. It's the honor of my life to brainstorm and plot-doctor together. Big squeezes and hugs and bisous.